163 G

THE
HOMESTEAD

Center Point
Large Print

Also by Linda Byler and available from
Center Point Large Print:

Fire in the Night
Davey's Daughter

THE HOMESTEAD

THE DAKOTA SERIES • BOOK I

LINDA BYLER

CENTER POINT LARGE PRINT
THORNDIKE, MAINE

This Center Point Large Print edition
is published in the year 2018 by arrangement with
Skyhorse Publishing.

The text of this Large Print edition is unabridged.
In other aspects, this book may vary
from the original edition.
Printed in the United States of America
on permanent paper.
Set in 16-point Times New Roman type.

ISBN: 978-1-64358-027-2

Library of Congress Cataloging-in-Publication Data

The Library of Congress has cataloged record
under LCCN 2018042775

CONTENTS

THE
HOMESTEAD

CHAPTER 1

As far as the eye could see, nothing but waving grass rustled in a wind that still carried a hint of winter. Brown and dry, it whispered the secrets that grew beneath its dying roots, as the sun coaxed tender green shoots of newborn grass from the snow-soaked earth.

If you looked closely, the beginning of a structure raised itself into the blue of the sky, thrust upward unfamiliarly, sharp and brown and out of place in the sea of grass, like the hull of a ship aground on the beach, the waves continuing their pounding as if the vessel had never been there.

Here, on the high prairie, the wind never ceased. Only before a storm did it become quiet, held back before it unleashed its power, multiplied by the calm, wreaking its havoc in the form of a deadly tornado or pelting hail driven by the storm's fury.

If you looked closer still, to the left you see faint wagon tracks that had crippled the waving grasses, crushing the brittle ones with each turn of the steel band that encircled the heavy wooden wheel, the plodding horses' hooves digging up the tender earth, erasing some of the weaker green shoots of grasses and delaying the stronger ones.

The trail curved away across the prairie until the distinct, sharp lines of the building jutted into your vision off to the right, marring the otherwise flat and serene landscape, the rough logs lashed and pegged firmly against the restless wind, and the steep pitch of a roof without lath or shingle.

The road turned down a small incline, rose slightly upward, and came to the mess of uprooted grasses, mud, and butchered logs dragged in from a place unseen. The whole scene was like a small wound on the immensity of the high prairie, smeared with wet salve. Off to the left stood a worn wagon, the dirty yellowed canvas straining against the ropes that lashed it to the bows bent into an upside-down U shape spanning one side of the wagon box to the other. It had once been a fine Conestoga wagon, but months on the road had aged it considerably.

It was the house that disturbed the blue of the sky and the waving grasses. Substantial in size, made of logs entirely, without a roof, windows, or doors, it was a structure being born nevertheless.

Two horses were tethered a distance from the wagon, the dusty harnesses slung across a steel-rimmed wheel. Granite buckets, the remains of a fire, an agate washtub and coffee pot, wooden troughs and crates, an assortment of stumps set around the campfire—all told of the human beings who traveled here to make a home in the vast and magnificent land, away from the East, from the congestion of religions and doctrines, and from brethren who bickered and fought among themselves like European starlings wearing their wide-brimmed black hats and broadfall trousers like an armor against evil worldly practices.

Mose Detweiler did not always know who was right and who was wrong. A simple, stalwart, dark-haired, sturdy man, he adhered to the doctrines of the Old Order Amish, the Christian sect founded in Switzerland by Jacob Ammann, who, in 1693, broke from the Mennonites over issues concerning excommunication and the practice of shunning.

By the twentieth century, most of the world's Amish lived in North America, their faith growing as they raised families according to their interpretation of scripture, and the rules and regulations written in the *"Mutterschprache,"*—the mother tongue of the Swiss and German lands from where many Amish trace their ancestry.

The Great Depression of 1929 had hit Mose like a ton of bricks; it flattened him and took away his farm with its wonderful black loam soil of Lancaster County, Pennsylvania. Unable to make the mortgage, steep by all accounts (his father and older brother had warned), the bank that held it crumbled under the weight of a worthless dollar. Mose took to making moonshine illegally and selling it to bootleggers for a few dollars.

After selling off most of the cattle and all of the sheep and pigs, what else could he do with the grain?

When the church discovered his secret, it excommunicated and shunned him. Shamed publicly, no longer able to hold up his head and look his brethren in the eye, he told his good wife, Sarah, that he was going West.

Her large brown eyes filled with the softness of tears, jewels of love and forgiveness. She said she would go, but not with ill feelings and certainly not with the curse of the ban. "You done wrong, Mose," she said softly, placing a hand on his solid shoulder as she looked into his brown eyes, watching them soften and become liquid with love. "Now make it right."

He hung his head, then, ashamed of his misdeed in the purity of her forgiveness. He went out, hitched up his horse and spoke to the bishop, repenting of his illegal work. He returned to the fold at peace.

So the family left, the shame of losing the farm riding with them on the high wooden seat. The many doctrines of the numerous Plain churches confused Mose, saddling him with a driving need to escape the noise and the cackling of a hen house with too many hens.

He wanted to continue in the doctrine his father had taught him, the simple belief that Jesus paid for his sins by His death on the cross. The

Bible commanded a plain and peaceable way of life, and that was all. It seemed to Mose that everyone around him complicated matters, stirring controversy with the wooden paddle of heresy. He didn't understand the endless prattle caused by dissecting Bible verses and examining them under a microscope of ill-feeling and tightfistedness. When he couldn't breathe love among his brethren, choked on the fumes of a hundred different voices spouting as many different views, he drove away on his Conestoga wagon with the most blessed among women by his side. His Sarah. His jewel. His finest God-given possession. In the light of her love he became a better man, for he knew he was simple and didn't comprehend many of life's intricacies and the complexities of other men's outspoken knowledge.

It had always been so, even in school. Quiet and subdued, he fell behind in class, suffering misery at the teacher's rebuke and dissatisfaction with his many shortcomings. Somehow, though, he had won Sarah, a dark-haired, dark-eyed beauty from Honeybrook who placed her hand in his and never left him alone or insecure again. She was his rock, his helpmeet, and his best friend.

The journey was arduous, but they were a stoic family. Their oldest daughter, Hannah, was tall, thin, and had her mother's brown eyes and creamy skin. But there the likeness ended. Easily riled, her full mouth frequently pouted contemptuously, a fire in her eyes like brown sparks, the least provocation setting off the shooting flames. Her adolescence was fraught with prickly ill-humor and dissatisfaction with everything and everyone around her. At fourteen she was the bane of her patient mother's existence, the thorn in her father's side, but the delight of her brother Manasses, known as Manny or, in Hannah's silly chatter, simply "Man."

Manny was twelve, dark-haired, sturdy, tall, and winsome, with eyes that were completely without guile. He adored Hannah, loved his mother, and held his father in high esteem. He was content with whatever came his way, so when the children were told of the move west, he merely nodded his head and agreed. He didn't know what the West was, but he figured it would be all right, as long as his father thought so.

Hannah threw a royal fit until Mose sent her firmly to her room with no supper. As she laid on her bed listening to her stomach growl, she vowed never to become a vanilla pudding like her mother—no backbone, no will, no nothing. She did not want to leave Lancaster County no matter how poor they were. Her father could get a job at the harness shop or the butcher shop or any place. She wanted to stay here with her friends Rebecca, Annie, and Katie. What was out West besides nothing? She guessed they'd all be dead by the time they got to the Mississippi

River, and if they weren't, they'd all be drowned shortly thereafter.

Eight-year-old Mary was dark-haired as well, but her wavy tresses were shot through with golden strands. Her eyes were light hazel, her skin pale with a dusting of earth-colored freckles as delicate as stardust. Mary was an astounding-looking child who skipped blithely through life, turning heads with her adorable smile. She carried her sheer unspoiled air of goodwill like an essence. At her young age, the West was a good place filled with bluebirds and colorful butterflies, fascinating bugs, and warm bunnies.

Mary persuaded six-year-old Eli, short, stocky, and dark-eyed with a thatch of thick black hair that always stood away from his cowlick like a mild explosion. He had inherited the same wild gene as his sister Hannah, so he was given to bursts of anger over slight irritations. Talkative, he voiced his childish opinions forcefully. As an infant he had yelled with colic day and night, aging his parents with relentless crying as his stomach churned with gas and indigestion, his feedings coming back up with the force of a water spigot. He fell down an entire flight of stairs at eight months, bumping his forehead until a blue-black egg formed like a frightening growth. His cowlick stood straight up and never laid back down.

Relatives cried, hugged, sized up the wagon,

and shook their heads. "Why don't you take the train?" one of them asked. But Mose was determined and Sarah was submissive. Eager to see the world, they trusted that the money would last and the Mississippi would be crossable. God would provide, and they'd be on their way with His blessing.

And they were blessed.

They made good time with the heavy horses suited for travel, the endurance bred into them. The hardest part was the cold weather, when the snows blasted them with tiresome fury. When a roaring campfire was not enough, they settled into a small clapboard house for a few months before moving on.

Sarah's lovely face had become gaunt and pale. She was short with the children, her hands riddled and crosshatched with chilblains. It was when she hid her eyes from her husband's searching gaze that he decided the cold and the monotony of days on the wagon seat were too much. So they stopped in western Indiana, in the forsaken little town of Salem, and took up residence in the other half of Mrs. Ida Ferguson's town house, built in 1848 by her husband's own hands, may he rest in peace. Hannah told Manny that Mr. Ferguson couldn't be resting too peacefully the way he slapped this cheap house together, then went and died and left his widow to stuff things like sheep's wool in the cracks.

Ida was short and buxom, a white apron encircling the vast circumference of her stomach. She wore it low and snug, leaving her hips to sprout like two appendages on either side, a resting place for her balled up fists, shoved snug by the weight of her lumpy elbows, scattered with blue veins and purple moles. Her nose was round and loose like a manatee, her mouth wobbly with relaxed skin, her eyes pinpricks of brilliant blue that fired good humor.

She put them up in the "harvesters' quarters," as she called the two rooms downstairs and two upstairs. It was drafty, the nails studded with frost like pristine mold, the rooms bare except for the minimum of necessities, the rough board floors scattered with bits and pieces of linoleum, frayed and cracked around the edges like a flapping, hazardous doily.

But there was a roof over their heads, and a rusty dysfunctional coal stove that was either red hot or barely producing heat, nothing in between. Their humble home was a source of comfort, a spot of warmth out of the wind and the constant smell of dirty wool, limp flannels, and unwashed bodies.

The first week in Salem, Sarah washed clothes in Ida's wringer washer and hung them on racks around the stove where they steamed with the good smell of lye soap and powdered detergent. She swept and scrubbed, lifted the derelict linoleum and swept underneath. She washed windows with vinegar water, ironed clothes, and soaked their white head coverings, which were now yellow and flattened from being stored in trunks and leather satchels.

They ate soup and fried meat, pots of oatmeal, and cornmeal pudding called corn pone. Sarah's cheeks were again pink, and her eyes soft and dark. She cleaned and cooked and slept in a bed with Mose by her side, like civilized folks, she said, not unkindly.

Ida visited every day, eyed Sarah's burgeoning figure, and asked how soon. Sarah's face flamed, and she kept her eyes downcast. "Not yet," she mumbled in a reply that barely made it past her lips. Ida watched her face, the spreading suffusion of color, patted her cheek, and said she hadn't meant to be nosy.

Hannah drew her eyebrows down and opened her mouth, but that was as far as it went. Her father kicked her beneath the table, his eyes sizzling with rebuke. These things were not spoken of, certainly not by a brash fourteen-year-old.

Ida missed all of this; her good humor rode on the wings of the blushing Sarah, so sweet, so grateful to have this house. Poor dear. What a journey! Why they had not taken the train was beyond her; but then, it was none of her business. She went home and baked them a molasses cake with crumb topping, opened a jar of preserved peaches, and took it over for their dessert. She sat on a chair by the stove and ate a large portion herself.

She cried when they left too soon, mopping her streaming eyes as she wished them Godspeed. She prayed fervently for Sarah every night before she went to bed.

The return of the cold, the flat monotony of the land, snatched the color from Sarah's face, turning her eyes dull and tired, like an unpolished rock. Her mouth was set in a straight line, her nose white and pinched, her eyes never leaving the brown, flapping haunches of the horses. It was only when spring arrived that she came back to life, the scent of new grass and south breezes filling her with hope.

Mose marveled at the land, the sheer, unbelievable magic of the empty space, immeasurable sky, and the distance from one line of cottonwoods to another. There was an occasional ranch, a cluster of houses, sometimes a small town, but mostly there was the endless sea of grass, the road before them, and the flat sky that turned from gray to blue and back to gray again.

Cold rains were the worst, draining their spirits, and sapping goodwill and energy. Roaring campfires dried out the worst of the discomfort, but dampness remained for days, leaving the children sneezing and coughing fitfully during the night.

Sarah wondered vaguely what would become of them out here in this wild, treeless land. Not one other Amish person to be with, to attend church with, to hold quiltings and hymn sings with, and no visitors to invite to your table. Would they all drift away, like miniscule seeds from a dandelion head, blown about by the winds of the world?

She watched her husband's smooth, untroubled face, thought of the small amount of dollars left in her cache, and wondered how they would survive. Must she go willingly, without question, hiding all her fears of the future? To second guess their decision now would serve no other purpose but to bring him down to the level of her pessimism.

Who would help her birth the baby? Who would know they had even arrived, let alone existed, needing help? Was there no kindly soul anywhere close? She felt her heart tightening, her stomach contracting, her pulse gaining speed. Her breathing became light and quick, and nausea rose in her throat.

"Mose." Her voice was quick and breathy.

He looked at her, shocked, his eyes widening. "Not already?"

"Oh, no. No. But, who will help when my time comes?"

Relieved, Mose laughed a genuine laugh filled

with good spirits and calm. He put his arm around her shoulders and drew her against him, rubbing the palm of his hand up and down the sleeve of her coat. "Ach, my darling Sarah, don't worry. I'll find someone."

When they finally rolled to a stop one day in April on the small rise close to the line of cottonwoods and box elders, with a creek winding among them, full and wide, overflowing its banks in the wet springtime, it was like a miracle, a mirage, something you believed you saw but that would disappear before you had a chance to touch the bark of those trees or the rippling water.

They set up camp and walked the property lines. Mose got out the documents as if they were sacred, read them aloud slowly, mispronouncing the words, but Sarah knew what it meant. They would homestead these one hundred acres. At the end of five years, they would be the owners of this wild and foreign land. Sarah scratched the red rash on her forearm, squinted into the late afternoon, and stopped her rising panic as she turned her body from east to west, then north to south. *A trail, a roof, a rider, please God.*

Her face calm, unruffled, she walked to the wooden stake that sectioned off their acres and began to shake uncontrollably. Grateful for her long skirt and the fullness of the gathered fabric, she gripped each elbow in the palms of her hands and held them, crushing her arms against her stomach as tremors of the unknown shook her.

All around was only the untamed land and the enormous sky with a white cold sun lending its half light. The wind moaned and blew ceaselessly, ruffling the ends of the brown, dead grass, pushing the faraway trees into a crooked, swaying dance. Brown birds, the color of the grass, wheeled across the sky at breakneck speed, squawking a shrill, short note before disappearing into the restless grass. There were no crows or vultures, no deer, only the incessant calling of the numerous prairie hens. A gopher stood on its hind legs and gripped its front legs in front of itself like a reverent little minister beginning a soul-searching sermon.

The wind spoke to Sarah of longing in a restless attack of homesickness so real it felt physical, as if a giant hand gripped her heart and squeezed. She lowered her head as hot tears squeezed from her eyes, trembled on her lashes, and dripped onto her stomach. When she turned her head to one side, the tears splashed on the wooden stake. Some fell into the thick brown grass, anointing the soil of North Dakota, her home, her place to live for the rest of her days on earth.

It was Hannah who marched down to the creek bed and swung an axe alongside her father. Her fierce energy finally had a productive outlet after months of travel. Her eyes flashed with renewed interest. She hacked and whacked and rode one of the horses to pull the logs to the site where their house would be built, her smooth white legs exposed until Sarah ran gasping in horror with a pair of Manny's trousers and told her to wear them; they weren't completely savage just yet. Hannah looked at her mother with narrowed eyes, asking who there was to see. No use putting on the constricting trousers.

Sarah spoke levelly, without anger. "Put them on. Get down off that horse and put them on."

The flash of rebellion from Hannah's eyes staggered Sarah. What was this? Resolutely she went to the horse's bridle, faced Hannah's anger, and repeated her order without taking her eyes off her daughter's.

Hannah was the first to look away, followed by a slumping of her broad shoulders. One leg swung over, a quick slide, and she landed on her feet like a cat. Springing up, she took a few steps, grabbed the trousers from her mother's grasp, held the offending garment up, hiked up her skirts and stepped into them, holding her skirts with her chin as she buttoned the waistband. Lifting the broadfall, she buttoned it without speaking.

Sarah held onto the bridle and stroked the faithful horse, still working after all those miles. For the first time she thanked God for the isolation, her daughter displaying an utter lack of discretion.

Turning, Hannah stood back, gathered herself again, so cat-like, Sarah thought. Hannah leaped, slung a leg over, grasped the reins and turned her head. The horse wheeled in response to the jerked left rein and galloped off in a spray of mud and wet grass.

Sarah lifted a hand to her forehead to shade her eyes and watched Hannah go until she disappeared into a hollow. That was the thing about this flat land, the deception of it. It wasn't as flat as it appeared; only the grasses waving in the restless wind looked even. Sarah shuddered without knowing why. She returned to the camp by the Conestoga wagon and continued her ironing.

She had set up her ironing board between two stumps, so she lowered herself to sit and iron. The sadiron was no longer hot. She attached the handle, placed it on the red coals and loosened the handle to let it heat up. Mary looked up from the book she was reading, smiling sweetly at her mother before returning to her concentration.

Sarah sighed and watched the light playing on Mary's gold-streaked head. Why did she bother ironing? There was no one to see, no one to care whether their clothes were wrinkled or soiled, or if they wore none at all.

She snorted, a derisive sound, surprising herself. Oh, this was only the beginning of having to think differently, of stepping outside her well-structured life. No longer would she be able to wash on

Monday, iron on Tuesday, plant and harvest and go to church and visit relatives and live among decent, God-fearing folks who lived together in unity. Well, mostly. How well she knew the unhappiness of her Mose, how the long and complicated talk of his peers bothered him, unsettled his simple way of life and his uncluttered thoughts. She knew too that he loved everyone and never thought ill of one person, in spite of not agreeing with him. Rufus Bontrager was the worst. Loud, obnoxious, cutting into other men's conversations to set them right with his own high opinion of himself, he rankled everyone's good humor. Mose always said he was loud, yes. And yes, a mite *grosfeelich*. But Rufus knew how to shoe a horse. He had a gentle hand in spite of his brute strength. When they lost their farm, he was the first to extend sympathy and shod both horses without charge.

Mose would never forget that act of kindness. And yet, he couldn't stay in Lancaster County. Ah, there was the mystery for Sarah. Would she ever understand his reasoning for going out and buying that still and making whiskey illegally to sell to disreputable men? The shame that followed, the women's unhidden pity as they let her pass along the row of benches in church.

Fresh shame washed over her, remembrance as painful as daggers. Her Mose. In the end, though, she reasoned a sensible answer to herself, that desperate men did desperate things.

Mose was just trying to save the farm and his good reputation. The hurt settled into her bones, evened out, faded, but stayed, like an arthritis only time could cure.

She missed going to church the most. The easy chatter of the women, the admiring of babies, young mothers bending to tie their little girls' head coverings, stashing their shawls and bonnets on tables or benches provided. Shaking hands, bending forward to give and receive the holy kiss, their traditional way of greeting one another. She could still feel the papery softness of Grandmother Miller's loose cheeks, the smell of starch from her covering, the wide strings beneath the soft, loose folds of her neck.

She lifted the sadiron and resumed ironing. A chill rushed up her spine as the grasses swayed and bent. The campfire hissed, crackled, threw sparks as the flames flared up by the wind.

Soon the chilly winds would stop. Soon the warm sun would win. Sarah became quiet inside herself knowing her time would be here then. They must find someone, somewhere. The quick panic that rose within her was successfully pushed back by her whispered prayers. She believed God was out here with them. She couldn't believe otherwise or she'd be swept away by her fear, her lack of trust in Mose, whom she had promised to obey, to love, to care for.

She put the ironing aside, shrugged on a

light coat, and asked Mary if she would like to accompany her to the creek bed to watch her father cut down trees. Mary eagerly rose to her feet, grasping her mother's hand and looking up into her face as they set off down the path made by the horses dragging logs up from the creek.

Soon it would be time for their evening meal, the preparations still unfamiliar after all these months on the road. Sarah could never feel as efficient or in control as she had back in her own kitchen. Now she always reverted to soups or stews or cornmeal mush. A campfire was an unhandy thing in spite of the grate and the iron rod set up between two sturdy posts to hold the blackened kettle above the fire.

Sarah squeezed Mary's hand and smiled down at her. "Soon we'll have a house, Mary!"

"Yes, we will. Dat said we will."

Ah, to be young. To trust with that childish, doubt-free trust that erased every worry. Sarah only hoped—with a doubt-ridden hope speckled with fear—that they would have a house and beds to sleep in by the time the baby arrived.

She thought of Abraham and Laban's flocks of sheep. The Old Testament described them as pure white or speckled with color—the impure ones. If she put her faith beside her small daughter's, her own sheep would be the ones spangled heavily with the impurity of brown spots.

CHAPTER 2

The walk through the heavy grass left Sarah surprisingly breathless, considering they were headed slightly downhill. Mary chattered by her side, sometimes racing foolishly after small brown birds she had no chance of catching. Running back to Sarah, bent over, her tongue hanging like a winded puppy, she waved her arms up and down in exaggerated effort.

Sarah laughed, the sound almost frightening in its unnatural, hoarse explosion. Mary laughed with her without noticing any change in the sweet mother she knew and loved. For this, Sarah was deeply grateful. She had to do better, to find a place deep within herself and draw on this source for strength and courage. Lifting her head, Sarah vowed to rise above the most difficult situation without allowing Mose or the children to see her inner struggle. There was a word for that, a Dutch word, but she could not remember it.

They came to the group of trees where the grasses thinned and the wide creek wound its way among them. At the far end there were the patient horses, tethered to each other, heads hanging straight in the quiet repose of a sleeping animal. There were five logs, straight ones, cut and ready to be hauled to the house, a pile of twigs, thin branches and brush, and another tree laying along the creek. At one end, Mose lifted the axe and brought it down precisely into the whitish crevice where it had struck many times before. Hannah whacked away at another tree in short, swift strikes, her face red with exertion, working twice as hard as Mose but accomplishing little except wearing herself out.

Manny was hacking small branches off the fallen trees, dragging them to the brush pile and walking with a sense of newfound purpose, his old gray hat brim flopping over one eye, torn away from the crown, and his dark hair spilling out like extra stuffing.

He caught sight of his mother, waved and grinned and called out to them before continuing his work. Mose stopped, wiped his face and turned, his face creasing with pleasure at the sight of his lovely Sarah and Mary. Hannah stopped, scowled, turned her back, and resumed her senseless whacking.

Mose laid down his axe and stepped away from his work to greet them. Dressed in patched denim broadfall trousers, an old blue chambray work shirt, the sleeves rolled above his elbows, the muscular arms straining every seam, he never appeared more handsome to Sarah. Gladness lit up her face, evincing radiance from within. The light drew Mose and had drawn him since he was young. "Sarah! So you came to see what we're doing? Good for you. And my best Mary."

He laughed as he kissed Sarah's cheek, one arm about her waist, drawing her close. She smiled up at him, their souls united in their searching gaze, seeking, finding, content for all the ages, being together, bound by their love.

When did she first think of Eli? Who spoke of him first? Mary or Mose? Was it herself? She could only remember the yawning pit of realization that Eli was not here with Mose.

"I thought he was with you." She was never sure who said the words first but knew instantly that something was terribly wrong.

Sarah's hands went to her mouth. Her brown eyes searched her husband's face as if she could gain entry to a reassurance in the depth of his brown eyes. "Where is he?" she whispered hoarsely.

"Wasn't he with you at all this morning? This afternoon?" Mose's voice was quick, firm.

"No. No." Sarah shook her head and pointed a shaking finger at Mose. "I thought he was with you."

"He wanted to come with me but I told him no. He was to stay with you."

Sarah's first thought was to run. She wanted to flee the terrible specter of a missing child on this immense prairie with its hidden hollows and swells, the grass waist high in some places.

30

With the realization that Eli was lost—she could not run from this fact—came the knowledge of hope, of bare spots where he could gauge his surroundings. She became rational, pushed back the panic, searched Mose's eyes. "He can't be too far. Did he not come with you at all?" she asked, her mouth becoming dry with her accelerated breathing. She licked her lips, tried to swallow.

"When I told him to stay, he was headed to the wagon. After that, I can't remember seeing him." His brown eyes filled with tears as his brow furrowed. He turned to the four directions, shading his eyes, searching the far-flung reaches of this strange and mysterious land.

Mary's eyes became troubled, large and round with concern. "Mam, he told me he was going rabbit hunting."

Sarah looked at Mary and grasped her shoulders with hands like claws, clamping down until she winced, shook herself away, and began crying.

"Tell me, where did he go?" Sarah ground out between clenched teeth.

Mary shrugged, sobbing now, her soft heart shattered by her mother. A kind of hysteria gripped her. Sarah began talking, moving away, moving back, babbling incoherently. The thought of their Eli, so short and stocky and manly, reduced to shrill cries of terror without knowing where he was and how he would find his family—it was almost more than her heart could bear.

He was her child, her baby. For six years he had been the youngest, the only one she had to cuddle and love, and now they had brought this innocent child to this terrifying, grasping prairie, this strange restless, treeless land of no mercy. A great sea of grass that was capable of swallowing children.

Mose came up with a plan. He told Hannah and Manny to stay together and keep calling, never losing sight of the treetops. Hannah listened to her father's words, her head bent to keep her emotions hidden, before saying that the whole plan was senseless on foot. Why not ride the horses? So Mose allowed it, watching both of the older children mount their horses and ride off up a small grade, the grass coming to their boot tops. Dimly they heard them calling, "Eli! E—li!" as the prairie and the sky swallowed them whole.

It was then that Sarah began sobbing—dry, harsh sounds of a mother's despair when a child is lost. Mose turned to take her in his arms, the sounds from her twisted face a form of torture to him.

"Don't, Sarah, my Sarah. Please don't. We'll find him. He's a tough little chap. We won't let him die. You and Mary go back to the house now and build a roaring fire. Maybe he'll see the smoke and find his way home. I'll start walking in the direction God lays on my heart. I'll see where He leads me by my prayers. Now go, my precious Sarah, put your faith in God. He'll take us through this valley."

He reached into his trouser pocket for a worn, wrinkled square of cotton fabric, lifted her chin and wiped her cheeks tenderly, searching the closed lids of her anguished eyes as if he could see through them and find his Sarah beneath them. As it was, the pain on her face became mirrored on his own. His smooth, untroubled features were now drawn, as lines appeared on his forehead and he became one with his heartbroken wife.

"Go now," he said gently, as he placed a kiss on her forehead. She stumbled away, the grasp of Mary's hand the only thing that kept her from falling. Mary was wide-eyed, serious, but too young to absorb the significance of a lost child in a strange land.

When Sarah looked up through streaming eyes that squinted painfully against the afternoon light, the prairie and the sky above appeared clouded in menace. The whole circumference of her world was ripe with portent.

They would not find six-year-old Eli. He had already been gone at least eight hours without returning, which meant he had gone too far to find his way back. These wide, harsh grating grasses never stopped their whispering, their rasping against each other. Their unstable movement deceived the eye with the appearance of sameness, and yet the height and depth was not similar at all. What if Eli stumbled onto a lowland, a swamp with mud underfoot and grasses above his head? He could wander for days in circles, never being found until it was too late.

The thought was too bitter, she could not tolerate the suffering of her small, squat son, the mighty one, the temper that flared like Hannah's. She kicked the red coals of the campfire, scattering the ashes, threw a handful of small wood pieces on top and watched it flare up. Dry-eyed with fear, she carried larger pieces of wood, rolling them expertly on top of the flames, watching the thick white smoke reach upward.

Oh, Eli, see this smoke. Look in this direction wherever you are. Taking a deep breath, she steadied herself, stood straight and searched the horizon, the far reaches of this endless land that contained nothing but grass. She shivered, hostility like goose bumps on her spine.

She had blindly followed Mose to this forsaken country, trusting his judgment, leaving her own will behind like clouds of dust curling from beneath those sturdy Conestoga wagon wheels. Here they were, cursed, *fer-flucht*. It was his disobedience to God with that insanity, that whiskey stilling. God is not mocked. What a man soweth, thus must he reap.

Oh, but he had repented though. Yes, he had, and truly. What had the bishop said? Though your sins are scarlet, I will make them white as snow. Clean like sheep's wool. Who was to know God's ways?

She threw another chunk of wood on the fire and watched the thick smoke curl, lift off, spreading upward, and on up. Look down on my offering, Lord. Accept it graciously the way you did for Abel all those many years ago. Accept my desperation, Lord, and return my son to me.

The sun's light was dimming now as it began its ascent into the waving grass. A chill crept across Sarah's arms and she shivered again. Darkness would come, inevitably. A darkness so black it would crush her if Eli was not found. She bit down on her lower lip, her teeth beginning to chatter with the new fear of day's end. She would not sleep, ever, until they found Eli.

But darkness came and with it a separation from any source of human comfort. Her husband and two oldest children were gone, for all she knew they were lost too, never to return. She paced the perimeter of the camp, tried to scale the walls of the house for a view of the darkness around her. Anything except to sit by the wagon and the half-built house with Mary quietly watching her with hazel eyes and helplessness.

Sarah could not comfort her daughter; she could not comfort herself. She felt cold toward Mary, a strange removal of feeling. She did not want Mary to see her like this. She wanted only Eli. To see his black hair sprouting from his hat, his open, laughing mouth, his snapping brown eyes, so alive, so eager and full of ideas, so restless in all of his imaginings.

Mary's whimpering about hunger brought a deep shame, a scramble to set things right. A slice of cold corn pone, some beans warmed by the fire. Sarah sat with her while she ate, an arm around the thin little waist. She assured Mary they would bring Eli back, and told her to put on her warm nightdress. Sarah tucked the girl into her bed in the wagon, with difficulty now, but she managed. Since the hour was much later than her accustomed bedtime, Mary breathed lightly, tucked her hands beneath her cheek and fell asleep almost as soon as Sarah pulled up the heavy woolen blankets.

Alone now, Sarah began pacing again, her hands clutched tightly over her stomach, causing a weird, rocking gait, but there was no one to see, no one to care. She cried then, loud, agonized wails until she was spent. She lay down on a blanket by the fire. Fear and doubt mixed with her heroic efforts at prayer. She could not concentrate. Her anxiety scrambled every coherent word until she gave up and lay there prostrate on her bedroll, a mere speck in this alien, unforgiving land. I just am, she thought.

I am only one person. God knows where I am, and He'll just have to take over. I can't pray, my bones have turned to ashes, and my strength is gone. I have no will. It's all right to give up, isn't it?

She thought of her own mother so far away, so unreachable, as if she no longer lived on the same earth but had spun off into the sky to some other world.

"*Shick dich*, Sarah."

How often had she heard the command as a child to behave herself? Yes, that was what she would do. She would accept the situation, give up her own will to God, and if He chose to take Eli to heaven, then so be it. At this thought, fresh tears squeezed from beneath her closed eyes, and she knew she wasn't close to accepting Eli's loss.

The night wore on, the half-moon lending its ghostly light, the stars blinking around it like silent listeners awaiting the outcome, offering their tiny pinpricks of light and comfort. The stars seemed close, a part of another world that looked out for people on earth, folks like her and Mose and the children, alone on the North Dakota prairie.

Sarah sat up, straining to see, to hear. There was only black night and silence. Even the wind had stilled. There was no swaying, no movement, no scurrying creatures. Only the silence laden with the knowledge that Eli had wandered off, that her husband and children were out there somewhere with the only two horses they owned, their only source of survival. That, the bags of seed, and the rain and the sun to coax them into germination.

She got up and tended to the fire once more. She thought it was useless to build it so fiercely if the dark sky swallowed the smoke without helping, the way the daylight would illuminate it. And yet she threw chunks of wood on the embers simply for the need to move, to do something.

She didn't know what time it was, too afraid of the time on the face of the clock in the wagon. One o'clock? Two? Would the time make a difference in her agonized waiting? Surely that was not a streak of dawn to the east. Please don't let it be the dawn. If they were out all night long and returned at daylight without Eli, she could see no way of being able to accept it, to comprehend with the settling of the horrible fact that her son was still missing.

She sat up. The earth spun, slanted on its axis, while a deep blackness engulfed her as the weakness spread through her limbs. Then—a smear of light on the prairie as if a star had fallen into the grass and shattered. There. Someone had extinguished it. A hand went to her chest to still her heart's pounding. Her eyes watered from intensely straining to see, to make the light appear. Perhaps it was only a giant lightning bug. No. There. There it was again.

She got to her feet, clumsily, whimpering now. It was a light. It was. It came on, closer. Voices. Real voices. Like a statue she stood, one hand clamped to still her heart, the other to her mouth to stop the trembling sounds that came from her throat.

There were horses. Ah, yes. There was Pete, with Mose. And Dan following with two riders. Hannah and Manasses. Manny. Somehow, this moment seemed too holy to call him Manny.

Was that a dark bundle across Mose's saddle? Sarah stood, straining to see, then took a few steps forward, her hand outstretched, reaching, hoping.

The horses and riders stumbled into the circle of light, the flickering fire illuminating the spent horses and the slump of the weary riders' shoulders. Mose called out, a quick high cry, in a foreign tone of voice she had never heard before.

Ah, yes. There was a hefty bundle across Mose's lap. Now Sarah could see the outline of a gray and rumpled hat, the shape of her missing son, her husband's strong arms around him. They came to a stop. Sarah reached Mose before he had a chance to dismount, her hands grabbing, claw like, her arms outstretched, muffled sounds no one understood coming from her open mouth without stopping until Mose had lowered her son into her arms. He was half asleep, filthy dirty, his hair stuck to the brim of his hat. When Sarah crushed him to her chest and rained tearful kisses on his face, he began to protest, turning away, spluttering and waving his arms.

"Eli. Eli. Eli." Over and over Sarah said his name, unaware of Mose or the other children's vigil.

"I'm all right, Mam. Stop it!" Eli protested hoarsely.

The horses were taken away by a dry-eyed indignant Hannah muttering to herself, a reluctant Manny following, having rather enjoyed the theatrics of his brother's return.

Sarah collapsed on a stump by the fire, her energy drained away by the enormity of her relief, the deflation of loss replaced by a sense of wonder and the dawning realization that Almighty God had heard her pitiful doubt-filled cries and had taken mercy. She could barely stay on the stump, her arms like water now, liquid, without substance. And yet she gathered her son to her breast, the rough wool of his coat a luxury, the softest fur imaginable.

"Eli, where were you? Where?" she asked, both laughing and crying. Mose sank to his knees, his arms going around his wife and son, his brown eyes searching Sarah's face, lit only by the fading embers of the fire.

But Eli didn't answer. He had fallen asleep. They laughed then, her and Mose, with a sound of bell-like joy, an exultation. A miracle. Their son had been returned to them. Together, they undressed him, washed his grimy face and hands, put him to bed beside the still sleeping Mary. Then Mose told Sarah his story.

They had ridden in wide circles around the creek bed. Keeping the treetops as their center they circled farther and farther, always calling, until their throats were parched by their hoarse cries. Darkness fell and hope with it. Mose could not understand why he had no guidance, no inner light. He asked God over and over, he explained. Stumbling around the seemingly endless prairie, only the North Star lending its light to keep their bearings, the horses became too weary to go on. Hannah complained about the senseless riding without an idea where Eli may have gone. Manny wanted to go back, rest, and resume the search in the morning. Mose could not face Sarah with empty arms and crush her with disappointment. So they kept riding.

It was Mose that ran his horse into the strand of barbed wire. Pete stopped, then shied away from the cutting of the sharp barbs, almost unseating Mose, but a cry went up from Hannah who immediately recognized the significance of a fence. Follow it and they'd find folks, other human beings in this forsaken place. She meant godforsaken but couldn't say it, having had her mouth slapped for it earlier and sent to the back of the wagon to ride with the horse feed—like a sack of oats.

They rode and rode, always by sight of the fence looming to their left. Sometimes, the prairie rose gently; sometimes it dipped down, but never very far or very steeply.

They found the outbuildings first. Black silhouettes, stark and unwelcoming in the dark, star-pricked night. Cattle stood around the barn like dark ghostly humps. A raucous barking rattled Hannah badly. There had to be five or six of them, all wolves or half-wolf. She fell back, holding Dan until Mose rode ahead. By the sound of them, they'd slay the horses and have them for dessert.

On they rode, past the corner post, beside an old wagon parked in waist-high grass, the dogs appearing like a dark sea of moving bodies, roaring and growling, leaping but never touching. Hannah wanted to turn her horse and get out of there but Mose said no, not before they spoke to someone.

They didn't have long to wait. There was the slam of a door, a shout of command, and the dogs' barking was extinguished like magic. A figure appeared carrying a lantern with a small orange flame burning inside the glass chimney, surrounded by tin and held by a thin metal handle. The opposite hand carried a rifle, long and low, the dark figure revealed only from the waist down.

"State yer business. If'n yer cattle rustlers, I

kin tell you right quick that if'n you don't leave this here propitty straightaway, ye'll be peppered wi' gunshot."

"No, no," Mose called out, his voice gravelly with exhaustion.

"Wal, what you here fer?"

"We lost our son, a little fellow named Eli. We're probably nine or ten miles away homesteading government land. Name's Mose Detweiler from Pennsylvania."

The bobbing lantern came to a halt, hoisted by one arm, it showed a grimy denim overcoat, a battered brown Stetson pulled low over a thin face, eyes barely visible, a moustache like a plastered-on chipmunk tail, a thin, scraggly gray beard, and a face like overcooked ponhaus. Silence spread through the night, thick and uncomfortable.

"Wal, I'd say we gotcher son. Little fellow, stocky on 'is feet, he is." Mose couldn't speak, afraid to show weakness in the face of this unknown character. He swallowed, felt the tears, and swallowed again.

The house was behind the barn, rising like an unkempt monster in a sea of mud. Lights glowed from the windows though, and somewhere was Eli. Somewhere behind those crooked walls with rectangular yellow eyes, perhaps his son would be safe and sound.

And he was. He didn't cry, only blinked and

43

blinked again. The lean woman sitting beside him was stringy and mean-looking like her husband, as if all the years on this harsh land had honed them into this toughness. But she smiled, said "Howdy," and that was most important.

Their names were Hod and Abby Jenkins. Lived on this here place all our lives, spoken proudly. Had three sons. Hod out riding, he said, checkin' cows. Stumbled on the sleeping li'l guy. Scared 'im, so he did.

They would come visiting. There was a road, a pattern of dirt roads. They had missed them all. Ranches dotted this land now. Surprised they could still get a grant to homestead. They'd be over, they said.

Mose's voice was an endless stream of rich gold oil that poured into the loneliness of Sarah's soul. There were people! Dirt roads! Even if it was nine or ten miles, that was a jaunt compared to the months and months of weary travel they had just come through.

Sarah had not realized she felt so alone until she knew they had neighbors. Real human beings. Flesh and blood. Someone to talk to, share lives, stories, find out about weather, crops, what could be done, what was profitable and what wasn't.

Here she was, holding her beloved son, delivered to her by God's own hand, the promise of folks living around them. People who built fences and lived in houses would come visiting.

Sarah breathed deeply, her eyes taking in the sweep of dark prairie, the sky above them, dark and starlit, the moon wan and impotent now, sliding toward dawn. The chill of fear and foreboding left with Mose's words, replaced by a warmer, more welcoming atmosphere, an air of hope, a breeze of anticipation. Perhaps it would be possible to feel content here, flourish even. Who knew?

Suddenly bone weary, her head drooped, her arms fell away from her stomach, as she tried to get to her feet. Mose came to her rescue, then held her lightly, too weary to think of further conversation. Hannah and Manny returned, spoke a few words before retiring to their bedrolls, arranging themselves into a comfortable position before nodding off.

Mose and Sarah knelt by the wagon, side by side, bowed their heads in silent prayer as each one silently spoke their gratitude to God. They retired for the night, rolling the heavy sheep's wool blankets on the canvas, drawing down the sides that allowed them a small amount of privacy beneath the wagon, still grateful, and immeasurably drained of strength.

Mose snored almost immediately. Only a minute had elapsed before the comforting sound of his breathing told her he was asleep.

Oh, she was blessed. Blessed beyond anything she deserved. Blessed among women. She reached over and stroked her husband's shoulder, then drew closer for the warmth of him, and shivered once before slumber overtook her.

In the waning hours of night, prairie dogs slept in the rich soil of their tunnels dug beneath the heavy growth of prairie grass. Rabbits tucked their twitching brown noses into their forepaws and rested, their ears flat along their silky backs. The firelight died down until only a few red embers glowed into the dawn of a new day.

CHAPTER 3

It was the cry of a meadowlark that woke Sarah, or some other familiar bird from Pennsylvania, she thought, without being fully awake. The sun was already high in the sky, which made her throw back the blankets and leap to her feet, thinking of the washing and the cleaning.

It was only after she stood on her feet, her hair scraggly, her dress rumpled and mud stained, the cold spring air sharp on her face, that she remembered where she was, how she had gotten there, the whole scene before her eyes a reminder of the shadow of hopelessness that had threatened to envelop her and choke life's breath from her body.

Squaring her shoulders, she took a deep breath and winced as ragged pains shot across her ribs. Ah, yes. This too, to be dealt with. Well, Mose had found someone, as he promised he would, so they were not alone.

She poured water into the coffeepot, set it on the rack above the fire, poured some into an agate bowl, grabbed a bar of Castile soap, and began to wash. She combed her hair, winced at the snarls, then twisted them along the side of her head. Using the very tip of the comb, she drew a straight line down the center of her head, divided the dark hair and twisted each side into a long roll before coiling first one, then the other, to the back of her head. She inserted steel hairpins with a quick, practiced precision. Satisfied, she placed a black scarf on her head, tied it beneath the thick, dark coil, and then began to prepare breakfast.

She shook her head a bit, thinking of her *wasser bank* back home. The kitchen cupboards lined along one wall, the deep sink where she placed her dishpans, the spot where the drain cover allowed the dirty water to drain out, the days she spent there, baking and cooking, and the wood-filled cooking range with the smooth cast iron top she cleaned with a piece of emery board until it gleamed like a polished mirror.

No use thinking about that. All she wanted was a roof over her head and four sturdy walls that kept out the night sounds. She hoped for the cleanliness of a floor, even if it was made of rough wood.

Her heart leaped at the thought of the possibility of a frolic. Inviting all the neighbors for miles around to have a day of building, erecting a house or a barn in a few days, the whole place swarming with straw-hatted and suspendered men, like a new hive of worker bees.

The sun's light dulled, the light fading out as if night were falling. Astounded, she lifted her head and saw a gray bank of clouds building up in the west. It was only midmorning but something was brewing, like a pot of coffee that had been percolating too long.

Well, if it was going to rain, she had better alert Mose and try to stay dry somehow with a canvas stretched between poles for a makeshift shelter. She rubbed her back when she straightened and searched her surroundings, with no trace of her husband.

As she sliced the boiled, congealed corn-meal mush, Hannah rose, disheveled and mud splattered. She stretched as far as she could reach then eyed the fast disappearing sun, the half-finished house, the weak morning fire out in the open, her mother's back rubbing, and her burgeoning figure. She snorted, stamping one foot.

"Mam, you know a storm is brewing," she said, pulling out hairpins and running her fingers through her thick, black tresses, spreading them around her face and shoulders.

"Yes. I believe there is a storm coming." Sarah stopped slicing the mush and turned to look at her oldest daughter. "Up already? I thought you'd sleep later, having been up all night."

"Yeah, well, we found him. We have neighbors too. They definitely aren't like us. Not Amish, that's for sure."

Sarah eyed her sternly. "What do you mean?"

"Well, after the wolf pack stopped braying, he

carried a rifle to greet us and meant to use it if we were cattle rustlers. What's a rustler?"

"I suppose a thief. What else?" Sarah answered. "Now get your hair combed, Hannah. Your father will be here soon."

Hannah obeyed, and Sarah turned back to frying mush. Sarah thought wistfully of the brown hens in the whitewashed chicken coop with the fenced-in yard surrounding it. Gathering the warm, brown eggs in the rubber-coated wire basket, washing them carefully, cracking them in the black cast iron skillet and watching the clear whites set to a white deliciousness surrounding the yellow yolk, like the sun in a pale patch of sky. She swallowed, her mouth watering for the taste of an egg. And freshly baked bread, yeast bread, white and so soft with the light brown buttery crust. She felt faint with hunger and longing then thought it may have only been the night's emotional chaos taking its toll on her well-being.

Fried cornmeal mush with a side of cooked navy beans; that was all they had. Hannah shook salt over her helping of beans, frowned as she scooped them into her mouth, and said she didn't care if she never saw another bean as long as she lived and that she was going to shoot a bunch of rabbits and prairie hens. At least they'd have meat and gravy.

Mose laughed outright and said she'd best help

get the house finished. He looked worriedly at the changing color of the sky and asked Sarah if she needed a shelter before the rain came.

"Well, what do you think? Should we just stay in the wagon?" Hannah pursed her lips as she listened to her parents. Always asking Dat, always following, going along with what he thought best. It drove her crazy. Didn't Mam ever have a will of her own? Not a thought in her head, other than what Dat thought? Gee. She was never getting married if she was expected to give her husband everything, including the contents of her head.

Take this whole catastrophe. Plopping his family down in the middle of a gigantic haystack, no thought for where he would get lumber or glass windows or shingles, just slapping logs into the form of a house, as if he knew what he was doing. She could not imagine that log dwelling keeping out the rain or the cold, the way he was going at it.

Hannah knew her place, though. She knew she could not say everything she thought and that about three-fourths of her thoughts were like seeds on unproductive ground: they withered before they took root and turned into words. Manny told her she needed to keep more of them to herself. It was not necessary to say everything she thought.

Well, maybe so, but Dat was going to need

help with that building unless he came up with a better plan. What was he going to use for a roof? She'd bet he hadn't thought that far, or perhaps he'd prayed that a roof would fall out of the sky and land on top of the walls.

Hannah scraped her plate clean, fishing the last bean from the side of her bowl. The sky turned gray, but a soft white gray, so perhaps the day would turn out cloudy, without sun, and no cold rain would fall.

Dat seemed in no hurry to accomplish anything, so Hannah wandered off to check on the horses. The wind was picking up. She noticed a sharp edge to every breeze, bending the grasses, ruffling them with gusts.

She lifted her eyes to the sky, taking in the shifting clouds. The now strange yellow light turned even the gray clouds a sickening color. Like vomit. The yellow light washed across the brown grass, turning it into a dark and sinister sea of ever-changing shadows.

It was late March, so surely this strange light and these churning, roiling clouds that erased the morning sun would not be the harbinger of snow. Or one of the Midwestern blizzards she had read about in her history book at the school she attended back home in Lampeter Township.

Hannah's large brown eyes took in the changing light, the bank of clouds. She wrapped her hands around her waist, her shoulders squared, wide and muscular on a tall, thin frame, her feet planted wide, leaning against the wind. She was defiance, strength, her unwashed hair in loose coils that stayed in spite of the growing gale.

As she stood and watched, the air took on a new chill in a few minutes. She shivered and wrapped her thin coat closer. Her calculating thoughts took stock of their situation. A sweep of prairie as far as she could see. The horses on their hobbles. The small pile of firewood, the fire out in the open, her mother bent over it. The only shelter, or some form of obstruction, was the four walls of the house, the stark rafters jutting into the sky, the Conestoga wagon with its worn flapping canvas.

Sitting ducks, that's what we are, she thought. Genuine sitting ducks. Greenhorns from the East who don't know anything about this high prairie and the weather that can wipe us all off the earth. Dat has so much faith. He'll just turn all soft and reverent, lift his face to the sky and place his trust in God alone, thinking He'll preserve us, and if our time is up, we'll go to our eternal home. Oh, I know how he thinks. Well, maybe I'm not willing to leave this earth quite yet.

With that, she stalked back to the camp and stood before Mose, who was eating his breakfast, hungrily slicing his cornmeal mush with his knife, a serene smile on his face, the welcoming light in his eyes as he watched Hannah's approach.

"Good morning, Hannah. Have you slept well?"

"Yes. Dat. Did you watch the sky this morning? Do you sense the wind?"

Mose finished chewing, swallowed, and then smiled. "Yes, Hannah, I did. I believe we're in for some hard rain."

"What about snow? It's only the end of March. We are not prepared to survive a winter blizzard, the way they arrive here in the West."

"Oh, I don't believe we'll have snow. The weather has favored us so far this spring. Our house will soon be finished."

Sarah sat on the stump, her plate balanced on her narrow lap, and looked from Hannah to Mose and back again. As usual, the decision was up to Mose. "I figure we'd better hitch up the horses and move out, find the Jenkins' place right quick. We can't survive snow and wind if it's a bad storm," Hannah said forcefully, spreading her arms, her hands palms up in a pleading gesture.

Mose finished scraping beans off his plate, deep in thought. He lifted his head to search the sky, watching the bank of gray building in the northwest. The sun was white, barely visible by the haze of yellowish gray smeared across it.

"Why don't we pray?" he finally asked.

"You can pray if you want, Dat, but I think we should get out of here. Now!"

"What about stretching the canvas across the rafters of the house? Could we quickly make a temporary roof? We'd have the four walls, such as they are," Mose said, his eyes searching his wife's.

"We could. But if this is a blizzard, how could we secure a canvas good enough to withstand the winds?"

Mose considered this, tugging at his long, dark beard. His eyes went to the clouds, and back to Hannah, his daughter, who was fast growing into an adversary, a presence he did not understand. A girl growing into a woman, outspoken with quick words and brute strength, the opposite of his soft, winsome wife and her quiet, accommodating demeanor, her willingness to let him lead in all things.

His first response to Hannah's plan was to reject it. A rebellion he did not understand welled up inside him. Who did this upstart think she was? His eyes went to the skies, back to the yellow brown of the moving prairie, ominous with the unnatural light that lay over the landscape like a threat.

He was still considering, mulling things over, when Hannah turned suddenly and pointed. Low on the horizon a dark, fast-moving blur that quickly came on, until they saw three riders bent low, their horses lathered, slick with sweat, their nostrils flaring red. They slid to a stop, breathing heavily, the riders flinging themselves off, the horses stretching their necks, tugging the reins from the riders' hands, then stood, intent on breathing.

It was Hod Jenkins and what Hannah assumed were two of his boys. In the harsh, yellow light he looked formidable with his dark, weathered face, his beard like frayed cloth, his clothes slick with grease and dirt. The boys were younger replicas of their father, tall and thin with angular features. Their hats were pulled low on their foreheads, their hair the color of the old tomcat back on the farm. Torn jeans and worn-out boots with crooked heels worn down from years of wear in all sorts of weather.

Hod wasted no time, minced no words. "Don't like the looks of this." He lifted a hand to the sky, a gnarled finger pointing in the sun's direction. "You better come with us. We don't have much time. I don't like the looks of this," he repeated.

Mose was at a loss for words. His gentle brown eyes worriedly searched the sky. Then his brow became smooth with his childish faith. Turning, he told the men he appreciated their concern and was thankful for good neighbors, but he believed the Lord would provide.

Hod let fly with a string of forceful words, telling Mose that he could think that if he wanted, but his thought of staying here unprotected on the high prairie was foolish. The temperature could plummet to a freezing low with strong winds and biting, icy snow. More folks than he could count had met their deaths, frozen less than a mile from home. "You don't mess around with Mother Nature, I'm tellin' you now," Hod finished.

Sarah stood, pulled her coat closer, shivered, and watched her husband. She could tell what he was thinking by the untroubled expression in his brown eyes. He wanted to stay and place his trust in God alone.

Manny came stumbling from his bedroll behind the wagon, his face alarmed at the presence of these men, their blowing horses, the dark sky and the sense of unease. He stood with his hair sticking up every which way, unwashed, his blue chambray shirt wrinkled from his night's sleep.

From the wagon, Mary and Eli's dark heads poked out from beneath the canvas, their faces alight, black eyes curious, without fear.

Hod waited, watched the sky, his boys' heads lowered, scuffing at the dirt with their boots, hands hooked in their jeans pockets.

But Mose was not stubborn or headstrong. He did not place trust in his own way. In the end he figured that Hod knew more about the weather in North Dakota than he did, being a newcomer and all. Yes, God did provide. God knew every sparrow that fell to the ground, but he also felt the wisdom of letting Hod advise him where the weather was concerned. And so he gave his consent.

Hod told them there was no time to waste. They

had best get that wagon going as fast as possible. His clipped words were obeyed. Mose brought Pete and Dan and hitched them to the wagon. Sarah and the children stored their belongings beneath a canvas in a corner of the house. They packed extra clothing in a small trunk. Hod told them to leave the food; there would be plenty at his house.

The riders went on ahead, leading the way. Mose drove Pete and Dan, prancing, misbehaving, jerking at the traces, pulling left rather than right. Sarah sat on the wagon seat clutching Eli as his head bumped one way then another. Mose sawed at the reins and tried to control the team.

Sooner than he thought possible, Mose guided the horses onto a good dirt road. In spite of the line of grass growing in the middle, it was more than wheel tracks in trampled grass. It was a good road.

Hannah stood, clutching the back of the seat for support and watched Hod and his boys ride. She had never seen anyone ride like that. It was as if the rider was merely an appendage, part of the horse, like an extra leg, something attached. It was a sight to behold, this skill of sitting on a horse so easily, a grace that stirred her senses. If it was the last thing she did, she would learn to master the skill of riding a horse, not just bouncing along, her legs flopping like a sack of feed.

Hod kept watching the sky, then held up a hand to get their attention. "Storm's movin' in awful fast. We still got an hour to go. If'n I was you, I'd get them horses going right smart."

Mose nodded. He had felt the change in the atmosphere, felt the air hitting his face turn frigid, slamming into his chest as if the buttons weren't securely closed.

Pete and Dan, the faithful brown Standardbred and Hoflinger cross, felt the storm's approach, the static, the wind and cold increasing as they trotted.

Sarah grimaced, holding on to the metal rim attached to the side of the heavy wooden seat, the wood and steel wheels jarring even with a slow steady trot. Now at every dip or hole in the road the thick mud was like glue. The horses tugged unevenly and threw them all around like corks in a bucket. But with the lowering skies, it was better to stay quiet, grit her teeth and endure the torment to her heavy body.

She felt Hannah's sharp knuckles through the folds of her skirt. She turned and found her daughter braced against the seat, her eyes burning dark with excitement, the storm mirrored in the depth of her gaze, watching the riders, a half smile on her face. She was enjoying the whole bit—the riders, the frightening weather— as if it was a deliverance, elevating her above the drudgery of their trip and the endless hard work that followed. Ah, Hannah, how will we be able to keep you with that spirit within?

The light was fading fast. The bank of yellow gray was changing to solid gray that spread over the enormous sky and the prairie below. Mose saw the storm, recognizing a fraction of its fury. His eyes widened as he leaned forward, bringing both reins down on the backs of the tiring horses. Sarah looked at him sharply. To goad a jaded horse was just not her Mose.

Hod yelled at the moment Sarah felt the first spit of snow. The atmosphere lowered, crushed the breath from them, as if a giant hand swiped through the air and took all the oxygen with it.

Hod pulled his horse back until he was level with Mose, who was concentrating on keeping the wagon intact and on four wheels. If there was an accident now, they might not make it to the ranch at all.

"Use your whip, if you got one!" Hod roared. "We got another few miles, but she's comin' fast. Keep your eye peeled for my buildings. If they get wiped out, concentrate on that spot. Your life and your wife and kids might depend on it."

Mose spoke sharply. "Hannah, help your mother get in the back."

"I can't," Sarah cried. Before she could muster any resistance, Hannah's powerful grip seized her shoulders, clamped down like a vice, and flipped her over the low back like a cat. Sarah cried out in fright. She grabbed an edge, anything within reach. It was the sturdy wooden trunk. She hung on like a drunk lost in his own dizzying world.

Mose was bringing the whip down on the terrified team, lunging and galloping, wild-eyed, the lather flying in white flecks into the howling wind. There was a gray whirling outside now. Through the small hole where the canvas was drawn together by a heavy ford, Sarah caught glimpses of a driving, slanted snow so thick it looked like the foam from the dishpan. She realized now they may never reach the Jenkins ranch. She had heard of folks dying in a storm, disoriented, frozen to death. But in March? In early springtime?

She heard Mose yell, calling hoarsely and still goading the weary horses. Above the wagon's clatter, she heard a faint call like the bleating of a sheep.

On rattled the sound of flying hooves, creaking wood, flapping canvas, the children's whimpers, Mose's voice like a hoarse scream. Another sound above the wind's howling and the roar of the snow. Again, that sheep's bleating.

The wagon slowed. Sarah felt it turn and tilt at a crazy angle. Mose's voice rose again. Sarah hit her head on the trunk as the horses broke into another frenzied gallop. Hannah yelled out to Mose in a panicked voice, screaming, "Left, Dat. Left. Bear left. I saw something!"

Mose did not hear, intent on the lagging horses, coaxing only a bit more speed. With an impatient snort, Hannah heaved herself up over the seat, grabbed the left rein and hauled it in, using both arms, her feet sliding off the dashboard now coated with ice and snow.

Mose tried to gain a hold on the left rein, but Hannah shouldered him away. Straight ahead a black hulk rose through the storm. Mose cried out, his relief putting him back on the seat, giving Hannah both reins. She kept her feet positioned against the dash, squinted through the thick gray turbulence, the whirlwind of snow, ice, and wind, elements that had the power to bring death to all of them.

When she pulled the team to a stop, dim figures appeared out of the black wall, pushed aside a part of it, the smell of hay, straw, manure, and oats, all pungent sweet smells from the interior of a barn, mixed with the roaring wind.

Hannah jumped down off one side, Mose the other, their hands like frozen chunks of ice as they fumbled to loosen the traces. Someone pushed her aside. Someone else took her arm in a tight grip and pulled her into the barn. Another person appeared out of the gloom and told her to stay; they would bring in the rest.

Hannah was startled into obedience long enough to step aside and allow the steaming, panting horses to be led through the wide door.

Foam, white lather, and sweat that had been rubbed against their skin by the chafing harness, dripped off their bodies. Their flanks quivered, their sides heaved.

Hod appeared carrying Eli, with Mary clinging to his hand. Manny led his mother through the door, white-faced, her lips twisted in pain. Mose was the last one in the door, his hat carrying a layer of snow, his face red with cold, his eyes still wide with the real danger his family had experienced.

The horses were cared for first, rubbed down with gunny sacks and given small amounts of water and hay. "No oats yet," Hod said stiffly. "It'll kill 'em, blowing the way they are." Mose nodded gratefully. He noticed the row of stalls, crude and makeshift but clean and mucked out, spread with fresh straw and plenty of hay, the watering trough clean.

"A' right folks. We need to get to the house and to do that, it'll take all the wits and common sense we got. We can't see more'n a few inches in front of our faces. Let's put the women folk between us." He turned, his gaunt, chiseled face taut with concern. "We ain't got no clothesline to hang on to, and this 'n's a humdinger. Biggest March storm I ever seed all my born days."

He called to his three sons, who stepped up in various stages of slouching, all tall, slim and crowned with the same battered wide-brimmed

Stetsons rimmed with dirt and grease. "Clay, you're first. Your sense of direction's the best. Like a homing pigeon. See if you can get us to the house. Now, whatever you do, don't let go of the hand you're holding. If you slip and fall, yell as loud as you kin, a'right?"

He pushed Hannah forward. "Take this 'un, Hank. Take her other hand." And so Hannah found herself grasping two gloved hands. The rest of the family was strung out, children between adults.

"You best start yer prayin' early," Hod said, but good-natured. Mose nodded. "You know if we miss the house we could all freeze to death wandering the prairie in circles. That's a human condition, a natural thing, to go in circles when it feels like yer goin' in a straight line."

Hannah thought he was making a big deal out of nothing until they stepped out into an alien world that contained a fierce cold. The whirlpool of snow and wind sucked all the air from your lungs and left you floundering to get only a fraction of what you needed, like a catfish on the riverbank before it was put on a stringer.

The cold slammed into her, through her thin coat and heavy skirt. Her hands that had been cold before were numb within seconds. There was no use trying to see through the gray, whirling whiteness of snow and ice. It was like being blind, but not black—only moving particles of white.

They kept moving forward. No one fell and no one hindered Clay's steady progress. The snaking line of human beings were being introduced to forces of nature they had no idea even existed. The worst they had ever experienced was a heavy, crackling, sizzling thunderstorm in the fertile valley called Lancaster County.

There was a bump and a shout. Clay had hit the corner of the house. More shouts went up and were snatched away by the powerful wind. Clay felt his way along the side of the house and found the porch. He stepped up on the porch and would not relinquish his hold on Hannah's hand until every last person was grouped on the porch, all accounted for and standing on his or her own two feet.

Only then did Hod raise a fist and brought it down on the doorframe over and over, a rhythmic banging that must have frightened the lone occupant within, Hod's wife, Abby Jenkins. Within seconds, the door opened a mere crack and a wrinkled face framed in fuzzy gray curls appeared, checking to make sure it was her husband and sons.

"You don't need to break down the doorframe, Hod. Git the little ones in. Watcha waitin' fer? Summer?"

Hod stepped back, extended his arm and pushed them all through the door where they tumbled, numb with cold, fear, and a real sense of having

CHAPTER 4

As the day wore on, they realized their miraculous delivery. They had never imagined God could create a storm of such intensity, with such a roaring, battering wind that sucked the heat up the chimney in spite of a good stove filled with massive chunks of wood. The glass panes in the windows rattled and jingled, lashed by heavy gusts of ice particles that scoured the house continuously.

Abby Jenkins was calm and in control, her lean, weathered face as tough as good leather, the frizz of gray curls sprouting out of her head with no rhyme or reason, no part in the middle, cut just below her ears and left to fend for itself. She wore a house dress with a row of white buttons down the front, the fabric having been adorned with flowers at one time, but washed and faded to a light-colored material with faint squiggles of color and held together by small safety pins in place of its missing buttons.

Her apron of sturdy oxford cloth pleated around her thin waist; woolen socks were pulled up halfway to her knees from severely tied sturdy brown shoes.

First, she brought a wooden clothes rack to the stove and dried all the Detweilers' outerwear.

Then she found seats for everyone, the long green sofa a luxury that Sarah sank into as she closed her eyes on waves of pain that rolled across her back. She gritted her teeth and willed it away, clutching Eli on her lap. Mary snuggled beside her, the child's hazel eyes wide with concern.

Mose sat beside Mary, watching his wife's face when he could. He felt out of control because of a situation he had not foreseen and had not even known existed. A belittling sense of shame and a stifling humility settled around him. For the first time in his life he questioned God, as if he was a bit put out that God had dared put them through danger that made them beholden to heathen folk. Their language was abominable in spite of their attempts to curb it for their visitors' sakes. He was not one to speak of religion to others. You had to be careful throwing out holy words in case you might be casting your pearls to the swine. These people likely didn't have a faith or believe in God. They appeared reckless, and the words coming out of their mouths were simply wrong. A sin, that's all there was to it. The Bible admonished plainly to let your yea be yea, and your nay be nay, and anything *dorüber* was unnecessary.

Manny and Hannah watched wide-eyed as they took in the talk that flowed so easily between the father and his sons, Clay, Hank, and Ken. Clayton, Henry, and Kenneth, Hannah thought.

Everyone appeared to have come from the same mold with almost identical slouches.

The house itself was surprisingly large and tidy for the plain appearance of the outside. A living room, complete with the large green sofa, a few rocking chairs, scattered rugs on a wooden floor gleaming with varnish, a few bureaus, dressers, and small cabinets with crocheted doilies. Most of all, the whole house had plaster walls that were painted just like the Amish homes back East.

The kitchen was substantial with a gigantic woodstove in the center, a long plank table, benches and various mismatched chairs. There were cabinets, a pantry, and a sink built into the simple cupboards that lined one wall.

Calendars hung above the table, from a feed store, granary, and a livestock market. Cast iron pans, blacker than night, hung from pegs on the wall, along with tin dippers and cups, saucepans, and an agate dishpan.

There was a bedroom downstairs for Hod and Abby and three upstairs, she said. There'd be no problem, her and Hod would move upstairs and she'd put clean sheets on the bed for Sarah and Mose. The kids could sleep on the floor. Hannah could have the couch in the living room. They'd make out and everyone would be fine.

And then she pulled an enormous blue roasting pan from the oven, took off the lid, and stirred the contents, releasing some mouth-watering scents

Sarah couldn't identify. With easy movements she unhooked a frying pan, got down a tin of lard and slapped a sizable amount into the heating pan. She disappeared through the pantry door and emerged with a parcel wrapped in white paper. Unwrapping it, she lifted a large slab of meat, threw it in the pan, followed by a few more, then another.

Sarah had never seen anyone fry so much meat for one meal. These were the years of scarcity, the Great Depression, when meat was rationed. Even a small beefsteak was hard to come by. Sarah would fry a small amount, cutting it carefully into tiny pieces and stirring in milk to make gravy that barely tasted of meat at all. In spite of herself, her mouth watered. Sarah pulled herself up from the couch and offered to help, but Abby waved her away. "I'm used to doing for my menfolk. It'd make me right nervous havin' another woman in my kitchen. Clay, git the table set."

Clay moved forward into the lamplight, hatless, his dark yellow hair sticking to his forehead in clumps, his face as red as a sunset below his eyes. His heavy plaid shirt hung in folds on his loose, skinny frame, but he moved with an easy, unselfconscious grace, as if it had never occurred to him that he should care what anyone thought of his appearance.

His eyes were blue, narrow, and surrounded

by skin weathered beyond his years. He had the most honest, frank gaze Hannah had ever seen, as if he didn't think bad of anyone and no one thought bad of him.

Hank was a bit shorter, wider in the face with the same lower level of red topped by that white ring where his hat hid his skin and hair from the elements. Odd-looking, but necessary, living on the prairie and working cattle.

Ken was the youngest, tall and thin with the identical phenomenon of red skin fading to that alarming, marble white. His face appeared youthful, unsullied by wind and weather. He caught Manny's eye more than once, grinned a lot, confident, swaggering, and like his brothers, unselfconscious.

Clay spread a long white tablecloth, and clattered dishes of various shapes and sizes. He splattered tumblers and silverware haphazardly around the table.

Abby turned. "There, we'll all fit. I'll sit beside Hod, then the kids can all slide along the bench there, and we're in business." She smiled her flickering smile that bunched her leathery skin into an accordion of creases as her blue eyes swept the room. "You must be starved, poor babies."

Sarah was dismayed to feel a swelling in her throat and the quick stab of tears. Surely she was stronger than this. But the truth was, she hurt all over, especially her lower back, and she was more than afraid of what it was. Ah, submission. So here she was, in an impossible situation, dependent on these kindly people, having no will or place of her own.

She felt Mose's eyes on her and turned to meet his worried gaze, assuring him with the light in her own dark eyes. I'll be fine.

When they were all seated, Hod spoke. "Now, it ain't our custom to do any prayin' before meals. But you folks has religion, I'm guessin', so you go right ahead if'n you wanna bless this here food."

Mose looked around the table and said, yes, they were used to praying before partaking of a meal, but always in silence, never speaking a prayer out loud. Hod nodded, said that was fine with him and bent his head. Everyone followed suit. Mose bowed his head, silently said his usual prayer, and waited for Hod to lift his head first. This was, after all, his home and his table, and by the customs of the Amish, it would be Hod who would end the prayer.

They sat and sat. Mose became uncomfortable, peeped at Hod, and was met by the top of his white, balding head. Thinking Hod must be more devout than he gave him credit for, Mose quickly lowered his head again.

Sarah cleared her throat and felt a blush of color suffuse her face as she thought how ridiculously long her husband was praying. Perhaps he was that grateful for their deliverance and the safety of this house.

There was a loud rustling, a cough and the clatter of silverware. Everyone lifted their heads, relieved. "I'm hungry. If none of you men will end the prayer, I will." It was Hannah who spoke. Sitting there in the lamplight without a smidgeon of shame, it was she who ended the prayer, so far out of her subservient place and quiet meekness that befitted women of the plain churches.

Mose was furious but quickly squelched his anger, gave a quick smile and a smooth "Why, Hannah. . . ." Sarah felt the beginning of a raucous laugh and pushed it back by lowering her eyes, her humility holding in her real emotions.

Hod looked at Hannah, really looked at her. His eyes shone. "Wal, Mose, I'll tell you right now. This young 'un's got some spunk. She'll make it." He nodded. "She'll make it out here, if'n no one else does."

Hannah gazed back at Hod, clearly pleased. She began to shovel an alarming amount of beans onto her plate followed by the crispy fried potatoes. Sarah couldn't help herself. She said, "Hannah, mind your manners. Perhaps there isn't plenty."

"What you talkin' about?" Abby spoke up. "They's always plenty at my table. I allowed for six extra. Let 'em eat. She's a growing girl."

After that, the bowls were passed, enormous blue stoneware bowls of beans cooked with tomatoes and onion, ground beef and bacon, fried potatoes and thick slabs of steak fried in lard and liberally salted. There were baking powder biscuits, so thick and light, and homemade butter. Sarah told Abby she must teach her how to make biscuits like these.

No one said much of anything. They simply applied themselves to their heaping plates of food. Outside, the storm continued, screaming around the corners of the house, whistling between windowpanes and walls, roaring across the level land with no obstruction in its way save for an occasional house or barn, which were like matchsticks compared to the power unleashed on them.

Hod said they might lose a few cattle but they'd felt it in the air, ridden hard, had most of 'em in the shed or corral. "Nothin' to do about any of 'em now. They ain't dumb. They'll find a shelter somewhere, left on their own."

Mose shook his head, doubt filling his eyes. "I don't know about this country. I had no idea the weather could turn severe this quickly."

Hod snorted, but not unkindly. "You got a lot to learn. This country ain't for soft folks or whiney ones that complains. Reckon if'n you want to make this yer home, you best hear me out.

"Fer one thing, you need to get that plow in the

74

ground. You need to finish that house and with just you and the kids, it ain't gonna happen. Your first year depends on the success of your wheat crop. You gotta get it in. Start a few calves and get your herd started. Me an' the boys'll be over. Get the house done."

"But . . . but . . ." Mose was at a loss for words. He shouldn't be needing all this help. It was not the way he had planned. He was from Lancaster County, Pennsylvania, the most fertile land in the East. He had planned on flourishing, raising corn and hay, and showing the West how it was done.

Already they had almost lost their lives, and here they were, dependent on these heathen who didn't pray before a meal, which told him they lived unthankful lives, and that was one of the seven worst sins. How could an Amish man of faith join with the man of the world? You cannot serve God and Mammon.

Mose pursed his lips and said, "Well, I do appreciate your offer, but I hadn't planned on growing wheat. I'm accustomed to our way of growing corn. And hay, of course."

Hod sat at the end of the table and stared open-mouthed at this young upstart. He thought, he won't last one year unless someone knocks some sense into that pious head. "Corn ain't much for this land," was what he said.

"Why not?" Mose countered.

"Wal, fer one thing, growin' season ain't too

long. Fer another, it don't rain when it's s'posed to. Wheat comes up early and ripens early. You get it shocked and milled before too much drought rolls around."

Mose shook his head. "Hard work."

"You skeered of it, or what?" Hod asked, eyes flinty with irritation.

"No, no. Oh, no."

"Yer money's in them cows anyways. You got all the hay growin' wild. This here's ranch country."

Mose nodded. This was all news to him. He hadn't planned on this. He had nothing but seed corn, and it was going in the ground no matter what Mr. Jenkins said. And he would not have to know that he didn't have enough money for a few cows and a bull to start his herd. He hadn't thought about raising beef cows. He had traveled all this way to a government homestead cultivating the thought of corn and milk cows, pigs and hens. He had no idea it didn't rain very much, or that the money they had brought was disappearing at an alarming rate.

So, according to this man, his own well-thought-out plan was not going to work. He would talk it over with Sarah, his support.

Abby saw to it that each child was comfortable for the night and assured them the storm would likely blow itself out in the morning. She hauled out blankets and quilts from chests smelling

76

of cedar, plumped pillows into flour sack pillowcases, and fussed over Mary's hair, saying wistfully it would have been awful nice to have a daughter.

"I'll be real nice to the boys' women if'n they ever show an interest. All's these men think of is cattle, the market, hay, and wheat. That's it." She laughed, still good-natured about her life in spite of living with these men.

"I got a few womenfolk neighbors. Now not between us, the way the men say. But there's Bessie. Bessie Apent. And Ruth. Ruth Jones. All married to ranchers, about five, six mile away. We'll get together every so often, exchange news and recipes. We listen to the radio and talk about what goes on in the world.

"Bessie's got four daughters. She'd love to marry 'em off to every one of mine. But I'll tell you, them girls is so fat and lazy, I dunno how she's ever gonna git 'em married off. She needs to git out and chase 'em around the corral a coupla times, melt some o' that lard off 'em. Big girls, not bad looking, but don't work hardly nothin'. Her husband runs the feed store in Pine. Pine's the town. Don't ask me why they named it Pine. They ain't any pine trees for hunnerts a' miles. Some say if Philip, that's Philip Apent, Bessie's husband, would get them girls to work, they'd have a right decent cattle ranch. But he has to hire help for whatever he does.

"Ruth Jones is a good friend. Salt of the earth she is. She'd give the shirt off her back. Has two daughters an' two sons. Names Lucille and Isabelle. They's awful nice girls. Work the cattle with their brothers. But seems like they don't have a hankerin' fer my boys. Somethin' about book reading and college. Want to go east to New York. I'll tell you right here, it ain't gonna work. Once this beg sky gits in yer blood, you never leave.

"New York City? They ain't gonna make it. Now you Amish. You don't marry outside a' yer religion, do you? What's *Amish* mean? Yer just plain down better than ordinary folk? I mean, same as them Catholic nuns dressin' themselves covered all over and not marryin' and stuff. Yer Hannah wouldn't marry outside her faith, is what I make it out to be."

Sarah answered her questions and explained about the Amish emigrating from Switzerland a long time ago for a place to practice their religion, how today there was a large group in Pennsylvania, but Mose wanted to see the West, so here they were. And no, normally girls did not marry outsiders. It would be a disobedience and a sadness to see their daughter overstepping the parental boundaries.

Abby nodded and shook her head wisely. She commented kindly, accepting Sarah into the realm of folks she kept in her heart. "We womenfolk, we have to stick together in the big country. It's all we got, an' if we can't get along, then the loss is ours, 'cause we all know we need each other. Stuff like, I'll give you my biscuit recipe, tell you how to make 'em, and you give me one a' yers. I ain't sure how Amish eat. You eat kosher, like them Jews? You fast and eat a bunch of purified fish and stuff? I'll tell you right now, there ain't no fish on the prairie. You eat hogs? Jews don't eat pork do they? If'n you don't, there's bacon in them beans we just ate. Hope you ain't left yer religion about my beans."

Sarah laughed outright. "No, no, Amish is different than Jewish, although we respect their religion. Jews are God's chosen people you know."

Abby narrowed her eyes. "You sure about that?"

Sarah laughed again, easily, and could see the suspicion of new and different cultures. Was it just Abby, or was it the West?

"Now that black shawl and bonnet you had on? You know yer gonna have to be careful where you go with that on. Folks'll take you for a witch. I mean it. We ain't used to that hereabouts. They'll not do you harm; they'll just keep about a mile between them and you. People get superstitious about ghosts and haunts and stuff, livin' alone the way we do. Might make us crazy in the head, probably."

"I won't go anywhere. Where would I be able to go? All I have is my family."

"Yeah, and looks like you got one on the way."

Sarah blushed and felt the swelling in her throat. "I do," she said softly.

"When's yer time?"

Sarah mumbled a date, then lowered her eyes. She mustered all her courage to meet Abby's eyes and asked softly if there was any help close by and how they should go about finding someone.

"Wal, there's Doc Elliot, but he's in Dorchester, thirty some miles away, which probably won't do you much good. I dunno. It's been awhile since I was in need of someone, so I'll ask around fer you."

"Thank you," Sarah whispered.

When she woke up in a stranger's bedroom, her children piled around her in dark bumps under someone else's quilts and pillows, she could not get her bearings or understand the dream that had awakened her. Someone was hitting her repeatedly until she woke covered in cold perspiration and a new knowledge of her fate.

Mose and Sarah's third daughter was born in the middle of a howling snowstorm out on Hod Jenkins's ranch, on the high prairie of North Dakota on March 31.

They named her Abigail, for Abby, who had woken right up, got dressed, and taken matters in hand, Hod hovering by the woodstove and smoking so many cigarettes in the lean-to out back, he almost froze.

She was a tiny thing, born five weeks early by Sarah's calculations. Abby's face grimaced and twisted as she fought her tears, her soft heart touched by this squalling infant, so skinny and helpless, born too soon, frightened and cold.

"Ain't no different 'n them scrawny calves that comes early," she chortled, digging out some small blankets. She ripped up some of the boys' long underwear and slipped the soft fabric over the baby for a makeshift gown. She wrapped the red-faced, black-haired infant in two old baby blankets and put a cut-off sock on her head. She handed her back to Sarah after her bath, cooing and fussing, her eyes wet with tears. It didn't matter how hard she tried to look stern, nothing worked. So she blew her nose, wiped her eyes, closed the bedroom door and made breakfast with Hannah's help.

They cooked a huge pot of oatmeal, fried cornmeal mush, made up a batch of biscuits, set the enormous blue coffee pot to boiling, fried some bacon, and made a pot of bacon gravy to ladle over the biscuits. She called the men, who tumbled into the kitchen in various stages of fright and embarrassment.

Abby set everyone straight by telling them it was as right and natural as the calvin'. She brought out little Abby, as she proudly called her, to show her around. Hod's face was alight with happiness, as proud of the little one as if she were his.

"Little Abby," he chortled. "Wal, Darlin', you got yer daughter!" The three boys looked into the pile of quilts and asked if everyone started off that tiny or if it was only Amish babies. Clay said she didn't look a whole lot different than a tomato, and Ken thought she should be kept in a box behind the stove, the way premature calves were.

Mose was clearly humbled, reverent, going about his devotion to his wife and newborn daughter with a newfound zeal. How could he ever have doubted God's leading? Clearly, he had given himself up to Mr. Jenkins's urging. Here they all were, his wife delivered of the infant that had so troubled her.

Again, he had won favor in God's eyes by relinquishing his own will, and the rewards were amazing. And so he loved his wife with renewed emotion and opened his heart to his tiny daughter named Abigail. A rather fancy name, but it was found in the Bible so he knew it must be all right.

The storm weakened in the late morning hours. By dinnertime the roaring of the wind, that scouring, whistling sound that buzzed at loose shingles and played with loose boards, had turned to harmless gusts. The sun shone on a white world with drifts packed against buildings and piled around fences and trees. As far as anyone could see, the snow lay in waves where the force of the gale had sculpted it. The sun's light cast a blue and green aura on the beautiful prairie, washed clean of all the ominous shadows.

Hod and Abby generously allowed them to stay, saying that Sarah could not travel and had no place to go if she could. The snow wouldn't last long, they said.

And it didn't.

By Sunday the grass was showing. Bare spots sprang up in the high places. The children wanted to play outside. They got on everyone's nerves until Abby shooed them out. "Like a buncha spring heifers, that's what they are," she laughed.

Sarah told Abby many times that this was all too much for her and they could go home. She would be fine in the wagon. Hannah was old enough to help with the family. But Abby would hear none of it. She shouldered all the extra work with alacrity, her curls bouncing on her head and her leathery skin creased into constant smiles.

"This ain't no bother, an' you know it. At the end o' March, we're all house crazy, fit to be tied, I'm tellin' ya. Here you all blew in, givin' me someone else to think about other'n myself."

Hannah was unimpressed with the baby's arrival, deeply ashamed of being so needy and pathetic to these English people. What must they be thinking? Being part of a poor, pathetic family of greenhorns was not the way Hannah wanted to live her life. The whole episode was intolerable, and then Mam went and had that baby. She told

Manny those boys probably thought they were all from the poorhouse somewhere. She didn't care that Dat made it sound as if he owned Lancaster County. Really? She knew very well what happened to the farm, the whiskey fiasco, everything. Here he was acting as if he had never done anything wrong in his entire life, and it simply wasn't the truth.

She became slavishly devoted to every move the three brothers made. How they shoveled snow and cleaned stalls. How they fed the livestock, saddled a horse, pulled on their boots, the way they wore their hats, their language, and above everything, the way they rode a horse as naturally and as easily as walking.

Manny was awestruck as well, except he felt as if they shouldn't imitate the way they talked. Dat had often warned against unnecessary words. Hannah shrugged her shoulders and said there was nothing wrong with it, not if their parents talked like that themselves. Maybe everyone talked like that out here in the West, away from ordinary civilization where people were packed together in cities and towns and worried a lot more what others thought of them.

"I'm never going back, Manny. These people suit me just fine. If we weren't so poor, I'd buy a saddle, a bridle, boots, and a hat, and I'd learn to ride and rope right along with them. You bet!"

Hod and Mose decided that Sarah would stay

at the Jenkinses' with the two youngest children, while Mose took the two oldest children in the wagon and drove Pete and Dan home through mud, defeated grass, and patches of snow. White geese flew far overhead, heading south, honking and whistling without ceasing. Hod said they were snow geese and would stop at Fall Lake. He'd have to take the whole family there sometime to see all the migrating birds.

The homestead was still there, the mud and the half-finished house, the logs and the sprawling trees in the creek bottom, the cache of food and belongings beneath the canvas.

Mose stood and surveyed the center of his domain and knew he could not finish the house without a loan. He had underestimated expenses for the months of travel, and now there was not enough for a decent roof, windows, and floors. There was not a person he knew for miles, except Hod, and he could not lower himself to ask him for a loan. He never spoke of finances, not even to his closest relatives, whom he thought would never know. But things got around.

They would manage. He'd learn how to make his own shingles. They could do without windows and a floor until the first corn crop was sold. They'd make do. Sarah would be willing, he knew. A virtuous woman, her worth was far above rubies. The truth, for sure. He never had to navigate life's path without her support. She would sweep her dirt floor, and if the roof leaked, she would set an agate dishpan under the leak and take it in stride.

Yes. He took a deep breath, filling his chest with appreciation of the good, moist air. The sun had risen in all its splendor. This was a land rich with the promise of wealth, with loamy soil and verdant grass, fair weather, and God's promises. He was a man blessed beyond measure.

And so he took his two horses, his two oldest children, his axe and his wedge, and went whistling to the creek bottom to fell more trees for the building of his house on his homestead.

CHAPTER 5

When Hod saw the log walls going up, he squinted, ran a hand over Mose's workmanship, and whistled softly. "It's a right good house you got here," he said.

Mose smiled his thanks, his eyes reflecting his goodwill. He nodded and said yes, he thought after those logs were chinked with mud, the house would outlive any of them.

"You got shingles or sheet metal for the roof? I'll tell you right now, the tin roof is the best in these here winds."

Mose stammered, his words didn't make much sense, saying he'd likely make his own, or something Hod didn't understand.

"You can't make yer own shingles. Not with these logs. Don't work. That's how come the folks here build sod houses."

Mose set his axe aside, pushed back his straw hat, and scratched his head. "Really?"

"Yep. These here trees in the bottom? They're too soft for shake shingles. Can't be done. I know. I'll take you to Dorchester, make a two day trip. We'll bring home the windows, doors, an' the roof."

Mose pondered Hod's kind offer, wishing there was enough cash in the box and ashamed to tell Hod there wasn't. He shoved his hands in his pockets, kicked at a clump of mud, then straightened, looked at Hod with the straight-forward look that reminded him of a child, and asked if he could get credit at the lumberyard.

"You need credit? You don't have money to finish?"

"No."

"How were you figgerin'?"

"Well, I thought I'd make my own shingles and doors. We could do without windows until cold weather, then my first corn crop would be ready to sell, and I could pay for a floor and windows."

Hod said this wasn't Pennsylvania; he better not count on a crop the first year. This was the West, and anything that can go wrong usually does.

Nonplussed, Mose smiled. "Like what? What can go wrong?"

"Wal, about a hunnert different things. This country ain't fer the weak."

Quickly Mose defended himself. "Oh, I'm not weak."

"Obviously, yer not. These walls couldn'ta been easy."

"That's right!" Mose was pleased to receive Hod's praise and felt powerful, as if he could get through anything the Lord chose to test him with. Anything. Out here in this level, uncluttered land, free of other brethren, those bickering, complicated fellow men who robbed him of his peace, his self-confidence knew no bounds.

"You know I have a good wife. She won't complain about a dirt floor. I can't go into debt. It would worry me."

Hod considered this, stuck both hands in the back pockets of his jeans, flapped his elbows a few times, pushed back his hat, squinted at the straight rafters and thought this man may well be able to figure something out on his own. He knew, too, the futility of the projected corn crop. And he thought of Sarah and her baby daughter.

"I'll tell you what, Mose. I got some windows stacked along the back of one of my sheds. We'll paint and putty, replace the panes o' glass. But you have to have a roof. Whyn't I pay fer the tin, an' soon's you can, you pay me back? How's that fer a pretty decent plan?"

"Oh, I'll pay you back. I certainly will," Mose said gratefully.

"Sure you will." Hod stuck out a hand, and they shook with strength, an amiable light on Hod's leathery red face and an eager, guileless one on Mose's.

So it was agreed by the pact of a good hand-shake. They made the trip to Dorchester with the two sturdy horses, leaving Sarah in Abby's care, and Hannah and Manny to fend for themselves in the middle of the prairie's expanse until their father's return.

Left to roam free, they explored their world on foot, took their father's rifle and shot prairie hens and rabbits, blowing the heads clean off, delighting in their marksmanship.

They skinned the animals, taught themselves to clean them and cut them apart into decent sized sections. They fried them in a cast iron pan over a bed of coals, in lard and cornmeal sprinkled lavishly with salt. They ate well, delighted in their freedom, slept late, and forgot to say their prayers until Manny reminded Hannah they hadn't prayed once, not even before eating all that fried meat.

Hannah eyed her brother, shrugged her wide, angular shoulders and said that praying before every meal they ate wasn't so all-fired important as Dat let on. You could wait and pray at the end of the day, when you said your goodnight prayer, or the end of the week. Same thing, so long as God knew you were hungry and thankful. You could even wait until the end of the year, if you wanted to.

Manny narrowed his eyes, pondered his sister's words until he came to the conclusion that she had no fear of God. No *Gottes furcht*, and told her so. Mose and Sarah would have quaked in their shoes if they heard their daughter's brazen answer. Manny showed no surprise, just stripped meat off a delicate prairie hen bone with his teeth and flung it over his shoulder into the deep black shadows behind him before shaking his head, wise-like.

"You better watch your words, Hannah Detweiler. You'd put our father in his grave if he heard you say that."

"He didn't hear me."

"Well, watch what you say. You're disrespectful."

"You think? Oh, hush."

Hannah sat cross-legged, her elbows resting on her knees, her hands loose, perfectly imitating the Jenkins brothers when they sat watching one another rope a calf or train a horse. If she would have had a fence to sit on the top rail, boots on her feet to hook her heels over the lower rail, she would have done that too. Manny did the same, whether he was aware of it or not.

The brothers were a wonder. They could do anything. Anything they tried, with loose-jointed skill, an unhurried grace, ambling through difficult tasks as naturally as if they'd been doing it all their lives.

Which, Hannah supposed, they had.

Her awe of them bordered on reverence. Their easy gait, the language they used, the way they stuffed a wad of pungent smelling dark brown tobacco into the side of their mouths and left it there, spitting a majestic stream of brown tobacco juice unbelievable distances.

When Hannah compared her own tiresome existence with the lives of those boys, it didn't seem fair being a girl, and an Amish one at that, with parents who set all these careful guidelines, recited those endless verses and Psalms from the German Bible, instilling the words of wisdom and the fear of God in their children. They were taught well. Behave, honor your father and mother, live righteously in love and truth, keep the Sabbath, fear going to Hell and missing Heaven by one wrong deed—it all hung over Hannah's head like irritable black ravens she wished she could shoo away.

What was the use of going through life when it was all so boring, so pale, like milk pudding without sugar or cinnamon? Take Mam. She'd live the remainder of her life walking behind Dat, her steps measured and careful, always obeying, always smiling into his kind eyes. They were always polite, always caring, always flat-out boring.

She was pretty sure Manny thought so too, although he was far too good-natured, too subservient, to say so. She doubted if he would ever stray very far from his parents' wishes, which were good and right.

A twinge of apprehension settled over her shoulders, as if this self-examination came with a price, and the cost was frightening her. So be it. Dat had no business packing her out here to the middle of nowhere, with not one other Amish soul around. Didn't he know in just over a year she'd be at the age when she'd begin her *rumschpringa*? Then what was expected of her? To have no company, no friends, and certainly no husband?

Manny's voice broke into her train of thought, derailing it precisely by his announcement that Clay asked him to help herd the cows to the corrals, as soon as they decided to do it.

"What?"

"You know, ride all over their land looking for cows and calves."

"Why not me?"

"You're a girl."

"What does that have to do with it?"

"A lot, actually. You're supposed to be in the house, helping Mam."

"She's taken care of, being with Abby."

"She's coming home, soon as this house gets done."

In answer, Hannah threw a few chunks of wood on the fire and flounced off to her bedroll in a huff. Manny watched her jerky movements, her stiff gait and elaborate thumping into her bedroll, and grinned. Here was a job for Dat. Good, kindhearted Dat.

The Jenkins men descended on the Detweiler house, wielding hammers and nails, bringing tin, windows, and doors. They cut and sawed logs for the floor, working long days before beginning their ride home, often through the dark. Hannah stayed with the men, keeping the coffeepot filled and heating the stews and soups Abby sent along.

Hod showed them how to chink the logs with a mixture of cement and mud, which Hannah tackled with her usual aplomb, shouting at Manny if he took a break or watched the men too long.

Mose was effusive in his appreciation, pumping the men's hands, emotion making his eyes shine with a gleam close to tears, which made Hod uncomfortable, not being accustomed to flowery speeches. But he guessed Mose was thankful, so he shrugged his shoulders, went home, and told Abby he believed Mose was a little soft in the head.

They brought Sarah home to the new house, pale and wan, but with a new eagerness to begin life in a house, living like civilized folk. It was small compared to her house in the East, but it smelled fresh and clean and had a good wood floor that had been sanded and oiled. That was plenty good enough for her, as Mose knew it would be.

They had no furniture. There had not been room to bring anything except the sewing machine, the trunk, a few dishes, pots and pans, extra clothing, and bedding. There was no fireplace and no stove, so the cooking was done outside, the stones set up in a circle, closer to the house.

The first thing Mose built was a sturdy table

made of planks, which he sanded smooth. One of Abby's tablecloths fit just perfect.

The breezes carried moist warmth, and the columbines began to bloom in the low places. A variety of birds moved across the sky of whispering grace. The air smelled different and infused a hope that had been elusive for Sarah.

Sometimes she stood at the doorway and watched Mose with the two horses and the plow, drawing a straight black line across the level prairie, tufts of grass sticking up like an old man's eyebrows. She thought of all that grass decomposing beneath the western soil, making possibilities seem like a certainty, a reality.

Then her heart soared, a song came from within her, and she felt a fresh will to continue, a desire to see what they could accomplish here, so far away from everything they had ever known.

In time, then, with the Jenkinses' help, they had a decent place to live. The house was small, the furniture sparse, but there was a lift, a good solid space under the eaves for the children's sleeping quarters.

Sarah had brought her flannel comfort covers, leaving the sheep's wool at home, reserving space for other necessities. So she stuffed these serviceable covers with thick, dry prairie grass, and the children slept well. Manny and Eli at one end of the loft, Hannah and Mary at the other. It was a wondrous roof; the gray tin didn't allow one drop of rain inside. When there was a storm, the sound was like a barrage of ice pellets thrown against it, though it really only was raindrops of water. Hannah loved the sound of it and the safety of lying cozily under this new roof.

Sarah never complained that she had to cook outdoors. There was no fireplace and no money for a stove, but she was grateful for the house nevertheless. She sang as she swept the floor with her homemade broom of willow twigs. She praised the Lord all her days for the roof and the good walls surrounding her at night.

She cared tenderly for little Abby, who was a good baby, lying in her little bundle of blankets because there was no cradle or crib for her. Mary was in awe of her, sitting on the one luxury they had brought from the East—the cane bottom armless rocking chair. Hannah tickled her under her dimpled chin and watched her mere seconds before directing her interest elsewhere. Babies were a bother, and they smelled.

Abby Jenkins shared more of the crumbling squares of white lye soap with Sarah, so it wasn't that the baby's diapers weren't clean. Sarah watched her oldest daughter warily. Her eyes followed her as she went through the door, pushed back the tide of alarm that threatened her calm, and wondered what kind of girl would be so unaffected by the innocence of a small infant.

How had they managed to raise this unruly

daughter, this distant person who showed increasing disinterest in all manner of spiritual teaching? When Mose read the German *Schrift*, she either tapped her foot as if she was irritated, or lifted her eyes to the ceiling while she strummed at her lips with two fingers, making a strange buzzing noise, which apparently Mose never heard, or if he did, he gave no indication of being distracted.

Sarah, however, was distracted. Always glad when devotions were over, she felt the stiffness leave her neck and shoulders, her breathing slow to normal. She could sense the lack of interest, but surely they would not need to raise a heathen in this wild and lonely country without sufficient people of religion to give her good company. How could they expect it of their children, wearing the white head covering if there was not another girl within a hundred-mile radius brought up in the doctrines of the Amish?

Sarah's way of dressing was very important to her. As long as she could wash, starch, and iron the large white head covering, she would wear it, and if it wore thin, she would patch it with fine and even stitches. Without it, she would feel unclean, exposed, naked. The head covering was instilled into her upbringing, infusing her life like a warm and fragrant tea, comforting, sustaining, a perfect guideline on how to live a godly life.

She thought of the Jenkinses often. Here was

an uncouth and worldly family, one who had no religious principles. And yet, their kindness knew no restraint. It flowed from them, an unexamined virtue they were completely unaware of, brushing away any grateful words with an air of unease, as if praise was an unaccustomed visitor, a stranger who made them nervous.

The diapers Abby had given them came from a store of good quality flannel from her high walnut cupboard in the living room, a massive, ornate piece of furniture that made Sarah wonder about the Jenkinses' background. Much too polite to ask about their past, Sarah had kept quiet and accepted the small favors, the tiny gowns adorned with old lace, the hand crocheted booties, yellowed with age, but wearable and comforting.

Abby's dry, weathered face had been a beacon of joy, the lines and wrinkles increasingly deepened as she smiled and laughed out loud with a coarse sound that came from her throat every time she held the tiny bundle. Until one day, a strange sound strangled the laughter. She sat back in the wooden rocker and gasped for air, trying to stop the sobs that began in the midst of her smiles.

"I had a little one once," she said suddenly, her voice raw with suppressed emotion. "I had myself a baby girl. As perfect as the rising sun and as welcome. We found her in her cradle, cold and still one frosty mornin'. Her life was not quite three months on, an' she was taken. I guess the Lord must have had need of her up there in His Heaven. I don't know. It still hurts after all these years. She was like a doll, my firstborn. Bitter, I was, for the longest time. But there ain't no use carryin' on if'n you can't have what you most want, so in time, it became a small pain instead of a big one. Clay came along then, and took a chunk of the pain away. Seems as if each baby that came along took some more of it with him. But now I remember back to how it all was."

She swiped at her eyes with the back of her hand, blew her nose with the square of muslin she always kept in her pocket, and shook her head. "Times come when it's hard to figger out the Lord. Why He does things the way He does. Not that I'm overly religious, mind you. Hod don't hold much with church going and prayin' an' stuff. But when you folks came along, it put me to mind of the time we used to go, singin' and prayin' and listenin' to the preacher yellin' about God and all kinds of them things."

She shook her head again, pondering. "I dunno."

Immediately Sarah's motherly heart took up the pain, understood Abby's ache, the longing she still felt, and she said softly, "The Lord giveth and He taketh away. The Bible is so clear about that. It was God's will."

"Yeah, well, I know. But I've come to doubt

God, livin' out here in this place where you can't count on nothin'. The dust and the storms and the cold and the heat, when yer crops shrivel and the cows can't hardly find a thing to eat until their ribs is like bed slats under their dried out skin, it's enough to make a person wonder if there is a God, and if there is, if'n He cares about this here prairie an' the folks that live on it."

Sarah murmured, "Oh, but His mercy is unfailing. His goodness is always with the righteous."

For an instant, Abby's eyes flashed, as if Sarah had angered her, and just as quickly, it was gone. When she spoke again, she had changed the subject to the amount of dark hair that adorned little Abby's head, and after that she never mentioned God in Sarah's hearing.

Had she angered Abby? Sarah did feel God would bless them here in this verdant prairie if she lived righteously, submissive to Mose and the way he ordered their lives. Had God not provided even now? She had not been able to see her way through the birth of little Abby, and the building of the house. Everything had seemed insurmountable, like a steep, forbidding mountain that was impossible to climb. Oh, her faith in God had multiplied, abounded, her heart filled with strength to go on, for He surely provided, even in the darkest times.

On their journey, when the horses tired, the way looked long, stretching before them like an invisible question. God had provided. It was only her own doubts and fears that had hampered her faith. She wanted to tell Abby this, share her testimony of dependence on a much Higher Power, fill the woman's heart with God's abounding mercy. But she was afraid Abby would not be open to it and that it would only anger or provoke her. Perhaps she had seen too much.

Mose hitched the horses to the sturdy new plow and went out to a section of land he felt was the most fertile, where the soil was thick with black loam and decomposed grass. He set the plow and called to the faithful creatures.

They lunged into their collars. Mose hung on to the two wooden handles and together they plowed a long, dark ribbon of upturned soil, clumps of grass sticking up out if it like misplaced whiskers. After a few rounds in the hot, spring light of the sun, dark streaks of sweat marred the horses' flanks, their nostrils were distended, blowing out with the force of expelled breathing.

Mose stopped, flexed his shoulders, pushed back his straw hat and surveyed the upturned ribbon behind him. Here was good soil, no doubt. Here he would prosper, his crops a beacon of good management that came directly from his forefathers, generations of men who had tilled the land and sowed the seed that had been blessed by the God who was rich with mercy and unfailing goodness.

With each turn of the good earth, his heart rejoiced in the Lord. He knew the corn he would plant would stretch on either side of his buildings, a waving sea of green, the wide, rustling leaves eventually producing large yellow ears of corn to feed the hungry children and animals, an abundant food supply, coupled with the endless sea of grass that could be harvested for the horses.

He hoped to obtain a calf from the Jenkinses, if the Lord so willed it. He thought he might be able to barter a few days' wages for it, perhaps longer than that, a few weeks, possibly, for a bull calf and a small heifer to start his herd.

Mose smiled at the thought of Sarah's delight in milk, cream, and butter, a veritable luxury, and one he looked forward to with keen anticipation. Yes, life was worth living. Oh my, how much it was worth! Out here in this powerful land, where God's presence hovered across the waving sea of prairie grass, the air was pure and as sweet as the nectar of a honeysuckle vine, free of the foul breath of other men's opinions. His spirit soared on the wings of the small brown birds that raced across the sky in acrobatic rushes of reckless flight. Uncharted, freewheeling, but crafted by the Master's hand, Mose thought, as he squinted into the brilliant noonday sun.

On into the afternoon they toiled, man and beast, using every resource they were given, struggling on across the land, tearing up the hardened grasses by the roots, tossing them aside by the shining plow slicing into the moist earth.

In the evening, Sarah stood at the edge of the field, her eyes wide with wonder. The thin line of plowed soil had turned into a broad, dark band, the clumps of moist earth sheared cleanly, glistening in the late-day sun. The soil was moist and heavy with promise, a harbinger of things to come.

She breathed deeply, never tiring of the sensuous odor of freshly plowed soil. It spoke of Mose's labor, a good man doing what God had ordained from the beginning, that man labor by the sweat of his brow.

She pushed back the notion that there were obstacles, the clumps of grass still protruding from places where the soil was not fully turned over. Would there be sufficient rain? Hadn't Hod spoken of drought?

Sarah hunched her shoulders, wrapped a hand around each elbow and stood, her head bowed as she murmured her lowly prayer to her God. One day at a time, Lord, one drop of rain at a time. *Himmlischer Vater. Meine Herre und mein Gott.*

The harrow bounced cruelly across the sturdy clumps of grass, jerking the hames of the horses' collars, rubbing them raw, their skin oozing drops of blood that smeared with the white foam of their sweat, turning it pink as the flecks dropped from them.

The sun was high in the sky, hot and getting hotter. Mose was perspiring freely. His legs and feet ached from the agonizing jolts as he stood on the rusted old harrow he had borrowed from Hod.

The morning was well spent, but his work seemed fruitless. Discouraged, he stopped the team, watched the heaving sides of the horses, noticed the raw places beneath the harness and became alarmed, stepping quickly to their sides. He looked back and his heart sank within him.

How would he ever get a crop into the ground with this rusty harrow and two horses? This grass was far more than he had bargained for.

He thought of the sturdy Belgians, the powerful, lunging teams hitched four abreast, easily drawing well-constructed, well-equipped harrows and discs and plows across soil that was easily turned and easily crumbled beneath the steel equipment. The corn planters were so new and efficient.

For one moment this journey fell on his shoulders with the weight of a sack of grain. He felt the folly of it. Or was it folly? Perhaps he was only discouraged and tired. To be back on the home farm, though, was like an invisible thread that pulled steadily, waking up thoughts and memories long buried.

His mother, plump and happy, always smiled

as she rang the dinner bell that called them in to her well-laid table. There was prosperity and happiness, so much food, such luxuries in the barn alone—cows, milk, butter, and cheese. There were hens in the henhouse laying eggs, clucking and cackling. His mouth watered thinking of two fried eggs with a side of scrapple after the hog butchering.

Suddenly, a longing to return seized him and shook him to the core. Just hitch up these horses and travel back home, resume life, swallow his pride, learn to listen to the arguments, and learn to appreciate other men's opinions.

His hands shook. Sweat poured freely from the agitation in his soul. He felt elated, ashamed, humbled, and uncertain.

What would Sarah say? Where did this thought come from, this seizing of his emotions? Only yesterday he had felt so certain of God's will leading them safely through adversity to the prairies of North Dakota. They were blessed indeed.

He wiped the sweat from his brow with fingers that fluttered, his mouth gone dry, his heart racing with a deep, unnamed fear. He looked up, expecting to see a black cloud covering the sun, turning the land gray and cold and barren. The thought of a flowing sea of green corn was replaced by a sick and colorless despair.

CHAPTER 6

Hannah snorted as she watched her father's pathetic progress, bouncing around on that ill-constructed harrow, the jaded horses plodding along. "Look at him, Manny. He is so determined to grow corn out here. There's an impossibility if you want to see one, and I mean it."

She had taken to hitching up the belt of her dress, imitating the way Hank and Clay tugged at their belts on their patched jeans. She stood with one leg crossed over the other, foot propped on the toe of her cracked and worn shoe. If she would have had belt loops, she would have hooked her thumbs into them. As it was, she balled her fists and pushed them against her narrow hips.

Manny stopped cutting branches from felled trees, shaded his eyes with his hand against his forehead, squinted, and nodded. "Horses are shot."

"I know. It's ridiculous. He'll kill them yet."

Manny shook his head and turned away. "He's our father," was all he said.

"Yeah, but he doesn't have too many good ideas. He never did. Do you know why we came out here to live? 'Cause he lost the farm and then tried to use up the leftover grain to make whiskey."

"He did not do any such thing, Hannah."

"Yes. Yes, he did, Manny. They kicked him out of the church. He had to join up again and do all that repentance stuff that sinners do. Then we left."

Manny drew himself up to his full height and addressed his sister in clipped tones. "I don't care what you say, Hannah. You lie. You say anything you feel like saying. You don't respect our father."

"Why should I? He's a dreamer. A loser. Not even Hod Jenkins can tell that man anything. Dat thinks Hod is a man of the world, so he doesn't amount to anything. He's not gonna listen to him. Hod knows he can't grow a decent crop of corn, not with those two spindly horses. And certainly not without bigger equipment. Hod's just humoring Dat, lending him that plow."

Manny stood, a man not yet formed, an ache in his youthful heart brought on by a young man's devotion to a godly father. He respected him, refused to believe in the hard, accusing words of his sister. She was the one with the problem, not his Dat.

The sun shone hot and bright, pressing down on his shoulders as he watched Mose slap the reins down on the horses' backs. They dutifully responded and clawed forward, their haunches lowered by the force of their efforts. He tried not to see the futility of his father's form bouncing around on top of the poorly built monstrosity on which he balanced. Beside him, he felt the prickly disapproval of his sister, but he said nothing when she snorted.

After that, they went back to work trimming branches from felled logs meant for the barn, tedious back-breaking work that kept them perspiring all morning. Hannah wanted that barn in the worst way, so her efforts were relentless, her energy unbounded. She was determined to have her own horse, a corral, to learn to rope and ride, and to drive cattle—all of it. She had a goal in mind and nothing would keep her from it. Nothing. If she had to build that barn with her own hands, then so be it.

Her dat was on the wrong track, so she figured it was up to her to keep things going if they were going to survive out here on the prairie. The only way she could see it work out was to employ Hod Jenkins and his boys, try and lay down her pride and accept whatever they saw as necessary. Otherwise, they'd never make it.

She straightened from her job, kicked a pile of branches, and watched as three riders approached from the south, their horses' heads lowered as they rode down the gentle incline toward the creek bottom. She swiped the back of a hand across her forehead and turned to watch.

How easily they sat astride their horses! If she never attained any other skill in life, it was all right if only she could learn to ride like that. It was an amazing feat, to become one with such a beautiful creature, to know its mind and become attuned to its instincts. To sit astride so high above the ground, to feel the wind and smell the endless fascination of the earth and the waving grass, the great nothingness of the landscape, knowing she was only a dot, a miniscule form in a vast, mostly unexplored region.

Who knew what lay twenty, thirty miles west? Or east? No doubt there were more ranches, folks like the Jenkinses, who ran cattle, some without fences to retain them. It was the way to make money, these cattle, tough, skinny creatures that plopped a calf on the still-frozen earth every spring, as regularly as the season changed.

You needed your own brand, though, the sign of ownership sizzled into their hairy flanks. Clay and Hank roped them with a swinging jute rope called a lariat. One arm swings a loop of it over his head with a muscular strength, a calculated grace that sends it over the running calf's neck. The horse immediately sensed his master's aim and stopped in seconds, haunches lowered, forefeet braced, as the rope twanged taut.

To Hannah, the taut lariat performed a song to her senses, like the strings of a guitar, the *verboten* musical instrument she longed to hold, to cradle in her arms, the form and sheen of it a thing of beauty, a vessel of sweetness that sang unbearable notes unlike anything she had ever heard. Its notes could evoke unnamed feelings of dissatisfaction, a glimpse into the unknown, a beckoning world she knew nothing about, like a promise of light and brightness at the end of a dark hallway.

She still hadn't reckoned it all out. It was like a jigsaw puzzle with half the pieces missing. But she watched Clay sitting on the top rail of the fence with the heels of those wonderful boots caught on the lower rail, the guitar balanced against his long legs, his hands plucking idly at the strings, as easily as brushing his horse's mane. Watching him laughing, nodding, his light blue eyes twinkling at his brothers who sang, their heads bobbing with the movement of Clay's hands, brought all these questionable longings. Her heart quickened, making her sit up and take notice of a world without the blackness of restraint and the laws that ruled her life.

Sometimes, when she was with her mother, the sweetness of her, the light around her an aura of goodness, she felt pulled by a rope as strong as a lariat to be like her, to live out her days in peace and contentment with whatever the Lord sent in her direction, plodding one step behind her husband. Just, well, taking it, "it" being whatever he decided, like pulling up her roots from Lancaster County and leaving her aging parents, severing the ties with her family with the sharp blade of his will. A stone was the only remnant of her past life that she kept, a stone where her heart should have been.

Glassy eyed with numbness, a deep keening, a mournful sound that stayed enclosed, tamped down with the strength of her will, her mother had remained seated on that wooden seat beneath the canopy of dirty white canvas.

Oh, Hannah had seen. She had felt every womanly sorrow along with her mother, knowing that the waxy contours of her face were the feelings so successfully banished, like her own.

Hannah figured they were here now, in this strange new world, so thinking back with yearning for the closeness of cousins, the kinship of grandparents and aunts and uncles, wasn't going to help a lick, so she may as well square her shoulders and get on with it, this living out here in this land full of nothing.

She looked up as the riders approached, watching the way they sat in their saddles, their limbs loose, relaxed, their hands idly holding the reins as if they weren't necessary for guiding or stopping their horses.

Hannah threw her axe, swiped at a thick strand of dark hair, and watched Hank's face, then Clay's. They both lifted their hats with that offhanded push they always applied, a gesture that puzzled Hannah. She thought perhaps it was a sign of good manners, like a handshake, only easier, but she wasn't sure about that. She smiled as her eyes met Clay's.

"Whatcha doin', Hannah?" Clay stopped his horse, threw a wrist across the saddle horn, put the other one on top and leaned forward slightly as he watched Hannah's face.

"We're cutting logs for the barn," she said, a smile playing around the corners of her mouth.

"You know you and him's gonna get hurt whacking them trees down," Clay said slowly.

"Him?"

"Your brother. You're nothing but kids. Your pa oughta be helpin' you some. Where's he at?"

Hannah shaded her eyes and pointed to the horses plodding methodically, their faithful noses almost touching the ground with exhaustion.

Clay's eyes narrowed into slits as he watched. His long, greasy blonde locks barely moved in the ever present wind, the cleft in his chin covered with blonde stubble, about a week's growth. His cheek twitched like a horse's hide when a fly bothered him, his jaw set. He shook his head.

"He's killin' them horses."

Hannah nodded.

"You know he ain't gonna grow no corn."

Hannah felt Manny behind her before she heard his voice, high and strident. "You don't know anything either, Clay Jenkins. You don't. God can bless my father and his corn crop."

112

Deeply ashamed, Hannah whirled to face her brother, eyebrows drawn, trying to shush him with her glare of warning.

Clay said slowly, "Well, that can all be, but looks as if he's gonna have hisself a job just keepin' them horses alive."

"God can do anything!" Manny spat out, his face white with childish rage and suppressed tears.

"I reckon."

Hank watched the plodding team, then turned his horse toward Hannah. "We come over to invite you and yer family to our round-up and neighborhood git-together in two weeks."

"Neighborhood? There are no neighbors," Hannah laughed.

Clay watched her face as she laughed, one of those laughs that came from deep within, that bubbled to the surface as clear and pretty as spring water in the Ozarks. He squinted, blinked, and kept watching as Hannah said that if there were neighbors, they sure were well hidden.

"Some of 'em are, some of 'em ain't. You get yer horses, we'll ride around and meet a few."

"Mam won't let me."

Manny nodded in agreement, eyeing the Jenkins brothers with distaste. He hitched up his trousers and told Hannah there was work to be done and the sooner they got to it, the better.

Then he turned on his heel and picked up his axe, his posture and vehement chopping giving away his disapproval.

"S'wrong with him?" Hank asked.

Hannah shrugged.

She met Clay's pale blue gaze boldly, as if trying to make up for her brother's bad manners. Suddenly embarrassed for different reasons entirely, she scuffed the toe of her old leather shoe into the wood chips and trampled grass, lowering her head to focus on the mud and wood chips.

"Hey, it's okay," Clay said in that slow, soft way of speech that he had.

He looked off across the grass to the house, where Sarah appeared in stark relief against the dark logs, her posture bent over the outdoor fire as she tended the pot hanging on a tripod.

"Yer ma never got a stove?"

"Not yet."

"Why'd the old man build a house without a chimney or a fireplace?"

Confused, Hannah lifted dark eyes to their blue ones. "What old man?"

"Yer pa."

"He isn't old."

"Just our way of talkin'. The old man's my pa."

"Oh."

Hannah looked away. Hank and Clay swung their wrists to the left, laying the rein on the right side of their horses' necks, shifted in the saddle, and were off in mere seconds.

Sighing, Hannah turned, slowly picked up her axe, and resumed her work halfheartedly. They must all appear like beggars, pathetic losers without a clue how to go about making a living. And that, precisely, is what they were. A hot wave of shame swept through her, followed by a pride so icy it stung.

Why couldn't they have stayed in Lancaster, where they were the same as other folks? Hannah thought of riding around to meet the neighbors on one of the sturdy, all-purpose Haflingers, dressed in her plain Amish garb with the large white covering on her head, without a saddle and without boots. She felt a sense of loss so keen she shivered.

It was the loss of being able to hold up her head, to feel as if she was a normal, attractive person of means, someone who knew what was going on in the world around her. She felt displaced, blinded by the vast world of the treeless plain, where the winds blew constantly, and the clouds hung in the sky, uncaring, void of color or meaning.

Sarah tended to her bubbling stew, wiped the sweat from her streaming brow, then hurried back to the house to hush her crying baby. She smiled warmly as Mary dashed to reach baby Abigail before her mother did, lifting the swaddled infant and clumsily patting her back.

Sarah sank into the armless rocking chair, so grateful yet again that they had had the good foresight to bring it all the way from home. As she fed her baby, her eyes grazed the interior of her home and again she felt deeply grateful. A good floor made of wood, sturdy walls, windows, and a door, the four necessities of a decent home. Beds to sleep in, a loft for the children, may God be praised.

Mose would *sark* for a chimney, he would. He wanted to get that corn in the ground first. Oh, he was working so hard to get started farming. A crop of corn would be all they needed.

She thought with satisfaction of the stew bubbling on the fire—potatoes, carrots, a few prairie hens, wild onions, garlic, and salt. It was a stew hearty enough to stick to her men's ribs. Her men.

Manny was growing so fast into a sturdy little man. She was grateful too for the gift of potatoes and a bucket of carrots from Abby Jenkins. What a treat to be able to change the daily diet of cornmeal and prairie hens. And so Sarah rocked, the stew bubbled in the open air, Mary ran out to play with Eli, the great open space beckoning, the world for them an endlessly unexplored place.

Sarah cared for little Abby with an even greater appreciation than any of her previous babies. Hadn't God provided? Oh, He had, and so much more than she could have comprehended, were it not for the fact that she held this perfect little girl, dressed in warm clothing, all taken from Abby Jenkins's chest, where she had stored away the clothes of her baby who had died. There was much to be thankful for, much to consider in the ways of the Lord, indeed.

A shout broke through her reverie, a far away sound that shattered her peace, as if a mere pinprick of noise became a harbinger of alarm. Her rocking ceased. Slowly she lifted Abby, closed her dress and held stock still, listening.

There. Another shout!

In one swift movement she gathered Abby in her arms, moved to the pile of blankets in the corner and laid her gently on her stomach, covering her with her own small blanket. She stood at the door and surveyed the flat expanse before her, involuntarily searching for Mose.

Her heart sank within her as she saw Mose circling the horses—or the lone horse left standing. The other was a dark mound on the upturned soil.

Sarah ran, leaving Abby alone in the house, calling to Mary and Eli. When she reached her distraught husband, she took one look at his red, streaming face, the panic in his eyes. Throwing up her hands, she asked what she should do.

"Water!" shouted Mose, as he bent to untangle taut harness pieces. Sarah ran back to the house, her skirt billowing behind her, the wind in her face. Her thoughts were racing over what a dead horse would mean: one horse left over, and they could not go on. She could not think about that now.

Grabbing the water bucket, she lowered it into the wood rain barrel until it was full, hefted it out with all of her strength, and walked fast, water sloshing over her skirt, the sound of Abby's wails in her ears.

Mose watched her approach, ran to grab the bucket, lowered it by the heaving horse's head, tried to lift it, coaxed, spoke gently saying, "Here's water, Dan. Water. Drink some water."

Sarah bent to examine the horse's eye, the lids falling heavily. The horse was covered in white foam, his sides streaming, the rivulets of sweat joining the foam, creating small crevices, and staining the earth where it ran off. She grimaced, seeing the blood seeping into the white lather, staining it pink, the dry nostrils expanding and contracting rapidly with the unnaturally quick breaths that came in desperate spurts.

"He needs water, Sarah."

"I know."

"How can we get him to drink?"

Sarah shook her head. "Loosen Pete."

"I did. Can't you see? He's not attached. He wants to stay."

They stood helplessly as the horse continued the fast, raspy breathing. The sweat continued to stream from him as he struggled to inhale and exhale.

"Can we get him up, do you think?" Sarah asked.

Mose nodded, grabbed the bridle, chirped, tugged at the bit, and kept calling his name over and over. Sarah watched the noble, obedient horse try to lift his head, scramble to regain his footing, scraping one foreleg and then the other along the partially tilled soil before a deep groan escaped him. His head sank forward, his body shuddered into a solid heap, and his breathing slowed until he was still.

Mose called his name again, urgently, but there was no response. "Is he gone?" Mose asked Sarah, a look of blank bewilderment in his brown eyes.

"Yes, Mose. He just took his last breath. He must have become overheated." Sarah's hand went to Mose's shoulder, moved up and down, a gesture of comfort, the caress of caring.

Mose lowered his face, and then lifted it to stare at Sarah. Her eyes opened wide, shocked at the incomprehension in her husband's eyes. "But, I can't harrow without Dan."

"No, you can't."

Mose hesitated, shoved his hands deep into his trouser pockets. "But how will we go on?"

Alarmed, Sarah soothed him, saying God would provide, thinking God would provide by borrowing a horse from the Jenkinses. Here was a case where they would evolve from God's testing and do the right thing by using common sense and the sound mind God had given them.

"But how will God provide?" Mose asked, as he brushed Sarah's hand away from his shoulder. Her hand fell away and for the first time ever she felt his reproach. Quick breathing beside her made her turn to see a white-faced Hannah, fists clenched, chest heaving, followed by an out-of-breath Manny, who came to a halt, peering down at the dead horse.

"So you really did kill this horse. I knew you would. You're nothing but a thickheaded farmer! Don't you know you can't raise a crop of corn in this soil without at least six horses and a plow twice the size of yours?" Hannah shouted, her white face reddening with the force of her fury.

Without hesitation Mose drew back his hand and smacked Hannah's face a glancing blow. "No daughter of mine will ever speak to me like that," he ground out.

Hannah's head snapped back, a red stain appeared on the side of her face and, for a moment, Sarah thought she would lower her head and take this as the chastening she deserved.

But in another moment, Hannah lifted her head, faced her father and spoke levelly, the words laced with a disrespect so potent it sickened Sarah. Hannah's eyes glittered and drew into narrow slashes of dark brown as she spoke.

"You killed that horse, Dat. You'll kill Pete, too, if you keep on. Didn't Hod tell you this is cattle country? Didn't he tell you? You won't be able to raise a crop of corn. You left Lancaster, Dat, now you're going to have to change your ways."

Mose stepped up to his daughter, his fists clenched, his jaw working. Sarah realized his intent and reached out to grab his arm and plead with him. "Come, Mose. Everyone is upset. Let's go to the house and eat our dinner. Bring Pete, Hannah. Manny, get the bucket."

They turned as one, this small band of people walking together leading the tired, sweating horse that remained across the level prairie with the grasses waving back and forth in the uninterrupted wind, each one carrying their own different loss and feelings of foreboding.

True to her word, Sarah calmly took up the stewpot, set it in the middle of the table, and got out the dishes they'd need. Hannah sliced a loaf of sourdough bread.

Manny put Pete on a tether after giving him small amounts of water and tried not to hear his weak, anxious nickering. Mose sat on a stump by the doorway, his head in his hands, his wide shoulders slumped forward with the crushing weight of his loss.

They all sat down together, bowed their heads, and prayed silently, although it was questionable whether Hannah prayed at all, the way she chewed at her lip and her eyes glittered like brass, the rebellion raging through her body. Manny and Eli bowed their heads low, squeezed their eyes shut, and said their prayers dutifully, not quite understanding what the death of a good horse entailed.

They all ate hungrily, sopping up the good, sustaining stew with slices of bread. Breakfast had been early and sparse, Sarah doling out the thin and watery cornmeal porridge.

The meal revived their spirits, and they kept up a conversation, a planning, of sorts. Mose took his rightful place as head of the house saying that God would provide another horse if they repented of their sins, lived righteously in godly fear, and prayed day and night. God had never let them down, and He wouldn't this time either.

Sarah bowed her head in submission, listening to her husband's words, wanting desperately to have a faith as great as his, although basic common sense knew there was only the Jenkinses and the begging—humble asking accompanied by the sense of failure—that remained. But she bowed her head anyway then looked up into his bright eyes, shining with a new and vibrant light. She smiled and said, "Yes, Mose, I do believe you are right. We will continue our work on the barn and see what the Lord has in store for us."

Happily and vigorously the children nodded,

content to live in the realm of a father who based his whole life on his faith. Manny, especially, was filled with a deep sense of the celestial, his face glowing with an inner light.

To see Hannah's face, then, was a study in light and dark. Her cheek still flushed from her father's administration of discipline. Her face was shadowed with anger and ill feelings playing across it like puffy, wind-driven clouds.

"Hannah, what do you think?" Mose asked, appearing to make restitution for his harsh discipline earlier.

No answer.

"Hannah?"

Still no answer.

Sarah looked at her eldest daughter with pleading in her soft eyes, but Hannah's eyes were well-hidden by the heavy curtain of her upper lids.

"Hannah, you will speak to me when I ask you a question," Mose said with conviction.

She refused to answer, as before.

Sarah had begun to rise, a hand on the table to steady herself, her mouth open to speak, when Mose's chair fell backward and clattered to the floor with the force of his rising. The kindness and warm benevolence with which he faced the world was erased by a black anger, the likes of which Sarah had never seen.

He grabbed Hannah's shoulders and shook

her, from behind, her head flopping like a fish, but only once. Hannah wriggled from his grasp, lunged through the door, and was gone before anyone had time to stop her. Sarah ran outside, calling her daughter's name, but she obeyed when Mose ordered her inside, saying she'd get over it. That girl needed her sails trimmed good and proper.

His words proved true. Hannah crept up to bed, avoiding the steps that creaked, thinking no one would hear. But Sarah lay wide awake, worrying and praying alternately until she heard Hannah's return, then wondered whether they were turning into uncouth heathens, same as the Jenkinses.

CHAPTER 7

As predicted, the miracle horse's arrival came in the form of Hod Jenkins and his boys, who rode over to confirm the announcement of the calf roping and neighborhood picnic.

They met Mose, who walked out of the house in the late afternoon, said he'd been resting, had a bit of a headache, blinking his eyes in the strong, hot sunlight. He scratched first one underarm and then the other and rolled up his shirt sleeves to reveal gray long-sleeved underwear. His hair was parted in sections, each chunk held together by a lack of washing. He yawned widely, revealing yellowed teeth caked with plaque.

Hod threw him a shrewd glance, figured this guy was going downhill without brakes, but said nothing, just threw himself off his horse, strode over to stand beside him, surveying the unfinished barn, the partially tilled field.

"Yer not up to par, then?"

"I beg your pardon?"

"Ain't feelin' good?"

"Well, yes. Just a bit of a headache."

Hod nodded, his eyes searching the man's circumstances. "Yer other horse run off?"

"No, he's dead."

Hod looked at Mose sharply. "He got colic?"

"No, I must have worked him too hard. He went down and never got back up. I don't know what was wrong with him."

"Yer horses gittin' only grain?"

Mose shook his head.

"So now what's yer plan?" Hod asked, shifting his toothpick to the opposite side of his mouth.

"The Lord will provide. He always does."

Hod chuckled, deep and friendly, the crow's feet around his eyes like fans crinkling out at the corners as his shoulders shook silently.

"Wal, neighbor Mose, if'n I was you, I wouldn't bet on a horse droppin' out of the sky, but whatever you fancy, I suppose."

They spoke of the coming roundup. Hod urged him to bring the family, and they left soon after. Hod took notice of all three of his boys trying to look for Hannah behind each other's backs and his chuckle increased to full blown mirth that he did nothing to hide. He just shook his head and knew the impossibility of all of it. Mose would have a fit. He chuckled again, shifted his toothpick, then looked to the left. His whole countenance changed to one of deep concern, then irritation.

"How's he gonna do that?" Clay asked, jerking his thumb in the direction of the field.

"His horse died."

"Yeah."

But, as was the custom, nothing more was said.

• • •

The bucket of carrots and the burlap bag of potatoes were stretched as far as they would go, the prairie hens Manny shot helping to round out the meals. But when Sarah found the bottom of the cornmeal barrel so close, she felt as if she could not take another day of her husband's alternating between headaches, reading his Bible, or disappearing into the bedroom to pray.

Hannah and Manny did their best to prepare logs for the barn, but progress was slow without their father's help, the logs becoming smaller and more misshapen. Every day Sarah kept up a positive outlook, swept her house, cared for the children, cooked the frugal meals, and encouraged her husband whenever he needed it, which, increasingly, bordered on the impossible.

When she looked back, the change in Mose was not slow in coming. Starting with the loss of the farm, the hard times when the animals' worth dropped so dramatically, the desperation without forethought of using up the leftover grain to make illegal liquor, the childishness afterward, and now this—yes, it was strange behavior.

To admit this to herself was frightening. How could she have escaped the fact that something was wrong with her husband? Should she try? Or should she accept it, unquestioning in her faith? She had no one but the belligerent Hannah, and they were barely on speaking terms.

When the cornmeal ran out, the last potato was eaten, and one wrinkled carrot remained, Sarah followed her husband into the bedroom when he went through the door to pray.

"Mose," she said.

"Do not disturb me, Sarah. I am entering holy ground."

"Mose, please listen. Our food is all gone. The children will be hungry in the morning. You must stop this. You must stop praying and fasting. You're only working yourself into a frenzy. Mose, we must do something about our plight."

"The only plight, my Sarah, is yours. When our faith falters, we have a plight, whereas we have heavenly peace when we trust in the Lord with all our hearts."

"But, Mose, listen to reason. God provides when we do what our minds can direct. If our food is all gone, we must find some. Don't you see?"

"No. My face is turned to God alone. Leave me."

Sarah knew now that she must be strong. She squelched the sob that tore at her throat and swallowed a hard lump as her eyes remained dry. The fright she kept at bay by moving about the house, caring for the children, putting them to bed, everything proceeding normally for their sakes.

It was the hunger in Manny's eyes that brought

on the boldness. She stopped Hannah midstride, laid a firm hand on her arm, and waited until she met her eyes. Sarah spoke in firm, even tones.

"Hannah, you must ride out in the morning. We have one wrinkled carrot and a handful of flour. Neither one are enough to feed anyone breakfast. Your father is not well. I have no hope of being saved from starvation but you. Can you ride to the Jenkinses for help?"

Hannah stared at her mother. "You mean he's crazy, or what?"

"He's acting very strange is all I can say. I'm afraid it's been going on longer than we think."

"You mean I have to go and beg?"

"Yes, you must."

"Mam, I'm ashamed."

"I know, Hannah. I know. If you want me to go I will, except I'm not a good rider. We have only the one horse, and he's not in the best shape to pull the wagon alone."

Hannah's gaze flickered. Her shoulders lifted and then slumped. "What do we need?"

"Everything, Hannah. Everything."

And so, midmorning Hannah rode out on Pete, the former beautiful, well-groomed muscular horse that had been worked too hard and spent months without grain. That was fine for animals accustomed to a steady diet of prairie grass, but not for this well-fed, well-cared-for Eastern horse.

His hair was long and unkempt, although Hannah had done her best to brush out the worst of the dirt and tangles. His ribs were like a small train track, with his belly hanging down, loose, muscle loss evident from every side. Even his well-rounded haunches that had been taut and firm now quivered with deep vertical lines every time he took a step.

Hannah felt hot tears prick her eyelids. She steadied herself with a deep breath and a measured squaring of her shoulders. Here she was, then, riding out to beg for food, set plumb down in the middle of nowhere, with people spread out like chaff scattered in the wind. Miles and miles of nothing but grass, driven in seventeen different directions by each gust of wind.

Dat was out of his head, it appeared, and Mam was as scared as a chicken with a fox in the henhouse, fluttering around the house with a smile that wasn't real. Just the corners of her mouth lifted to keep everyone else calm and let them think everything was fine with Dat, who held his head and moaned. Nothing to eat, a dead horse, and a stalled corn crop. If they all got on the train in Bismarck and went back home, there would be hope. Grandparents and aunts and uncles would all ask the church to help them with a fresh start.

A cold fear swept through Hannah. This was the

first time she was close to admitting defeat. But this ride to the Jenkinses had to be done. They could not survive on prairie hens and gophers. An occasional herd of antelope could be seen in the distance, but they moved swiftly, far away, a blur of brown and white, so that was out of the question.

She hoped she would not miss the road to the Jenkinses. She kicked her heels into Pete's side and was rewarded by flattened ears and the beginning of an easy lope. Her teeth rattled, her head was jarred on her shoulders, so she kicked him again, slapped the end of the reins against his neck, chirped, and urged him into a gallop.

Pete's hoof beats sounded dull and muffled on the track through the grass that served as a road. He soon tired, and reverted to his bumpy trot, then down to a slow walk.

Hannah sighed, loosened the reins and looked around. It was a bright May morning with blue skies flecked with thin white clouds, like a bride's veil, she thought. It was as if the brilliance of the sky was too bold, too bright, out of the *Ordnung*, and needed to be covered with a thin layer of white. Not that she'd ever be an English bride, having a worldly wedding and wearing a long white gown with a lot of her back bare for anyone to see.

Once, back home, she'd seen all those beautiful dresses in a Sears, Roebuck & Co catalog from 1931. She had pored over them for days, whenever her mother wasn't looking, eager to see how differently the lace draped around the tiny waists, down to the great swelling flow of the skirt just brushing the floor.

She smiled to herself, thinking of the Amish way. She had been to weddings. In awe of the solemnity of the occasion, the sober-faced row of ministers, the bearded bishop speaking about Ruth and Boaz (what kind of name was that?), and all the other love stories in the Bible. *Heiliche Schrift.* Holy Bible. All that seemed dim and faraway, like a tarnished memory, one that had too many days and too many miles between now and back then.

When her cousin Edna was married, her white Swiss organdy cape and apron was stiff and brand new, pinned up under her chin and close about her neck in modesty and *dehmut.* Her face was white and frozen, like a porcelain doll, as she sat erect and unmoving for the four-hour ceremony. When they (finally) stood in front of the bishop to say their vows, Edna looked as if she would fall over in a swoon, that's how scared she was. Well, Hannah had decided right then and there that she'd be scared into a faint too if she had to marry Samuel Stoltzfus!

He was thin as a stick and just as ugly. Mam had told her back then already to stop saying those things. It was brazen, loud-mouthed, and not spoken in Christian love. She guessed she should have sugared it down a little by saying only that he needed a few good home-cooked meals and that he wasn't handsome.

But it was true. Samuel was homely looking as all get out. Edna was no beauty, but she was a lot better looking than Samuel. She hoped they were happy in their little rental property. She should write to Edna. Dear Edna, we're starving and Dat's crazy!

She smiled to herself thinking of Mam's letters to her relatives, the eagerness in her voice when Abby offered her paper and pen, stamps and envelopes. Like water to a dying person.

No doubt her letters spoke of only goodness—Abby's birth, the new house (she wouldn't mention not having a chimney), the Jenkins family's generosity. Oh, it would all be sweetness and light—how Mose was tilling the soil, how Manny was turning into a man, so strong and able to help Mose. It was Mam's way, the Stoltzfus pride, the ability to squeeze every drop of goodness out of the most horrid situation. Keeping the moldy cheese curds of life to herself, letting others see only what they could gather from the buttermilk that flowed from her cloth.

Well, that didn't sit right with Hannah. You were who you were, and if people didn't like it, then that was tough. Out here on the prairie there was no one to worry about, no one who cared what you wore or how you talked or if you were clean or filthy dirty from a day's hard work.

She shaded her eyes with her hand and searched the surrounding area for signs of a barbed wire fence, a roof, or some sign of civilization. She should soon be at the Jenkinses' place.

She leaned forward, patted Pete's neck, and spoke to him, telling him he was a good horse, it wasn't too far, and then he could rest. On the horizon, she saw a darker blur against the sky. She watched until she could see it was a spring wagon, or buckboard, as they called them out here. It was pulled by a lone horse. Who could it be, other than the Jenkinses?

Warily, she watched them approach, clouds of dust billowing behind the rattling buckboard, the horse trotting at a brisk pace. She slowed Pete, waiting by the side of the road, thinking perhaps they would want to speak to her.

Keenly aware of her poor horse, her dress, her white head covering, wearing men's trousers, and riding bare back with no shoes, Hannah kept her eyes lowered, overcome with shame.

"Whoa!" The rattling buckboard came to a halt, the black horse hitched to it prancing impatiently. The seat was high, which made the couple appear even larger than they were.

"How do!" yelled the red-faced, heavyset man on the right. Hannah nodded, smiled only for an instant.

"My, my, here we have a girl," the woman burst out, identically heavyset and rosy-hued.

Hannah thought fleetingly of two well-fed happy piglets, but banished the thought immediately, thinking of Mam and her admonishments.

"You from hereabouts," shouted the man, more a statement than a question.

"Yes."

"Where?"

Hannah turned and pointed back the way she had come. "I'm Hannah Detweiler. My father's name is Mose. We just arrived five, maybe six, months ago. We're from Pennsylvania."

"Ah, hah, homesteading are you?"

"Yes."

The woman's hair was braided, then wound about her head like a crown. She wore no head covering, and her dress was a brilliant hue of pink, mostly made up of pink flowers and green vines. There was a row of buttons down the front of her dress, also pink. Her face was about the same shade of pink as her buttons, with a pert little nose and two bright blue eyes. She was actually pretty, in a pink sort of way.

Her husband wore a hat that was not a Stetson, the way the Jenkins men wore. It had a soft, floppy brim, and it looked as if it was made of leather. His shirt was white, and he wore a leather vest that he had no hope of closing over his well-rounded stomach.

Hannah swallowed, thinking of all the good, rich food they must enjoy, being so well fed and amiable.

"Where are you off to?" asked the woman, leaning forward eagerly, her eyes searching Hannah's face.

"To the Jenkins place."

"That far? Oh, we didn't tell you our names. My goodness gracious. We are Owen and Sylvia Klasserman. We live over thataway." She pointed a short, square finger to the east, the sleeve on her dress riding up to reveal a pink, flapping underarm.

"We must come look where you live. Detweiler, you said? We're always happy to have new neighbors. We've lived here for thirty-some years now. Arrived here at the turn of the century. We're from Sweden. Rode the whole way across the Atlantic when we were young, full of spit and looking for adventure. We sure got it, let me tell you. There ain't one speck of bad weather God forgot to send on these Dakota plains, I can tell you right now."

Hannah smiled now, revealing her white teeth.

"My, ain't you just the purtiest thing! Too bad my boys is all married." She narrowed her eyes, touched her own braid on top of her head, and asked if she was a nun, from the Catholics.

"No, we're from the Amish, in Lancaster County."

"What are they?" the man broke in, curiosity beaming bluely from beneath his hat brim.

Hannah shrugged. A deep sense of shame kept her mute. How to describe their way of dress? Their beliefs? They would laugh at her if she tried. Perhaps they weren't Christians, didn't even believe in Jesus or anything. She wished she didn't have to wear this covering anymore. It was just so strange looking, so out of place in a world where there was no one else just like you.

"Just people like you," Hannah muttered, hating the self-consciousness that welled up into a blush. She felt the warmth spreading across her cheeks.

"Ain't that the truth? Throw us all together in a pot and what you get is vegetable soup. All good, all together, a fine flavor."

Hannah swallowed, thinking of her mother's vegetable soup in the fall when she cleaned out the garden, cut and sliced, diced and chopped, cooked and stewed potatoes, tomatoes, lima beans, green beans, carrots, onions, celery, parsley—and flavored it with beef broth. It was so good with applesauce to cool it down.

"Wal, we best be on our way. We're on our way to the Apents. They got a steer down, so we'll help with the meat."

Hannah nodded and wondered who the Apents were and where they lived.

Owen picked up the reins, clucked to his horse,

and with a wave of fluttering hands, the large black horse drew them away.

Hannah was hungry now, and thirsty. She hoped she'd soon be in sight of the Jenkinses' buildings, or at least see a few cattle dotting the green grass, black dots on green fabric.

Someday, their own acreage would appear just like that. Branded cattle growing fat on the lush grass, a barn filled with hay in winter, the cattle driven to market, money in the bank. She'd already named the place the Bar S for Stoltzfus, her mother's maiden name. Right now it was the Bar Someday, a future planned, the biggest obstacle persuading her father and Manny, who was as obstinate as Dat.

She rode on, gratified to recognize the rolling of the land, the hollows and swells invisible from a distance but close to the Jenkinses. But as faithful Pete neared the outbuildings of the ranch, a sick feeling clenched her stomach. For a moment, she felt like throwing up. Where was her courage, her bluster, when she needed it?

Angrily she swiped at a bothersome horsefly and decided she'd best get this over with. No one else was going to do it. She hoped Clay would not be in the house, with his week's growth of blonde stubble on his cleft chin, his lazy blue eyes that watched her, as calm as pond water on a still day. Blue.

There was only Abby, her gray, curly hair

flapping about her thin, wrinkled face, her eyes welcoming Hannah from beneath leathery lids. She was out in the yard hanging up the last of the day's washing, shaking out denim jeans with a flick of her skinny wrists, pegging them to the sagging wash line as if a strong gust of wind would take them away.

"Ya ride all the way over here by yerself then, did ya?" was her way of greeting Hannah.

Hannah dismounted off Pete's back in one easy motion, tried to throw the reins the way the boys did, but one caught on the horse's ears and she had to stand on her toes to pull it free.

"Yeah, I did."

"What brings you?"

"Well, my mother sent me. We're . . . well, we're out of food. The potatoes and carrots you brought are gone and my father—my father is acting strange. He doesn't seem to be . . . thinking the way he should. You know our horse died, his corn crop isn't going to get into the ground, and he's upset. We just need a bit of help until we can pay you back."

Abby kicked the wicker clothes basket against the wooden clothesline pole, untied the sack of clothespins from around her waist, and shook her head. She looked off across the shed roof, a scowl marking her face, drawing the lines taut, downward, as if a clamp scrunched up her cheeks. Her small blue eyes snapped.

"That man shouldn'ta brought you out here. This ain't no country for you folks. You best git back on home."

Hannah scuffed her bare toe into the dust, unable to meet her gaze. It was too sharp, too penetrating. "We can't," she said, finally.

"Why not?" Abby asked, her eyes watching Hannah like a hawk's.

Suddenly, Hannah hated Abby with a raw anger that shocked even her. Up came her face, her dark eyes blazing with a black glitter. "We don't have money to return, that's why!" she shouted. "You know we don't. You just want to hear me say it. We're poor, we're half-starved, and my father is slowly losing his mind. So how do you expect us to go back home?"

"Honey, here, here. I didn't mean it that way." Abby stepped forward as if to hug her, at least to protect her with an arm about her heaving shoulders.

But Hannah shrugged her off, turned and shouted, "Don't touch me. Go away and leave me alone."

She gathered up Pete's reins, draped them across his mane, grabbed a handful of hair and stood back, ready to fling herself on his back.

Abby's bony hands reached out, grabbed Hannah's arm, and tugged her away from Pete. He looked as if he didn't have the strength to return to the homestead.

"Look here, young lady. You ain't talkin' to your elders thataway. You best git yer wings clipped, or you ain't havin' no friends hereabouts."

"I don't care!" Hannah yelled.

Abby stepped right up and grabbed her arm in a grip like a clamp. "You better care," she shouted right back, "cause I can tell you, in this here country, you need folks to help you out sometimes."

Hannah said nothing, just stood by her horse's neck, a handful of his mane twisted in her grubby fist. She glared at Abby like a trapped animal.

"Let goa yer horse," Abby commanded. "Come on, let go. You best come on in and help me get dinner."

"No!"

"Fine. You and yer horse are so hungry and weak you'll drop halfway home. Suit yerself." With that, Abby walked away, picked up her clothes basket, and walked across the scrubby yard up onto the porch. She flung the empty basket on a metal chair and let herself into the house with a backward glance.

That made Hannah so mad she couldn't see straight. She leaped up on Pete's back, kicked her heels against his knobby sides, startling the horse into a clumsy lunge that unseated her and landed her by the corral fence with dust all over herself, the chickens squawking and flapping their wings as they dashed to safety behind the fence.

Thundering hooves rounded the corner of the barn. Three horses slid to a surprised stop, their riders grinning down at her. The spectacle of a young girl sitting in the dust, her riderless horse a few paces off, face suffused with anger, dark eyes popping and snapping—it was all hilarious to them. Not accustomed to young women, they laughed without restraint, not aware that their laughter was neither polite nor proper.

"That sorry old nag dump you?" Hank chortled.

"Slid right off, did you?" Ken asked with a wide grin.

Clay said nothing, just sat on his horse and looked down at her with that slow, easy light in his blue eyes.

Hannah fired a round of defensive words that hit them without making a ruffle in their denim shirts. Still laughing, they dismounted and walked toward the barn shaking their heads.

Except Clay, who walked over and offered her his hand. "Want up?"

"I can get up by myself." In one quick movement Hannah was on her feet and dusting herself off with rapid strokes of her hands. She straightened her head covering, tucked a few strands of hair beneath it, and glared at Clay.

"Yer lookin' awful puny. You folks gittin by?"

It was the way he said it that upset her most. Her glare and her defensiveness melted away as his kindness seeped through her belligerence.

She swallowed and felt the prickle of hated tears, her face changing expressions like a soft, spring squall of warm rain.

She shook her head, swallowed again and whispered, "Barely."

Clay stepped closer. All she could see was his blue denim shirt front, the pockets with flaps buttoned down over them. She smelled the horse, the prairie grass, the wind, his tobacco, and a masculine scent that made her want to touch his shirt pocket and straighten the one corner that stood up as if blown by the wind.

She looked at the pocket, then dared to lift her eyes to his open collar, his tanned dusty neck, and the cleft in his chin. She had no nerve to meet his eyes. They were too blue, too slow and easy.

He saw the dark hair, thick and wavy, the eyebrows on the perfect brow, twin arcs of dark perfection. Her eyelashes lay on white cheeks, so thick and long it was ridiculous. He'd never seen anything like it. He was gripped by a longing to see the dark eyes beneath those unbelievably perfect eyelids, a longing that left him shaken and weak-kneed.

He hadn't expected this. He sure hadn't figured on any such feelings for this girl wearing that white head covering, her father like a prophet straight out of the Old Testament.

They were worlds apart.

Clay Jenkins knew plenty of girls. He knew

too that he could have anyone he set his mind to. At twenty-two years old, he was up for grabs, in many of the local girls' minds. So far, he'd never met one he wanted to spend the rest of his life with, let alone marry one and raise a brood of children.

"Barely, you said?"

Hannah nodded. "My father isn't right. Something's wrong with the way he's acting. My mother isn't used to fending for herself. She does whatever Dat says. Our food is all gone. The garden doesn't look too promising. You know our horse died. We would go back home to Pennsylvania, but our money is all gone too.

"So I rode over for help. Mam made me come. She doesn't know what else to do. The children are hungry. We've been eating prairie hens, but it's not enough to keep hunger away."

Clay had never felt anything close to what he was feeling now. It wasn't pity, not even sympathy. Her words were pressed out from beneath a covering of pride. He saw the courage it took to speak about their situation, the force of her will, the desperation to help her family. He knew that she was the only one who could lead this group of well-meaning, misled Christians. He guessed that was what they called themselves—Christians. He couldn't seem to pronounce Amish correctly.

"But that doesn't mean we can't make it here

on our own," Hannah continued. "We just need to borrow some food until we can pay it back, if that's all right with your parents anyway."

She stepped back and gripped her hands behind her back. She looked into his eyes, hers masked by her fierce determination to hang on to her pride. She looked too thin herself, with the faint blue shadows of hunger beneath her dark eyes.

"That bad, is it?" Clay asked, hating the way his breath caught as if he'd been running up a hill.

"It's pretty bad, yes."

"Did you talk to Ma?"

"Yes. She made me mad."

Clay laughed, wanting to take her hand but didn't. Hank and Ken followed them back to the house, sat with them at the dinner table waiting for Abby to dish up the potatoes and roast beef. Hod joined them, stomping onto the front porch with the force of a tractor, yelling to Abby that these cats had to go! There were about half a dozen too many around here!

Abby lifted her head from the hot oven door and told him if he touches them cats, she'd chase him off the ranch with her varmint-killing .22 rifle.

Hod laughed, removed his hat to reveal his white forehead that began after the red stopped, about halfway between his eyebrows and his hairline. Hannah looked at the boys' foreheads, and found them to be the same, only not as pronounced as Hod's.

Hannah took the heavy plate filled with boiled potatoes dotted with browned butter and chunks of beefsteak as large as her fist. She tried to eat slowly but found herself having to lift her head repeatedly and lay down her fork to keep from wolfing down her food like a dog, putting her face in her plate without bothering to use fork or spoon.

Clay watched her, the same unnameable feeling welling through his chest until he felt as if his heart was floating in moving water. Everything in the room spun before righting itself, and he figured he'd better watch himself. These feelings were far harder to handle than a bucking mustang or a wild steer.

CHAPTER 8

The Jenkinses cared for the Detweilers, bringing more potatoes and onions and carrots, cold-packed beef in Mason jars, flour, baking powder and salt, cornmeal and coffee. They brought a milk cow and two calves.

Hod sat down with Mose and explained in detail that their only hope of carving out a life for themselves here in North Dakota was raising cattle. Abby told Sarah they may as well get on the train and go home, which didn't sit well with Mose at all.

He had, by this time, mostly given up on his fasting and praying, seemingly humbled that the Lord he knew so well had hidden His face from him for reasons he did not understand. He told Sarah in a quiet, subdued tone of voice that yea, though He slay me, I will trust in Him, just as the Bible tells me to do.

Sarah's heart swelled with love and something akin to worship. To have her Mose back with sound reasoning and peace of mind was more than she deserved. Surely now things would begin to look up.

The Jenkinses brought a horse, a contrary old nag they hitched to Pete in the harrow. At this, Pete threw a fit, crow hopping, shaking his head, and flattening his large ears. But Mose trained him well, and eventually, the team tilled the soil and planted the corn seeds in the ground.

They named him Mule. His ears were only a fraction smaller than a mule, and he beat every mule Mose had ever seen for crankiness. The most important thing was that he served his purpose well and Mose was thankful.

For a time, then, things progressed for the Detweilers. The barn was finished in due time, such as it was, built with logs and rusted tin patched in pieces. But it was free from the Jenkinses, so no one thought to complain.

The whole family helped drop the corn seeds, even six-year-old Eli. Mose drew a homemade tool with one horse that dug furrows, and everyone followed with the precious seeds, dropping them not too deep and not too shallow.

The days grew warmer. Puffy clouds hung in the sky like pieces of cotton stuck to the blue dome above them. The wind blew, but it was a warm, friendly wind, a playful breeze that tugged at the women's skirts as they bent over the soil and sent their white covering strings dancing, slapping them against their faces.

The large square of tilled soil by the house, flecked with clumps of stubborn prairie grass, they called the garden. It was, by all means, a primitive patch of half-tilled soil that swallowed the seeds, leaving Sarah with the feeling that if anything sprouted out of that wet, clumpy ground, it would be a miracle.

But it did. Little by little, the beans and potatoes and onions showed tender green plants shoving up from the earth, and Sarah's eyes filled with tears of gratitude. Such hope!

No matter that things had been hopeless, here was promise. Here was a sign from God above, who looked on them with benevolence, love, and mercy. His ways were so far above her own. All she needed to do was continue to trust, even when the way grew so hard there was no light at the end of a long and dismal tunnel.

Manny became an expert shot, killing prairie hens, which Sarah learned to skin expertly, eliminating the need to boil water and pluck feathers, a time consuming, tedious task. The small amount of meat on each one was sufficient to keep protein in their diet and with the bread baked with flour the Jenkinses had donated, Sarah stretched the potatoes and carrots as far as she could.

The roundup day arrived with Mose refusing to allow his family to attend, saying they had no fellowship with the world. They were a peculiar people, set apart to be holy unto the Lord. Sarah agreed, hiding her grudging heart, covering her longing for women's company with her head lowered in submission. She could see her husband's point, especially with regards to

Hannah. She was so set in her ways, so determined and quick to mouth her opinions, like throwing rocks neither Sarah nor Mose could always dodge.

When she heard they would not be going to the roundup, she said her father was right; they were peculiar people, completely strange. They didn't fit in anywhere, like a boatload of slaves brought over from Africa, the ones she read about in school. All they were good for in the western country was being stared at, poked at, and made fun of.

Mose drew himself up, took a deep breath, and did not look on his daughter with anger or rebuke. But there was no kindness in his voice either. He told her if she didn't learn to curb her tongue and respect her elders, she would become a slave of the devil. Didn't she know the tongue was untamable and like a ship without a rudder unless she learned to master it—may God help her. Sarah stood by her husband, her gentle brown eyes filled with rebuke.

Hannah went out to the calves and changed their tethers, pulling up the long pegs driven into the ground, moving them to an area where grass was more abundant. She stood with her hands on her hips and decided there was no difference between her and the calves. She was pegged tight to her Amish heritage by her father's views, and there wasn't a soul around to pull up her peg and change her position either.

She noticed the ribs beneath the hair on the

calves' sides, the way their necks appeared too thin, and decided this was no way to raise calves. She marched back into the house and approached her father without shame.

She told him what she thought, mincing no words. A calf tied by a rope to a peg in the ground was not the way things were done out here. Barbed wire was out of the question, the ever-present ghost of being poor hovering over them. So why didn't he brand these little calves and the one cow so they could roam? That's how it was done.

Mose listened to his daughter's voice and thought that here was a more daunting job than all the acreage he had been given by the United States government. Here was a challenge so steep it made the prairie appear bridled in comparison.

His own daughter.

She was beautiful by anyone's standards, with a head on her shoulders and a voice unafraid to be heard, opinions aired so freely and as naturally as the wind rushing past their house.

His head hurt. He gripped it with both hands and shook it back and forth like a wounded dog.

Hannah burst out, "Stop that!"

And still his head hurt.

The two oldest Jenkins boys rode over after Hannah asked them to acquire a branding iron for them. She named their homestead the Bar S, just the way she planned. She told Clay without preamble, leaving him scratching his head and wondering what other ideas were floating around in her mind.

"You know I'll have to go to town for that, don't you?" he asked.

"Why?"

"They have to make your brand if they don't have it."

"Who?"

"The horseshoe guy."

"Who's he?"

"Someone who makes horseshoes."

"How's that done?"

"You'll just have to come with me and see."

But Mose and Sarah were adamant. Absolutely not. Their daughter would not be riding into town in the Jenkinses' old pickup truck with Clay at the wheel. To begin with, any form of automobile was the workings of the devil. Any contraption that ran by itself was devised by his cunning. God surely would not allow anything like that to be put on this earth—a machine breathing fire and brimstone, like an instrument from Hell itself.

No good would ever come of it. Mose trembled at the thought of those fire-breathing monsters rattling all over God's green earth, leaving plumes of black smoke, with leering, grinning, ungodly people at the wheel. His judgment was harsh, in black and white, labeling cars as evil; and that was that.

So Hannah stayed on the homestead, helped her mother with the washing, cooking, and cleaning, all the while fuming silently about the plight of the calves tied to their pegs. She washed sheets and pillowcases with a mad energy, rubbing them across the hated washboard as if she hoped it would bleed from her frenzied rubbing.

Sarah watched Hannah from the doorway, holding the baby in her arms, her face untroubled and still beautiful in spite of the long, arduous journey and the hardships she had endured since.

Hannah twisted a white sheet from the rinse water, her face grimacing in concentration, water sloshing down her dress front, the soggy garment now clinging to the womanly curves of her body. Going without an apron again. The *Ordnung* meant nothing to Hannah, of this Sarah was now convinced. The rules of the church were an unwelcome tether, a binding to authority that, to her, was unnecessary. A burden, a prickly collar she wore with disdain.

Suddenly irritated, Sarah called out, "Hannah, you're wet. What if someone came to visit and there you were, half-dressed?"

Hannah lowered her eyes and turned away without answering. "Come," Sarah said gently. "Put your apron on."

"Why would I put an apron on? There's no one coming to visit, and who cares?" Hannah spoke with resentment, her eyes black like coal.

"God cares," her mother said, this time a bit firmly.

"Who says?"

Oh, the impudence of her own daughter! Sarah was dumbfounded and had no ready answer. To quote the Bible to her would only cause more irritation. She must speak to Mose. Turning, she went inside, hefting Baby Abigail on her shoulder, her smooth face now gray with a certain weariness she could not explain. She would not stand in the doorway trading barbed remarks with her eldest. Tears pricked her eyelashes and a lump of despair formed in her throat.

"Yea, though I walk through the valley of the shadow of death, I will fear no evil." The comfort of this Psalm spoke gently to her as she laid Abby in her box in the corner. Yes, she would not be fearful of the evil that would constantly waylay her daughter. With that attitude, she was an easy target for the devil and his wiles. She would trust her God and leave it to Him. He had created Hannah and would care for her. She would be a devout mother, praying constantly and giving all her cares to God alone.

Why, then, instead of peace, did Sarah experience foreboding? An ominous black cloud seemed to raise its head on the horizon, and the wealth of waving summer grasses suddenly turned harsh, as if they whispered of an impending doom.

Sarah shivered and turned away from the window. It was time to begin the day's bread making. She lifted the lid of the agate kettle, where the sourdough starter was kept, took out a cupful, and replaced the lid before turning to the flour container, alarmed at the weight of it. So light. What would she do when the flour ran out? She knew they could not depend on the Jenkinses forever. Their assistance had been more than generous. How could they keep asking for more knowing there was no income?

The sun laid a square patch of heat and light on the oilcloth tabletop. Another sunny day. Every day the sun shone, the heat became more intense, the wind blew and blew and blew, unstoppable, never ceasing. Sarah wondered as she watched the tender green shoots of corn as the wind tossed about the leaves of the fledgling plant. The corn would need rain. The sun hiding behind gray clouds, raindrops beginning to fall, first a tiny, wet splash, then another, until the earth was moist and lovely. The rain smelled wonderful, an earthy aroma of moisture and promise and God's goodness. But each day, that seemed a thing of the past.

Surely God would send rain. Surely.

Sarah kept a calendar of her days, marked them off with a large X across the square. She kept a careful account of the weather in her diary, writing each day's work, the children's growth, ordinary goings on with a family of five. At home, in Lancaster County, she had always recorded where church services had been held, who gave the sermon, and the number of visitors present.

Her whole being seemed to fold in on itself, until she felt as if her very breathing became constricted, so sharp were the pangs of her homesickness, her longing to see her mother, her sisters, her grandparents. To be among them, one of the Stoltzfuses, a happy, well-adjusted *freundshaft*, a group of people so near and dear she could feel their presence, here, today, in this crude house made of logs in the middle of this unbelievable prairie.

Unbelievable, yes, it was. Living in this treeless, mountainless land, without neighbors or any roads of significance, without an income or a church to rescue them from the raw poverty in which they lived. What was her duty?

Should she always be submissive, when she felt in her bones that there'd be no corn crop, no money, only debt to the Jenkinses? Should she always trust Mose? Yes, that was the right choice. The Bible clearly stated this truth, the ministers expounded the women's path as followers of their husbands, calling him Lord, as Sarah had called Abraham and God had blessed him beyond all understanding.

So Sarah looked upon the stunted corn sprouts, watched sadly as the heat of the sun and the wind's ceaseless pounding tormented the brave growth they had planted with their own hands.

Two weeks without rain, then three. A month passed, with the sun rising in unfettered glory each morning, a giant, orange ball of pulsing heat, surrounded by a brassy blue sky that contained only wispy plumes of thin white clouds that hurried by, as if they were ashamed to be seen on this otherwise perfect day.

In spite of the constant heat, the corn must have dug its roots deeper into the earth, finding enough moisture to keep growing. Mose exulted in every healthy cornstalk. He fashioned sturdy hoes from straight tree limbs and sharp rocks, sent Manny and Mary to the cornfield to hoe thistles and other weeds that threatened to choke the corn.

They became deeply tanned, their dark hair bleached to a lighter hue, yet they never complained of the backbreaking work, obeying their father without question. Sarah always walked out to the cornfield with a tin pail with a lid on it, to bring them a cool drink of well water.

Hannah refused to hoe corn, in spite of her father's orders, or his threats. Mose and Sarah discussed this refusal and decided to leave it. As long as she performed her other duties, they saw no reason to bully her into submission. Her hatred would only intensify, they felt.

The sun shone on the little homestead, the rough-hewn log house and adjacent barn for which *shed* was perhaps a more fitting description. The buildings were not too far from being hovels, both for the human beings and their animals. The children played around these buildings, in chopped, scythed grass, trampled and dusty. A clothesline was strung between two sagging log poles, but it was serviceable, the clothes drying fast in the hot, dry wind.

Sarah still cooked outside on the fire surrounded by rocks taken from the creek bed, a tripod on each end, the blackened cast iron pot in between, the earth trampled around it by Sarah's bare feet as she bent over her cooking. Little Eli played with sticks and bark, made grass huts, and generally ran wild, often with Mary by his side, if she wasn't needed to watch Abby.

Their clothes became too small in time. Mary's dresses were snug across her chest, tight beneath her arms, and much too short, but the one remaining tuck had been left out, so there was nothing to do but wear short dresses. Sarah patched trousers again and again, until the denim fabric ran. The boys lived with ragged edged holes in the knees of their pants; they were like open mouths to Hannah, shouting of their shameful poverty.

The corn turned color, slowly, into a dry, olive green, the leaves curled into harsh tubes that mocked the whole family, rattling in the wind, tossed and twisted piteously. Sarah's gaze swept the endless blue sky. Mose returned to his headaches, gripping both sides as he swayed back and forth in abject misery.

Again, hunger became their constant companion. Too proud and too stubborn to ask for help, they survived on prairie hens, the few onions and scraggly carrots they pulled from the garden, the soil packed down, jagged with cracks where the dried earth had shrunken like a toothless old man.

One morning in July, Hannah ate one bite of prairie hen for her breakfast, laid down her fork, and announced in a tone as bitter as horseradish that she was riding into town to look for work.

Mose looked at his daughter, his eyes popped and snapped in the most uncharacteristic manner, and he told her she was doing no such thing as long as she was under his care.

Hannah shouted then, her voice raised so that the baby woke and began to cry. "Care! What care? Every one of us is starving, our clothes are wearing out, and you say we're under your care? I'm going, so don't even try to stop me. I'll get a job doing something, and I'll return home every Saturday evening with whatever I'm paid. I am not going to the Jenkinses ever again, to *beg!*" The last word was a shriek laced with anger.

Mose's eyes settled back into their sockets, and his heavy lids fell halfway and stopped. He spoke quietly, his words measured, his tone soothing.

"Well, my Hannah, if you feel the need to have more earthly goods than what the Lord has provided for us, then I suggest you take up the Bible and read about the lilies of the field, how Solomon in all his glory, a wealthy man, mind you, was not arrayed like one of these."

"I don't need earthly goods, Dat. We can't eat lilies, and Solomon's not here either. I'm hungry, that's what. So I'm going to do something about it."

"Which town, Hannah? Surely not to Dorchester?" Sarah asked.

"Of course not. To Pine. I'm going to Pine. But if I can't find work there, I may have to go to Dorchester."

"You may not have one of the horses," Mose spoke with authority.

Hannah snorted. "What would I do with a horse? If I perish of hunger, it'll just be me, you'll still have your horse."

Sarah gasped. "Won't you reconsider, Hannah?" she asked.

"Why would I? We're all going to starve out here on the prairie. We can't eat grass. The corn is shriveling up in the heat, and we just sit here like ducks waiting to be shot."

Manny's eyes flashed. "Dat knows what he's doing, Hannah. Why do you have to do something foolish?"

Mary and Eli began to cry in earnest, the

usual breakfast harmony shattered by Hannah's announcement. They were too young to understand Hannah's undertaking, too young to know how their lives were rimmed with desperation. They only wanted Hannah to stay, to stop frightening her parents.

Mose spoke then, in tones dripping with patience and loving forbearance. "My Hannah."

Before he got any further, she shot up out of her chair, launched by her complete disdain of him. "Stop calling me that! I am not your Hannah. You don't own me the way you own Mam. You own her only because she allows it. Let me tell you, when I come back, you'll be in debt, trying to pay me back for providing for your family, a job you aren't able to do."

Before she left, she tied on a clean gray apron on top of her ill-fitting faded blue dress. Barefoot, her clean covering patched where the straight pins had torn the fabric, her face was like stone, hard with resolve, compacted with bitterness.

Sarah tried to hold her, grabbed at her arm, and tried to draw her into an embrace. But Hannah would have none of it, shrugging free of her mother's pitiful attempts at restraint.

Sarah began to weep, softly. "Just be careful, Hannah. Be wise. Don't let anyone persuade you to do wrong. Men are not always trustworthy. Here, take this."

She pressed a cold, gleaming half dollar

into the palm of Hannah's hand, her fingers grappling for a hold on her beloved daughter's hand. "Please, please be careful. Remember that you were raised Amish. You cannot go out into the world without conscience. Keep your way of dress. Let no man seduce you. Take your small prayer book, the German one, the one Mommy Detweiler gave you last year. Was it just last year?"

Sarah took a deep, ragged breath, wiped her eyes with her apron, her voice trembling when she told her not to allow anyone to give her a ride.

"Hannah, we are Amish. We are not of the world. We are forbidden to ride in cars. We must always bow our heads and pray before and after meals. Your head must be covered with your prayer covering. Remember the Lord Jesus, who died for you. When you feel the need to be baptized . . ." Here Sarah's voice dwindled to a whisper, then stopped.

"Then what, Mam? Huh? Then what?"

"Don't, Hannah." But she raised her eyes level with her sixteen year old daughter, saw the hard, unwavering truth in her dark, fiery eyes, shrank from it and tried to erase it by lifting a hand as if to ward off a blow.

"You expect me to travel a thousand miles back home to become a member of the Amish church? You know it's not possible. I won't

162

spend the rest of my days alone because my Father chose to leave the only way of life I had ever known."

"We didn't leave a way of life, Hannah. We are still Amish, born and raised, keeping the faith."

"And how will I? How will I ever marry or have children of my own, with not one other Amish in these woebegone parts? Huh?"

Sarah began weeping softly again, a torn handkerchief held to her face, shaking her head from side to side, as if that move alone could dislodge this hard truth. Hadn't it hung between mother and daughter long enough? A gossamer veil, mocking their camaraderie, blown against one or the other repeatedly, an annoyance that couldn't be denied.

Here is where Sarah was torn. To be blindly submissive to a husband who had just not taken his children into consideration when he thought of making this move.

Had it been the correct way? Already she understood the way of a woman. Hannah was grown, and longed for the companionship that Sarah had also longed for and had found in good, gentle Mose.

But here was her own daughter, flesh of her flesh, heart of her heart. The urge to hold her was so strong it felt as if her arms were made of iron, too heavy to hang from her shoulders. She lifted tormented eyes to her daughter's.

"Hannah, I can't promise you that your life will be easy, if you choose to do this. Just make sure that you pray every morning and every evening. A young girl needs guidance from a personal relationship with Christ. *Mitt unser Herren Jesu Christus*, Hannah. Oh, that we could both be seated on the bench in a house in Lancaster, listening to our beloved Enos Lapp. Sometimes it feels as if I'll just break in two with homesickness, missing the ones I love."

Hannah's hard brown eyes misted over, like polished coal. She turned her back, her shoulders squared, before facing her mother.

"Here comes Dat, so I'll say this quickly. Don't worry about me. I'll make it on my own. And I'll pray, whenever I think about it."

There was no embrace, only the sight of her thin form in the faded blue dress, her covering strings slapping in the wind, walking away from the log house with the ring of stones and the smoke wafting away from it.

Sarah lifted a hand, lowered it. A fierce, possessive pride gripped her soul. She wanted to shout words of encouragement, knowing her daughter was capable of anything. Anything. She was young and beautiful and talented, smart as a whip and not afraid to speak her mind.

Sarah swiped at her streaming eyes, the vision of Hannah becoming a blur among the waving prairie grass. But there was a consolation now:

her trust in Hannah she could acknowledge in secret. No one needed to know.

And when Mose mourned his daughter's absence, Sarah lifted devout eyes that effectively curtained the small spark of pride she tended well.

CHAPTER 9

The day was hot, so by midmorning, Hannah was wiping her face with a corner of her apron.

She was following the road to the town of Pine, consisting of a small group of crude buildings with a cattle auction, a feed store, a gas station, and, if she remembered correctly, a large general store and a café. Maybe more, she wasn't sure. She'd only been there once.

She gripped a small black valise that contained a change of clothes, her prayer book, a comb, and a toothbrush. The half dollar was in her pocket, a deep patch of fabric sewn to the front of her skirt. She had used a safety pin to secure the top of the pocket, so she wouldn't lose the most precious of all her meager possessions.

The road stretched before her, perfectly straight, on level ground, disappearing into a V on the horizon. Sometimes, grass grew along the middle; only the sides of the road were bare, gray, and dusty, the grass parched and brown. Heat shimmered across the plains, the light white hot against her eyes. She squinted, then closed her eyes for a moment and stumbled on a tuft of grass before opening them.

The light was unbearably bright. Or hadn't she slept much? Probably not, the way she'd tried to untangle everything during the night. She could see no way out of her family's desperate poverty, as long as Mose kept up that childish, undying optimism. It was almost pitiful, the way he assured himself constantly that God would send a miracle, a gift, and save them all. No matter that the hot winds blew and shriveled the corn, or that they were all skinny and hungry, every prairie hen shot to death for miles around.

And still he prayed.

You had to admire a man like that, she supposed. Admire him for his determination, if nothing else. Pity for her mother was like a dagger, only for an instant, before she steeled herself against these unwanted loopholes of emotion. She couldn't go all soft like this.

The soles of her feet were beginning to hurt. She was thirsty, but that couldn't be helped. Like a camel, she'd drank her fill at breakfast, hoping it would last all day.

Who would hire her? They were in the throes of the Great Depression, whatever that was. She'd heard her father and Uncle Levi discussing the United States currency, the closing of well-established banks, the crash of the stock market. She didn't actually know what the stock market was, but if it broke down, it must be important. She guessed that if wealthy people were in trouble, the poor would face some rough times, for sure. Well, it couldn't get any worse than their plight, that was another thing sure.

Even if those calves grew, they couldn't sell them. They were meant to be breeding stock, according to Hod. It could take five or ten years to build up a sizable herd. The corn was nothing but a loss. Which meant that someone had to get a job. Become gainfully employed. Do something that put a few dollars pure profit in your hand. Enough to buy flour and cornmeal and a bit of shortening.

Her mouth watered, thinking of biscuits and sausage gravy. Or fried mush and shoofly pie. When had she last eaten a piece of pie?

A speck in the distance took her mind off her hunger. The Klassermans again? Surely they weren't on their way home. They never had been true to their words, coming to visit them. Just as well. She would have been deeply ashamed to allow those well fed individuals to see how bad off they really were.

Yes, it was a wagon. Wait. No, it wasn't. It was an automobile; the dust rolling behind it was too dark to be purely dust.

Now she heard it, the *poppa-poppa-poppa* sound of the engine. The car slowed as it approached, the windshield splattered with dust and insects, gleaming underneath its layer of dust nevertheless. A deep shade of red. The center of the wheels were silver, the spokes like pinwheels.

Hannah stepped off to the side, allowing the car to pass, which it did not do. When it came to a stop, Hannah immediately observed that the driver was a young man, unaccompanied, which spelled caution in capital letters, plus an exclamation mark.

"Howdy, sister!" The voice was loud, brash, without restraint. The face was tanned, smooth, and boyish, the eyes as blue as Clay Jenkins's.

Hannah didn't say a word, just stood there by the side of the road with her covering strings blowing and her dark hair shining in the sun.

"You some kinda nun, or what?"

"I'm no nun."

"Well, you look like one. Where you going?"

"To Pine."

He put both hands on the steering wheel, leaned back, and whistled. "You got a ways to go."

"How far?"

"Eight, maybe nine miles."

"No, I don't."

"Hm. Huffy, are we?"

Hannah stalked off. She wasn't about to be ridiculed, called a nun, and then told a lie about the distance to Pine. Who did he think she was? She didn't bother looking back and wasn't surprised when she heard his approach from behind.

"Get in," he called.

"No."

"Why not? I'll take you to Pine. I'm going that way."

"You are now. You weren't to begin with."

He rolled his eyes and whistled.

She walked off. He followed her, slowly. "It's getting hotter. Get in. Come on. I'll be nice. There's nothing to be afraid of. Not with me. I wouldn't hurt a fly. I mean, flea."

Hannah walked on.

"Aren't you going to talk to me? You are a nun, I can tell."

"Just leave me alone. I can walk to where I'm going."

"Where you going?"

"To Pine."

"But where in Pine?"

"None of your business, you know."

"Come on, I'll give you a ride. Do you drive?"

Hannah said no and walked faster.

"What's your name? I'm Philip Apent. Phil, as everyone calls me. You can call me Phil."

Hannah stopped and glared at him, her dark eyes polished with impatience. "I'm not calling you anything. Now leave me alone!"

After he had roared off in a black cloud of exhaust, Hannah wished she would not have been so cautious, so obedient, so everlastingly conscious of her mother's words. The sun was hot enough to fry an egg on this dusty road. Her throat was parched, shriveled together like a hog's intestines on butchering day. Her feet were scratched and aching. Well, there was nothing to do but keep going and hope for the best.

The land was the same the whole way to Pine. Nothing but sky and level land and grass. Occasionally, the dry dusty smell changed to a more earthy one, which made her wonder if she was close to a creek or a water tank.

She saw the windmill first, then the town. A church spire. A grain bin. White buildings, gray ones. Now that she saw this group of homes and established businesses, an overwhelming shyness, a shrinking inside of her, made her stop and consider this bold venture.

Times were tough. This was the Great Depression. There were no jobs, no money, nothing much available. Hod Jenkins had spoken of his family's self-sufficiency, how fortunate they were to raise cattle, and own the ranch free of debt.

Who would hire her? Who could afford wages?

Her mouth dry, her knees weak, her heart pounding in her chest, she approached the first building, the side of a white clapboard house with a foundation of fieldstone.

A white sign, faded and peeling, hung from an L-shaped wooden post that said, "Welcome to Pine."

Nothing seemed welcoming. A wide, dusty street, with wood-sided houses facing each other, like two sides of an argument, their false fronts held aloft by weathered gray braces that no one had bothered to paint. A hardware and feed store. Better not.

The café was next, a yellowed building that had been white at one time. A thin plywood sign above the door said, "The Waffle Café." A sparrow had built a nest in the bottom crevice of the sign, sending a spray of white offal over the screen door. The windows, two of them set side by side were so dusty on the outside you could not see if there was anyone inside behind the greasy pink curtains that were hung halfway up the frame on sagging rods. There was a yellowed sign in the window that said, "Waffles, 25¢. Everyday Special."

Hannah's mouth watered. Without hesitation, she opened the screen door and stepped inside, the bell above the door tinkling with the force of Manny's .22 caliber.

All heads turned in her direction. Bold, curious eyes, eyes accustomed to knowing everyone that stepped through that door.

Quickly, Hannah found an empty table, slid into it, her eyes lowered, her hands clasped on the table top. It took awhile until someone had the nerve to approach her. These prairie folks had probably never seen a woman or a girl wearing a head covering.

When someone did come over to her, Hannah assumed it was the owner, a buxom woman who was so tall she seemed to touch the ceiling. Dressed in a fiery red housedress, layered by a greasy white apron, her yellow hair stacked in a loose bun on top of her head, her lips painted the exact shade of red as her dress, she was as intimidating as a runaway horse.

"Hi, honey!" she boomed.

"Hello."

"What can I getcha?" Her eyes were kind. Curious, but kind. Hannah smiled up at her.

"I'll have a large glass of water, please. And a waffle."

"You want chicken gravy on your waffle?"

Hannah thought of prairie hens and shook her head no.

"Syrup? Butter?"

Hannah said yes, that would be fine.

When she brought the glass of water, there was ice in it, clinking invitingly. Hannah drank thirstily and asked for more.

The owner of the café was named Bess. Bess Jones, sister to Ruth Jones. Did she know Ruth Jones?

Hannah shook her head, then offered the information Bess wanted from her. She had walked to Pine. Mose Detweiler was her father, and she needed a job. She did not mention the hunger, the failed crop of corn, anything. Nothing about her dress either. Let them figure it out.

Bess sat opposite Hannah at the table with a thick

173

white mug of coffee. She brought out a package of Lucky Strike cigarettes from her skirt pocket along with a silver lighter that was square and smooth. She expertly flipped up the lighter's top, ran her thumb along a small wheel, then put the cigarette in her mouth and lowered it to the small flame. She breathed out, spewing a cloud of smoke toward the ceiling, then hooked two fingers into the handle of her mug and swallowed her coffee.

Fascinated, Hannah watched every move. Her fingernails were long and red and mirror smooth. How could that be? How could she cook like that? Didn't it hurt, drawing all that smoke into her throat? That explained her deep voice. At first, she'd thought a man had spoken when Bess greeted her.

But the waffle was so good, the water so cold, the café cool and inviting. Bess had kind eyes, so she'd ignore the rest.

"So tell me, honey, how old are you?" Bess asked, squinting through yet another cloud of smoke. Reaching out, she drew a heavy ash tray toward her, tapping the quivering, gray ash into it.

"I'm sixteen."

"And you need a job?"

"I do, as soon as possible."

Bess looked at her sharply. "Why?"

"Well, we just arrived not too long ago. We lost our farm."

"Whaddaya mean, you lost your farm? You

mean because of this awful depression, or what?"

"I guess. I don't know. We traveled from Lancaster County, in Pennsylvania."

"On the train?"

Hannah was tempted to nod her head. Who would know if she lied? She could save herself some humiliation. But she said, "No, we drove a team of horses and a covered wagon."

The waffle was gone in about five memorable bites, dripping with butter and syrup. She was still hungry, but it had to be enough. She picked up her water glass, swallowed.

"Real pioneers, are ya?" Bess asked, smiling broadly. She leaned back, tilted her head to survey the room and nodded in Hannah's direction.

"We got ourselves a pioneer girl." She laughed, a hoarse cackle, not unlike a crow. A few heads nodded and looked in her direction. One said, "Aw, Bess, give her a break."

"She don't need no break. She's a big girl. Ain't you? What did you say your name was?"

"I didn't say."

"Oh, well, you can tell me, honey. I'm your friend. You want another waffle?"

Hanna shook her head no, the fifty cent piece heavy in her pocket.

"Sure you do." She lifted her voice and yelled, "Mabel, another waffle, with a side of bacon." Turning to Hannah she asked, "So what did you say your name was?"

"Hannah. Hannah Detweiler."

Bess gave no answer, simply lit another cigarette, and watched her with squinty eyes. "You're hungry," she said finally.

Hannah nodded.

"So, if I give you a job, I can't pay you much. Times are lean. I don't need anyone, really. And I don't know what folks will say coming in here, with that thing on your head and all. It won't make 'em feel right."

Hannah considered this, thought of taking off her covering. She knew she would feel downright exposed, sinful, and rebellious. But if it fed her family, would it be all right in God's eyes?

Bess nodded in the covering's direction. "What are you? Jewish? Catholic?"

Hannah didn't want to say the word, knowing this woman would have never heard of the Amish, and how would she explain? But there was no way around it, so she said, "Amish."

"Never heard of 'em."

Hannah nodded, thanked the cook when she brought her waffle, then concentrated busily, spreading butter on the hot waffle, watching it melt and run into the squares of sweet dough, her mouth watering.

Bacon. When had she last had a slice of bacon? A few years ago. It was crispy, salty, and perfect. Her heart was soft toward this large, garrulous woman dressed in red. A woman of the world, and one to be avoided at all cost, she could hear her father say. But she had fed her and thought nothing of it.

"So, what can you do?" Bess asked now.

"Everything."

"Everything?" An eyebrow raised, followed by a burst of raucous laughter, a tap of a red fingernail on her cigarette. "Honey, you're a babe in the woods, is what you are. You'll be devoured by wolves, let me tell you."

Hannah looked up from cutting her waffle. "I can take care of myself."

She was met with another peal of hoarse laughter that seemed to ignite the few men lounging around the greasy tables, snorting and sniveling like mockingbirds.

Hannah popped the last bite of waffle in her mouth, chewed, pushed back her chair, and looked at Bess, her eyes two wet coals of anger. "Go ahead, make fun of me. Thanks for the waffles. You won't see me in your stinking café again. Plus, you better learn to take care of yourself, smoking the way you do."

With that, she walked out, the fifty cents still pinned securely in her pocket, leaving Bess with her mouth open. She didn't close it until the screen door slapped against its frame, leaving a small shower of dust in its wake.

Hannah was furious. She walked fast, her fists clenched, hating everyone in that dirty eating place. Filthy, cheap, smelly. Who did they think they were?

She walked past more houses, weedy alleys between them, littered with old boxes and tin cans, pieces of rope like dead, dusty snakes. The sidewalk was made of cement, but it was cracked and dirty, and some sections lifted up at the corners as if a miniature earthquake had rumbled underneath. Or prairie dogs.

To her left there was a large plate glass window with "Rocher's Hardware and Mercantile" printed across it in square capital letters, each one exactly alike. She stopped and considered the mercantile part. Ladies' stuff? Fabric, yarn, and house wares? Fueled by the waffles, her spirits high, she decided to enter the store and see what happened.

The door was heavy, wooden, also painted red, with a massive handle that ran horizontally along the middle. She pulled, then tugged back harder, before looking and reading the word "Push." To her acute embarrassment, a tall thin man wearing a white shirt stood inside grinning broadly at her.

"It won't open by pulling," he informed her, still smiling.

His head was so bald it shone like a pale, polished apple. A luxuriant moustache covered every inch of space between his nose and mouth, like a limp animal tail, but clipped and groomed to perfection. A pair of round, gold-rimmed spectacles hung on a string around his neck. His eyes were small and squinty looking, as if he needed the spectacles on his nose instead of hanging from his neck. Hannah didn't hesitate to tell him that the "Push" should be in larger letters.

"You think? Well, maybe I'll have to see about that."

Hannah walked past him, her large, dark eyes taking in everything. Every shelf was piled with men's tools, pipes, copper tubing, rubber hoses, nails, screws, seeds, and fertilizer, just about anything they could have used at home.

One side of the store was stacked with fabric, bolt after bolt of gaily colored material— flowered, patterned, plaid. There was heavy denim for work pants, suspenders, buttons, thread, needles, pins, just about anything any woman would need to sew for her family, plus dishes, buckets, pots and pans, mops and brooms, towels and washcloths. The list was endless.

Hannah walked up and down the narrow aisles stuffed with goods and thought of her mother's patched stockings and aprons, the broken comb the whole family used. She nodded brusquely at curious customers, or kept her eyes lowered, intent on fingering an especially fine piece of cloth, riffling through buttons as if searching for a special one. She noticed the dust, the chewing gum stuck to the floor, cigarette butts tramped flat, bits of thread and dried grass, clumps of yellow earth, bits of newspaper. The buttons should be sorted by color and size to make it easier for the housewives to find a button to match a certain fabric. Same way with the dress material. Much better to stack it together by color—blue plaid, blue flowered, navy blue, sky blue.

She stood still, took in the lone electric bulb hanging from its greasy black rope like a malevolent eye, barely giving enough light to distinguish the blue from the green, much the same as the conglomeration of buttons.

Why didn't he add more of those light bulbs, clean them up a bit? She wasn't accustomed to electricity, but she bet it was much the same as a lamp chimney all smoked up.

She stepped aside to let an elderly lady pass, then walked up to the counter before she lost her nerve. "Mister?"

The man was taking down a dozen eggs in a wire basket, but he stopped and gave her his full attention, his eyes telling her he was in a hurry but wanted to hear what she needed.

"You need me to work for you. Your store needs to be cleaned well, and you need better light. I could rearrange your fabric, sort buttons, and clean windows. You could make many improvements in here."

The owner of Rocher's Hardware and

Mercantile had been in business for close to thirty years. Out here on the plains, with folks scattered around for miles, none of them could afford to buy too much at any given time. So to survive, he'd learned to cut corners, keep his overhead down. His boys had both worked in the store until they went east to a college in Ohio, which left him scrambling to stay efficient, with this depression clamping a lid on any thoughts of bettering himself. His wife was, sadly, crippled with arthritis, her knees painfully swollen, her fingers becoming more twisted each year.

This odd girl, though, with that ungainly white thing on her head. "I would like to have you in my employ, but times are not good, as we all know. I couldn't pay you any wages to speak of."

Hannah answered immediately. "You wouldn't have to. All I'd need for a month or so for my beginning wages would be ten pounds of flour, ten of cornmeal, some salt, and a bit of sugar. Oh, and a ride home on Saturday evening, if it could be arranged. Plus, I'd need a place to stay."

"Harry!" The voice came from the back, loud and demanding, capable of turning the man immediately, as if the strident voice had strings attached to his hands and feet, puppet-like.

"Yes, dear." That quick, he was gone.

The bell above the door pealed. All the light coming through the door was darkened by a stout figure wearing a short sleeved dress, pulled in at

181

the waist by a thin strip of fabric, which divided her effectively into two parts, a rounded upper and a more rounded bottom. Her face was as red as a sour cherry, and as shiny, her yellow hair in a braid on top of her head.

Mrs. Klasserman. She was followed by Mr. Klasserman, who was mopping his own florid, shining cheeks with a great red handkerchief as large as a pillowcase.

"My lands, it's hot," Mrs. Klasserman said. "When it gets this hot, there's a storm cooking out there somewhere. You mark my words."

She sailed past Hannah without showing any sign of recognition, then realized that Harry was not behind the counter, where he was supposed to be. The heat had put her in foul mood. She was in a great hurry and needed only twelve black buttons for her Sunday serge. She was not about to wait.

She blinked, her eyes adjusting to the dim interior. She saw Hannah, followed by a smile of recognition, saying her name, both the first and last one correctly.

"Are your folks well? Never thought we'd run into you way out here in Pine. We must come and visit now. I told Owen I'm ashamed to go anymore, not having taken the time to meet your folks."

Hannah smiled, acknowledged her kindness, and told them Harry had been called to the back by his wife. She was sure he'd be out as soon as possible and offered to help her locate the black buttons, which took only a few minutes, with Hannah pouring a whole scoop on the countertop for Mrs. Klasserman to search for herself. When Harry did not appear, Hannah found the card taped to the wall with a list of button prices. She decided on a fair amount for twelve black, steel buttons, collected the money, and scooped the buttons into a small paper bag she found. She handed the bag to Mrs. Klasserman, smiling and accepting her thanks with a polite, "You're welcome."

When Harry returned, Hannah stood by the counter with her hands clasped behind her back, radiant with the feeling of ownership and accomplishment the transaction had given her. She wanted this job. Harry Rocher had a sickly wife, and his store was an unusual hodgepodge of items thrown together with no one to arrange things in an inviting manner.

She watched his face and saw the gray weariness, the lines drawn deeply around his mouth, the twitch in the muscle of his cheek. She stepped up to the counter and said, "So, would you consider my offer? My family is homesteading, and my father is without money. If you would allow me to be in your employ, I'd make a difference. I could help your wife with the cooking if you have a place for me to sleep.

I'll do my best in return for enough food to feed my family for a week. That's all."

Harry Rocher looked at her, this able-bodied, fresh-faced girl with flashing dark eyes and, no doubt, an assertive manner. He desperately needed help but could not afford to pay her. Quickly he calculated—ten pounds of the food she had mentioned would cost a few dollars. Perhaps he could throw in some lard and a partially opened sack of sugar that had turned hard. He thought of the widow Hennessy's oatcakes that hadn't sold. It would be a shame to feed them to the hogs. There was nothing wrong with them.

He looked at Hannah and knew how desperately poor some of these homesteaders were. He slowly nodded his head.

CHAPTER 10

The new chapter of Hannah's life that began with her job at Rocher's store would, in many ways, prepare her for the future God had planned for her.

Harry Rocher introduced Hannah to his wife, Doris, a slim woman who must have been pretty at one time. But, ravaged by a cruel disease, her hands were little more than pitiful claws that scrabbled to hold a comb or a glass of water. She was an unhappy woman, obviously despising the town of Pine and all its inhabitants. For more than thirty years, she had longed to return to the East, and three decades was an interminably long time to someone who would rather be elsewhere. It was her husband's will for them to live on the plains, but her love and loyalty also chained her to the prairie. Corroded by bitterness and dissatisfaction, she mostly kept to herself and spent her time reading or talking on the telephone to relatives back East. On good days, when the pain in her hands subsided a little, she wrote letters or played Solitaire.

She told Hannah to find her own way up the narrow staircase to the room on the left, Bob's room, but he wouldn't be home for at least nine months, perhaps a year. Harry followed her, opening windows in the stifling heat, turning back covers, running a hand across the dresser top, and shaking his head after examining his fingers.

"Everything, just everything, shouts neglect," he said quietly, so Doris would not hear. "Perhaps you are sent by God, an angel worker."

Hannah stopped short, astounded. Here was a man of the world, Dat would say, and he talked religion, just like Dat? Well, she could bet the fifty-cent piece in her pocket that he hadn't fasted and prayed and carried on the way Dat had. Likely he'd went about his life, patiently doing what he could, as best he knew how, balancing his work and the demands of his sickly wife.

Huh? Hard to think of herself as an angel worker. A few hours ago that Bess had called her . . . what was it? A waif? No, a babe in the woods, whatever she meant by that dumb saying. Well, an angel she was not, but she'd try hard to make a difference in this place. It appeared to have been much better at one time, especially this upstairs bedroom.

The furniture was made of good quality oak, just like at her aunt's house back home. The mirrored dresser was small, but had an ornate frame to hold the mirror, attached by dowels so that if you pulled it away from the wall, it swung forward or backward. The bed was a luxury Hannah couldn't even think about, having slept on ticks, those buttoned up covers filled with stinking dried hay. You could never get away from the feeling of being in a barn, sleeping in a haymow, but then, it was better than sleeping on the ground or a bare floor and waking up with your legs as stiff as a stovepipe.

She sat on the edge of the bed, marveling at its firmness and luxurious softness at the same time. Real pillows, clean white sheets. The walls were finished with a grayish white paper that had the texture of burlap. Ohio State pennants hung on the walls with framed black-and-white photographs of groups of boys kneeling or standing, wearing what looked like uniforms, a football in the foreground. She wondered which one was Bob, and what the name of their second son was.

There was a straight chair, a clothes rack, more pictures, a few dull brown rugs scattered on the floor, chintz curtains blowing in the hot breeze that sucked against the screen when the wind changed direction. Everything was dusty, the window screens, the sills, the curtains, the tops of every article and piece of furniture. She went over to the window and looked down, but could see only the rough side of another building not more than six feet away, plus weeds, tin cans, empty Coke bottles, and piles of what looked like horse manure scattered along the narrow alley.

There was no sense living in this squalor.

The townspeople needed to get busy and do something about the appearance of this derelict little place. But first things first, she supposed. She'd go downstairs and get acquainted with Doris and her kitchen and see what Harry's plans were. She tingled all over with the anticipation of returning home with the flour and cornmeal, to see her mother's happiness and her brother Manny looking forward to a good meal. As often as he tried to disguise the hunger in his eyes, he would be rewarded with corn cakes and pan-baked biscuits. She ached to do anything to feed her family and lift their spirits, so alone out here on these plains.

As far as her father was concerned, she felt nothing except perhaps a mild disgust. He needed to take responsibility for the well-being of his family. It was hard to have respect for someone who walked around with his head in the clouds, dreaming of all the miracles waiting just beyond the horizon, in the time when God's provision would wondrously manifest itself. Oh, he didn't doubt that a black cloud would appear one day, move over the homestead, and soak that corn.

Hannah shrugged, shook off her reverie, went to the mirror, and looked at her reflection. Skinny. She was thin. Her eyes were huge, and her face looked thin too. Ah, well, hopefully she could eat here. Taking a deep breath, she turned and made her way down the steep, narrow staircase.

Doris looked up at her with a wan smile. "Harry says you can cook. It will be wonderful to have a bit of help in the kitchen. Are you acquainted with a stove?"

Hannah looked around the kitchen and saw the white appliances, the refrigerator, and what appeared to be a square white object with black coils on top. "A wood stove," Hannah answered.

Doris introduced Hannah to electricity and all its wonders. Wide-eyed, Hannah discovered a quart of ice-cold milk in the refrigerator, just where Doris said it would be. And you can keep butter and meat in there for days without spoiling, she explained. The stove became red hot at the flick of a button, the heat contained in the black coils.

Hannah learned to cook well with Doris hovering at her elbows, a certain delight now smoothing her unhappy features. For one thing, Hannah made Doris laugh. Her blunt, unapologetic way of viewing the world and its inhabitants, and the colorful way she described her family filled Doris's gray world with small rays of brilliant light, pinwheels of imagining, little bursts of unexpected humor that elevated her existence to a higher level of happiness. She could picture the drab homestead, the beautiful children (Hannah was a beauty), the submissive Sarah, the dreaming Mose. Doris knew Hod Jenkins and had seen Abby in the store, but didn't know them personally.

By the end of the week, the house had been cleaned to a spotless sheen, the floors swept and scrubbed, the windows washed, and the screens taken down and scrubbed with soap and water. Dust flew, and Doris held her breath as Hannah whipped about the house, rocking precious china dishes and lamps, shaking rugs with so much energy she was afraid they'd fall apart.

Hannah swept the store, but the rearranging would come later. She felt she was not acquainted with Harry as she should be before suggesting ways his goods could be better displayed and more appealing to women's eyes. There were so many changes to be made, so much to do in a week's time that Hannah plopped into bed bone-weary every night, wishing Manny could know what it was like to sleep on a mattress with a good soft pillow again.

On Saturday afternoon, then, Harry told her firmly that she could not walk home. His wife would accompany him, and they would drive her out to the homestead. For all Hannah's pluck, she found it extremely difficult to tell him her father would not want her to ride in a car.

Harry was bagging her flour and cornmeal, preparing a tin of lard, and gathering bits and pieces of leftover merchandise to give her. For a moment, he stopped what he was doing and asked, "And why not, do you think?"

"It's our religion."

"You can't carry these things the fifteen miles home. Not in this heat, and the day fading already."

"Does someone have a buggy? A horse?"

Harry shook his head and said, of course, but you'd kill a horse driving all those miles in this heat. So if she wanted to go home, she would have to ride in his car.

And so Hannah did. She sat in the back seat of the glistening black car, which shone in spite of an ever-present layer of dust. The seats were upholstered and springy, in a kind of smooth leather, although it seemed too slippery to be leather. She sat stiffly, her feet braced side by side, her knees held together by her fear, and watched steadily out the front windshield through a gap between Harry and Doris.

They rumbled away from town, picking up speed. The wind rushed in through the open window, lifting her white covering by its strings and tugging it away from her head. The pins that held it to her hair pulled horribly, so she grabbed her covering strings and tied them beneath her chin.

The speed was frightening. She had never moved across the earth like this. The level prairie moved by as if it was propelled by a large, unseen object. The car sputtered and clattered. Harry gripped the steering wheel with both hands, but never moved it much, neither right nor left.

The car slowed when Hannah gave directions, then slowed again, bumping over ruts and deep holes, grasses growing in over the track that served as a road. Doris tugged at the thin scarf she had tied over her coiffed hair, then closed her window, cranking a handle that raised or lowered it.

Dust rolled in through the opened windows. Harry sneezed, then cleared his throat. Black dots appeared on a rise to their left, which puzzled Hannah. Whose cattle were they? They had already passed the road that led to the Jenkinses' so perhaps there was another ranch they knew nothing about.

Nervous as they approached, Hannah slid forward, gripping the front seat with both hands, asking Harry to drop her off before they reached the homestead.

"I will not let you carry those parcels by yourself," Harry said, turning to look at her while the car kept moving by itself.

"We can't do that," Doris said matter of fact.

"My father will not be pleased. I'm afraid he won't be very kind or welcoming." Hannah faltered in her speech, ashamed of her father, ashamed even more of the conditions in which they lived. The crude barn, the unfinished house made of crooked logs, the campfire in the yard, and the ruined corn crop. Since she had spent a week in town, their glaring poverty, their poor management of trying to raise corn, the garden struggling through the grass that threatened to reclaim the tilled earth, the thin children with the too-short pants and dresses, patched and ragged, assaulted her. Yes, they were ragged. Yes, they were thin. All of this seemed to press Hannah down into the smooth surface of the seat, shrinking her to a small black blob, an unnoticed, unworthy piece of failed humanity that had no business living in town, eating the Rochers' good food, sleeping in a clean, comfortable bed, and acting as if she knew something about the store when, in truth, she was nobody. Raised surrounded by a secular community a thousand miles away, blindly following a delusional father with a broken wife by his side, she was now returning to the unpresentable situation they accepted as home.

A fierce pride, coupled with anger, rose up in Hannah. She hated being poor. She could not face her father or her mother. This feeling left her scrambling for a handhold, as if she was climbing a steep cliff and could not find a way to keep pulling herself up. It would be easier to stop trying, just let go of all of it, and fall. Tumble down, down, down until her body collided with the earth, folded in on itself, and perished. All of this went through her mind in a second, the knowledge of her station in life, the confrontation of who she was, where her roots lay, and from where her father had pulled them up to transplant them in this forsaken country.

Is this what her father meant by dying to self? All of that talk about being born again? You just fell off a cliff and gave up, figuring your life was no longer your own? She resisted fiercely, the thought of turning into her mother, going about her days with a song on her lips, no strength of her own, like a rubber band pulled this way and that, always depending on her husband, going through life without questioning anything.

As the homestead came into view, Hannah looked out of the window of the car and thought bitterly. This is where it got you, here in the middle of nowhere, starving, her head as empty as a stone. Well, it wasn't for her. She still had her wits about her.

As Hannah expected, her father was taken aback, to state it mildly. His eyes popped in his head when he saw the car approaching, his pain and disbelief evident when Hannah got out of the car, clutching the groceries to her chest like a peace offering, her face a mixture of bravery and confusion.

Harry stepped out, greeted Mose with a handshake, introduced himself, and told him they'd brought his daughter home. Doris remained seated, her face bland with hidden feelings, surveying the log house with careful, measured eyes.

Hannah tried to slip past her father, going

around him from behind, but he turned and caught her with a sharp, "Hannah!"

She stopped and turned, her eyes bright and unflinching.

"I thought we told you not to ride in cars. You have openly disobeyed."

What was there to say to that? Hannah ground her teeth in anger. Now why couldn't Dat have waited to cut loose until after Harry and Doris had left instead of displaying his righteous little sermon here and now? "I brought food. I couldn't carry all of this." She thrust the heavy parcel out to show him what she had brought.

When her father's eyelids came down, and he spoke the inevitable, Hannah remained standing, clutching the cornmeal and flour as if his words could take it from her.

"I have prayed that God would send us a blessing, but I didn't think He would send it in the devil's machine. So I propose, Mister . . ." he faltered, forgetting Harry's name.

"Rocher," Harry supplied.

"Yes, Mr. Harry Rocher. Our religion doesn't hold with riding in cars, so I suggest that Hannah will not be in your employ in future. Also, the food you have so graciously brought, according to my way of thinking, has been tainted by riding in an automobile. So I would suggest that you put it back into the machine that brought you."

Hannah had never felt so helpless, or outraged.

She opened her mouth to speak to her father, but could not utter a word. She could only stutter.

Her father smiled at her, then walked toward her to take the food she clung to, as if her very life depended on it. "Hand it over, Hannah."

"Dat," she began, feeling tears of rage and frustration prick her eyelids. "You need this flour and cornmeal. You can't do this to Mam and the children. We . . . you, are hungry."

At the thought of Sarah and the little ones, Hannah saw the flicker of reconsideration, felt his weakening, and she resolved to stand her ground. "You can't go on, Dat. We need to sit together and talk this over. I have a job now. I work for these people. They can't afford to pay me, but they can spare us some food."

"Very well, then. But you must not ride in the automobile." Turning to Harry, he said that Hannah would return on Monday by horse, which was their way. As for the food that had ridden in the *verboten* vehicle, there may be a time when common sense was involved, and this may be one of those times.

So Harry and Doris Rocher rode back to the town of Pine, without meeting Sarah, having caught only glimpses of the children, their curiosity riding home with them. Harry shook his head and told Doris he had never seen anyone quite as strange as that Mose Detweiler, but Hannah seemed normal enough.

For one evening, Doris forgot her own woes and talked in a lively manner, thinking up ways in which they could be useful in helping that family. Harry watched his wife's face, the expression in her eyes, the way she waved her hands for emphasis, and thought that a miracle had happened right here in their car in the middle of the high plains.

The evening meal was something to remember. Sarah worked the dough as if it was made of diamonds, each pat of her hands holding anticipation and gratitude. The children crowded around the bubbling cornmeal mush, sniffing, laughing, and clapping their hands. The smoke from the campfire made their eyes water. They coughed and scampered away only to return for more.

Hannah spread the tablecloth, brought out the dishes, poured the cold well water. Sarah warmed the prairie hen gravy. The bread baked over the fire in a covered skillet. The mush was thick and salty, filling their hungry stomachs with heaven-sent manna.

Sarah watched her family eat until they were full. Now they were happy, light-hearted children, their cheeks flushed with the warm food. She took pity on Mose, trying hard to contain himself, to eat without wolfing down the food, but his eyes gave away his glittering hunger from within.

Sarah knew the dull ache of an empty stomach herself. Nursing Abigail, she could not have gone on for many more days without a better supply of food. All week, she had considered asking Mose to hitch up the team and go to the Jenkinses' for help, although knowing he would not allow it. At night, when the baby cried, not satisfied, it seemed as if the corners of the dark room contained a black portent, a foreboding of unseen hardship, and her soul felt weak with trembling.

But she must be strong. She could see the despair in Mose's eyes, the way he plied his religion to keep it at bay, the futility of his constant vigil and his expectation of a miracle. There was a certain hope in the way he watched the half-grown corn wither and curl in the blazing sun and the increasingly hot winds. He built a barnyard for the cow and two calves, which brought Sarah to a weak belief that he may be willing to change, to take what Hod Jenkins kept telling him into consideration.

But tonight, with their stomachs full, Sarah did not want to bring unwanted worries to the table. Tonight, she would enjoy having Hannah back, relishing the new-found maturity she displayed by accepting the food as payment.

They talked while they washed dishes, Sarah listening to Hannah's expanded world with awe. She gave a small laugh, eyes wide as she listened, thankful for every scene her daughter allowed her to see. They giggled like schoolgirls, thinking what Mose would say about Bess. Then Sarah turned to Hannah and asked if she honestly would promise to stay out of the café. She believed Bess was kind, but likely the men that frequented the café would not be very good company.

More than ever, the crude house and barn seemed primitive to Hannah. It was pitiful in its raw state, as if unlearned children had decided to build stick structures. The logs were thin and crooked with yellow, cracking clay clapped between them, the roof gray and rusted brown in long streaks.

The outdoor cooking was the worst. Like Indians. Sarah did not seem to mind, but living the way they did chafed at Hannah's spirits, like ill-fitting boots rubbing blisters of shame. But she was here now, in the company of her family. So she would not let the state of their lives drive away the comfort of being with them.

They sat around the fire late into the evening, the logs burning down to embers, a soft glow encroaching in the west as darkness crept across the sky, pinpricks of stars poking their way through. At night, the wind slowed to a whisper. The grass stopped its constant tossing, as if knowing it was time to go to bed and rest while the world closed its wings and slept.

Eli and Mary sat close to Mose, leaning on his legs with their elbows, their eyelids drowsy, the heat of the fire putting them to sleep. Sarah held Baby Abigail, although she was sound asleep, loving the feel of the small, pliant form in her arms. Manny sat cross-legged, staring into the fire, his dark eyes hiding any form of emotion, his handsome face etched in stone.

Hannah watched her brother and wondered. What had occurred this past week while she was gone? Manny loved his father, stood by him, and defended him with his whole being, in spite of Dat's erratic behavior.

Hannah broke the silence by asking about the calves. Mose said he believed they were doing well. Hannah asked if they were still tethered on ropes.

"No, they are in the barnyard now."

"Always? Don't you let them out to graze?"

"No, we don't. We give them grass by the forkful." Sarah's eyes cautioned Hannah.

"You know, the Jenkinses' cows pretty much roam at will. They don't go far, and if they do, they are branded. Everyone knows whose cattle they are. We haven't branded ours yet."

Mose nodded.

"Clay has a brand made at the farrier. The Bar S for Stoltzfus, Mam's maiden name."

Mose looked at Hannah in disbelief. "You took that on yourself, then, to name the homestead into a place called a ranch, the way our worldly neighbors have done? We are not of the world;

we are a peculiar people, set apart. We are God's chosen, so we do things differently. Who gave Clay Jenkins the right to carry on with the name of our ranch, I mean, homestead?"

"I did."

"Without my permission?"

"Yes." Hannah hung her head, her gaze dropping to her hands in her lap.

"So, you are planning on turning this productive little homestead, a humble place of abode blessed by God, into a ranch with a worldly name?"

"Dat, we have to. Don't you see? We have no choice. Look around you. The corn is withering on its roots. This is normal weather for early summer. They don't grow corn here. They raise cattle. The grass is abundant and it's free. The cattle grow fat and we sell them. That's how we survive. Until the herd is built up, we need to have a paying job to stay alive."

Mose pursed his lips. "The rain will come, Hannah."

"And what if it doesn't, Dat? Do you have any plans beyond the withered corn, already dying in the field?"

"God will provide."

And then Manny spoke in a deep voice, a man's voice, bringing Mose to attention. "Dat, I want to be an obedient son, and you know I always have been. But Hannah's right. Perhaps this is a test for our faith, a test of our will to survive these first years. Already we would have perished without the help of our worldly neighbors. We are no longer among our own people, so we need to accept advice and help from those around us. I met a man named Owen Klasserman when I was out riding, a heavyset man who speaks German. Their ranch is closer to us than the Jenkinses'. He says, too, that cattle is the way to make a living in the Dakotas."

A long speech for Manny. Mose listened to his son's words and considered them, Sarah could tell. With the respect he had for his son, his words meant more than if Hannah had spoken them. For a heartbeat she waited for her husband's reply and when none was forthcoming, she continued to wait, knowing Mose would think for a long time before he spoke.

She got up, put Abby to bed, and returned to find her husband waving his arms forcefully, speaking in loud tones. She stood in front of the house in the darkness with her arms crossed, watching the red glow of the fire and her husband's waving arms. As she listened, his voice seemed like rocks thrown on the roof, and a genuine dread gripped her.

"Who are you to be telling your own father?" he shouted.

Eli and Mary rose to their feet, fleeing from their father's rant to take refuge in Sarah's arms. Quietly she put them to bed and knelt with them to say their German prayer. She kissed them goodnight before returning to the fireside to sit with Mose, his speech now done. A cowed silence, rife with unspoken words, settled over them.

The fire glowed. Mose got up to add a stick of wood, sparks shooting upward to the magnificence of the vast night sky. Somewhere, a wolf howled its eerie call of the wild across the rustling night grasses, immediately followed by the high yipping of a coyote.

And then Sarah spoke in a voice filled with peace. "Children, I do believe your father and I can see that what you are saying is true. But it is hard for parents to accept the counsel of their children, knowing that we are older and wiser and have been here on earth longer than both of you. So, we should be the ones who guide and direct you. However, our situation borders on the desperate, and without the aid of our English neighbors, we will likely not survive. My whole heart yearns to return to Lancaster County, the land of my childhood, the home of our dear parents, and aunts and uncles. But that too is an impossibility with no money for train fare, and no resources to make the long journey with horses and wagon.

"Hannah, you are doing the one thing that for now will save us from starvation. Manny, you are right. We need to learn to adapt and accept help from those around us, whether they are people of faith or not."

Here Mose broke in. "Believers should not be yoked to unbelievers."

Sarah went on, "We are not yoked, my husband. We are here in a harsh land where folks need each other, and without that, we will surely perish. So we will continue allowing Hannah to work for the Rochers and try our best to grow the food we can, watering the garden and branding the calves, which looks to be a necessity. Then we will wait on the Lord, and see what He has for us in the future."

CHAPTER 11

On Sunday afternoon, Clay Jenkins appeared riding a black horse that still tugged at the bit in spite of having traveled the miles between them, carrying the branding iron he had picked up at the farrier's that week.

It was fortunate that Mose was asleep, that Hannah stood by the barnyard fence watching his arrival, painfully aware of her threadbare blue dress that was too tight across her shoulders, the torn black apron tied around her waist, her bare feet.

The welcoming light in his blue eyes, the way he lifted his old brown Stetson, and the blonde hair falling over his forehead put her at ease so that she smiled her welcome in return.

He proffered the iron. She stepped up to take it from him, lifted it carefully, examined the insignia on the bottom, and ran her fingers over it as if the shape of the cast iron was the shape of her future. She looked up at him, her dark eyes thanking him.

"I guess you know I can't pay you for this."

He nodded and said, "It's all right." Then, "Mind if I get down?"

"No."

He dismounted in one easy movement, then

stood, so tall above her, and asked if she'd want to walk with him.

Hannah glanced at the house and noticed the lack of activity. She nodded her head, her heart pounding in fear of her father. Clay knew he would be unwelcome, but was determined to take this chance when it presented itself.

They walked side by side, Clay leading the horse, down the grassy track that served as a driveway to the buildings.

The air was hot and windy, the sky a dome of blue heat, the grass waving restlessly, tossed by the constant current of air that tugged at her skirts, flapped the strings of her covering and loosened her dark hair from its restraints.

The horse blew from his nostrils, the way horses do, with a rumbling sound that made Hannah jump.

Clay laughed. "Thought it was your pa comin' up behind us?"

Hannah laughed that rich laugh that came from deep inside. Clay looked down at her and saw only the top of her head, the band of white that was her covering, and the dark hair blown loose by the wind.

She looked up then and caught his gaze. "He'd be yelling long before he got this close."

"He don't like me much."

"No."

"Well, what I came over for was to give you

the branding iron, but also to see how you all are gittin' on. I can't see how you're livin' half decent with no food, and I don't believe money's plentiful around here. I guess to say it right, I'm plain worried about you."

Hannah sighed. She gazed off across the prairie and then stopped walking. Looking at Clay, really looking at him, she told him there was a time when her pride would not have allowed her to say how bad things actually were. But now, she'd have to.

Clay switched the reins to his other hand, tipped up his hat, and waited. With a proud lift of her chin, Hannah told him about going to town, relating the whole story in minute detail, to the filth in the alleyways, Bess at the café, the room she slept in at the Rochers', and Doris's unhappiness.

"I just want to be able to keep my family. The children are hungry." Defiance flashed from her dark eyes, carrying the knowledge of her father's disapproval.

Clay showed his disbelief. "Whyn't you ride over? You did once."

"I'm no beggar."

"But it wasn't begging. You did what you had to do."

"I know."

There was a silence, long enough that Clay was aware of her, so sharply aware of wanting to comfort Hannah and take away the unfair burden that had been laid on her too-young shoulders. She was tied to her father by her strict upbringing and would become her mother when she was married. He could see this plainly. Slowly, her spirit would change.

"So your mother wouldn't go against your father?"

"No. Well, not really. She did give us a little speech last night, although in her own timid way, which I suppose will help somewhere down the road. But in the meantime, the situation is real. Someone has to come up with a plan to put food on the table."

"Looks like you're doing it. Right plucky of you."

"You think?"

"Yeah."

"There was nothing else to do."

"So tell me, Hannah, when you get married, will you be like your mother?"

"Who would I marry? There are no Amish within hundreds of miles. I want to get married. I figured that out soon after we left home."

"You can't marry a normal person?" Clay asked seriously.

Hannah laughed. "You're saying you are normal and we aren't?"

"Something like that."

Hannah thought for awhile, then shook her

head. "I'm still young. I don't know what would happen if I met someone and fell in love with him. If he wasn't Amish, my parents would never allow it, so I could never receive their blessing. That's a scary prospect. Besides, I don't know what love is, or how to fall in love. How does a person know when that's about to happen?"

Clay gave a short laugh. "I've been in and out of love 'bout a hunnert times."

"See what I mean? It didn't work for you. Probably never will for me."

Clay dropped the horse's reins and asked if she would sit for a spell, then bent to flatten some grass by the side of the road. Grateful to rest, Hannah sat facing him, her legs curled beneath her skirt, her dark eyes on his face as he removed his hat. His hair was so long she couldn't tell if he had the telltale blue-white forehead of every man on the plains.

He did have a nice face, she decided. The squint of his blue eyes, the straight nose that appeared to have been smashed once, or at least broken, the cleft in his chin, his smooth skin already had the makings of fine lines and fissures around his eyes from the unforgiving weather.

She did not let her gaze linger on his mouth for reasons she did not understand. Perhaps it was too perfect. She had never seen a mouth with that kind of perfection. It was unsettling, so she looked at his nose again, but that was too close to his eyes. So she settled on a region somewhere beyond his shoulder.

He told her that her family would need help getting along. Did she know that? She said yes, she did know that, but figured as long as she stayed on at the Rochers' store, she could supply sufficient food for all of them.

"What about your pa? Couldn't he find work someplace? Or your brother?" Clay asked, watching the way her eyes grew darker, thinking on things.

"Manny will have to, eventually. Even if it's for food, the way I'm doing."

"Your pa? He wouldn't work for wages?"

Hannah shrugged.

"You dread goin' back to town on Monday morning?"

"No, not really. I'll like it better once I know everyone."

"When's those boys comin' back from college?"

"Not now. Maybe in six months or a year. I don't know."

Clay said he'd never wanted to go to college. All he wanted to do was buy his own spread and raise cattle his whole life long. That was all he knew.

"Do you want to get married and have children?"

"Yeah. Probably, if I can."

"Why couldn't you?" Hannah asked. Clay shrugged and thought, *because I can't have you. I would get married right quick, Hannah, if I knew I could have you.* But he didn't say it.

"Yeah, well, same for me, Clay. There's no one close, so I'll probably remain single and work to feed my family."

Suddenly she sat up straight, a fierce light of determination in her eyes. She told him she was going to learn how to rope and ride if it was the last thing she ever did!

Clay looked at the sun and told her there was time to ride home to his place and practice in the corral. Would she?

She couldn't go home and get one of the horses. Her father would never allow it, with Clay and on a Sunday.

"You always bring your pa wherever you go? Come on. You can ride with me."

Hannah felt the blush before it colored her face, then kept her eyes downcast, afraid to let him see how badly she wanted to do just that. She became so flustered, she could not think of an answer fast enough, so she started to laugh, which came out in a mixed-up sob, the hysterical sound of a young girl's heart.

Clay stepped closer, reached down, and pulled her to her feet, searching her face, not understanding what had caused the sound coming from her throat.

She yanked her hands out of his, stomped one foot, and told him to go away and leave her alone, accusing her of bringing her father when he wasn't even close, and if he was, she'd do exactly as she wanted anyway.

With that, she ran off toward home, her feet pounding the dry, hard earth, tears of rage and frustration welling up as she ran.

Clay called after her, then thought better of it. He gathered up the reins and made his way home, thinking the less he saw of Hannah Detweiler the better. But he knew too that he would look forward to their next encounter, which he planned for next week, when he would go to Rocher's Hardware for some bolts. Or nails. Or something.

Hannah rode the faithful Pete to work the following morning, beginning at daybreak with a parcel of cold mush in the pocket of the clean brown dress her mother allowed her to wear. It was a dress kept for church on Sundays, but since there was no church to attend, what was the point? She wore Manny's old pair of trousers underneath, for modesty.

She looked down at her mother from her seat on the horse in the half-light of dawn, when everything was still and as pristine as an angel's wing.

"Are you sure you'll be all right, Mam? You have enough to eat, enough to get by 'til Saturday?"

"Oh, yes, Hannah. With the prairie hens Manny shoots, I feel sure we'll have enough."

"Then I'll be off. Good-bye, Mam."

Sarah touched her daughter's knee, gave it a little tap of affection, and let her eyes tell Hannah how much she cared. She raised a hand, stepped back, and said, "Bye."

The day was sharp and cool, the prairie appearing like a dark ocean, the tips of grass waving like ripples of a current in a vast body of water. The sky was gray, tinged with the color of ice, the sun's advance below the horizon bringing a soft shade of pink, like a bunny's ear.

Hannah always thought the velvet pink of a rabbit's ear was the loveliest color she had ever seen. Someday, she might have a dress of that shade, if she worked hard enough.

Her cousin Samuel had a whole pile of rabbit hutches on the east side of their barn. He raised them to see at Easter, but since the Depression, no one wanted to waste their money on things that weren't necessary; a rabbit wasn't something you absolutely had to have. Someday, though, she would own a pale pink dress and a row of rabbit hutches painted white. She would clean the cages every day, give the rabbits fresh hay and cool water, get them out of their hutches and let them nibble on green grass and hop around on their long hind legs before replacing them in their cages. Perhaps rabbits couldn't survive the cold Dakota winters. Well, she'd put the hutches into the barn for the winter.

She wondered if Samuel's family lived in the same state of poverty as her family did. It probably was hard times to Samuel, but she'd bet their living conditions would be a rare luxury to them. To Mam anyway.

Her thoughts rambled along in the past, remembering times when she would have never imagined having the responsibilities that were on her shoulders now. They were like a hard, wooden yoke chafing her neck and bowing her into submission, she guessed. But she wasn't beaten yet.

The sun burst on the horizon, painting the sky in crimson, orange, and yellow. The sun's rays rode on the birdsong that came alive as the morning progressed. Chirps and liquid trills, short light chants, and shrill whistles, all the merry sounds from numerous birds flitting among the grass and racing across the sky in showers of dark-colored winged acrobats—but Hannah missed them completely, immersed as she was in her own thoughts.

When the town of Pine came into view, she slid off Pete's back, ashamed to be seen riding into people's scrutiny of the Amish girl who was forbidden to ride in cars. How many people in the town knew about her, now that the garrulous Bess had her in her teeth? She'd shake her like a dog, leaving her to pick up the pieces by herself, no doubt.

Well, in this town, her father did not follow her. She was her own person. She squared her shoulders and walked with her head up, leading the horse through the back lot in the small fenced-in area behind it, as Harry had instructed her. She made sure the stable was accessible, that there was water in the trough, and then removed the bridle, petting good old Pete with love and affection. She removed her trousers as quickly as possible and hung them on a nail beside the bridle. Taking a deep breath, she began her day in the other world, the realm of life that was lived among *auseriche leit*. Outside people. People of the world.

Doris greeted her, dark circles under her eyes and a tired, half-lidded expression. The kitchen was a mess! Harry's relatives had been here, Doris explained. They were quite the company, she said, leaving her with a mountain of dishes and never offering to help with them.

Hannah eyed the sink, laughed, and said that the mountain was still there all right, which made Doris smile. She kept smiling as Hannah emptied the sink, banging pots and pans, scraping dried food off casseroles and cast-iron pans, water splashing out of the sink and dribbling down the front of the cabinet, and soapsuds as high as her elbows. Her shoulders erect and her head bent forward, Hannah threw herself into a frenzied attack on the towers of dishes. In no time at all, the pile was gone—washed, rinsed, dried, and stacked neatly in the cupboards. The electric stove shone like a mirror.

Doris sat in her rocking chair, her feet propped on an upholstered footstool. She wore a clean yellow housedress covered with a sunny print of daisies. She had a simple crocheted afghan over her lap, the radio on the small dark table beside her spilling the morning news, an electric fan whirring from the opposite side.

Hannah remained in awe of electricity and its amazing ability to be carried on a wire stretched between poles for hundreds of miles, a substance you couldn't see contained in one wire. It sizzled into homes, turning them into well-lit dwellings with hot and cold water coming from a spigot by the mere turning of a handle, keeping refrigerators ice cold, and stoves red hot. A man's voice came from a wooden box called a radio, and a telephone on the wall transmitted your own voice to someone else through a wire, allowing you to hear the other person's voice as well.

She figured there had to be some smart people in this world, much smarter than herself, but that was all right. Being Amish, she'd never have a need for electricity. It was amazing, nevertheless, and she planned on enjoying every luxury as long as she was here in Pine working for the Rochers.

216

She told Doris her dress was lovely, like a field of flowers on a sunny day, which made Doris smile again, reaching up to fix her hair so that it fell just so over her ears.

"Now, what do you have for me to do today?" Hannah asked.

"Why don't we take this week to do all the housecleaning here in the house?" Doris replied, anxiously searching Hannah's face for signs of disapproval.

"Sure. That would be great. You just want me to do it the way I was taught by my mother?"

"Oh, yes. I'm sure the way you clean will be fine. I just have one request, and that is that you use the Murphy's oil soap for the furniture and floors."

"Right. Okay. I'll get started then."

Hannah turned on her heel and went up the stairs. Doris heard scraping and banging, bumps and footsteps, before Hannah ran down the stairs with an armload of sheets, quilts, and curtains. She carried them to the laundry room behind the kitchen, a sunny little alcove containing the wringer washer and rinsing tubs, a shelf with powdered soap, vinegar, bluing, and cakes of lye soap. Other shelves held cardboard boxes and the remains of geraniums planted in coffee cans that had died years ago. The shelves were littered with dead flies and bees, the windows were hazy with grease and dust, their curtains hanging haphazardly on bent rods and a film of spider webs like lace over everything.

Neglect, is what it is, thought Hannah. Here was a woman without enough spirit to even attempt to keep things up. Harry should take his wife home to the East if he took the teachings of the Bible seriously enough to give his life for his wife, as Christ loved the church. Or something like that.

That was her whole grievance with Dat. All of his pious show, his holiness, didn't amount to a hill of beans with her the way he brought Mam out here to live without a plan, and now look at all of us. Living like poor squatters, starving, corn dying in the field. Anger brought rebellion to the storm of her thoughts, stuffing quilts through the wringer with a vengeance.

Before lunchtime the clothesline was pegged full of flapping quilts, curtains, and sheets. Hannah was upstairs wiping down walls, polishing windows, and washing floors when she noticed her arms becoming weak. Dark spots floated in front of her eyes and the room began to tilt and spin. Quickly, she sat on the edge of the bed, then realized how hungry she was.

Should she ask Doris for lunch? Make it herself? Either way, she had to eat or she'd fall over in a faint. So she made her way down the stairs and found the kitchen empty. There was a note telling her that Doris went to her doctor's appointment and to help herself to food in the refrigerator.

She ate cold fried chicken, like a dog, she thought wryly, tearing at the tender meat that fell away from the bones. She ate mouthfuls of sweet pudding, slabs of cheese, crackers, and a dish of cold oatmeal. Because she was alone, she could lower her head and shovel the food into her mouth, acting like the starving person she was.

The nausea that rose up immediately after the gorging of food surprised her, and when she miserably retched up all of her lunch soon after, she wiped her mouth, sat down against the wall in the bathroom off the kitchen, and cried. She cried because she loathed herself for eating like a pig. She cried for the state of poverty her whole family was in. She cried mostly for being in this dingy, dusty little town, living with people she barely knew. And she cried because she was so angry at her father.

Why couldn't Dat go out and get a job? He was the one who was shirking his duty, going through life shining with religion, without seeing to the basic needs of his family.

And then she was done. She wiped her eyes, straightened her shoulders, and checked her appearance in the small cracked mirror on the medicine cabinet, just like the one they used to have at home.

She went back to work after slowly eating a slice of buttered bread and honey and was still cleaning when Doris returned. She wondered vaguely whether Harry had accompanied her to the doctor's office and who would have watched the store while he was gone.

Hannah cleaned all afternoon, then brought in the sweet smelling quilts and sheets, while Doris ironed the curtains with an electric iron that stayed hot. She never had to heat it the way they heated their sadirons over the fire at home.

The evening meal was reheated leftovers and Hannah ate slowly, savoring each bite of the delicious scalloped potatoes and corn and applesauce. She had a large slice of spice cake and more of the pudding. She felt full and satisfied. Her spirits lifted as she washed dishes and offered to help stock shelves in the store.

It was a joy and a pleasure to work in the unorganized, dusty store. She filled a bucket with soapy water and started in the back, where the sewing supplies and fabrics were kept, removing everything off the shelves, scrubbing, dusting, and rearranging.

Finally, she realized she was weary. Bone tired. Her shoulders ached, her lower back hurt, and her feet felt like lumps of iron. She pitched the dirty water out the back door, wrung out the rag with her hands, and called it a day.

She tumbled into her bed after washing up in the bathroom and fell asleep without remembering to pray. She slept a deep and restful sleep so that when she awoke, she was surprised to find herself disoriented, not realizing where she was.

The night of rest had done wonders for her outlook, and she thoroughly enjoyed her time finishing the upstairs cleaning. Doris said at lunchtime that she could have a break to eat her soup and bread and then sit down with her for a talk.

The kitchen tidied, the afternoon sun shone through the back windows as the fan whirred by her chair. Hannah appreciated the homey atmosphere, the way the chairs were situated side by side with the sofa along the opposite wall, the patterned rug in between. The rose-patterned wallpaper was in soft pink and a mellow green, which was duplicated in the pillows on each end of the couch.

The wide door between the kitchen and seating area allowed the sunny light to shine through, leaving a glow in a room that would have appeared darker without it.

At first, seated beside Doris, Hannah felt self-conscious, but only for a short time. The way Doris asked questions and the kindness with which she accepted Hannah's answers was encouraging. Often, Doris would shake her head and murmur an expression of pity or disbelief, but always politely, never making Hannah feel like the oddity she knew she was.

"So," Doris continued, "that covering on your head symbolizes submission to God first, then your husband. But you aren't married, so why do you wear it?"

Again, Hannah reminded her that there wasn't always a clear reason. It was a rule, called the *Ordnung*; it was part of their belief, the way they were born and raised into their culture. The head covering on girls likely portrayed their recognition of God, their obedience to the *Ordnung*, and their obedience to the verse in the Bible about women having their heads covered.

"But I cut my hair short without guilt, knowing that same verse says that if a woman's head is uncovered, let it be shorn. So how can that be?" Doris asked.

Hannah smiled, then laughed. "Well, to put it the way I see it, you were born to English parents . . ."

Doris interrupted, "Not English."

"I don't literally mean English people from England. We Amish call anyone who is not Plain, people like you and Harry, we call them English. Maybe that goes way back to the Mayflower and the Puritans, I don't know."

"But you're not Puritans or Quakers."

"No. We're from Switzerland, from a group started by Jacob Ammann."

"Hmm. That's interesting. But what I have a hard time with is why would your father have brought his family so far out here to this . . ." Her voice trailed off, and she waved a disfigured hand weakly, then let it drop. "It's just such a big land full of nothing. Nothing. Dust and dirt and poor people living on ugly ranches, scrabbling to make a living, raising horrible cattle, and riding around on horses, shooting each other."

Hannah threw back her head and laughed, the deep laugh that affected everyone who heard it. Doris smiled, put a hand to her mouth, then laughed out loud, a sound no one ever heard from her. "I'm serious. I hate it."

Hannah stopped laughing and thought a minute before replying, "I don't hate this land. I rather like the emptiness of it, the wildness and the great big nothingness. I could live here for the rest of my life if our situation was different. We are dirt poor, which I'm sure you could tell when you drove me home."

Doris shook her head. "It's just so sad. And your father is such a strict man. Does he really feel the way he spoke?"

Hannah nodded. "Yes, he does, but he forced himself to take the food because he knows his family is starving."

"But he needs to change his mind. He needs to see that God is not so harsh and does not require such stringent rules."

Hannah nodded and again stayed quiet. So deeply were values ingrained in her conscience, she knew it was better not to speak too bitterly against her parents, no matter how often she rebelled. No, she did not believe such restrictions were required for herself or her mother, sisters, and brothers, and yet it seemed wrong to openly belittle her own father to a woman like Doris who was not born among the Amish.

She didn't know. She was only sixteen.

"Tell me, Hannah, as a young girl who is very acceptable to young men, I would think, will you marry someone of another belief?"

Hannah shook her head. "No, not if I obey my parents."

Doris looked bewildered, then shook her head. "But he brought you way out here! For what?"

All Hannah could think of was the poor management, the loss of the farm, the public shaming of being excommunicated for the distilling of his grains, the long, arduous journey to a land of poverty, and near starvation. What kept her from being honest, from going against her father and belittling him to this woman the way she often did alone, in her thoughts?

It would be so easy to abandon ship. To tell Doris how she actually felt. To convert to their faith and take off this covering that labeled her as odd and different. To wear sunny, daisy patterned dresses and cut her hair in a flattering style. Sometimes she hated her father and wanted to do something just like that to hurt him, to see him on his knees begging her to come home. So far, that kind of hardness was impossible for her to obtain, or to be comfortable with.

CHAPTER 12

Sarah stood in the doorway of the house, the hot summer sun searing the dry dust at her feet, the sky spreading before her pulsing with a brassy light, the heat baking even the clouds into obscurity. The wind was strong today, moaning about the tin roof, rattling loose edges, the grass rattling and brittle, browned and bleached by the soaring temperatures and the constant hot wind.

She squinted, trying to see where the corn had been, but was hardly able to see where Mose had tilled the soil. The prairie reclaimed the land quickly, as if the tilling and growth of foreign plants had been an affront to it, the grass having been there for many centuries.

A calf bawled in the barnyard. Sarah turned to see Mose hoist an armload of hay across his crude fence, then stop to lift his soiled straw hat and wipe his brow. Manny was at work behind the barn using a scythe the Jenkinses had loaned them to cut grass for the winter's supply of hay.

Hod had insisted he'd come over with the tractor and the mower, but Mose would have none of it. He didn't even own a pitchfork, a fact he hoped to keep hidden from his neighbor. Mose just did not like accepting charity from worldly people, although there had been a time, when

Abigail was born, he had been appreciative. Enough was enough. With Hannah working in town, they had become self-sufficient once more.

Sarah watched him taking turns with Manny at the scythe. It all seemed like such senseless hard work, with the horse standing in the shade of the barn. But if they had no mower, she guessed there was no alternative.

A wail from the baby made her turn, pick her up, and croon and cuddle. She sat down in the armless rocker to feed her, and quickly became sleepy, dozing off, waking and dozing again.

A cry from the barn woke her. Startled, she scrambled to close her dress front and hoist the baby to her shoulder for a quick burp, before going to the window. Oh, it was Hod and Abby!

Exhilaration filled her, like a drink of cold, sweet peppermint tea. Here was company. A woman to talk to, share details of their lives. Oh, how she missed the camaraderie of other women!

Abby sat on the spring wagon, her back straight as a stick, her green plaid sunbonnet tied so tightly below her chin, her face appeared pinched. Her dress was, or had been, a violet purple at one time, but had faded to a gray lavender, the row of purple buttons marching down the front like a colony of ants. Hod beside her, his Stetson pulled low, his clothes faded and worn, like Abby's, his face creased with dozens of deep lines and crevices, chiseled and molded by years of extreme weather.

Sarah called, "Get down, get down, Abby! Oh, I am surely glad to see you. Get yourself down and come on in!" She realized she was babbling, but didn't care.

Abby came striding across the dusty yard, glancing at the smoldering ashes in the fire ring made of stones, and greeted Sarah in her own inimitable way. "Sarah, you know, you folks will start a prairie fire, sure as I'm born. Why that lazy Mose don't get you a cook stove is beyond me. He coulda laid a fireplace."

"Well, Abby, it is certainly good to see you. I am so glad you came over. I've been wishing for another woman to talk to for so long."

"Where's Hannah?"

Sarah led Abby to the armless rocker, took the remaining chair herself, and balanced the baby on her shoulder. "She's in town working for the Rochers. I guess they own a store, the way she said."

"Is she being paid?"

Ashamed, Sarah lowered her eyes. "With food."

"Enough?"

"Yes, I believe so."

"What did she bring?"

And so Sarah told Abby the story of Hannah going to look for work, eliminating any distress, any hunger, and of her return, without mentioning

Mose's reaction to the automobile that brought her. This was Sarah's way, to erase the desperation and heartache and replace it with sunny optimism. It was good, her glittering unshed tears a dead giveaway to how bad matters actually were.

When she had finished, Abby said curtly, "Well, you can keep talkin' but it's as plain as the nose on yer face, yer starving. There ain't nothin' to eat, lest you started chewin' hay."

Sarah laughed, a fine, tinkling laugh without humor. So near were the tears of their affliction to the surface that she bit her upper lip hard with her lower, her eyes wide, watching Abby's face. The dear, kind face, like an angel with wrinkles and well-washed clothing. She would never forget this woman as long as she lived.

"Hod come over to try and talk some sense into Mose. We're willing to loan you the money to go back East on the train, back to yer family. This weather, you know, is why. It'll turn into a drought, maybe the worst one we've ever seen. Hod says there's sun dogs and it don't rain; the storms aren't coming. The wind is from the southwest an' we ain't gittin no rain. He says the crick'll dry up right soon, an' he ain't sure how good the well is you got here.

"Thing is, you ain't got money in the bank, no cattle to speak of, and jobs is hard to come by. Hannah won't make enough to keep all of you goin', you know that."

Sarah nodded, bit her lower lip, and pondered her words. Finally, she spoke. "Abby, I would get on that train today, with your money. I would gather up my children and board that train, return to my family with nothing but pure joy, the greatest joy, Abby. But I know Mose will never return."

"He will have to. This kind of weather is nothing to mess with. There's always the fear of having no water for the cattle."

Sarah shook her head, her large eyes apprehensive. Hod and Mose came through the door, lifting their hats and wiping their foreheads exactly alike. The day was very warm, too warm to be operating a scythe, Hod said, clucking his tongue.

Mose smiled. He looked pale, a bit peaked. Sarah had dark circles under her eyes, her hands looked thin and claw-like.

Hod stated his case in forthright language. It was hot and dry. It would likely get hotter and drier. They were concerned for the Detweilers' welfare, willing to pay the train fare home.

Mose sat on the crude stump at the makeshift kitchen table, his head lowered, his hands between his knees, without watching Hod's face as he spoke.

Abby reached for the baby, crooned, and snuggled her as she smiled a beatific smile of contentment, holding this baby girl, the real live baby of her past. Sarah watched with tenderness.

When Mose looked up, Sarah recognized the steel behind the heavy lidded eyes. Hope dashed to the ground, smashed like fine china thrown with force. "I don't believe we'll take up your offer. I have no need to return to Lancaster County at this time."

Hod became agitated, his blue eyes opening wide beneath their busy gray brows, the wrinkles and lines around his mouth lengthening and deepening. "You're crazy, Mose!" he burst out. "You ain't gonna survive a few years of drought. You have nothing to go on. 'Less you git a job in town, and they're scarcer 'n all git out. Ain't nobody payin' good wages. Me and Abby, we can do what we can, but you got the children to think of and nothin' put by."

"We are, in fact, surviving well. Hannah, our daughter, is employed at Harry Rocher's store."

"For what? He can't pay her big wages."

"She brings home sufficient food, week by week."

"You need to get them calves out of the barnyard. Did you brand 'em yet?" Hod was almost shouting, veins sprouting blue on his neck.

"Not yet. I understand they roam quite a bit, and I only have the 320 acres. One claim."

"How'd you get a claim?"

When Mose told him about signing the paperwork and getting his government papers, Hod wondered if a word of it was true. For all he knew, these people were merely squatters the government would drive out if they weren't here legally. But he liked Mose. He genuinely liked the fellow, and gave him the benefit of the doubt, sitting there in his crude house.

"Another thing, Mose. You're gonna have to come up with some kind of indoor heat. You know that fire thing you got out there's gonna put the whole prairie to flame one o' these days."

Abby nodded vigorously, keeping time by patting the baby on her back with her gnarly fingers, like misshapen twigs.

"Well, here we do have a problem then. I have no means of procuring a stove. Nor do I have the resources for a fireplace."

"What d' you mean, no resources? What's that supposed to mean? Sure you have the resources. They ain't very big, them rocks in the crick, but you could build yourself a decent fireplace, you and the oldest boy."

"I have no cement."

Suddenly Abby burst forth, her words as if someone were pounding on piano keys. "Well, you sure don't have anything else, either. No money, no food, and no ambition to try and make life better for yer wife and five beautiful kids. You best listen to me and Hod whilst you have the chance. Get on home. You ain't cut out to be pioneers in

231

this hard land. It ain't gonna deal kindly with any of you if we're reading the signs right."

A woman speaking in those tones was like a cheese grater on Mose's well-being, scraping and mangling the respect he held loosely for women to begin with.

"You are implying that I have no ambition," he stated, wounded.

"I sure am."

"Who, then, built these dwellings?"

"Why, I'll tell you who built 'em. Mostly your two kids, an' Hod, an' the boys, that's who. You was too busy readin' and prayin'.

Mose sighed as a sad smile crossed his features. "Well, neighbor Abigail, to all Christians, persecution must come. I forgive you for your misunderstanding of our circumstances. Many were the nights when I lay tossing and turning, pained by the soreness of my muscles."

Abby muttered something that sounded like, "Good for you," but no one was sure, so the conversation took a turn to other subjects of interest, including the rapid regrowth of the prairie grass after a field had been tilled.

Sarah sat in her chair, shocked and humiliated in turn. She knew there was far too much truth in Abby's words, but loyalty to her husband came easily. To admit Mose was making a mistake was like being pushed off the face of the earth to go spinning into a vast galaxy without gravity.

Her safety lay in obedience, one step behind her husband, her will given over. When he stopped, she stopped. When he moved on, so did she. When he climbed on the covered wagon for the western sojourn, she followed in body and spirit. She well knew their dire situation. She knew. But to rebel, take the children and return, was as unthinkable as just that, being pushed off the earth. Better to stay where she felt safe, at peace, her place secure in the realm of her husband's wishes.

"I would offer you a drink, but we have no tea or coffee," she said.

Hod assured her they didn't expect anything, and they soon took their leave as Eli and Mary watched wide-eyed, their mended, threadbare clothes another testimony to this family's hardship.

The following day Hod and Abby returned, driving a pickup truck with wooden sides flapping and rattling, the back loaded down with a kitchen stove with a rusty top and one leg missing, stovepipe and chimney blocks, and enough bags of cement to build a chimney.

Hod didn't waste many words, just told a gaping Mose and a tear-eyed Sarah that this thing had been settin' in the shed since they got an electric stove. Mose may as well roll up his sleeves and begin mixing cement because they were getting a chimney, before the whole prairie went up in flames.

Abby brought towels and sheets and pillowcases. She had a whole cardboard box of fabric, needles, dishes, and all the groceries she could spare, which was a sizable amount from her well-stocked pantry and cellar.

She brought two cupboards, one to set on top of the other, for kitchen space, and a table that suited well as a sink, the height perfect for washing dishes in a dishpan. She barked orders to the men, telling them where to set the stuff, busily carrying in boxes herself.

The three boys followed about an hour later on horseback, clattering up to the house on their foaming, wide-eyed mounts. Hod took to scolding, telling them it was far too hot to race them horses, but then he laughed. He'd been young once himself.

When the sun began its western descent, the Detweilers had a chimney and a cook stove. The cement was dry, and the stove was set up with a sturdy square of cement block replacing the missing leg. Abby helped sand down the rusted top, which they cleaned with ammonia water and lye soap.

They made steak and potatoes, with cabbage from Abby's garden. They ate slice after slice of custard pie, a delicacy that seemed impossibly delicious. Sarah's eyes shone as the children ate. Mose was effusive in his gratitude.

They sat together on the front porch, the yard

strange without the fire ring. When they started a small fire in the cook stove, the smoke leaked out of the new stovepipe, setting Eli and Mary both to crying, thinking the only safe way to build a fire was outdoors until Sarah explained it to them. She was so glad to be rid of the outdoor cooking, now that she would not need to do it any longer.

Drinking coffee was a luxury both Mose and Sarah had almost forgotten. Abby taught Sarah the Western way of making coffee, with no fancy percolators or other gadgets. "You just throw a handful of coffee grounds into the water and keep it boiling awhile," she said, producing a cup of steaming hot bitter liquid that could easily have been stretched into two cups.

So the neighbors parted amicably, although Abby made a point of ignoring Mose, neither looking at nor speaking to him. Mose was all right with that. Having been raised in a family of nine sisters, nothing surprised him. It rankled him, though, to be called lazy. As far as he knew, he'd never shirked any manual labor a day in his life.

Mose and Sarah lay side by side on their tick filled with hay and talked as the crescent moon hung in the sky, surrounded by the kingdom of blinking stars. The heat hovered inside the house, but there was a cool breeze blowing through the open window.

"I feel as if we have been visited by a miracle," Mose said, his hands behind his head, his elbows sticking up like wings on either side of his head.

Afraid that her husband would resume his fasting and praying, Sarah quickly assured him that it was only the Jenkinses' generosity, their caring, that made it possible to live closer to normalcy. She added the fact that they should not live on more charitable donations. "Wouldn't it be better to make our own way?" she asked, timidly.

"Yes, yes, it would. I'm praying about it, asking for the Lord's leading. You may not think so, Sarah, but I am sincere. I believe I have overstepped my boundaries of faith, that point where it blurs a line with determination, and even where you start blending reality with unreality."

Sarah felt a love and gratitude well up inside and turned to stroke his chest and face, a caress of true love. "Oh, Mose, for some time now I've been afraid for you—almost afraid of you from time to time. You were so determined, so not your usual self."

"I can see it now, Sarah. I have blurred the lines, and my family has suffered the consequences. Hod's visit has brought up reality very sharply. Do you think a drought of that proportion can occur here? Years? Hod said years."

"I don't know. But we do have well water."

"The well is old. Remember? It was almost like

an accidental caving in, the well was so easily dug. And who knows? If a long-term drought should occur, will we have water?"

"We'll see. Do the Jenkinses feel the winter will be dry too? Or does the snowfall replenish the moisture? We didn't think to ask."

There was a small space of restful silence, a moment when the breathing between them was a harmony of their hearts, a married couple who had both come through the fire that heats the dross to form a golden vessel, the purity and comfort of their union.

"Yes, for now, we are provided for, once again. But we will both continue to pray." Then, "Sarah, do you want to return home?"

"Oh, I do, Mose, I do. If it was only me, I would be on the train tomorrow. But I know you would not go willingly."

"As much as you want to go, I want to stay. The clamor and shifting for position, the greed and desire for the best farm, the best cattle, the constant overload of relatives and church members, the endless discussions of hay and corn and religious doctrine—I am seriously in fear of Lancaster County."

"But, Mose, perhaps it is only in you. No one else seems to mind it. They rather enjoy it as a way of life. Surely God is blessing that fruitful land and will multiply the heirs of farms for generations to come.

Mose shook his head from side to side. "Then I, alone, am a failure. A heretic, if you will. I have failed to keep the farm, failed to keep the *Ordnung*. I was abused by my brethren when I was only doing what was necessary to keep the farm. The distilling of grains. Who decided that it was worth being excommunicated?"

In his petulant tone Sarah heard the self-righteousness of the spoiled youngest son and thought, yes, he had failed in many ways. He was failing again. But did that give her the right to return without him? Oh, she could. Fiercely she knew that she could but never would. She was bound to him by the holy vows of matrimony. She had promised to care for him, for richer or for poorer, in sickness and in health. Yes, they were poor beyond anything she had ever imagined, her husband's mental health had been in serious decline, and could possibly still be, although his talk tonight was encouraging.

"The bishop, I suppose," she said, mildly, covering all her thoughts.

"One person?"

"No, Mose. You know these decisions are conferred."

"Not always."

So there it was, the impossibility of their return. Her husband harbored a sore bitterness toward the ministers of his church, a canker sore that rose on his skin, which might never burst and heal. His

238

outward display of religion, keeping the *Ordnung* to the letter, his tight-lipped conservative manner, it was all a hooded cover-up for his own seething rebellion toward higher authority. Clearly, his choice to live in the middle of nowhere, surrounded by a level sea of grass, made perfect sense. It was the staking of his own claim to be free of his own failures. And he kept failing, but blindly.

When Mose took her in his arms and kissed her, the tears had already begun to flow. Later, when he lay softly snoring, she cried with the raw abandon of the brokenhearted, her face stuffed into the goose down pillow from home.

But in the morning there was a song in her heart and a light in her eye, seeing that Mose had started a small fire in the gleaming new stove that stood in the kitchen on three legs and a block of cement. She got down the cast-iron frying pan and fried mush with newfound pleasure, and gave herself up to her life on the plains as the slabs of mush sizzled and sputtered.

Every morning she thought of Hannah and prayed that she would stay true, unspotted from the world. She missed her fiery oldest daughter and the abandon with which she viewed the world. She wouldn't be a bit surprised if Hannah never stayed Amish. How could she? She was already too aware of Clay Jenkins. Would it matter to God if she had been brought out here to live by a father who would not conform?

239

In her heart, Sarah was thrilled by the budding romance, the way mothers are when their oldest daughters grow to the age where boys notice them. She had seen them leave together and didn't have the heart to call them back.

When Baby Abigail awoke, Mary tumbled down the stairs to reach her before her mother did. Sarah ran to playfully snatch her away, grabbing Mary's waist to set her aside. Mary screeched and reached out to smack her mother's arms. Sarah laughed and handed a delighted, cooing Abby to her sister, then set a pot of porridge to boil. There was coffee to be made too, a rare and wonderful treat.

To think of cutting and sewing fabric, turning it into new dresses and shirts, was beyond anything she could imagine. She felt so warmhearted toward Abby; somehow, she must think of some way to repay all she has done. Surely her kindness paralleled, even overrode, any kindness she had ever received from members of the close-knit community back home.

That day, the Klassermans arrived, driving their spring wagon up to the house and calling out in a blend of jovial voices. "Hey, ist anyone to home?"

Sarah rose from scrubbing the wooden kitchen floor, shocked to hear the strange voices, shocked to see they had company yet again, which was unusual. For a moment, she felt afraid, alone and unprotected the way she was.

So she was weak-kneed with relief to see the pink, portly pair seated cozily side by side on the high seat of the spring wagon, mopping their brows. The patient horse, as well fed as his owners, was already stretching out his neck for a nap.

Sarah walked to the spring wagon, leaving Mary with Abby. "Hello," she said, wondering.

"Vy, hello." They introduced themselves as Owen and Sylvia Klasserman, come over from "Chermany." Neighbors to the east and closer than the Jenkinses. They had met their daughter on horseback.

Sarah looked off behind the barn but saw no sign of Mose, then beckoned them to get down and come inside to visit.

They were happy to do just that, grunting and grabbing the steel rimmed wheel to heave themselves off their high perch. Sylvia laughed as she alighted, said that age and extra weight took its toll in getting on and off that wagon these days.

She had brought a German chocolate cake, a thing of magical flavor and texture. Sarah served it with cups of coffee, being careful to give Eli and Mary their share, their large eyes in awe of the wondrous cake.

Sylvia's round face looked crestfallen though as

she looked around the primitive home. She tried to compliment the housekeeping, but through her eyes, accustomed to a house with papered walls, painted trim, and linoleum, it was a shame, a shame. The beautiful children. The tired yet beautiful mother. So little. These people had so little, and they had a pantry full and overflowing.

Sylvia held the baby. Owen eyed her fondly. "We'll come back often," he promised. He knew his wife's love of babies, never having had children of their own. But they enjoyed a loaded table, a good meal bringing them contentment.

Sylvia chortled and chuckled, holding the baby with an obvious sense of glee. "Oh, but Mrs. Detweiler, if you'll chust let me half the baby ven I come to visit, I will be the happiest voman on earth."

"Why, of course you must come. I often wish for the company of other women. I grew up in a close-knit family, with mothers and grandmothers and sisters and cousins nearby and everywhere."

"Where are you from?" Owen inquired, polishing off the last bit of cake, relishing even the last crumbs on his knife.

"We are from Pennsylvania, from Lancaster County, where a group of our people have settled. We were farmers who fell on hard times. The Depression had hit us hard, and we could not make our yearly mortgage. So my husband, Mose, wanted to try homesteading on 320 acres here."

"You haven't been here long, have you?"

"No, not quite a year yet."

"I see." Owen looked around at the misshapen logs, the slapdash chinking, which looked to be mostly clay from the creek bottom, and the peeling, rattling windows. Here was a winner, he thought. But he smiled at the children and asked about cattle, nodded his head in understanding when Sarah told him they had a start with a cow and two calves.

"You should do all right in about five years," Owen said.

Sylvia nodded. "It takes awhile. We started on 160 acres and own about a thousand now. We're running about 300 head of Black Angus cattle."

Sarah observed the buxom Sylvia and thought of her on a saddle, riding the range and throwing a rope. No, she decided, that that was an impossibility. "You are part of this operation?" she inquired politely.

Sylvia threw up one hand; the other was clamped to the baby's back. "Just the records. Only the bookkeeping, nothing else. Owen oversees the entire operation from horseback, though. He's a good rider and has a good horse. Seems in this area, that's what counts. A good horse."

"Do you raise any crops at all?" Sarah asked, curious.

"We grow oats for the horses, and I hear there's a few chaps trying winter wheat over the other side of Dorchester. I look for that crop to be taking aholt here, with sowing it in the fall and cutting it before the hot, dry weather begins. I think with tractors becoming more common, that will likely be the crop for profit, if any."

Talkative and amiable, the time flew till Mose came in for dinner, surprised to find a visitor's team tied to the fence.

He found the Klassermans very informative and helpful in the ways of the land. They agreed with the Jenkinses about the drought, about most things, actually. Politely they did not inquire about their income or lack of it. They just took their leave with polite goodbyes and promises to return.

The minute they were perched on the high wagon seat, Sylvia was making plans for the old davenport in the parlor, the table on the back porch, the blankets in the cedar chest she would never use, the canned pickles and red beets, all those whole tomatoes canned in wide-mouth jars none of us enjoy. The faster Sylvia talked, the faster Owen nodded his head, bringing down the reins on the horse frequently until they jostled and bounced over the rutted road at a frolicsome speed.

CHAPTER 13

Hannah fed her horse, stabled him in the small barn along the back alley, stroked his face, and told him to be patient; the week would be over before they knew it. He snuffled around in his box of oats, chewed, and lowered his head as if to assure Hannah he was fine as long as he was fed.

She turned to go outside when she heard voices coming from beside the barn, men walking along the back alley, carrying their lunch buckets, on their way to work, she supposed. She stepped back, allowing them to pass before making her way back to the house. That was the thing about living in town. There was no way you could avoid folks and their ordinary, everyday comings and goings, having to greet them amiably in spite of wanting to push them out of your way, just getting on with your life unhindered, the way they did out on the homestead.

For that is what it was, a homestead. A place called home, no matter how primitive or how far they sank into the endless crevice called poverty. She missed the wide open space, the purity of the endless wind, the rustling of the grass—everything.

But here she was, no closer to the one thing she

245

yearned to do, which was rope cattle, learn to ride the plains with the Jenkins boys. She guessed if she ever wanted to do that, she had to stay alive, which meant she was stuck here in this dingy town to scrabble for food, like a possum looking for eggs in a henhouse.

With a sigh, she went into the house, to find Doris in her housecoat, yawning and pouring herself a cup of coffee, her hair flattened from her night's sleep. She seemed almost like a child, young and vulnerable, as if she needed care, someone to hold her and help her face the day that was dawning hot and bright and dusty.

Doris whimpered a good morning, then sank into the rocking chair with her coffee, drawing an orange patterned afghan across her lap. "This dust. This endless dust. I declare, it will be the death of me."

Hannah stopped, looked at her, and could not think of a word to say. So she shrugged her shoulders and said she never heard of anyone dying from breathing dust, but she guessed you could if you wanted to. Doris threw her a tired glance, wrapped her hands around her mug of coffee, and sighed deeply.

Hannah got out the cast-iron frying pan and scrambled eggs, made toast, and poured juice. She called Harry and told him breakfast was ready.

They sat down together, Harry bent his head

with his hands clasped on the table top to pray audibly, in his own words, thanking the Father for his food, may it bless their bodies and so forth, a practice so new and strange it made Hannah want to hide under the table in shame. She had never heard anyone pray out loud, much less using their own words. Dat would always take the lead, lowering his hands beneath the table, bowing his head in silence, each family member learning at a young age to pray their prayer in private. The Amish all did that. Hannah had never questioned this, but now, she needed to know why all praying was done in silence. She'd ask Mam.

When his prayer was finished, Harry shoveled in his scrambled eggs, praised Hannah's toast, and asked her how she'd done it.

Hannah told him she'd fried it in the pan, with butter, the way they always did at home. Doris didn't eat eggs, the toast was a bit greasy with butter, so in the future, would she do hers dry?

Hannah washed the dishes in a fury. She had no patience with this whining, sickly woman. Doris needed to get out and do something, anything, other than sitting at the hair-dresser or pitying herself. She needed about a half dozen kids to care for, that's what.

She wiped the cast-iron pan and flopped it into the cupboard, stalked past Doris without saying a word, slapped the door open that led into the store, and set to work.

Customers came and went, spoke to Harry, picked up their purchases, the bell above the door ringing constantly. Hannah stayed in the back, by the low windows, arranging and rearranging, wiping down shelves until the water in her bucket turned black from the years-old dirt and dust.

When she came to the jumble of ribbon, thread, elastic, snaps and buttons and braids, pins, needles and pincushions, she stood back with her hands on her hips and surveyed the dusty mess. Lifting her hand to wipe at the beads of perspiration forming on her brow, she left a smudge of gray dirt across her forehead.

How could this man sell anything? Even if he was living in hard times, there was no sense in this. She marched up to the counter where he stood cleaning eggs from a wire basket, wiping each one methodically with a rag and stopping to examine an oversized lump of dirt stuck to a large brown one, before taking a fingernail to scratch it off, letting it fall on the countertop.

Hannah swiped it to the floor. "You know, Harry, this place is so dirty that I can't see how you stay in business, selling things that are covered in dust and soot and crap!" she said forcefully. "You blame Doris and her poor health, but I hope you know you don't try, either."

Harry looked at her. "Well, well, what is this? Why do you say this?"

"It's offensive, that's why. Trying to make a

decent living is not easy for anyone right now, but the place could be more appealing if it was clean."

Harry put an egg in the carton, carefully, then said that if that's how she found things, then go ahead, go right ahead and clean and change whatever she thought best.

That was exactly what Hannah wanted to hear. She turned on her heel and marched smartly back to the hopeless jumble of sewing notions and began to blow the dust off each individual spool of ribbon and thread. She threw each one into a bin and was just starting to wipe down the shelves when Harry's voice caught her attention.

"She's in the back with the fabric," she heard him say.

Hannah was standing on a wooden crate, reaching up as far as she could, when someone called her name. She turned to find Clay Jenkins looking at her, almost level with her height. Her knees turned weak and her mouth became dry as the air around her.

"Hi." He smiled his lazy, relaxed smile and melted Hannah's resolve, just tipped it over like butter in a hot frying pan.

She was so glad to see him she could not keep her lips from parting into a smile of true gladness, a welcoming he understood. "What are you doing in town?" she whispered.

"Needed a bunch of staples."

"Staples?"

"Yeah, the kind to fix a wire fence."

"Oh." Flustered now, Hannah wasn't sure where they were kept. She looked past him as if to go around him and show him, wanting to impress him with her expertise as a salesperson.

"Hannah."

She looked at him.

He reached out a hand, touched her cheek where a smudge of gray dust had smeared across it. "You think you might need a ride home on Saturday afternoon?"

"I rode Pete here."

His eyebrows lifted and then settled back down. "So I can't give you a lift, then?"

"Not in the truck. Dat doesn't allow me to ride in one."

"If I came with the buckboard?"

"Buckboard?"

"You call it a spring wagon."

"Oh. Well, no, not if I have Pete. No. Guess it won't work."

"What about the food they give you as wages?"

"I'll strap it on, somehow. Pete is just like a pack mule." She smiled to assure him she'd be fine. She wanted him to leave her alone; at the same time, she wanted him to stay.

"Can you have off for an hour or so? We can go to the café and get a soda or something."

Immediately, the specter of the red, brassy Bess

filled her head, and she lifted her startled eyes to Clay's achingly blue ones. "I can't. Harry needs me here to finish this."

"Do you mind if I ask him?"

"No, no. Don't ask. That's fine. I'm not hungry. Or thirsty."

He touched her shoulder. "Hannah, that's not why I asked you to go. I want to talk to you. Just sit across a table and look at you and listen to what you have to say."

"Clay, I can't be seen with you. Not here in town. My father will never allow us to . . ." She stopped.

"I didn't ask you to marry me, just to have a soda."

Humiliation and anger boiled up, turning her face dark and staining it a deep color of shame. "Clay Jenkins, you stop that. You just stop saying things like that, making me feel like a pathetic idiot. Leave me alone. Just get out of this store and don't come back. You have no right to talk to me like that."

And then, after that forceful speech that should have turned him on his heel and blown him out the door and down the street, he reached out and cupped her chin in his hand, smiled that smile that took all the strength from her legs, and said, quiet and low, but not in a whisper, "I'll see you around, Hannah."

He took his good old time leaving too, stopping

at the front counter and talking to Harry while he cleaned that disgusting chicken dirt off those eggs.

The whole encounter was too humiliating. Hannah attacked the shelves with so much energy she knocked down five bolts of fabric that landed on her bucket of filthy water, almost upsetting it. By this time, Hannah declared it was one hundred degrees in the filthy store! She was already worn out and the day still stretched out like a long summer's drought.

He didn't have to leave so soon. She wanted him to stay so they could have an ordinary conversation the way normal people do. She wanted to talk about horses and roping cows, things that interested her. She didn't want him touching her cheek or her shoulder. Not her chin either, talking to her as if she was as old as Eli.

If this didn't stop, her future roping cows was fast going down the drain. She couldn't learn to rope and ride with all three of those boys if this was how things were going.

All week that same dark cloud called Clay Jenkins hung over her head, putting her in a prickly state of mind. The one good thing that came from his visit was her never-ending energy, banging and lifting, arranging articles in eye-catching displays and placing the new signs she made beside them. Customers began to notice and comment about Mr. Rocher's new arrangements. Old spools of trim and braid, dusted off and placed in a wicker basket with lace and yarn sported a sign that read, "Special 10¢," sat in the middle of the aisle on a walnut end table. Hannah dug out bolts of cloth that had been buried beneath more popular patterns. She cleaned and displayed them by draping a corner of the fabric loosely over the bolt so that the women could touch it and run it between their fingers to examine the texture more closely.

Talk began to flow. Beth Apent told Bess at the café, and Bess told Ruth Jones, who had come in for a waffle with chicken gravy. Harriet Ehrlichman sat on a barstool and listened as Bess told her what she'd heard about Harry Rocher's store. Harriet told Sylvia Klasserman when she came into town for some chicken feed.

Sylvia clapped her hands and said she knew Hannah and had been out to see her family. Then she lowered her voice and said it was pitiful, just pitiful the way that poor family lived. She held her hand to the side of her mouth and told Harriet how they'd traveled the whole way from Ohio—or was it Pennsylvania? Anyway, they didn't have a cent. That Harry likely paid her in peanuts, old tight-fisted thing. And that dusty wife of his was enough to drive you straight up a wall, not that it would be an easy feat, at her size. Harriet chuckled along with Sylvia and said they'd go down to the store next time Sylvia came to town.

• • •

On Saturday, the temperature shot up to 105 degrees, and the wind stilled until it became unbearably hot. Harry worried about Hannah riding home, but she assured him she'd wait until later in the day to start out, after the temperature had cooled to a more comfortable level.

He taught her how to run the cash register, so it got alarmingly late, well past six o'clock, before she had gathered all her provisions into a gunny sack and slung it across Pete's rump, well-tethered to the saddle that Pete was now proudly wearing. Harry allowed her to use it if she would always return it on Monday morning.

So Hannah set off for home, eyeing the sun's descent, planning to push Pete to arrive home before nightfall.

She was glad to be away from the buildings that seemed to stifle the breath from her. Away from the untidy lots filled with patches of red root and thistle, broken tin cans, and all kinds of refuse, just an accumulation of stuff people pitched out of moving automobiles or off horses hitched to faded old buckboards—and anything that carried folks to town.

Someone had thrown a feed sack filled with half-starved mewling kittens on the doorstep of Harry's store, which made Doris wrinkle her nose and call them rats. So Harry left them in the weedy, overgrown lot as well, saying the townkids would either rescue them or get rid of them, one or the other.

Hannah would have loved to take a cat home for Mary, but they could barely feed themselves, let alone a cat. Someday, she would bring a full-grown cat home, a good mouser, one that was self-sufficient, the way their barn cats had been back home.

Pete's head nodded, his heavy mane fell on either side of his neck, cream colored, thick and dusty, the way the top of a horse's neck always was. She rode comfortably, her bare feet resting on the wooden stirrups, heels down, the way the Jenkins boys had told her. She sat straight, the reins held low, but not loose. They had told her to do that too.

The heat hung over the flat land, like an oven that had been turned off but still retained the radiance of the coils in Doris's electric stove. The grass hung limp, baked, and defeated. The road stretched before her, the yellow brown of the dirt cracked in long, jagged tears where the ground had become steadily parched, drawing together, packed down and covered with dust.

A layer of dust covered everything everywhere. Every blade of grass, every rooftop, every living creature. It lined Hannah's nostrils, filling her mouth with a powdery taste, and it coated the gunny sack filled with the week's provisions for her family.

Every day the sky remained the same hot blue. Every day the sun rose, a huge, orange circle of untamed heat, the light blinding and brassy with the dry, unchanging fiery temperature.

They said this was common. Summers were always dry. But the grizzled old men wearing their slouched, greasy hats made of leather, the ones who came from Utah, the gold miners and trappers, some of them with slovenly, unkempt Indian women who came to town looking for trades—they all said there'd be a real drought this time, the likes they ain't seen in many years.

Fear shot through Hannah's stomach when she heard it, thinking of the sprouting cattle herd, the two horses, the weak, shallow well. How would anyone survive if there was no rain for years? They'd be forced to move. The cattle would die. Dat would resume his fasting and praying. Hannah shuddered, reached back to touch the sack of food, assuring herself of the next week's survival.

She watched the sun. The heat no longer shimmered across the prairie the way it had at midday. She shifted in her saddle and spoke to Pete to move him along. She couldn't goad him into a trot with the awkward pack on his back, so she'd have to keep him stepping. In the distance the sun had already slid lower in the sky.

She had a good feeling about the pack, or rather, its contents. The usual flour, sugar, and cornmeal,

256

but this time there was more coffee, tinned milk, canned peas, a round of hard, yellow cheese, and a side of bacon covered in green mold that had been left hanging in the widow Layton's attic too long.

Layton had brought it into Harry and wondered if he'd trade it for a few necessities. He said yes, not having the heart to turn her away with that little flock of pale, wide-eyed children. How could he?

Hannah respected Harry for his choice, respected him even more when he wrapped it in brown butcher's paper and sent it home with her. As a last-minute kindness, he added a large sack of dried navy beans, so Hannah could hardly wait to present her mother with the beans and bacon.

She'd carefully cut away the mold, breathless and intent on each slice of her knife, knowing the salted meat would not be spoiled on the inside. She'd soak the beans overnight, add a bit of onion, simmer the soup on the back of the stove all day, and bake fresh bread with so much care, resulting in a meal that would be a spread of pure thanksgiving.

She came to the crossing where the road turned east, lifted the reins and urged Pete on, now watching the sun with a sense of agitation. Had she started out too late?

"Come on, Pete. Hurry up." Pete quickened his steps, his ears coming up and flicking back at the sound of her voice. If only she could made him break into a good, fast gallop she'd soon be home. She thought of loosening the pack and holding it across her lap, but that might be foolhardy with those tin cans flopping and banging around. Perhaps she should have accepted Clay's offer.

She urged Pete on again, felt the clapping of the gunny sack against her legs. The trousers were so thick and irritating, being alone and no one to see her riding, she decided to stop Pete and get rid of them. She pulled on the reins, slid off the saddle, and lifted her skirt to work on the buttons with one hand, holding on to Pete's reins with the other. She could soon tell that wouldn't work, so she dropped the reins and returned to loosening more buttons.

She didn't know old faithful Pete could take off like that. One second he was there; the next he'd dug his hind feet into the hard, dry soil and taken off in a flash, leaving Hannah with the unwieldy trousers half buttoned, standing in the middle of the road and yelling until she was hoarse.

Then she shed the trousers and began to run. She ran until the sweat rolled down the side of her face and the neckline of her dress was wringing wet. Her breath came in gasps of pain, but still she ran.

Twilight settled across the immense, level land, cooling the air. Hannah slowed to a walk, shaded her eyes for a sign of Pete, but there was none.

He had vanished over the horizon, the gunny sack tied to the empty saddle and flapping wildly. With a sinking feeling, Hannah knew there was not even a slight possibility the sack would stay on.

There was nothing to do but keep walking and hope the sack would fall off on the road, food intact, so she could carry it home. But what if Pete took a shortcut, traveling straight across the prairie, dropping the sack in high grass where it would never be found?

That would mean they'd go begging to the Jenkinses again, or she would, since no one else took that task upon themselves.

She wouldn't go this time. Absolutely not. She would not go crawling back to Clay after refusing his offer of a ride home.

She calculated she still had five or six miles to go. Frustrated, she stood in the middle of the road and screamed, stamped her foot, and screamed again. There was no one to hear, no one to care, so why not? Here she stood, carrying the stupid pants that had caused all the trouble to begin with. She wanted to fling them into the tall, dry grass and leave them there.

With the twilight came the birds' evening calls, their wheeling across the cooling sky that was still misted with a rose color, the afterglow of the setting sun. The birds' songs made her feel a bit better, along with the pungent, earthy smell of the dry grass. The flat plains stretched away on every side, the grasses now appearing shadowed, unmoving, an immense expanse of nothing, yet everything. The sky, the air, the earth beneath, the sharp tang of the listless wind; it was everything to Hannah.

This was her home. A clean, unfettered place that spoke of freedom. The magnificence of being in a world that was so vast, so immense, dwarfed every care, every fussy little worry in her head. Here on the prairie, all the pressure, the tugging on her mind about ordinary things, simply evaporated.

So she set off with one foot in front of the other, and she walked. Darkness fell, the stars poked their blinking little faces through the dark night canvas of the sky. The moon appeared above her in a thin crescent.

The darkness deepened. Hannah thought she should be coming up on the creek bottom shortly, or at least be able to see the tops of the cottonwood trees. But still, just dark blobs in a dark world.

Was she still on the road? She guessed she must be, or else she'd be in tall grass, although this wasn't much of a road.

Ahead, a light flickered and went out. Hannah's breath quickened. Was she close to home? No, they had a chimney now, and a cook stove. It couldn't be Mam's cooking fire.

Hmm . . . There! There it was again. A fire. But who would build a fire in the middle of all this dry, blowing grass? Surely no one in their right mind.

Certain now that it was a fire, she moved slowly toward it and saw the hulking figures squatted before a ring of torn away grass with a crackling fire in the center.

She stopped. To walk up to two strange men in the dark of night would be unwise, that was sure. On the other hand, what if they had found her sack of food and were helping themselves to it, having a hearty meal with the only food that would mean her family's survival? Well then. She had only one choice, foolish or not.

She kept walking, then thought better of it and stopped. Perhaps if she got closer and listened to their speech, she could tell whether they were trustworthy or not. Her instinct told her to make a wide turn through the grass and slide silently through it, like a wraith, a ghost. They'd never know anyone had ever crossed their path.

But the food. What about the food? She hesitated, then began to walk until she was so close she could see the spit with the broiling animal roasting on the fire.

Two men. Hats like the trappers and gold miners.

"Hey!" Hannah called.

They turned toward her voice, their faces

shadowed but illuminated on one side by the firelight. Their eyes appeared like slits in their faces, their noses were the only thing visible, protruding from faces covered in dark facial hair.

"Hey yourself."

Hannah stepped forward, the trousers bunched in her hand. "You didn't come on to a gunny sack filled with food, did you?"

Slowly, they both got to their feet and turned with their backs to the fire. They appeared completely black now, like menacing ghosts that had stepped straight out of some book her father would never let her read.

"Wal, what's comin' down th' road? A vision. A angel's come to visit."

"A crown on 'er haid," the other one remarked. Their voices were raspy with age and life, but not unkind.

"I'm Hannah Detweiler. My horse ran off when I was coming home from work. He had a sack tied onto his saddle."

"No ma'am. We ain't seen no horse. But we ain't been here that long. We is Peter Oomalong and Bradley Hopps. Jest travelers makin' our way. Some people call us tramps, or hobos, but we ain't either one. Just folks like other folks, makin' our way."

Hannah stepped past the fire, thanked them properly, and ran like the wind, stumbling over stubbles of dried grass, putting as much distance between them and herself as she possibly could. She calmed herself by walking again, straining her eyes to find the tops of trees, the creek bottom, anything for a sign of home.

Then suddenly, there it was—a pinprick of light that was the window of the house. She walked slowly now, savoring the new feeling of safety contained in the lighted window.

She found her family in tears, Mose and Sarah pacing the floor. Pete had returned, riderless, the food intact. The only thing that had gone wrong, the beans had spilled from the paper bag into the gunny sack, but they could be washed and used just the same.

Sarah held Hannah in her arms, and Hannah did not resist. Mose was reverent in his gratitude. Manny was pale-faced, but as brave as he was able to be. Hannah recounted her story, which left them shaking their heads in bewilderment.

"It just isn't like Pete. He's never done anything like that," Manny grinned, saying that the thought of Hannah taking off the trousers in the middle of the road must have scared him.

Sarah said there would be no more riding home from work, ever.

CHAPTER 14

The dreadful news of Sarah's mother's passing arrived in a letter from her sister. Hod had gone to town, brought back the letter and watched Sarah's still lovely face crumple and fall, her large dark eyes straining to contain the endless reservoir of tears that would follow. She would have fallen if Hod had not reached out to support her, which is how Mose found his wife weeping in his neighbor's arms.

Sarah would not be comforted, her grief like a great swelling of darkness in her body that shut off the light and life around her. Mose led her away from Hod to the armless rocking chair, knelt before her, and dried her tears. He spoke many words of comfort, quoted scripture in soft tones that Sarah failed to hear, so completely was she swallowed by her grief.

Hod stood, shifting awkwardly, cleared his throat before offering them money for the train fare.

"Do you want to go, Sarah?"

Sarah shook her head and whispered that she'd been buried weeks ago. Hod ground his teeth, the muscles in his cheek working. How could this man take his wife to a region such as this with none of their own kinfolk near? Obviously, the

Amish were a close-knit group, like birds or animals, one kind stuck to their own. This Hod understood, and as time went on, their existence here, dependent on others, made no sense.

He sent Abby over with an agate roaster of beef stew and dumplings. Sarah was composed but fragile with the force of her grief. Hod sent Clay with the truck to fetch Hannah, saying the family needed her until Sarah was better, which Clay did, trying to hide the happiness he felt.

He had a hard time persuading Hannah to go with him. She stood like a statue, her arms crossed, and listened as he spoke of her grandmother's passing, her face white and resolute, not a tear in her eyes.

"I'm not going back in the truck. I told you. Before."

"Yes, you are. Your mother needs you."

"And what if Dat sees me pulling up to the house? Then what?"

"He ain't gonna do nothing."

"You don't think?"

"No. He's real worried about your Ma."

"She's not my ma. She's my Mam."

Clay didn't answer. He wanted to smack her the way she was acting, all hoity-toity and holier-than-thou. When he didn't answer, she didn't know how to take it, just watched after him when he strode out of the store.

He went out and sat in the truck, figured he'd

wait about a half hour, and if she didn't get her royal self out, why then he'd just go back home without her.

Ten minutes passed, then twenty. He was just about to start the motor when she yanked the door of the truck so hard he thought she might pull it off the hinges. Still mad, he warned her not to pull on that door like that. She'd pull it right off.

"Oh, get over it," she answered rapidly.

Clay didn't say anything, just started the truck, turned the steering wheel and moved out into the street, reached down to shift gears when it was necessary. Keeping one hand on the wheel, he stared straight ahead with a deep scowl on his tanned face.

Hannah slouched back in the corner of the truck, as far away from Clay as possible, which was still much too close. She had never been able to study him in such close proximity, so she took her time, noticing the way his light hair hung down over the back of his gray shirt collar, the plane of his nose, the set of his jaw, the way his mouth turned down at the corners. He had pockets on his shirt, and wore jeans with a leather belt and a big silver buckle, which was way out of the Amish *Ordnung*, especially that silver clasp on his belt. Or whatever it was.

His hands were big, the fingers long and the backs covered in fine blonde hair. When Hannah

266

had finished sizing him up, she crossed her arms and looked out of the window to her right, decided if he wasn't talking, then she wouldn't either.

The truck rattled and bounced over the cracks in the road. The hot wind puffed in through the window as the level land flew past, and nothing was said.

Finally, Hannah had to know why he was riled, and asked how they found out her grandmother had died.

"A letter." And that was all he said the remainder of the trip. Hannah flounced out of the pickup and slammed the door as hard as she had yanked it open, then fled into the house as the truck pulled away.

Well, be that way then, she thought, before she entered the house to find her mother quietly sitting in the armless rocking chair, holding Abby and weeping with soft little moans into her blanket.

Hannah stood before her, uncertain. "Mam," she said softly.

"Oh, you're here. They said you were coming. That's good." She lowered her head and laid it on top of Abby's blanket, the tears resuming with soft moaning sounds of devastation.

Unsure what to do, Hannah remained standing, awkwardly, her arms at her sides, thumbs tucked in her closed fingers, one bare foot propped on the other.

"Don't cry, Mam."

"I won't. Not much, anyway," came the muffled answer.

So Hannah went to work, trying not to compare this dwelling on the homestead with the one in town. Everything seemed so dull and brown and rough, especially the floor and the walls. She missed the sink and the cupboards and the clean, sanitary bathroom with everything in order. And here, well, this was her home, so she would have to accept it.

She cooked the simple evening meal of corn-cakes and beans, glad to see Manny's surprise when he spied her. The children were quiet, watching their mother's face as she picked at her food. Mose ate well, with concerned eyes lifting to his wife's face every minute.

Hannah decided enough was enough, with that awful, quiet ride home from Pine, and now this. It was like living in a tomb. No one laughed or spoke. The wind rustled the grass and blew in through the window as the children's spoons clanked against their plates. Dat cleared his throat or swallowed noisily, liquid sounds that rankled Hannah's ill humor to begin with.

Suddenly, she pushed away from the table and said she was going outside. She couldn't get away from that house fast enough. Blindly she ran, not caring where she went. Eventually, she flopped down on the grass and laid on her back, her breath coming in short, hot puffs. The sky loomed over her, a gigantic lid of heat that would not let her breathe.

So Mam's mother had died. She was dead to Mam the day they had left. She knew then that she'd never see her mother again. Or did she? Who could tell, plodding along behind Mose the way she had done. Her father, Mose. What a dreamer! Now, here he was, watching his wife's face with all that loving worry and concern, which wasn't worth the effort it took to lift those pious black eyebrows.

Hannah felt the old resentment rising up. She didn't care that she ought not to think these negative thoughts. If he could only lay down his self-righteous life and take Mam home to her family, his own life would be free from all of this concern. He knew how she struggled. He knew it. Then why stay here?

But to go back home would be strange too. They would be not only strangers in their own community, but, perhaps even worse, failures. He'd lost the farm. He'd lost everything. They'd all say that.

No, this was home. These 320 acres were their homestead, their own proof that they could make it. They could face every adversity, every drought, every storm, every winter, everything. Poverty wouldn't put them under, either. Poverty was the worst. In life, you needed certain things

269

to survive. You needed food and clothing and money.

Well, they'd beat poverty too. They would. Somehow. With God's grace, Dat would say. And yes, she agreed fiercely, with her determination and God's grace. His *byshtant*. His standing by.

She pictured the squalid buildings, surrounded by acres of grass, with a God who stood as high as the sky, standing by, ready to defend them, His arms outstretched, His robe white, His countenance like lightning. No one had ever seen God, but He was there all right.

That was one thing she never doubted, the presence of God. From the time she was a wee toddler, she had known there was a Heavenly Being watching over her, the Good Man, *der Gute Mann*, as her parents had taught her. So now, when they needed Him, she believed He would bring them through these daunting obstacles.

She started by telling Hod to come over and show her how to brand their calves. Of course, it was Clay who showed up, by himself, which she figured would happen. She was glad he came; he owed her an apology.

She took good care to brush her hair, wash her face, and pinch her cheeks. Her dress was plain brown, faded, and worn thin, but that could not be helped.

She met him at the barnyard, smiled, and said

that these calves needed to be branded, and the cow too. It was time they were turned loose. Someone was going to have to teach her how to rope.

Manny was summoned from the hayfield, followed by her father, who seemed amicable, offering to help wherever he could, which was nothing short of a miracle. Hannah eyed him warily, however, wondering what holy lesson he had up his sleeve this time. She knew he was suspicious of the Jenkins boys.

He set to work building a fire, though, and watched with a smile as Clay let Manny ride his horse and showed him how to coil and hold the rope. "It's in the wrist, I guess," he drawled, in that easy relaxed manner of his. "Let them out, Hannah," he said briskly.

So Hannah opened the barnyard gate, watching from the fence as the calves charged through it, their tails held out like broomsticks, kicking and bawling and acting as crazy as loons, in Clay's words.

"Ride after 'em. Run 'em down. Bring 'em back," he called to Manny. It was obvious the horse knew more than Manny did. He took off as if there were coiled springs in his legs, dodging along with the calves, leaving poor Manny clutching the saddle horn just to remain seated. He couldn't attempt staying in the saddle and twirling a rope at the same time, so he galloped back, the horse fighting the reins every step of the way.

"I can't do it," Manny said, his eyes alight.

"Takes practice."

"Your turn," Clay told Hannah.

It couldn't be that hard, she thought to herself, as she watched Manny dismount. She clapped his shoulder for reassurance, then climbed into the saddle without looking at Clay, hoping she knew enough to climb astride a horse without looking like a cow. She figured she'd better let the horse do the chasing because, like Manny, just staying on was all she could manage.

The calves lowered their heads and came bawling, only to veer away at the last minute, the horse turning with the calf, almost unseating her. Determined not to grab the saddle horn as the horse veered left, Hannah slipped right off in the opposite direction, landing hard in the dry grass, with a crunch, on her right shoulder.

The horse stopped.

She heard footsteps and saw Clay and Manny looming above her.

"You hurt?"

"I don't think so."

She sat up, felt her arms and gingerly stretched her legs, but everything seemed intact. She stood up, brushed off her skirt, and asked Manny if he wanted to try again.

He did, so she stood with Clay, watching

Manny at his first attempt at roping. This time, he stayed on but accomplished nothing as far as the roping went. Breathless, he galloped back, his black eyes sparkling, his straw hat lying in the grass, his dark hair tousled. He was laughing.

"It's impossible to ride and swing a rope at the same time," he called. Clay laughed.

"You can practice on a fence post awhile. That's what I did."

Hannah mounted again and stayed on this time. But like Manny, she couldn't touch the rope, much less think of lifting it or throwing it over a calf.

Then Clay said he'd get the job done, and it was a breathtaking sight. It was as if he and his horse were one, both thinking the same thing before doing it—turning, stopping, galloping full speed from a standstill.

When he rode along the plunging calf, his wrist flicking the rope up and over his head, throwing it out with the ease of long hours of practice, the horse stopped, sat back on his haunches, pulling the rope taut and flinging the bawling calf to the ground. It was only a matter of minutes before the hot branding iron sizzled its way through the coarse, black coat into the calf's leathery skin, branding it forever with the Bar S brand.

The old cow was heavy, close to 1,800 pounds, Clay guessed. She had horns like thick tree limbs protruding on each side of her head. Red-eyed and belligerent, she stood in the grass, pawing at the dirt and raising clouds of brown dust.

"She don't like us, so everyone watch out. You don't mess around with this kind. They can be as bad as a bull any day."

Clay galloped off, swinging the rope. The cow charged, bellowing her anger, but the horse dodged easily, prancing like a bullfighter in the ring.

The dance between horse and enraged cow was something to see, like a poem someone put into motion. The horse's flanks were dark with sweat, and a splotch of moisture dampened the back of Clay's shirt.

The cow was tiring, so the rope slipped easily over one horn, but she shook the rope loose and took off in a wild plunge straight toward the fire and the branding iron—and Mose. He leapt toward the fence and got a leg up to step away from the bellowing cow. She charged for the fence and hooked one horn into his suspenders, flinging him to the ground. Clay yelled and goaded his horse. Hannah screamed, a hand on each side of her face as she watched the cow grind her horns into her father's flailing body. Repeatedly, the animal twisted and turned, her goal clearly to rid herself of this adversary that had disturbed her peace.

Clay rode up to the blindly enraged cow. He kicked at her and prodded her away from Mose, yelling all the while. Manny stood rooted in horror, his face contorted with the intensity of his feelings.

The cow lifted her head and came charging toward Clay and his horse, leaving Mose lying in the dust, a shadowy, dark figure behind the brittle, waving grass. Clay turned her into the barnyard and slammed the gate before they all rushed to Mose's inert form.

Manny screamed, "Dat! Dat!" before prostrating himself by his father's side, reaching out to touch his chest.

Clay knelt, his face as white as his shirt. "Mose. Mose. Can you hear me?"

Hannah lowered herself slowly, kneeling beside Clay, nausea welling up into her throat, horrified to see her father lying by the fence so bloodied and battered.

Clay laid a hand on Mose's chest, then threw his hat aside to put his ear to his torn and bloodied shirt front.

"Mose. Mose."

His eyes were open, his mouth in a grimace of pain. He was breathing in short, painful gasps. But he was breathing.

"Get yer Ma," Clay ordered. "I'll get the doctor."

Mose was whispering, struggling to breathe, the dust and dirt slowly stained dark by the blood seeping from his wounds. Manny stayed by his father's side as Hannah raced blindly for the house, calling, calling hoarsely for her mother, who raised eyes that were cloudy with mourning to absorb this bizarre thing Hannah was saying.

The children were told to stay in the house and watch Abby. Like an old woman, Sarah made her way slowly to her dying husband, held his hand, and told him she loved him one final time. At peace, Mose took his last breath, secure in God and his wife's love, the two things he valued far above any earthly possessions.

Hannah would never forget the picture of Sarah kneeling by Mose's side, her head on his battered chest, tears flowing. A heavenly light surrounding them in the gray dust, their union immortalized by his death, the only sound the waving of the grass—or the rustling of angels' wings. Who could be sure?

The song of the heavens was the angels who came to take his spirit home, the soul that often yearned for a home, for Mose often found the earth riddled with too many complexities, too many cares, and too many people he did not understand. A simple man, Mose was one who would find death a victory.

Sarah understood this, and she understood her husband. She truly knew him—his failures, his triumphs, his every breath.

When Clay returned with the doctor, all that remained was a small group of people dressed in plain, worn garments, with tears flowing, but an acceptance buoying their spirits with the power of a solid rock. Clay told Abby at home that he'd never seen anything like it.

Mose was carried to the house by strong men who arrived from town and from neighboring ranches, men the Detweilers did not know and had no idea they existed. In the middle of her numbing grief, Sarah wondered at the kindness of the *ausriche*, these worldly men with leathery faces and grizzled beards. They were like the Amish, come to help at a time when they were needed.

The yard filled with automobiles. Women dressed in flowered prints, bright plaids, some in trousers, wearing lipstick and coiffed hair like bonnets of curls, brought casseroles and fried chicken, cakes and pies. They gathered Sarah and Hannah into embraces of perfume and expensive talcum powders, left traces of red lipstick on dry cheeks, like rose-colored benedictions of concern.

Here, on the high plains, they had all known devastation and loneliness. Plain or worldly, hardship and loss were a way of life. So when the news of Mose Detweiler's death reached their ears, they knew what it would take.

The Amish relatives in Lancaster County were notified, a telephone call to the local police barracks in the city of Lancaster was sufficient.

With the heat so prevalent, a small group helped wash Mose's battered body, dressed him in his white Sunday shirt and trousers, and laid him tenderly in the rough casket Hod and the boys fashioned in a hurry.

Sarah moved as if in a gray dream filled with dark shadows of longing and despair. She did what was required, fed and cared for Abby, thanked the unknown flock of brightly dressed women for all their kindnesses, seeing them as through a mist of grief that blended all the bright colors back to gray.

It was only at night that she allowed herself the blessed relief of sobbing, howling into a pillow pressed tightly against her mouth. The loss of her mother had stripped her of the warmth of remembrance, leaving her scrabbling for a firm foot stone to step through the iciness of the unrelenting river of grief. The homesickness was one thing, worn like a collar around her neck that ceased to chafe with time. But never to see her mother again, never talk to her, was more than she could bravely carry.

And now her husband, Mose, the light of her life, the reason for her existence, the pillar of strength on which she leaned. Yes, he had weakened, but it was a test of faith that he had come through admirably. She couldn't see how she would survive without him.

She chose a plot not too far away. How could

she have him buried on the flat prairie covered with blowing grass, the plain stone marker gone from her sight and her mind?

South of the house. Southeast, where the morning sun would find the gravestone and caress it with light. When she stood on the porch, she knew he would not be far away.

Owen Klasserman read the German scripture, words of promise and hope that Sarah could only hear through the noise of her shock and anguish. It was comforting, though, to hear the German read the way she had been brought up, sitting on a hard wooden bench in various homes, listening to the scriptures and the sermon in the German language.

Hod and Abby were there, and the boys, dressed in clean shirts and jeans, holding their hats awkwardly by their sides. Owen and Sylvia, Harry and Doris Rocher, and a new pastor from the First Church of God in Pine, a tall, lanky fellow who spoke with so much kindness the tears rained down Sarah's face before she could begin to constrict her throat to hold them.

They lowered the casket into the dry earth and covered it as the dust whipped away on the hot wind. Manny had been a pillar of strength throughout the ordeal, but the cakes of hard soil hitting the wooden casket was a finality he could not contain. Miserably, he lowered his head and began the anguished sobbing of a boy, not yet a man, but no longer a boy.

Hannah stood, her eyes lowered, her mouth in a tight, grim line, showing no feeling, no emotion. She just wanted this whole ordeal to be over so she could begin her life, taking care of Sarah, and figuring out how they would proceed. Her thoughts spun, caught on irritation, dangled on pegs of grief, flying through her head propelled by remorse. If only she had been a better daughter. Half the time, she hadn't liked her father and had barely tolerated his pious attitude. Now he was gone, and there wasn't a thing she could do about it.

Wouldn't he have a fit, though? All the automobiles that had come to be at his funeral. All the worldly people who stood to bury him, with the relatives chugging along somewhere in a train between here and Ohio, probably. She'd bet they weren't too happy. Mose had gone off to North Dakota after his humiliation, and here he was dead.

Well, she wasn't going back, that was for sure. They couldn't drag her back with a logging chain. She simply wasn't going.

Hannah stood in her black dress with the cape pinned over her shoulders, the apron around her waist, barefoot, refusing to put her feet into those too-tight shoes or pull the prickling stockings over her legs. Her shoulders were wide and erect, her feet planted apart in a stance of firmness, a strong-minded figure, obstinate. Her chin was lifted high enough that folks took notice.

Here was a stubborn one, they thought. Here was one different from the rest. Beside her stood her mother, surrounded by the little ones, her shoulders rounded, bent forward with the weight of her heartache. The children were wide-eyed, observing the way Owen spoke, seeing the clods of dirt, wiping their eyes from the dust, without understanding very much at all.

Their beloved Dat had been ground into the earth by an enraged cow, but he went to Heaven to be with God and Jesus and all the angels. Yet here he was, being put beneath the earth on this great big prairie that would swallow him forever, and they'd forget where he was. So they clung to their remaining comfort, their mother's skirts, and Mary cried because she couldn't bear to see her father buried.

The sun blazed down on the small group surrounding the grave. The searing wind blew skirts and dust and grass, till they turned one final time and made their way back to the house.

The women who ministered to Sarah were dressed in black or gray on this day of Mose's funeral. As gentle as doves, their kindness like a healing balm, Sarah allowed them to heat the food, care for Abby, and sit beside her with a hand on her shoulder as they murmured words of comfort and encouragement.

Doris Rocher's face glowed with an inner light as she set casseroles, pies, and cakes on the table.

There were not enough plates (this woman had so little) but they made do with bowls, allowing the men to eat first, then rinsed the dishes and set the table for the women.

The food was so delicious, so bracing, in this time of shock and unreality. Manny found comfort in the rich potato-and-cheese casserole, the home-cured ham and green beans, applesauce, cabbage slaw, and the mound of baked beans well-seasoned with bacon. Hannah piled her plate to overflowing, consumed every bit, spoonful by spoonful, then ate two slices of custard pie and a thick chunk of yellow cake sprinkled with sugar. Mentally, she calculated the days the food would last before they returned to their steady diet of cornmeal and beans.

The pastor was friendly, with smile crinkles at the corners of his eyes, round spectacles somewhere between the bridge and the tip of his nose, a ready smile, and hands that were made to comfort with a warm touch. He noticed the bare room, the primitive furnishings, the abject poverty that lived in this simple house with these plain people whose pillar of strength had been taken away by God's Hand.

He pulled up a chair and sat beside the grieving widow, who refused every attempt the women made to get her to eat. Didn't she want to taste the beans? The pie?

She would not. Her face as white as the puffy

clouds in the sky outside, her large dark eyes deep wells of pain, she sat holding Abby as if holding the baby was her only link to reality.

She had borne so much, been brave in the face of so many obstacles, but this cruel taking of those most beloved to her had shattered her strength, drained her resolve, and rendered her as limp and pliable as a wet dish rag, unable to will herself off the armless rocker.

Abby Jenkins stayed all night. She sat beside Sarah and stroked the back of her hands, without uttering a word. She put the children to bed, swept the floor, cleaned the stove top, and sat with her suffering neighbor far into the night, before finally succumbing to drowsiness.

And Sarah sat alone, wondering how soon the Lord would allow her to join Mose. She was tired, tired of this life on the prairie, tired of the prowling poverty that threatened to pull her into its deadly, gnashing jaws, tired of Hannah's rebellion, tired of being alone.

There was no reason for her to go on.

CHAPTER 15

The relatives arrived, a flock of familiar faces clad in black. Wide black hats, large black bonnets, black dresses, trousers and vests, shoes and stockings. They arrived in two buckboards pulled by a team of sweating horses, this day as sweltering as each one before.

They removed their cardboard boxes, suitcases, and satchels, the black garments carrying a coat of gray dust.

Sarah stood in the doorway, dressed in black, thin and pale, the tears already streaming silently with no other display of emotion. There were firm handshakes, a deep searching of eyes, but no hugs. Only the common, traditional way of greeting.

Sarah's father. Older, broken, but the same tall man, not stooped, alive and vibrant, smiles tinged with sorrow, but no tears. Strong. This man was so strong, so able. Sarah found herself longing to stay with him, return to the fertile land of her childhood, take his strength for her own, and rest in it for the remainder of her days.

Two of her sisters, Fannie and Sadie. Tears flowed like water. Her brothers, brave and stalwart, their eyes blinking furiously to stop the tears. Her Aunt Eva and Uncle Henner. Ah, but they had aged. Brave to come all the way on the train.

Her father spoke first. "Ach, Sarah. So this is where you are. Isn't it something?"

Sarah managed a smile through her tears. "Yes, it is, Dat. It's very different."

"Here you are, and *der Herr* has seen fit to take Mose. Tell us about it. Tell us what happened, Sarah."

But it was Hannah who spoke, with help from Manny. The sisters, like magpies, like fussing house wrens, their hands over their hearts, gasping and exclaiming, broke in with voices filled with disbelief.

How could this be? How? What kind of animal did they raise out here on the prairie? To kill a man.

"Oh, but it's happened before," Sarah's brother Dan broke in, nodding. "Remember Kaiser Elam's Jacob?"

"Ah, yes. Yes. Forgot about him. That was a bull, though, wasn't it?" Fannie asked.

"No, a big cow. Just had a calf. They can be dangerous."

The hot sun chased them inside, seeking shade. The sisters were shocked at the living conditions, the aunt pitying, but they all tried to hide their feelings from Sarah, who seemed proud to show them the rough walls and dingy floors.

"We built the house together, Mose, Hannah,

and Manny. We had help from the neighbors. Hod and Abby Jenkins and their boys," she explained.

Her father nodded, pleased to know they were not alone.

They talked for hours and ate the food leftover from the funeral. They renewed the old bonds, precious as fine gems. They exchanged news, mulled it over, exchanged it again, and the fine soup of happenings nourished Sarah's starved heart and gave her a spot of color in her thin, white face. She smiled and laughed and her eyes regained their sparkle.

Hannah watched her mother's transformation and fear struck her heart. She'd go back. She'd ride that train back home, Hannah knew it. Her breath quickened, her eyes dilated to a bitter black. Resolve welled up like dark oil and filled her mind. Every atom of her being resisted the idea of going back to Lancaster County, to plod the well-trod road of her forefathers, the jobs, teaching, working in the fields and gardens, being a *maud*, the girl who lived with other Amish families in time of need, when there was a new baby or housecleaning in spring or church services. Keeping up with everyone's expectations of a well–brought-up, obedient young Amish woman, following the same road as her mother.

She felt real nausea well up. She could not leave this land. These 320 acres were theirs. All they needed to do was stay here another nine years and the homestead would be all their own. Her and Mam and Manny and the little ones.

When Clay rode over that evening, her heart beat rapidly. Without a backward glance she raced out the back door and down to the barn, her eyes wide, her lips parted in greeting, motioning him to step behind the barn so no one would see. He led his horse in the direction she indicated, searching her agitated face.

"They're here. All of Mam's family. Well, not all of them, but a bunch. They can't see us. Mam will want to go back."

Clay looked at her, then whistled softly and shook his head. "You think she will?"

"Oh, Clay! You should see her. She's a different person. She's alive. She talks and smiles and even laughs. She's eating again. I know why. There's hope for her, thinking of returning."

"You'll have to go?"

"Of course. How could I stay?"

"Do you want to go?"

She shook her head from side to side, her brows lowered over her dark eyes, spots of color infusing her tanned cheeks.

"Why don't you want to go, Hannah?"

Suddenly confused, she looked away from him to the right, where the cottonwood treetops swayed in the wind. "I don't know. I just don't want to. I don't want to go back and be exactly what everyone else is. A *maud*, a teacher, then a wife, with a whole pile of babies, turning old and fat and, well, like Mam."

Clay's eyes lit up with merriment, then he laughed, a slow, easy sound that Hannah loved to hear. "You're something, Hannah."

She looked at him, and she should not have. His eyes were filled with so much longing, she knew it mirrored her own feelings, and this was not anything she could have prepared herself for. Swept away by the light in his eyes, she was captive, a willing prisoner, propelled forward into his waiting arms. He held her there against his wide chest, her cheek resting against the flap buttoned over his shirt pocket. She wanted to be held closer, to stay there forever while the rest of the world went away.

"Clay . . ."

"Shh. Don't talk, Hannah."

He bent his head and lifted her chin until her eyes found his, blazing with a new and fiery light. His kiss was soft and tender, his lips asking questions, claiming her love, then wondering if it was possible.

Hannah had never felt a man's lips on her own. Shocked, her first instinct was to step away, smack his face, and ask him how he dared. But the need to be close to him, closer still, was so overpowering that her own arms crept about his waist and drew him to her, the world turning liquid with stars and butterflies, and the sweet breezes and light.

"Hannah!" The voice tore through her spinning senses as she wrenched her arms away from Clay. She stepped back, a hand going to her mouth, her eyes wide with horror to find her Uncle Dan standing at the edge of the barn, his wide-brimmed hat squarely on his head, his brown eyes spitting indignation and outrage.

"*Voss geht au?*"

Hannah opened her mouth, but no sound came out of it. Clay regained his senses, cleared his throat. "I'm sorry. We just . . ."

"You just what? Hannah, come with me. I believe your mother will want to know this." Glaring, he looked at Hannah until she started to walk away from Clay. He reached out a hand, as if to keep her, then dropped it helplessly and stood rooted by his own sense of having overstepped his bounds.

Slowly, he gathered up the reins, swung into the saddle, and without a backward glance he rode away.

Hannah walked behind her uncle, her head bent, her eyes blazing into the grass at her feet, unprepared to meet the shame that would be showered on her. The discipline that would follow was unthinkable.

Why had she kissed Clay? What had compelled

her? She knew any feelings for Clay Jenkins were an impossibility.

The time of sitting in the house with the posse of relatives was worse than if Uncle Dan would have blurted out the awful scene he had encountered behind the barn. She made small talk, her agitation making her face flush, then drain to a chalk white, her eyes black with shame and remorse.

Dan waited to tell Sarah until they had a moment alone, so Hannah lived through hours of fear and unknowing, before Sarah approached her on the porch, in the still of the night.

Hannah felt the soft presence of her mother before she could see her. The heat had evaporated into nightfall, the grass quieted, the moon rising in its perfect symmetry in the east, the vast night sky sprinkled with the stars that were still uncountable, as they had been for Abraham of the Bible.

"Hannah." When there was no answer, Sarah wasn't surprised, so she pressed on. "Dan told me about you and Clay."

"So?"

"Hannah, you must try to understand. It isn't allowed. He is not of our faith. He is a boy—a man—of the world. We are a Plain sect, set apart, living in a culture he would not understand. It can't be love. You are too young to know your own heart. Our bodies sometimes betray us.

Loneliness, fear of the future, a need for safety, these can all be mistaken for love. A young girl can be swept away by infatuation, a need that is nothing close to what God wants us to have, the real, spiritual kind of love that is lasting and by far the most important love, blessed by Him."

"I didn't say I loved him."

"Then why were you in his arms, Hannah? He was kissing you."

Hannah choked, hearing her mother say that word, almost like an obscenity. Her face flamed in the dark and she turned it away.

"Listen, *meine dochter*. Clay is very handsome. No doubt he has had plenty of experience with girls and knows every wile to captivate a young girl's heart. You were ripe to be falling for him with Mose, your father's, death. Please don't tell me it is nothing. The kiss meant something."

"You're going back, aren't you?"

"Don't change the subject."

"But you are going back." It was a statement, each word a stone thrown in Sarah's direction, stones she could not dodge.

"Yes, I am planning on returning."

"I knew it!" Hannah shouted.

"Shh! You'll wake everyone."

"I don't care. I don't care if they all wake up and come down the stairs to point fingers at me. You can go, Mam. Just go, you and nice, obedient Manny and the little ones. I'll stay right here. This is our home, this is where we belong. We built this house, and we will own all these 320 acres of land. Dat is in his grave, here. Here, Mam. Not in Lancaster County." She rose from her seat on the steps by the power of her passion.

"Hannah, listen to reason. We can't live here without Mose."

"And why can't we? He did nothing but fast and pray and dream and read his Bible. He didn't know a thing about making it on the prairie. He didn't know his foot from his elbow when it came right down to it. Look at the way he penned up those pitiful calves. He was so stubborn, so dumb."

Hannah drew back, but not fast enough to save herself from her mother's solid, open-palmed smack that hit her cheek, twisting her head sideways with its force, promptly followed by another, then a claw like grip on her shoulder, shaking her firmly until her head spun.

"Stop it! Stop saying those words, Hannah Detweiler. You are blaspheming against God and your poor, dead father," Sarah panted, her throat hoarse with pain and emotion.

Hannah didn't cry. She stood with blazing eyes that appeared like black, glistening pools in the moonlight, her fists clenched, her feet planted firmly.

"I don't care what you say. He was not the reason we got this far. It was all the help from the Jenkinses, and you know it. We'd all be dead, starved, lying like skeletons, our bones picked by buzzards, if it hadn't been for you and me. You were the one who sent me to the Jenkinses for food. I was the one who rode into town for food. He was off on a tangent, wishing God would help us. Wishing!"

Hannah was crying now, her face contorted, hot tears of shame and hurt and rebellion splashing down her cheeks.

"It was his faith, Hannah, his faith. He believed until the end, and will be rewarded in heaven."

"That may be so. But *we* did the work. We used our God-given talents and found food. Barely enough to keep us, but *we* did it."

Sarah sighed and sat back down on the porch steps, lowering her face into her hands. "How could our lives come to this? It all started with Dat's dreaming back in Lancaster County and losing the farm."

"It was the Depression. We're not the only ones who were unfortunate." There was nothing to say to this. It was uncontested truth.

Hannah said, "We're here, now. I'm not going back."

"Because of Clay Jenkins?"

"No."

"The homestead?"

"Yes."

"Then you're going back. You will have to obey. Please Hannah. It's your duty."

"You can't make me go with you," Hannah stated flatly.

"You can't stay here."

"Could Manny stay?

Sarah sighed. "He says he'll go back."

For a long moment they sat in silence, absorbing the night. Was anything ever as wondrous as the prairie at night? The moon was twice as brilliant, unfettered, shining with a blue-gold brilliance that washed the grass in tinted white shadows. The soft rustling was like a plucking of nature's guitar, a moving music of sighs and longings, the call of one melancholy heart to another. The boundless territory of nothingness, when a lone person could disappear into a small black dot, insignificant, unnoticed by the human eye, but much closer to God than ever before. He reigned absolute here on the plains, with nothing to come between a mortal and her Maker.

Together, mother and daughter breathed in the solitude and let it wash out the hopelessness, the anger and passion that goaded it, until their spirits became restful. Yet they did not speak, both realizing they had reached an impasse.

Hannah would refuse. Sarah would not allow it. There was no sleep for either one as they lay on the hard wooden floor by the kitchen stove until the old clock banged out the hour of morning.

Stiff, tired, and obstinate, Hannah dragged a

comb through her hair, dressed, and left the house long before the relatives were awake.

There was no dew, not even a trace of moisture after months of no rain, so Sarah set out in her bare feet to check on the calves. They never strayed far, and she wanted to make sure the brands were not bleeding or infected.

She walked briskly, as fast as her skirts would allow, her eyes searching the dry grass for the telltale black calf backs rising above it. After she found them, she called, "Sook, sook, sook," gently, the way she used to call the calves in Lancaster. They allowed her to walk up to them and she rubbed the tops of their heads, ran a hand down their backs, parting the thick, black hair, till she came to the Bar S brand.

The Bar S—her own project, her own idea. The S standing for the heritage that was her mother's name. And here she was, faced with the awful prospect of following her remaining family away from this, away from everything she loved, all her hopes and dreams.

Her goal was to own a herd of cattle. A good bloodline, like the Jenkinses and the Klassermans. Decent buildings, a better well, horses in the stable, not horses like Pete and that leftover pile of bones the Jenkinses had sent over.

She'd work at the Rochers to support the family. Manny would have to get a job. After she became good at running the store, she'd demand wages. She'd put every nickel, dollar, penny, and dime in a jar until she could build up the herd. With the sale of the first calves, she'd dig a better well, and think about a windmill.

She could probably do better than the Jenkinses. They were all an easy going lot, in many ways. Especially Hank and Ken. Probably the reason she liked Clay best was that he came around most often and seemed to be the one with the most ambition.

Take all that junk lying around, which didn't seem to bother them a bit. Hannah figured her ranch would not look like that at all. Everything would be in its place. She'd plant trees and water them with water from the new well, the windmill pumping it up out of the ground.

At breakfast, she didn't talk and avoided the cold stares by remaining invisible. She ate coffee soup and fried mush, thinking what a treat coffee soup had turned out to be. Buttered bread sprinkled liberally with brown sugar, placed in a bowl with a cup of hot coffee poured over it. Aunt Eva had brought a can of tinned milk, which only made the coffee soup better.

She wasn't going to let anyone see her taking pleasure in her meal. She simply sat at the corner of the table and ate deliberately, spoonful after spoonful. Sarah seemed pale and edgy, but if anyone noticed, they said nothing. Hannah looked up once to find Uncle Dan's accusing eyes probing her face and felt her face flame before lowering her eyes.

Old goat.

It was her grandfather who opened the subject of returning, like lifting the lid off a beehive, the bees filling the room with their terrifying buzz. "So, we need how many tickets to return?"

An icy silence crept across the room. Fannie said he didn't have to know ahead of time, they could purchase the tickets at the station. Sadie said certainly not.

Uncle Dan said Fannie was right, everybody calm down.

"But everyone is agreed to go?"

"Yes, I believe so," Sarah said quietly, without looking at Hannah.

"We need to get the train in Dorchester, right?"

"How will we get there?" And so on.

First of all, the horses had to be taken to the Klassermans, who were closer than the Jenkinses. The cow and calves could be turned loose, they'd find their way to the water, and had plenty of grass. There was nothing to do about the stove and the beds and the table, although no one said what they were truly thinking, that they weren't worth a red cent anyhow.

Sarah worried about Abby Jenkins's dishes, her tablecloth and fabric, all things she had given them.

All around Hannah, plans swirled, buzzing in

her ears, tormenting her head like a fever. They, none of them, were considering her refusal. They forged straight ahead, pushing her along like that blade on the Jenkinses' tractor, pushing a load of snow ahead of it.

It was now or never. Loudly, actually louder than she intended, Hannah blurted out, "You don't have to worry about anything. I'll be here to *fa-sark* everything. I don't intend on leaving the homestead. This land will be ours after nine years, and I don't plan on giving it up."

All eyes turned to her. Mouths hung open in disbelief.

"Ach, Hannah, stop chasing rainbows, you silly girl," her grandfather said.

"I'm serious. I have no plans of returning."

"But you must. You can't stay here. Surely you know that."

Hannah shook her head. "I can stay, if Manny will stay with me."

Sarah opened her mouth, then closed it. She met her daughter's eyes, shivered at the light of determination, helpless before it. She began to cry, lowering her eyes, then her head, reaching into her apron for a handkerchief.

This angered Sarah's father and Uncle Dan. "Hannah, you are an *ungehorsam* daughter. Nothing good will come of this."

Hannah met their eyes, unflinching, unmoved.

"God is not mocked. What you sow, that shall

you reap. You have already taken up with an *ausricha*, that despicable man you were with." This from Uncle Dan.

Audible gasps went around the room. Sarah slid down into her chair, flinched until her features looked folded.

"What man?" shouted Fannie.

"What do you mean?" barked Sadie.

"Hush. Everyone hush. I will not put up with this public shaming," said Uncle Dan piously. "It was nothing."

Hannah exhaled, grateful for his words. She sincerely hoped it was the end of that subject, or the way it was headed.

As luck would have it, the Jenkins family arrived that afternoon, the parents driving the rusted out pickup truck, the boys following on horseback, tanned and lithe, easygoing and full of laughter.

Hannah yearned for Clay. She yearned to be with him alone and be rid of this flock of people dressed in somber black, with their dire predictions and spouting the evil that would come to pass if she disobeyed.

Her mother's tears, though. They fell red hot on Hannah's conscience. That was the lone reason that Hannah finally admitted to herself that she simply could not do this to her mother. She knew if she stayed, her mother would not have a moment's rest if she traveled home to Lancaster

County without her. So she, herself, would lay down her own will, the flesh, and stay with Hannah. She'd follow Hannah in much the same way she'd followed Mose, cowed by the will of another person, a sheep to the slaughter.

So she sought out Clay, made sure there was no one to see, and slipped behind the barn, away from prying, curious eyes. He asked her what the plans were.

"I have to go, Clay."

"You said you wouldn't go."

"I know. Oh, I know. But my mother won't go without me. She'll stay here, give up for my sake, and I'll be like my father. Someone she gives her life for, a person she follows, in spite of her own unhappiness. I can't make her do that."

Clay kicked at a clump of grass, his hands in his pockets. "What about us? Is that simply not possible?"

"What do you mean?"

"A future together? You know, getting married an' all."

"I'd have to leave my faith, my family, and my life as I know it."

"Stay, Hannah." He clasped both of her hands in a grip of iron. Hannah winced. "Stay with me," he whispered brokenly.

All of her yearned toward him. She wanted to do just that. Stay here with him. Together they could have a prosperous ranch. Would their love be strong enough to bridge the divide between the two cultures?

Hannah saw herself take off her large white covering, let down her long dark hair, shed the plain, homemade dresses, and put on the gaily flowered shirtwaists, the flesh-colored stockings, and high-heeled shoes. Eventually, she'd wear jeans and shirts, go to dances, drink beer, and paint her lips as red as a cherry. She'd change over to a woman of the world and be like everyone else. Never again would she belong to her family, her relatives, in the true sense of the word.

She'd never joined the church, never taken vows, so she wouldn't be excommunicated. She'd just not be a part of it any longer.

She'd be like her cousin, Harvey, who had run off to join the army. They talked to him when he returned, but with a certain reserved, careful way of speaking, as mistrustful as a wild steer. He was a man of the world, especially because of joining the war effort—oh, doubly so. He was an apostate, a heretic, responsible for breaking his mother's heart, bringing his father to an early death. Some said there was no hope for his soul. He would burn in hell for all eternity for going against his father's wishes. Cursed is he who brings sorrow to his mother.

At the tender age of sixteen, Hannah grappled with all of this, confronted by a handsome young man who pleaded with her to stay with him in the land that she loved.

With a cry, a plea for help, she flung herself into his arms and clung to him, trying desperately to rid herself of her own conscience. Her *bessagrissa*. The knowledge deep within that she knew better than to disobey her mother, caring nothing about her feelings of despair, living only for herself, selfish, unthinking, without natural love.

They had a few moments of stolen kisses, with Clay's tears mingling with her own, his arms around her like velvet, steel beneath the softness, their longing and denial a battle that had only begun.

"I'll go back, Clay," she whispered, brokenly. "I'll listen to my poor mother. But the rest of my life, I'll try and figure out a way to come back to you. I will. We can write. I have your address."

Clay groaned as he pulled her closer. This final time together was the worst kind of torment he had ever known. He had never fallen so hard for anyone. All the relaxed manner he had ever known could not have prepared him for the agony of their parting.

CHAPTER 16

The train chugged into the station, plumes of black smoke rolling from the smoke stack as if the devil himself was in charge. Which he probably was, Hannah thought bitterly. Her black shoes and stockings pinched her feet and chafed at her heels. Her breath, sour with the morning's coffee soup, irritated her as much as the prickling at her waistline where her apron was pinned too tightly.

The mountain of suitcases and cardboard boxes was embarrassing. They looked like a bunch of immigrants from another country, everyone dressed in crow-like black. Aunt Eva looked like a crow, with that monstrous nose of hers. Probably the reason she never wore her spectacles was because they'd never fit on top of that nose. Her eyes were as sharp as a crow's eyes too; she saw right through you.

Manny sat beside her, his tanned face quiet, serene, his eyes darting everywhere, taking in the sights and sounds around him. He didn't speak to Hannah; he merely ignored her, knowing the mood she was in would not bide well with him.

Sarah could not hide her childlike wonder. The pure happiness of returning to the land of her youth, back to her childhood home, was almost more than she could grasp. Every click of the train wheels sang a song that traveled to her feet, through her body and into her heart. Home, home. I'm going home. Never more to roam. Never would she return, never.

She hardly slept and didn't mind the grimy soot that seemed to coat every available surface with black dust. Even the inside of her nostrils were stopped up; her tongue was dry with it and her teeth clacked together as if they were grinding eggshells. Tenderly, she held the baby and cared for Eli and Mary with a heart that bubbled over with joy and anticipation.

She felt as if she would never need to eat another meal. This unexpected homecoming was all the sustenance she needed. It was only at night, when the train slid through the darkness, that she closed her eyes and saw her husband's wracked body, the pitiful gasping for breath, the final moment when he had to let her go, that she shuddered, reliving the pain and the onslaught of grief that followed.

She would never be free of this and didn't want to be. She remembered Mose as a strong, healthy man, a lover of life, her heart's desire, a tender man who loved his wife and children beyond all reason.

They had a layover in Chicago. The children huddled around their mother with large, frightened eyes, taking in the enormity of this strange, bustling world of people, cars, trucks, and hissing locomotives. Hannah stood with Manny on the platform of the great station as they peered up, up, and up at buildings so tall they could not imagine them staying upright in a wind storm.

"But Hannah, what are these buildings made of?" Manny asked, breathless with wonder, his large dark eyes unable to absorb it all.

"I don't know. Steel? Cement? Who knows, Manny?"

"We didn't learn much about things like this in school, did we?"

"Not much."

Then, "Hannah, you didn't want to come back, did you?"

"No."

"Because of Clay?"

"No. The homestead."

"We can't go back without our father."

"Sure we can. I will, someday."

Manny watched his sister's face and knew she meant it. He smiled at her, his youthful face beginning to show signs of manhood.

Hannah touched his arm and grinned. "Don't worry, Manny. I won't go without you. I know you'll want to go when the time is right."

Their arrival in the city of Lancaster was uneventful, the train sliding smoothly into the station. Two of the uncles came to greet them and hustled them into wagons with teams of horses.

There was so much talk, so many greetings, so much formality and recounting of her father's death. Hannah was bone weary, completely sick of the fuss, the endless whirl of coming home, that she slouched down in the back of the wagon, drew up her knees and closed her eyes. She thought of Clay and his eyes when he pleaded with her to stay.

It was dark, late in the evening, when the horses trotted into the driveway that led to Sarah's father's house. A sprawling house built of gray limestone, with wooden additions, a black slate roof and a wire fence around the yard, it was everything Hannah remembered.

Sarah cried with the joy of being at home, a place she didn't think she would ever see again. Empty and cold without her mother, carrying the loss of her husband like heavy armor, the room seemed to fold in on her chest and squeezed the breath from her body.

Her father sensed the immense upheaval in his daughter's spirit and took the children to their rooms, showed them where to wash, and produced the suitcases that held their nightclothes, leaving Sarah to lay her arms on the tabletop, her shoulders heaving with sobs. There was too much grief, too much to absorb, the awful pit of her grief yawning before her, the joy of coming home lifting her to new heights, only to return to her grief by the kitchen of her childhood without her precious mother.

She became aware of her father standing beside her, quietly waiting until her sobs subsided. He handed her a folded white handkerchief. "Will you be all right, Sarah, through all of this?"

Her swollen eyes still leaking tears, biting her lip to regain her composure, she nodded, then wiped her eyes and blew her nose. "It's just so empty without Mam," she wailed, on a fresh note of despair.

"Yes, it is that. It will never be the same. But we are not put on this earth to stay. Our home is not here, and the Lord truly does give and He taketh away. Her time was up, in spite of those who are left behind missing her so badly."

"As was Mose's time," she whispered.

"Ya. Oh ya, Sarah. I'm so glad you accept that. It is the truth. We can never blame ourselves or circumstances for a death. God cuts the *goldicha fauda*, the golden thread of our existence, and that is that."

So with a calm heart and a weary body, Sarah went to *die goot schtup*, the guest bedroom, the room with sheets that smelled of dried lavender, quilts that smelled faintly of moth balls, green window blinds, and freshly starched white curtains that were hung halfway up the ornate trim work, which was varnished to a high gloss.

The kerosene lamp illuminated the old oak sideboard that had been her grandmother Stoltzfus's bonnet cupboard. The gilt mirror hung above it, and the old, hand-embroidered family record. Even the pitcher and water glasses with painted fruit. It was all here, just the way she remembered.

She washed in the basin provided by her father, slipped into her old nightdress, and lay between the smooth, cool sheets on the firm mattress she had once been used to. Never in her life had she experienced such luxury, almost sinful comfort. Clean, soft, and smelling of lavender, Sarah pressed the palm of her hand into the pillow beside her head—empty.

So this is what widowhood was. An empty pillow beside her, only the memory of Mose's dark head remaining. A fresh wave of longing seized her, the grief and sorrow pressing her into the mattress.

Ah, dear God, dear God, how can I bear up under the weight of this loss? Silently she prayed, silently she cried gulping sobs. She simply could not sleep alone. She threw back the covers, tiptoed across the room and down the hallway to the children's room, found Abby and lifted her soft, sweet body into her arms, then laid her in the bed beside her, becoming sleepy in an instant, her arms wrapped tenderly around her precious baby.

She would need to care for her children, was her last thought before a blessed slumber overtook her.

Sarah awoke to find the sun's rays poking between the green blind and the window frame. Cows lowed in the barnyard, and the birds twittered and chirped their morning song in the oak branches outside her window.

The sounds of home. She really was home. She dressed quietly, leaving Abby asleep, then tiptoed down the stairs to the empty kitchen to comb her hair and wash her face.

The sun's early rays that lit the kitchen illuminated the cupboards and dry sink, the basin by the kettle house door, and the old woodstove that contained live red coals, even in summer. The homemade rag rugs scattered across the linoleum looked worn and muddy, the floor itself scuffed and dull. The windows were greasy and unwashed.

Well, here was her work. Here she would live with her children, do for her father the tasks left undone in her mother's absence. Filled with a new sense of purpose, Sarah drew a deep breath, then began to open doors and drawers, searching for food, knowing her father and two younger brothers would be hungry after the milking.

A disgruntled Hannah took all the light out of the kitchen. Belligerent, refusing to comb her hair, she sat on the sofa, yawning, stretching, doing anything she could to ruffle Sarah's good humor.

Finally, exasperated, Sarah turned with her hands on her hips. "Hannah, if you won't try to cooperate, then return to your bedroom until you can face the day in a better state of mind."

"What state of mind do you think I should be in? Huh? I hate Lancaster County. I don't want to live here with our doddy. I'm not going to milk those stinking cows, either."

"Go to your room, Hannah. Go." Sarah's voice was icy with disapproval.

Hannah didn't go. She didn't want to return to that stuffy upstairs bedroom smelling of mothballs and feet. Someone's feet smelled like spoiled cheese, the kind that had green mold growing over the rind. So she sat on the davenport that perpetually smelled of cows, glared at her mother, then shuffled off to comb her hair.

Sarah's hands shook as she measured oatmeal into the boiling, salted water. So this is how things would be. How could she have tricked herself into thinking Hannah would give in? A sense of unease followed her to the henhouse, where she lifted the wire basket from the peg on the wall, reached under the brooding brown hens to find the perfect eggs underneath.

An egg. A real miracle. How long since she

had had an egg for her breakfast? Likely the eggs would be rationed, the way they always were. Only one apiece. There was too much money to be made by selling them at the market, or peddling them to the neighbors. Oatmeal, coffee soup, and fried mush were much cheaper and filled stomachs sufficiently.

But these eggs were glorious orbs of deliciousness. Her mouth watered, in spite of herself. A golden yolk in the middle of perfectly cooked white, a slice of firm, spongy homemade bread fried in butter, torn into pieces and dipped into it, was a rare treat she had often longed for in their crude house on the Dakota plains.

Now, on this perfect day, with birdsong trilling and whistling around her, the oak and maple trees like a benediction from God alone, the deep green of the mowed lawn, the irises and gladioli, the marigolds and petunias in a border along the stone house—so much beauty around her she could scarcely take it all in. The brilliant yellow of one marigold was a miracle in itself.

She paused to admire the perfect red of the flowering quince bush and breathed deeply of the pungent pine boughs. She picked up a pinecone from the carpet of pine needles on the ground and held it to her cheek, rolling it in both hands to release the scent.

Today, she would visit old neighbors, laugh and talk and weep. She would renew old bonds, revel in friendship, become alive to the sounds and sights of her world, her senses filled with the compassion and love of her beloved church members.

Hannah would come around. She would learn to like the hustle and bustle, the friendship of other girls her age. So strong was her longing to stay, she resolved fiercely to make Hannah become obedient, to force her to comply. Why couldn't she be like the other children? With God's help, she would nip this blossoming rebellion in the bud before it bloomed into a scarlet life of sin. She had come this far, and she would complete the journey to fit back into the mold.

Her father and two brothers, Elam and Ben, walked into the kettle house, the room where the laundry and washing up were done, a smile on their faces, sniffing the tantalizing aroma of fried bread and eggs, the steaming coffee for coffee soup.

"Good morning!" Sarah trilled.

Hannah, perched on the edge of the davenport like a displeased crow, glared at her mother's happiness.

Her father returned her greeting warmly. Elam and Ben nodded and smiled. "It's so nice to come into the kitchen with breakfast waiting. It makes me miss Bena more than ever." Her father ducked his head to hide the emotion he felt so strongly.

Breakfast was a happy affair, the children

tumbling sleepily down the stairs, Mary carrying a waving and smiling Abby, Manny sheepish for having overslept on his first morning.

Her father smiled at the one egg apiece rule that she had remembered. "Eggs are dear, especially now in these hard times. Most folks can't afford the laying mash, so the hens don't produce the way they should. We get over a dollar a dozen in town."

Hannah shoveled her egg into her mouth, spoke with her mouth full, "I'd kill the chickens and eat them. Fried chicken is better than eggs."

Elam and Ben both looked at her sharply. Sarah's heart sank, the delicious breakfast like sawdust in her mouth. Blinking rapidly to repel the tears that constantly lurked so close to the surface, she rose to dish up the creamy oatmeal.

To her relief, her father smiled slowly, challenging Hannah. "And why would you do that?"

"I said, fried chicken is better than eggs."

"But after the chickens were all eaten, you would have neither one."

"So. I hate chickens."

Sarah stared at her daughter, astounded at this flagrant display of rebellion. She had not spoken one suitable word all morning. A tightness in Sarah's chest accelerated her breathing. She opened her mouth to speak harshly to Hannah but was stopped by her father's eyes.

"Why is that, Hannah?"

"They're stupid. Pecking and flogging, *mishting* all over everything."

Elam and Ben threw back their heads simultaneously, howling with laughter. "You have to agree, Dat," they chortled.

Her father laughed along with the boys, then told Hannah if that was the case, they'd try and keep her out of the henhouse, which evoked a reluctant smile from her. And so it went.

Every day was a rediscovery of joy, renewing old acquaintances, working on the home place, doing for Dat and the boys. Her sisters were regular visitors, flocking into the yard like garrulous birds, dressed in greens and purples and blues.

But Hannah constantly chafed at the restraints that held her. She felt suffocated by the towering trees, the still and stifling air, the barn hovering over the house, rearing its head like an overprotective guard. Sometimes she felt as if she should lean all her weight against it, move it away. It was built too close to the house, in her opinion.

The smell of manure clung to everything. It was spread on the fields with a rattling contraption drawn by horses. It clung to the cows' tails and there were piles of it in the barnyard. It permeated every denim coat and pair of rubber boots that stood on the woven rug inside the door.

Thunderstorms and rain showers were frequent,

loading down the unmoving air with dense humidity that drew sweat until it ran down her face. Her dress back was soaked with it as she bent over picking lima beans and string beans, tomatoes and cucumbers.

The only bright spot in her restricted, clamped-down world was her unmarried uncles, Ben and Elam. Hannah made them laugh. She was always surprising them. Girls her age did not talk the way she did. She viewed the world through thorny glasses, unafraid to voice an opinion, no matter how colorful or prickly.

The aunts supplied the Swiss organdy fabric for a new white cape and apron and a new covering so she could attend church services. New shoes and dresses materialized for all the girls so they could be seen as decent, hiding any signs of the poverty in which they had lived.

Hannah forgot how itchy that stiff Swiss organdy was. She grumbled and complained; she couldn't get the pins in straight, her hair wasn't rolled right, and her bob on the back of her head was too loose. "I don't know why we have to roll our hair along the side of our heads. Whoever invented that was just plain ignorant."

Sarah peered around Mary, who stood in front of her mother. She was pinning the white organdy apron around Mary's narrow waist, looking pretty herself in a purple dress with a black cape and apron pinned perfectly.

That was the thing about being Amish, Hannah thought. There were so many ways of being neat and just as many of being sloppy. The *leblein* sewn on the back of each dress—the small piece of fabric sewn to the waistline—was where the sides of the apron had to be pinned to with precision, so it would hang straight and even on each side.

Same way with the pleats pinned on the shoulder of the cape: perfectly aligned down the back, the neckline in front not too low (that projected *hochmut*, or "loose morals") or too high and certainly not crooked.

The hemline of the apron should be aligned with the hemline of the dress, the double row of deep pleats in the back, below the *leblein* as straight as a pole. It was all about neatness, modesty, precision, and if it came right down to it, perhaps a tinge of fashion as well.

The fancy girls' head coverings were smaller, their hair combed in loose waves. Dresses could be shorter or belts on aprons wider. Anything tight or form-fitting was considered risqué, but some girls tried to get away with it, creeping out of the side or back doors before their fathers caught sight of them.

So Hannah went to church services for the first time in many months, in a district that was not her own (they had lived close to the town of Intercourse), in a foul mood, dissatisfied with her appearance, without knowing a single person.

She rode with Elam, Ben, and Manny. Twenty-one-year-old Elam and twenty-year-old Ben were dark-haired, dark-eyed young men. Good-humored and easygoing, they enjoyed life on the farm, their social activities, horses, and girls. Both of them could have had almost anyone they chose from the flock of young ladies they hauled to and from hymn singings and Saturday night barn parties called hoedowns.

Elam, especially, at the age of twenty-one, was considered quite a *ketch*, the girls clamoring for his attention in their covert glances and witty remarks.

None of the youth drove a buggy with a top on it, as was the custom at the time of the Great Depression. They only bought a *doch-veggly*, literally translated as a roof wagon, after they married, if they could afford one. If not, they continued traveling in the courting buggy, a one-seated buggy with a lidded box in the back, a rubber blanket to pull up over the people seated on the lone seat fastened to a hook with a leather strap. A sturdy black umbrella was poked down along the side, where it was within easy reach, in case of rain or snow.

When there were three or four individuals to take, the driver merely plopped himself on someone's lap, and they rode in layers.

This morning, Hannah and Manny were seated, with Elam and Ben perched comfortably on their laps. It was a fine morning, already uncomfortably warm, the sun an orange ball of heat, the air moist with humidity.

The horse was black with four white feet, a long blaze of white down the length of his face, his neck arched like a show horse, his small curved ears turned forward. There were white porcelain rings on the harness, which were there only for show, although usually the young boys would try to pass it off as a necessity. The buggy was gleaming after its wash with buckets of soapy water, the spokes of the wheels throwing off sparkles in the sunlight.

"You may as well own a car," Hannah blurted out.

"What?" Elam was incredulous.

"Why do you say that?" Ben asked, pretending innocence.

"Your horse and buggy is all about *hochmut*. You can't tell me you don't have loads of pride in this horse. I bet it's the fanciest horse in Lancaster."

"God made this horse. We are not out of the *Ordnung*," said Elam, testily defending himself. He did have pride, but to be told it to his face was a different thing entirely.

"God doesn't make cars. Men do," Ben agreed.

"Puh. Men can't do a thing unless God gives them the knowledge. We're supposed to have cars or God wouldn't allow it."

"Perhaps their knowledge is of the devil."

"Oh, now you sound like Dat."

"Hannah, your father is in his grave, may he rest in peace. You should not be talking like this."

"I don't care what you say. You still sound like him. I can't stand the way Amish people speak about anything they reject. Just because they can't have it doesn't make it wrong for everybody else."

Elam and Ben both shrugged, held their peace. She spoke the truth, and they knew it. Each man's conscience had to account for himself and not another person, especially those who were *ausriche*.

Unapologetic, Hannah rode to church, figuring those two needed to get off the tower of their own goodness, get back down, and live like the rest of the world. Life pinched your backside sometimes. It sure did.

Here she was, then, pushed into this strange room with a gaggle of girls dressed in a colorful display of Sunday finery, the white capes and aprons like a mist of purity. They were all shapes and sizes, dark-haired, blonde, some with facial pimples, others with clear skin, large noses, small perfect ones, bad teeth, and beautiful smiles.

Hannah shook hands, a twisted half-smile of self-consciousness plastered on her stiff features. Her hair was rolled too loosely, resulting in *shtrubles*, loose hair that floated free, the first mark of a sloppy, ill-kempt girl. Her cape was pinned wrong too, the pleats down the back crooked, one sticking out the side, the other plunging straight down the opposite shoulder. Her stockings were too heavy. *Who would have made her wear those hideous stockings?* the observant girls wondered.

Some of them knew who she was, had heard of Mose and Sarah Detweiler and their ill-timed voyage to the West.

The room quieted as they examined this tall, dark-haired girl with the unfriendly expression, the too-dark eyes that threw their own glances back at them making them uncomfortable. The silence became strained; a few ill-timed and out-of-place giggles erupted. No one welcomed her. Most of them were simply at a loss in the face of Hannah's belligerence, if you could call it that.

Everyone was relieved when the lady of the house came to tell them it was time to be seated. They filed in after her. The girls were accustomed to being seated strictly by their age, but no one was brave enough to ask Hannah how old she was.

Hannah stood watching as one by one they formed a line and walked out the door on their way to the barn. A small girl who looked no older than twelve called out, "Wait!" She pointed to Hannah. A heavy-set girl, her wide face friendly, stepped back and motioned Hannah forward with a wave of her hand.

She fell into line then, wondering if it was all right for a sixteen year old to be seated with the school-aged ones. Nothing to do for it now. A deep dislike for the girls her own age, for Lancaster County, for tradition, and for everything about this day, this church, and her own life settled about her shoulders like the ill-fitting white cape she wore.

She wanted her own Sunday on the prairie back in North Dakota, where she was free to roam, to ride horses, and to watch the calves; to contemplate the grass blowing every which way by wind that smelled of clean, dark earth and dried plants; to reflect on gophers and prairie hens and wet mud and trickling water in the creek bottom, where dragonflies perched on weeds and the breeze rustled the cottonwood leaves like a song; and thinking, most of all, that Clay Jenkins might ride over, which he sometimes did.

Hannah missed him with an acute sense of absence that was always brought back to earth by their impossible situation. Sometimes, she wondered to herself if his love would be deep enough that he would become Amish, follow her culture, and submit to the *Ordnung*'s ways. And quickly she knew he wouldn't.

To imagine Clay perched on a courting buggy, driving along the well-kept roads of Lancaster County, the thick green corn growing like a forest on either side; a life of order, hard work, and restrictions was a joke, and she knew it with a sense of hopelessness.

He was as free and unfettered as the wind, his life revolving around a wide space of choices without demands. A whole other lifestyle. A heap of old boards and tin and automobile parts, wheels and unkempt weeds around the barn, broken fences patched with barbed wire and dry boards the cows would easily break through again—none of it mattered to the Jenkinses. If the fence wasn't repaired immediately, it posed no real problem. The cows and calves that broke through would be rounded up sometime, and, if not, the Jenkins men enjoyed chasing and roping them on horseback.

This glaring difference was like a slap of reality, sitting on the hard bench, a head taller than any of the girls around her. It was bad enough being so tall without having to be seated in a row of much younger girls.

Well, she knew one thing: she was going back.

CHAPTER 17

The remainder of the church service passed in a haze of remembering. The need to get away from this stifling, bustling colony of relatives and friends she was sort of acquainted with consumed Hannah. Perhaps she could manage to act like everyone else—friendly, bland, saying just the right thing at just the right moment—enough so that everyone would approve of the widow Detweiler's oldest daughter.

What a nice young woman, they'd say.

What was *nice?* By whose measure were you *nice?* Which words and actions came under *nice?* It was a high ceiling to measure up to, that was sure. The whole world of being proper, well brought up, soft spoken, and sweet, was a world in which she simply wasn't interested. She wanted to live a life that was real—to herself and her own dreams and expectations, not someone else's.

Her mother, though. That was the one bond she could hardly bring herself to break. To tell her outright that she was not staying here but returning to North Dakota was almost more than she could think about. Sarah wouldn't agree, but to keep Hannah, Sarah might offer to follow her back to the homestead, like the willing servant she was.

Hannah didn't help sing. The swells of the German plainsong around her brought an unexpected lump in her throat, a surprising and unwanted emotion. After services, she slouched in a corner of the room, without taking part in the conversation, her glowering expression keeping everyone at bay.

No one spoke to her while she sat at the table to eat the *schnitz boy*, jam, and bread and butter, pickles and sour red beets, so she didn't bother waiting on tables or helping with the dishes.

Visibly relieved when Manny came to ask her if she was ready to go, she rode away from the church service with pleasure.

Elam asked if she wanted to go along to the hymn singing that evening.

"No!" Hannah shouted.

"Whoa," Ben laughed.

"I don't know anyone, no one talks to me, so why would I?"

"The West has changed you, Hannah."

"You didn't know me before I left, so how would you know?" Hannah was bristling with enough anger to repel any advances on her good humor, unknowingly separating herself from anyone in the courting buggy.

"Yeah, maybe so," Elam replied quietly, leaving a silence to settle around the open-seated buggy the remainder of the ride home.

• • •

Hannah locked herself in the guest room and wrote a letter to the Jenkinses, not just to Clay. No use him getting all kinds of ideas about her missing him, which she didn't.

"Dear folks . . ."

That didn't sound right so she erased "folks" and wrote "friends." Better. In North Dakota your folks were your family, and there was no sense in letting Clay think she was part of the family, which she wasn't.

"How are you?" Should she include "all"? If she wrote, "How are you all," they might think she was trying to write or speak the way they did, with their *y'alls* and their *fers*.

She erased the whole question.

"We're here in Lancaster County at my mother's home place. The barn is much too close to the house, everyone knows everyone else's business, and the relatives are like a large gaggle of geese. They all look the same, except some are older than others."

Here she paused, wondering if she should tell Clay about her plans. Perhaps she shouldn't, since the plans for how she expected to go about it weren't solid yet. But they would be. She just couldn't be sure how she planned to go about it.

"The corn here in Pennsylvania looks like a never-ending forest of upright stalks with huge yellow ears. It rains regularly. If North Dakota

325

had some way of watering the fields, my father's idea might have worked. But you can't grow corn without water. Doesn't rain out there.

"I can't ride horses here. My grandfather would be shocked. Girls just put on their neat dresses and capes and aprons and ride around in dumb buggies and say exactly the right thing in the right tone of voice, which I suppose I'll have to learn." (Let Clay think she was not coming back. That would be good for him.)

Midway through her letter writing, there was a firm knock on the door, followed by, "Hannah!"

"What?"

"Go along to the singin'. You know Rebecca Lapp."

"Is she there?"

"Usually."

"I don't have anything to wear."

"Yes, you do. What's wrong with what you wore to church?"

Silence.

"Come on, Hannah. You have an hour to get ready."

"Who else is going?"

"Open the door."

Hannah slipped the paper and pencil into a drawer, then unlocked the door, peering around it to find Ben in the dim light of the long hallway.

"What?"

"I think you should try being part of our group.

Give *rumschpringa* a fair chance. Come on. You shouldn't lock yourself away from the world we live in. You can't go back, not for your mother's sake, Hannah."

"No one talks to me."

"Not with that expression on your face."

"What expression?"

"You know. Mad. You're plain mad."

"No, I'm not."

"Come on. I'm leaving at seven. Get ready."

With that, he left, but Hannah could tell he genuinely wanted her company, which was something, wasn't it? But still . . .

Torn, Hannah wallowed in indecision. It would be so much easier to return to the West if she could alienate herself successfully. Why try and enter the world of *rumschpringa*? What was in it for her? She didn't need the company of other young girls, did she? They talked about stupid things that held absolutely no interest for her. They giggled and laughed and simpered about things she didn't think were one bit funny. They were just plain dumb.

She didn't like the way they all had the same goal. Getting married. Finding a suitable young man and getting married. It was considered the highest honor, the ultimate destination.

Hannah couldn't understand that very well. She wanted to get back to the homestead, learn to rope and ride, install a windmill and a tank, run the best herd of cows for miles around. Her and Manny.

It was all right, this bit of excitement with Clay. He was someone to talk to and admire. But what she wanted from him was certainly not marriage. She wanted his experience, his knowledge of the West, the cows, all of it. This kissing thing wasn't anything. She had no plans of falling in love, which was a term that hung on the edges of idiocy.

What all that love thing entailed, she had no idea. She wasn't about to be trapped, like a groundhog in the steel-toothed jaws of a rusty old trap like Manny used to set on the edge of the cornfields. Anyone who was smart could plainly see what marriage brought. Look at Mam. She had no life. She gave her life to her husband, and to God, and look where she landed. No, this thing of giving your whole life and will to a man— incompetent creatures, half of them—was for the birds.

Then for a fleeting instant, she heard her mother's beautiful voice and saw her happy, serene face as she sang to Abby in the crude house, rocking in the armless rocking chair that had ridden in the covered wagon, the whole way out there. Was there a peace, an underlying happiness that blossomed like a rare and beautiful flower after you did the unthinkable— surrendered your own will?

Hannah's own will, getting out of life what she

wanted, was what made her happy, so there. She wasn't like Mam.

She did get dressed, then, in her own haphazard, slipshod way, her dark hair sliding out the back of her covering, loose strands on her forehead, her apron crooked, too low in the back, too tight.

She kept the brick wall of belligerence firmly around herself. She thought that if Ben wanted to drag her to the singing, he wasn't going to be rewarded with a different person.

The home where the hymn singing was held was a typical Amish farm, with a white house and barn, a cow stable, corn crib, outbuildings that housed chickens and pigs, and some horse-drawn farm equipment. Dusk was falling, enveloping the farm's perfection in a glow of sunset, before the mist of twilight set in.

The thought of being married, gardening, milking cows, having a dozen children, living in this congested valley of rich soil and expectations, set Hannah's teeth on edge.

"Now what am I supposed to do?" she asked Ben, after he had pulled up to the farm, surrounded by other open seated buggies and horses being led to the forebay of the barn. Groups of young men stood around wearing colorful, long-sleeved shirts with black vests and trousers, black hats set at rakish angles, pretending they didn't know she sat in Ben Stoltzfus's buggy like an oddity.

Ben hopped off the buggy, told her to go into the house and look for someone she knew. Rebecca Lapp would likely be there.

Wishing she hadn't come, or could go sit in a cornfield until this dreadful singing was over, she climbed off the buggy, walked across the driveway and up the sidewalk to the house, carrying herself as if the chip on her shoulder was more important than anything else.

It didn't get any easier once she was inside. The kettle house was lined with girls of every description, the only difference being the absence of white capes and aprons, which were worn only to church. Now they all wore capes that matched their dresses, with black belted aprons around their waists. A colorful gaggle of hopeful geese, she thought.

A dark-haired girl stepped forward, proffered her hand, gripped Hannah's, and said, "Welcome. Are you Mose Detweiler's daughter?"

Hannah nodded, her reserve masking any relief she may have felt.

"I'm Katie Esh. We used to be in the same church when you still lived here in Lancaster. Remember Simon Eshes?"

Hannah nodded.

"I'm sorry to hear about your father?" The sentence was spoken as a question.

Probably wonders if I'm sorry he died, knowing he failed at farming and then did something as despicable as that whiskey thing with the leftover grain.

"Yeah, well, things happen." She didn't need to know more than that. The poverty, the homestead, the crude house, was all hundreds of miles away, hidden from their scrutiny, so that was the end of the conversation.

Rebecca Lapp found her and set up a hysterical giggle of greeting that chafed Hannah like an ill-fitting shoe. Held to Rebecca by duty and good manners, they exchanged news of the past year, insipid words like dandelion fluff blown on a stiff breeze.

What did Hannah care about her job picking produce on their farm? If she wanted to break her back picking strawberries and beans under the hot sun in the humidity of Lancaster County, it was none of Hannah's business, or her interest. So that conversation melted away as well.

Relieved to be sitting at the long table made of church benches on wooden racks built for that purpose, opening the thick, black *Ausbund*, the book of old German hymns written by their ancestors in the prison in Switzerland, in Passau, to be exact, where they were imprisoned for their Christian faith.

That's what happened to history, Hannah thought. Way back then, the Amish were persecuted, hunted for their beliefs, and thrown into prison for believing on the Lord Jesus. They were real Christians, saintly in their martyrdom, tortured and burned at the stake, their passage into Heaven secured by their unshakable long-suffering faith.

Now, through many reprints of this very same book, these songs remained in use at every hymn singing, every church service, still honored and loved. But so much had changed since then.

Prosperity in America had directed the Amish down a new path of farming, building, other thriving businesses, and the *Ausbund* was no longer understood and revered the way it was hundreds of years ago. As is the way of all people, one slowly gets off track from the devotion of these writers, composing in dank prisons. God was everything then. God was all they had.

Very nearly, Hannah could identify with their forefathers. Her family surely hadn't had much more, there in North Dakota. Plus, her father had held true faith and a real belief that God would look after—*fa-sark*—them all.

Had God done that? Had her father given his life for his faith? Or was the generosity of the Jenkinses and the Rochers the only thing that pulled them through? Was everyone too blind to see the real part of life?

The sacks of flour, cornmeal, and the other provisions she toted home from the town of Pine were real; they didn't fall from the sky like manna for the children of Israel. They were given by the generosity of an English person, an *ausricha*. Her father had eaten the corn pone like a starved person, lifting the spoon rapidly, convinced his fasting and prayer had secured it. Pensive, her lips in a tight line, without joining the singing, Hannah sat along the table with dozens of other girls, like a mystery.

The young men filed in, hatless now, their hair combed very carefully, parted in the middle, hanging loosely halfway down over their ears, cut round in the back. The collars of their purple, green, and blue shirts were closed according to the rules set for men's clothing. Their rich baritones enhanced the girls' voices, until the room was filled with a beautiful cadence.

Later, the wild boys filed in, seated themselves along the benches in the back against the wall. Their hair was combed up over their ears, bangs fluffed and combed sideways, shirt collars hanging open, a few in short sleeves. They slouched against the wall, talking to each other, laughing, openly having a great time, disregarding the watchful eyes of the gray-bearded elders in their presence.

They didn't hold Hannah's interest. She was curious, watching them with dark eyes that smoldered, her thoughts miles from this room, in North Dakota. Tall and upright, her wide shoulders in their usual position of defiance, her mouth closed and not singing, she bided her time, filling her thoughts with subjects that mattered.

The first youth that led the pack of *ungehorsam*—young men—was much older than the rest, Hannah could tell. He was scruffy looking, as if he hadn't shaved well. His hair was dark as midnight, as were his eyes. Big eyes, with lowered black brows and no smile. While the others carried on with their pinching and punching, he brooded.

Hannah noticed this all without a trace of interest, merely observing in passing his unhappy face.

His name was Jeremiah Riehl, and he was twenty-three years old this past March. His father could see no other alternative than to ask him to leave, not being able to raise a family of nine boys with his rebellious example like poison, spreading it around without fear of parental authority.

Like a weed in a field of young rye grass, he was torn out and disposed of, his father white-faced and grim, his mother dry-eyed and staunch, like a post shoring up his father's decision. A well-meaning relative took him in and regretted it later. The boy had no scruples, no conscience. He ran with the town boys, got drunk, drove a car, returned to his relative's house to eat and sleep and sneer in his face.

But years of patience paid off. The relative's wife wrote Bible verses on scented stationery, left them on his nightstand, loved him unconditionally, and saw through the veneer of evil rebellion. Here was a hurting child; here was a soft-hearted boy who sought his parents' approval in strange ways that neither understood.

The soft heart was coated with the steel of nonconformity and the need for vengeance. His saving grace was the relative's interest in good horses, the gift of a fine thoroughbred, presented with eyes blinking back tears, received with surprise, and resulting in the first chip in the coat of steel surrounding his heart.

By the age of twenty-two, he was known as Jerry, the horse dealer. He bought and sold horses trucked into Lancaster County and bred his own line of Standardbred road horses for the Amish and riding horses for the English.

He developed a keen eye for good horseflesh, inheriting his sense of business from his father and the drive to succeed from his steel-willed mother, who managed the house and surrounding gardens with an iron hand. Cuffed and pinched from the time he was a toddler in diapers, belted by his father for every misstep, his soft heart bruised, then broke, then covered itself with hard rebellion, taking a long and difficult journey beset with wrong choices.

Here he was, then, tempered by his difficult past, seeing in front of him the only girl who had ever held his glance.

He blinked, blinked again. His heart rate picked up considerably, his hands became sweaty, his breath shallow. Pride lowered his eyes, caution kept them glued to the thick book in his hand.

Eventually, he looked up. Like a wild, unkempt mustang she was. Untamed, her free spirit evident in the set of her shoulders, the set of her mouth. She was more than beautiful. She was like a vision. Her eyes were huge, set in her small, heart-shaped face. A perfect mouth. So different from the other girls, with that hair.

Who was she? Where had she come from?

When the other girls began their ridiculous water drinking and giggling, passing around hard candies and chewing gum, she merely sat without a trace or sign of interest. Obviously unhappy, she was like a tethered, untamed horse, pawing at the ground, resenting the halter and rope that held her to the singing table.

How long did the singing keep going? He had no idea. His whole world stopped, held by the vision of this mysterious girl in front of him. When his group of young men rose to leave the room, for the first time in his life he wanted to stay.

If he left, she might not be there when he returned. He had to know who she was. Always the last one to return for the remainder of the singing, he had to stay, talking, laughing, spending time outside, away from the parents and more obedient ones.

To hide the fact that he was eager to return, he was the last one in, now seated much farther away. When the cookies and popcorn were served, she rose from her seat on the bench and made her way to the door with Rebecca Lapp.

Tall. She was much taller than Rebecca. She moved like a princess, her head held high, gliding, not walking. She didn't speak to anyone. Quiet. She was a quiet girl.

Jerry did his best to hide his interest, now much more than a spark. A flame had begun, and he was swayed by his lack of power in the face of it. Inwardly he writhed helplessly as the sight of her hammered painfully at his efficiently armored heart. All of his failure and inability to please accosted him like a river of molten steel, ready to replace any sign of breaking away the coating that was already secured.

The cookies and popcorn passed through his hands unnoticed. "S' wrong with you, Jerry. Aren't you hungry?" Laughing, Jerry grabbed a cookie and bit off half of it. Oatmeal, like sawdust in his dry mouth.

She returned. He choked on the crumbling cookie. Laughter and backslapping. He looked up in time to see those large, black eyes on his own red, spluttering face, holding so much disapproval.

Then her eyes slid away with a lowering of her eyelids, an unconscious natural look that set his heart to its accelerated racing, as if it was not a part of him but a mere projection of his weakness.

So he stood in a dark corner of the yard and watched. It was Ben Stoltzfus who came to claim her for the ride home. His girlfriend from another county? There were Amish in Berks County, where they had originally settled when they emigrated from Switzerland.

Nonchalantly, on the outside, every sense honed for a response, Jerry dropped the question. "Ben after a woman?" He had to repeat himself, before anyone heard, the boisterous crowd rife with Sunday evening shenanigans, as usual.

"Naw, that's his niece."

Words like ambrosia. A sweet nectar sipped from the cup of promise. "Really? That's his niece?" He could have slapped little Amos when he snorted about all that happiness about only a niece. What was up with that?

So, he was more observant, but spoke nothing afterward. He watched Ben back his horse into the shafts, the tall girl holding them aloft, expertly lowering them, quickly fastening traces and britching. Ben said, "Better watch it, Hannah. He rears when he's riled up."

Hannah. That was her name.

"Want me to hold him?" Her voice was low, almost like a youth. Low and husky.

"Afraid you can't get in."

"I'll be all right."

And sure enough, the nervous horse rocked on prancing legs, gathered himself on his hind legs, ready to rear and come up on those muscular hind quarters to paw at the air with his front feet. But the girl was too quick. Without fear, she yanked down on the bit and said, "Hey. Oh, no you don't." She stood her ground like a soldier.

Jerry knew expert horsemanship when he saw it. His chest felt constricted, choked with emotion.

The horse stood, recognizing her fearless command.

"Get in!" Ben called.

"I will when I'm ready. He needs to learn to stand." By this time a crowd had gathered. Hannah was oblivious. She held firm to the bit, stroked the horse's white blaze, and murmured something.

Someone called out, "He's not a dog! He'll come up the minute you stop that, you know."

She never bothered answering. Jerry watched as she slowly loosened her hold on the bit and said, "Whoa," firmly, then walked to the buggy step and climbed in without hurrying.

Ben lifted the reins, and in a flying leap they were off in a spray of gravel, the light courting buggy swaying, fishtailing, righting itself before disappearing into the dark night.

They rode through the warm summer night at a fast clip, the humid air turning Hannah's *schtrubles* into curls, moistening her skin, and ruining the crisp white organdy of her covering.

Ben whistled, enjoying the fast trot of one of his best horses, thinking of a perfect time to ask Rebecca Lapp for their first date. He already planned on Hannah helping him out, which was the real reason he had urged her to go to the singing with him in the first place.

"My covering is ruined," Hannah lamented.

"The other girls wear bonnets. That protects them from the damp night air."

"I hate bonnets. They smash your covering worse than the night air."

"Really? I wouldn't know."

"I guess not. You don't normally wear one."

They laughed. Ben thought she had an attractive laugh, deep and genuine. Too bad no one hardly ever heard it.

Then Ben said, "Hey, go along to Stephen Zook's on Saturday evening. There's a hoedown in their barn."

Hannah's voice caught, faltered. "I don't know. I don't know how to play."

"You don't have to. You can sit and watch."

Hannah shook her head. "Probably not. You know I don't have much interest here. I will be going back to the homestead as soon as I can. I have no intention of letting those 320 acres go to waste."

"But Hannah, you have to think reasonably.

Your mother will never want to go back. How can you think of going, with or without her? Give up those acres of land. You can't do it."

"Manny and I could."

"How?"

"Cattle. A windmill. Horses. Ben, the land is free! Think of it. Free! All it takes is a bit of guts to get started. Once those cattle get going, we'll be rich. Acres and acres of free grass. You know we don't have a penny. If we stay here, we'll be sponging off grandfather for the rest of our lives. Or I'll be slaving in produce fields, teaching school to a bunch of snot-nosed little kids who don't listen to the teacher. I don't want to get married like everyone else. I'd be tied to housework and diapers for the rest of my life. Besides, what if I end up with a genuine loser and have to live the way my mother always has?

"I'm going back, Ben, and no one will stop me. I'm different than most of the girls you know, so get over it."

CHAPTER 18

Hannah's grandfather approached her about getting a job. In September, picking was at its peak, and she could make good money picking tomatoes and lima beans at Uncle Henry's. He was concerned that Sarah didn't have enough to do, her grieving turning her into a thin, sorrowful person.

"It seems as if you do the biggest share of the work, which gives her too much time to sit and think. I don't believe this is good. Everyone has to move on, forget about themselves. Hard work is a good cure for grief. It is as the Lord intended. Besides, you need to think of footing some of your own expenses soon. It doesn't sit too well with the other children that I am your sole provider."

Hannah felt an instant surge of rebellion. "Oh, they don't think you should provide for your widowed daughter, do they? Well, then, I suppose I'd better get to work, huh?"

"Yes." Her grandfather failed to take the hint of sarcasm in Hannah's voice, merely accepted her response as a willingness to comply, went peacefully on his way with the two brown mules and the wagon, back to loading corn for silo filling, the heat of the day marking his straw

342

hat with a darker rim of perspiration around the crown, where the black band was tied with a knot.

Safely out of her grandfather's hearing, Hannah let loose with a volley of rebellious words like bullets pinging across the kitchen.

Sarah's face was pale, tired, and weary, despite a temporary bright spot of color on each cheek from the heat of the cook stove, where she was boiling tomato juice to make ketchup. Glass jars lined the countertop, scalded and sparkling clean. Mary was playing with Abby on the green marbled linoleum, pulling a small wooden duck by a string, the orange feet flapping rhythmically with each step. Abby laughed and waved her arms, then fell to one side, where she rolled, happily grabbing her bare feet. Mary giggled, then went to blow kisses on her little round belly.

Manny and Eli were helping the silo fillers, driving teams of horses while the men hoisted the heavy bundles of corn.

"Hannah, watch what you say."

"Why? No one can hear me. They're all just afraid Doddy is going to spend his money on us instead of stashing it away at the bank so that when he dies, they all get a nice check. Their inheritance. Greedy, greedy. Well, I have news for them. I'm not picking produce. I won't break my back so they can have more inheritance."

Sarah wiped the back of her hand across her forehead, then turned to sink onto a kitchen chair, hitching up her skirts only a bit, just enough to cool herself a little while remaining chaste.

"Hannah, you make me so tired. Why can't you do this for us? I know my sisters are right."

"What?" Hannah shrieked.

Sarah lifted confused eyes to her daughter's angry ones. "We can't be like a leech to my father's money."

"What about the church? Isn't that what alms are for? To keep the widows and orphans? The poor? Well, we qualify under poor and certainly widowed, so there you go."

"Hannah, listen to reason now. As long as we are able-bodied, we deserve to be employed, to make our own way. You can do this for us. Your father provided for us when he was alive, now it's your turn."

Without glancing at Hannah, she rose to her feet to stir the bubbling tomatoes on the hot stovetop.

"Well, Mam, if I have to be the breadwinner, then I'll do it my way. I'll make money all right, but it will not be here. I'm going back to the homestead, me and Manny."

Sarah gasped, a hand went to her chest. "You can't!"

"And why can't I?"

"You just can't, Hannah. We almost starved. The winter is coming."

"So? We have firewood."

344

"You know I don't ever want to leave Lancaster, my family, my church. My heart is here with my loved ones."

Hannah threw her argument like a knife. "What about Dat lying alone under the prairie sod? What about 320 acres of prime grassland to fatten cattle?"

Sarah moaned softly, began to weep, making small mewling sounds that failed to break Hannah's resolve.

Why couldn't her mother brace up and be her own person? Simpering through life depending on everyone else's judgment rankled Hannah, spreading thistles into her own fiery ambition, irritating her to the point of anger. "I'll work in the fields but Doddy Stoltzfus is not getting all my money. Some of it is mine. I'll save it for my train ticket. Mine and Manny's."

Up came her mother's face, followed by the sound of honking into her handkerchief. "Yours and Manny's? What makes you think he'll go with you? He's not like you. If I ask him to stay, he'll obey me."

Hannah had no answer to that. Sarah looked at the clock, gasped, and sent Hannah down to the cellar for potatoes. The silo fillers would be hungry, twelve men who had not eaten since their early breakfast.

Hannah washed and peeled potatoes, cut them in chunks, and put them on to boil, adding a stick of wood to the cook stove. "It's hot enough to fry an egg on the table," she grumbled.

"Be quiet. Hurry up and quit complaining," Sarah said roughly.

Hannah threw her an unapologetic look and fried the chunks of pork in lard, added salt and pepper, while her mother grated cabbage for pepper slaw. They boiled long yellow ears of corn, cooked navy beans that had been soaking all night and seasoned them with bacon and molasses, tomato juice and pepper. They sliced the red and succulent tomatoes in thick circles, and piled homemade bread on ironstone trays, with deep yellow churned butter and raspberry jam, in addition to applesauce and small green pickles.

For dessert there was chocolate cake, ground cherry pie, cornstarch pudding, and freshly sliced peaches sprinkled with sugar. Tall glasses of sweetened meadow tea acquired a sheen of moisture along the outside of each glass, the humidity soaking everything, man and beast alike.

Sarah wrinkled her nose as the men filed into the kettle house to wash up precisely on the dot of twelve o'clock. From noon until one o'clock, the men refueled themselves and their sweating horses.

"They stink!" Hannah hissed to her mother.

"Hush, they'll hear you."

She thought Ben and Elam's foot odor was unbearable. The smell was like cleaning the cow stable on a rainy day. She grimaced as she watched the long hair and ratty beards being sloshed with soapy water and dried on one towel for all twelve of them, their thin, short-sleeved shirts sticking to their backs with perspiration and dust. Ruddy faced and muscular, these husky men were used to manual labor, heat, and humidity, eagerly facing whatever came their way.

Silo filling was an event, a neighborhood get-together. Each farmer had his own silo, his own cornfields, but the work went so much better with a group, many horses and mules, the camaraderie of their neighbors a boost to everyone. Showing off their strength and tirelessness, they encountered plenty of friendly jokes and ribbing, especially the one who was perhaps a bit over confident.

Hannah served them with a minimum amount of breathing, especially when she refilled glasses of tea or retrieved empty serving dishes. She had a good notion to pinch a clothespin on her nose, but she was sure her grandfather would be mortified. Didn't these men ever bathe? They should be thrown into the watering trough.

Chewing with alacrity, talking around mouthfuls of mashed potatoes and gravy, wiping their hands on the tablecloth or, some of them, on their shirt fronts—it was the worst display of manners she'd ever seen.

Was this how the Jenkins men ate? She hadn't had too many instances to remember. She knew Harry Rocher did not talk around his food or wipe his hands on the tablecloth. But he was English, and they were fancier in their eating habits. Likely she had been accustomed to this behavior her whole life long; now grown up and having seen some of the world, she had a new perspective on scenes like this. She had no plans of becoming anyone's wife, ever, so her worry about cleanliness and table manners was unnecessary.

She wondered if the Jenkinses had received her letter. Would Abby be the only person to write back? Or would Clay send her a letter? And if he did, what would she make of it? There was an ocean of culture separating them. No matter how hard she tried to make it go away, to minimize its length and depth, it was there, inaccessible, uncrossable, without a deep and abiding pain that would cut into her mother's already grief-battered heart. There was no easy way out.

She served the chocolate cake and pudding, followed by the ground cherry pie, amid yells of approval, yellow-toothed smiles, gulps of tea thrown down throats with heads tilted back, and calls for more coffee.

Ephraim Hershberger watched the daughter of

Mose Detweiler and thought someone had their hands full with that one. Her expression was enough to pickle red beets, sour enough to curdle milk. She probably didn't want to live under her grandfather's direction, rebellion sticking out of her like porcupine quills. If she was his daughter, she'd be taught a thing or two.

To watch her response, he yelled out, "This coffee has grounds in it," followed by a brown, tobacco juice grin.

Hannah didn't skip a beat, pouring tea. Didn't look at him, either. "Shut up and eat them!"

A howl of delight from Emanuel Yoder. An intense look from her grandfather. A whispered, "Hannah!" from the pale-faced widow, Sarah.

Washing dishes with fury, spraying water and soapsuds across the linoleum, Hannah silently took her mother's admonishing, listening wearily as she quoted scripture about the virtues of a good woman.

"Hannah, you are choosing to be prickly. You are choosing to go through life irritated by the slightest thing, caused by your inability to give up. Such a flagrant display of disrespect, Hannah. It isn't funny."

"One of the men thought so."

"Your grandfather didn't. Your punishment will be to stay home from any of the *youngie ihr rumschpringas* this Sunday."

"That's not much of a punishment. I don't want to be with the *youngie*."

. . .

So that was the reason Jeremiah Riehl searched the barn floor most of the evening, the harmonicas' lilting tones setting the dancers' feet flying across the oak floor of the gigantic bay between two others filled with hay.

She wasn't there. All evening, he kept up his hope, until at midnight he finally gave in and went in search of Ben Stoltzfus, who was about to leave, in a sour mood himself, having lost his main ally when Hannah refused to accompany him to the hoedown.

"Going home already?" was his way of greeting Ben.

"Yeah. It's late."

"Need help?"

"With what?"

"That horse."

"I'm not driving him."

"Oh." Then, "where's your niece this evening?"

"You mean Hannah? I couldn't persuade her to come with me."

Without sounding disappointed or interested, Jerry let it go, changing the subject to the horse he had for sale, if any of his brothers needed a sound driving horse. They exchanged pleasantries the way two well-brought-up young men would, before Jerry asked how come Hannah had never joined the group of young men and women before this.

"Her dad is Mose Detweiler. Was Mose Detweiler. He was killed."

"Oh, that guy. Moved out West. Where was it? Montana?"

"No, North Dakota."

"Yeah, I heard about that. Sort of different, wasn't he?"

"Hannah's like him. She doesn't want to be here. Says she's going back. They're homesteaders, or were before he died. She's determined to keep those 320 acres. She'll break her mother, you watch, and her fifteen-year-old brother. She wants a windmill and a herd of cows. Dry as a desert out there. No other Amish. Got a mind of her own."

Jerry let it go at that, grateful for that bit of information. His interest only increased. He vowed to make her acquaintance, somehow, before she left. He could do no more than wait and hope she'd show up.

He could never drive up to the Samuel Stoltzfus farm and ask to speak to her; the culture in which they lived completely forbade it. All matters of the heart were conducted in secret and never mentioned until long after a couple had actually begun seeing each other. It would be considered brash beyond reason to approach a young woman in the light of day, let alone on the home farmstead.

He figured he'd been patient before, he could

be again. He turned and went back to the lively sounds of the Saturday night hoedown that suddenly appeared drab and colorless.

Hannah stayed true to her word and began picking tomatoes on Monday morning. A fine mist settled across the tomato field as she picked up the first wooden crate of the day, bent her back, and began to find the ripened fruit under the prickly stalks.

All morning Hannah's back stayed bent as the late-summer sun burned off the mist and she continued to pick tomatoes. The backs of her legs ached, then her lower back. She stood up, stretched, rubbed her back, then bent over and threw more tomatoes in the crate. Teams of Belgian horses pulled flatbed wagons across the level fields and hauled the loaded crates to the cannery.

She became aware of a shadow crossing ahead of her, looking up to find the farm's owner, Daniel Lantz, standing in front of her with his arms crossed. Tall and wiry, his beard like a stiff, brown brush, his straw hat creased and worn, he drew his eyebrows down across his small brown eyes and said, "I've been watching you."

Hannah was hot and aching with fatigue, her mood at a genuine low, wishing she'd brought a jug of water. Her throat was so dry she could not have swallowed her saliva if there was any available.

She glared at him and thought, what a scarecrow.

"You're throwing the tomatoes. You'll bruise them. You need to place them in the crate, not throw them."

"Is that right?"

Taken aback, Daniel opened his mouth and closed it again. "I was just saying, if the skin of the tomato breaks, it makes a real mess on the bed of the wagon. You just need to be more careful in the future."

Hannah stood in the warmth of the sun and glared at him with so much dislike that he felt as if he was in the presence of danger. Turning on his heel, he left without a backward glance.

Hannah picked tomatoes for awhile longer, filled the last crate, and stalked out of the tomato patch with her head held high, her shoulders erect, and never returned.

She refused her mother's pleas, Manny's embarrassment and obedience, and said she'd do anything else to earn money, but she was not picking tomatoes for that picky stick man.

So Sarah had to go to her sister's quilting and answer their questions truthfully, saying no, Hannah hadn't yet found a job, leaving out any information where Daniel Lantz and his tomato picking was concerned. Often ashamed of Hannah's belligerence—where did it come from?—she found it only increased here in

Lancaster County among so many friends and relatives.

Rachel drew her eyebrows as if made from elastic. "But, Sarah, you need to take that girl in hand. She is one *ungehorsam* girl. You can tell by the way she walks, so stiff and unfriendly."

Yes, yes, Sarah knew. She knew. But a mother's feathers are often ruffled by being admonished about her own children, and Sarah was no exception.

Who was Rachel to speak? That little Samuel of hers had been expelled from school in eighth grade. Annie told her that, and here sat Rachel, all high and mighty, telling her where she was going wrong with Hannah.

But being the cowed, humble person she was, Sarah agreed with Rachel outwardly, nodded her head, and said times were hard during this Depression, but they would keep trying. She told them about Hannah working in Harry Rocher's store in the town of Pine, thinking they would approve, but she was met with cold stares of disapproval for allowing Hannah to stay the night at an Englisher's house.

Sarah bent her head over the quilt, wondering how she could possibly have missed this quarrelsome bunch of women. Their disapproval was like a kick in the stomach, taking all the life's breath from her, leaving her bewildered and alone. How could any of them understand being poor to the point of desperation? Yes, times were hard, they knew, but not to the extent that Sarah did. They had no idea of the panic of scrabbling a tin scoop around in an almost empty sack of cornmeal, of children who went to bed hungry. Yes, hungry. To admit that even to herself brought back the cold fear of actually having to starve. Or crawl to the neighbors.

Perplexed, bewildered, Sarah stayed quiet, kept her peace. She could not keep thoughts of pity from crowding out the love she sought to keep. Yes, it was pity for herself, perhaps, but in the face of this cold-hearted onslaught of not understanding, the blatant unfairness was like a slap. Jesus said the poor would always be among us. Every fair-minded Christian, surely including her own sisters, recognized the poor and gave what was available.

"You don't have much to say, Sarah." This from Rachel and Emma, well fed, their crisp white coverings pulled over the oiled hair combed severely, so perfectly obeying the laws of the church, outwardly at least. Respected and well-liked, a beacon of shining examples by the way they dressed, they hid their refusal to accept Sarah's plight well beneath their wide black capes.

Sarah merely shook her head, her mouth unsteady with the tears so close to the surface. Lydia eyed her sharply.

"Did we hurt your feelings about Hannah?

Well, I do feel sorry for you, but you know we're right. You do need to take her in hand."

"How?" Sarah burst out, so out of character, this meek and quiet sister defending herself with one harsh word. Down came the eyebrows, everyone's attention grabbed effectively. "Tell me how," Sarah said harshly.

"How did she get like that in the first place?" Emma wanted to know.

Sarah shook her head. She had always been like that. *Vonn glaynem uf.* Since she was small, she had been obstinate, her will unbreakable. Nothing fazed her; fear was not in her vocabulary. Had the move to the West only worsened the nature she had been given at birth?

"Nothing like hard work to break that stiff will," Rachel began. "Uncle Jake's Suvilla got in her head she wasn't going to be *gehorsam* and he sent her to his brother Sam's, as *maud*. They had the twelve children in fourteen years, milked twenty cows by hand, and grew strawberries. She was busy from four in the morning until nine at night. Really did the trick. She was glad to go home, glad to help her mother after a few years of Uncle Jake's wife, Lomie."

Rachel chuckled, comfortable from her viewpoint on the self-appointed tower on which she had hoisted herself by her own opinions.

"Isn't Suvilla the one with mental problems?" Sarah asked, quietly.

"I guess she does have some affliction of the mind, but only because she won't give up. The devil has plenty of room to stay as long as that will isn't broken."

Emma nodded, pulled a long thread through the quilt top, then dipped her head for another round of pushing her needle up and down to create tiny, even stitches on the nine patch Rachel had pieced from scraps.

"That's what Hannah needs to do," Lydia said, staring at Sarah.

Sarah laughed outright, a sound that came from her throat without intention. "She wouldn't go. You don't realize, you cannot make Hannah do anything."

"Oh, really?" Rachel's voice dripped with disbelief and something close to mockery. "That sounds more like an excuse than anything else. Mothers that do that—stand by their children when they know full well they are in the wrong—will only suffer sorrow and heartache down the road."

Sarah bent her head to the quilt, incredulous. Her own sisters. Her blood relatives. It seemed to her as if the dearest to her heart, the ones she had missed most, had turned into coldhearted stone objects she no longer recognized.

Was it their mother's passing? Was it grief that caused them to become sisters with attitudes so alien to Sarah's remembrance? Compassion had been shelved, for one thing. They were perfect, in their own eyes. "Oh God," Sarah cried silently. "Have I experienced a time of awakening in North Dakota and returned to find myself changed? Or has the Depression done this to us, to them?" Well she remembered the openhearted giving, the jars of honey and preserves, and the pieced baby quilt when Hannah was born. They had done her peach canning, her applesauce, gaily coming and going in their dusty buggies pulled by spirited horses, fussing and clucking about their sister's first baby, Hannah.

Emma gave days of her time, getting her started on making little broadfall-type trousers for Manny and pinafore-style aprons for Hannah. She only remembered her sisters as kind and loving. She had spent days dreaming of her return, of being taken back into their generosity, of their open arms waiting to receive her, and of their listening as she spoke of the journey.

Oh, they had been sympathetic. They cried and wiped tears, discreet in their grief, reserved as was the Amish custom. But this coldhearted judgment of Hannah? The admonishing about being under her father's care?

This she could not grasp. Was it greed? A tight-fisted lust for money? Surely they had not fallen so far away from what God intended his Christian church to be.

Sarah searched her own soul as she sat quilting, smiling acknowledgment when necessary, joining softly into the conversation when it was expected of her. She filled her plate with unimaginable food, the serving dishes piled high with parsley potatoes, serving platters of fried chicken and stewed tomatoes and dumplings. Yes, times were hard, jobs hard to come by, scrimp and save and make do. With this food so plentiful?

Mentally, Sarah shook her head in wonder. She didn't care if she never saw another cup of cornmeal as long as she lived, but this thought she did not share with her sisters. They would blame Mose and bring up the whole shame of their past. Then start in about Hannah.

No, best to let it go. And she did, to the best of her ability. But that night, alone in the comfortable bed, where Mose's pillow lay untouched beside her, she cried. She talked to God. She asked Him for guidance. There was the monumental problem of Hannah. Should she take Rachel's advice? Make her go work for a stranger? How would she do that?

She knew there was no way to force Hannah to do anything. To return to North Dakota was like facing a giant beast and its open, slavering jaws ready to devour her. She quaked with a lack of courage. She knew her own cowardice. To again be subject to that kind of desperation was simply unbearable.

To stay, living with Hannah's powerful rebellion, was another beast, almost as fearsome.

Give her time, some said. But Sarah knew. She knew Hannah would not bend. She would never forget the 320 acres of land, her strong love for the plains, the freedom of the wind and the swaying grass, the horses and yes, likely Clay Jenkins was at the back of all the rest of it.

So what if she made the sacrifice to return for Hannah's sake? Should mothers sacrifice for their children?

Sarah wasn't sure that going back to the prairie would only send her daughter back to Clay, an *Englisha mon*. She would leave the faith, leave everything she had ever been taught.

The next day, Sarah had a long talk with her father. She poured out her heart to her remaining parent, who listened attentively and recognized the problem for what it was, not what he wanted it to be.

Wise, aged, experienced, he pondered Sarah's plight, then went off to drive the corn binder in the late September sun.

CHAPTER 19

Hannah was lost. Low scudding clouds threatened a serious downpour. She was in Elam's open courting buggy, by herself, and had already taken a few wrong turns. Fred, the bay driving horse, was exhausted, his head lowered, his sides heaving, leaving Hannah in a mild state of panic. Justifying herself by blaming the stupid Lancaster County roads, she stopped the horse, which happily obeyed, and looked around her.

That was strange. There was a fairly high ridge, or at least a small mountain, to the left of her. All of Lancaster County spread out to the right, the woods, green fields and brown ones, dotted with white houses and barns, cement silos, and fences. Hannah snorted with impatience after acknowledging that she simply didn't know where she was.

Well, she couldn't drive Fred up that hill, he'd likely die. So she guessed she'd have to turn around and ask someone. The thought of actually driving into a strange place to ask for directions was irritating, but the only smart thing to do.

"Git up, Fred." Slowly, he complied, lifting his weary head and starting back the way he'd come.

Hannah had heard through a friend, Lydia, that there was a job available at a feed store, weighing corn, measuring and mixing feed, and waiting on customers. She was told it was about ten miles away, in Georgetown. She thought she'd already gone farther than that. Mam had wanted her to use the neighbor's telephone, but she despised that contraption. Dialing made her nervous, always afraid she'd put her finger in the wrong circle. Then, when she did hear a voice, it was crackly and unintelligible.

Against her mother's wishes, she left early, despite her grandfather's warnings that it would likely commence raining. She told him if it rained she had an umbrella, laughed off his warning of driving a horse and holding an umbrella at the same time.

So here she was, caught in a very sudden and serious downpour, digging around under the seat for the large black umbrella while holding on to both reins with one hand. Large drops of cold rain splattered on her back. She pulled on the reins and stopped Fred under the overhanging boughs of a large tree, thinking it would afford a bit of protection, which it did not, large drops falling off the swaying leaves.

This was a fine mess. She decided the best course of action was to turn into the drive leading to the closest farm, seeing the way the wind was getting up. The house was built of brick, the barn white, with the usual huddle of maple trees around the yard, the clean barnyard and well-kept grass surrounding everything.

No one was about when she stopped by the hitching rack. Feeling foolish, she quickly hopped off the buggy, her white organdy covering already clinging to her head by the force of the rain. She eyed the house, then the forebay of the barn.

Should she pull up to the watering trough, get her horse and buggy out of the rain? Would that be too bold?

"Hey!"

She turned to find a man standing just inside the wide door of the forebay, beckoning her with his right hand.

"Better get in out of the rain."

Sheepishly, she led her tired, dripping horse to the watering trough, looking to thank the man who had allowed her to get out of the cold rain.

"You're pretty wet," he observed.

No beard. Single. Hmm. Hannah observed this in one swift glance, her dark eyes fringed with wet lashes, her covering thoroughly drenched, her dress clinging to her with no coat for warmth.

"Who are you?" she said, quick and to the point, as always.

"You can call me Jerry."

"Jerry? That's different."

"Why don't you unhitch?" He almost added, "Hannah." It was her. It was. He felt as if a rainbow had descended out of the gray, wind-driven clouds and produced a miracle. A very wet and obviously irritated miracle!

"How did you get yourself into this predic-ament?" he asked, grinning at her across the horse's back, working loose the snap that held the britching to the shaft.

Her eyes flashed. "Looking for a feed mill, if you have to know."

"Whereabouts?"

"They said Georgetown, but there's an awful hill. Growing up here, I never realized that mountain was there."

"May I ask who you are?" As if he didn't know.

"I'm Hannah. Mose Detweiler was my father. He died in North Dakota."

"I heard about that."

"You did?"

"Yeah."

What else had he heard? All the stupidity associated with her family? She said nothing as they unhitched Fred. Jerry took the horse to a stall and gave him some feed and hay. Hannah wanted to follow, taking notice of the long middle aisle with stalls on either side. This was obviously one huge horse barn, housing more horses than the average.

She thought of the thin-necked, pot-bellied, long-haired nags of North Dakota, fed on grass and water, wherever they could find it, branded like cattle, half of them as wild as deer. She wondered what Clay would say about some of these horses' heads appearing above wooden half-doors.

Hannah was intrigued but too proud to move down the aisle and gawk like some poor beggar. Which she was.

"I am a horse dealer," he offered.

"Mm." Feigning disinterest, Hannah walked over to the barn door, her arms crossed about her waist. She was cold but determined he wouldn't see her shiver.

He thought about asking her into the house for lunch, which was where the rest of the family had gone, but he couldn't bring himself to do it. He wanted to keep her here, in the forebay, lit magically by her presence.

"Would you like to see the horses?"

"I could, I guess." She turned and led the way. He noticed she was almost as tall as he was and that her covering really was ruined by the rain. She could have worn a torn rag on her head and she still would have been the most beautiful girl he had ever seen or imagined.

"This is Duke."

"Hm. High and mighty name."

"He's a high and mighty horse."

She turned to look at him, her eyes wide. "Is he really?"

"Yes, he is. The best. His offspring are amazing. I can get hundreds of dollars for a foal."

Intimidated, Hannah didn't answer. From one stall door to another, she viewed black or brown horses, mostly for driving, sold to Amish men who knew a good horse with plenty of stamina when they saw one. She was quiet, unafraid to reach out and stroke foreheads, to cup a hand below a mouth. She was used to being around horses.

He was so full of questions, and so afraid to ask them.

They returned to the door of the forebay, watched it rain. Her hair was as glossy and black as her eyes, her profile like a princess. She was cold. She rubbed her hands across her bare arms, her voice shook.

"Are you cold?" he asked.

Immediately she snapped, "No!"

"We could go inside and get something warm to eat. Coffee."

"No."

Relieved, he asked how far she had to return.

"I don't know. Far."

"How will you get home? It doesn't appear to be letting up anytime soon."

"I'll wait."

And you'll be out here tomorrow morning, he thought. But he didn't say it. This girl was not the normal Amish type of girl. She was unfriendly, barbed. Quickly, before his uncle and nephews returned from the house, he said, "So, how was it, living in North Dakota?"

She shrugged, then turned to look at him and saw his friendliness, the dark light of genuine caring, and something else she couldn't name.

She saw that he wanted to know, though, and not only for the wrong reasons.

"It was a lot different. Wild. Windy. Nobody around. We almost starved. My father was, well, not too capable. We lived like destitute people. It was scary. Dat tried planting corn, but it shriveled up in the hot sun. We didn't have a windmill like the other ranchers. We didn't have cattle. One of our horses died."

Hannah waved a hand, as if to dismiss the whole telling. "I'm going back. I hate it here. We have 320 acres of land from the government. All we have to do is live on it for ten years. Prove our claim. I'll make a go of it. We have two young cows and one old, mad cow, the one that killed my father."

Soberly, Jerry nodded his head. "Heard about that."

"Dat didn't fit to the West. He was a dreamer. He thought if he planted corn some God-given cloud would float above it and dump rain on it." She looked wide-eyed with surprise when he laughed, genuinely laughed, loud and long.

"You're not very reverent about your poor father."

"Well." Then, "It doesn't rain out there. Drought is common. The cattle roam around, branded, so the ranchers know which cows they own. I want to learn to ride and rope, have my own cattle. But my mother . . ."

She stopped. "I shouldn't be telling you this."

"Why?"

"I don't know. I just shouldn't. Who are you anyway?"

"My name is Jeremiah Riehl."

"And?"

"I live here with my uncle. My past is nothing to be proud of."

"What did you do? Kill someone, or what?" She was surprised again when he laughed like before.

"My dad and I had a fight. We didn't get along. My fault, a lot of it."

Instead of a suitable comment, she changed the subject back to North Dakota. "You should see the horses in the West. Some of them, well, most of them, are as ugly as goats. Tough, rangy, pot-bellied mustangs that can go twenty miles without breathing hard. Like the people. If it wouldn't have been for the Jenkins family, we'd probably all have starved to death."

Jerry glanced at her sharply. He felt his own bitterness in the word "starved." He didn't doubt for a minute that she would go back and continue to make choices driven by her unforgiveness, much the same way he had.

"How will you go back?"

"I don't know. I can't go back without money this time. I was on my way to Georgetown for a job at a feed mill. I have to save some money before I can go back. I'm thinking maybe my grandfather will allow me to take a loan. The Jenkinses are keeping the horses and three cows. We need a better well and some way of pumping water out of it, likely a windmill. The creek is probably dry by now."

Her speech was laced with passion, her planning shone in the intensity of her eyes, her hands moving in agitation. Jerry watched her face like a man hypnotized. He thought, *How could this girl survive in the West with all the uncouth characters, the claim jumpers, the cattle thieves, and the law sometimes helpless?* He saw the challenge and accepted the unreality of her plans. She would not stay in Lancaster County.

They went into the house and Becky served them bowls of steaming vegetable soup, slices of homemade bread, and apple butter. The fire in the cook stove felt so good that Hannah chose the chair closest to the heat, bent her head, and ate hungrily, the way a person who remembers an empty stomach does.

Becky knew enough to stay quiet, watching Jerry. Hmm. Shook up, he was.

When Hannah had finished her soup, she pushed the bowl away and began spreading apple butter on a slice of bread, her actions deliberate and concentrated. Jerry noticed the length of her fingers, the long, slim hands and arms. He pretended to eat, more than what he was actually hungry for.

"Well, if you don't want to drive your horse across the ridge to Georgetown, I could probably take you in the *doch-veggley*."

Hannah looked up from spreading the apple butter. "No."

Jerry raise his eyebrows and swallowed the retort that came naturally.

"I don't want the job. I'd have to drive a horse over that ridge every day from my grandfather's farm. I won't do that."

She pushed her chair back, surveyed the kitchen, the children around the table, and the window above the sink where the rain splattered and ran down in slices. "I'll let Fred rest awhile and eat something. Then I'll be on my way."

"Not in this rain," Jerry protested.

"I won't melt."

Becky didn't doubt for a minute she wouldn't melt. Like a stone, this one. "Would you like to borrow my bonnet?" she ventured kindly.

Hannah reached up to touch her ruined white covering. "Wouldn't help much now."

No smile, no appreciation for the offer. She rose, tall and slender, raised her hands to the heat of the cook stove and said firmly, "*Denke* for the soup. I'll be on my way."

Jerry opened his mouth, closed it again. He followed her out and helped her hitch up Fred, all the words he wanted to say crowding his chest. He watched helplessly as she sprang onto the buggy, pulled up the sodden gum blanket, lifted the reins, and looked at him.

"I'll be all right. A little rain never hurt anyone. My father would have given anything for a few drops of this to save his field of corn."

He had to say it. "Don't go back. Don't go without letting me know when you're leaving."

"Why would you have to know?"

"I would be worried, I guess." What an impotent answer! A limp, pathetic version of the desperate plea he felt in his heart, his whole being straining to keep her from making the same mistake her father had made.

"Yeah, well, that's nice of you, but I'm going. Somehow, I'll raise the money."

He didn't doubt she would do just that. The only comfort he could take with him after that was the length of time her eyes stayed on his, the amount of softening that took place in her hard, black gaze.

She drove out of the forebay into the driving rain without looking back or saying goodbye.

She came down with a terrible fever and sore throat. Her chest was filled with infection, her breathing came in short gasps, and her face was flushed and hot. The doctor was summoned from Lancaster, who pronounced her ill with double pneumonia in her lungs. He left medicines and pills and came back twice, begging Sarah and

Hannah's grandfather to put her in the hospital.

Oh, never. The cost was much too high. Sarah tried every remedy she knew. She summoned her sisters, who came and stood over Hannah's bed like flapping crows, their voices hurting her head. She turned her face away, refused to open her eyes, willing them out of the house.

Onions. Raw, boiled, fried, slapped on her chest sizzling hot. Time after time, Hannah raked the stinking poultice off her chest and slammed it on the floor beside her bed, gasping for breath from the little effort it took to move her left arm.

Sarah steeped comfrey leaves in boiling water, added honey, and brought the cup to Hannah's papery lips, which was all she could do. Hannah refused to swallow the vile stuff.

Rachel said mustard and Echinacea poultices would be good. Emma suggested burdock root tea, which Sarah knew would not get past those clamped lips. They applied burdock leaves on her chest, hot and steaming, but odorless, which Hannah accepted. She fell asleep after that, resting deeply.

Back in the kitchen, Sarah shook her head at her worried sisters, taking their concern as a token of the love she had remembered, the love she held to her heart when she journeyed west with Mose.

"She'll likely get better," Emma commented.

"I would think so. Who is going to pay the

doctor? He's been here how many times? Likely it will fall on Dat's shoulders." This from Rachel, shaking her head with long sighs of resignation.

Sarah assured Rachel she would do everything in her power to repay her father, who had already done more than enough. When Hannah recovered, she'd get a job, they'd see to it. Manny was already a big help to Elam and Ben. Hannah had been on her way to apply for a job at Rohrer's Mill when she had gotten caught in the rain.

"Rohrer's Mill?" Emma shrieked.

"What in the world, Sarah?" Rachel gasped. "A girl like Hannah working at a feed mill with all those men. That wouldn't be fitting. I would not let my daughter within a mile of that place. But then, you can't control Hannah the way I can handle Susie and Fannie."

Sarah nodded agreeably. This was true. She couldn't. But Hannah was not the type to like men. She was wooed reluctantly by Clay Jenkins. Wouldn't these sisters have a fit if they knew?

Suddenly, the need to stand up for herself was so strong it was like bile in her throat. Sarah coughed and cleared the passageway for the words that had lain dormant too long.

"Hannah could handle the job at the feed mill. She doesn't like men as a rule. She could hardly serve the table of silo fillers. I would trust her completely. She is a determined girl, but if it can be directed in the right way, she will be a talented young woman someday."

Her sisters stared at her, openmouthed. "Now you're taking up for her. I'm surprised at you, Sarah."

"Since I've said that, I'll say more. I will not stay here with Dat. Everyone in the family resents our living off his charity, which is understandable on your part. My decision is made. I will ask Dat for a loan to return, start our herd, and with God's help, we will prosper on the claim of 320 acres. Mose lies under the North Dakota soil, and I know now, that is where I want to be. He loved me in a way none of you could ever know.

"Your love is buried beneath your greed and avarice. All you know is to get ahead, pay off your farm, and snatch up another. You may believe my Mose was a failure, but he was the most successful man I have ever known, if you count the wealth of his love. Oh, he saw it. He saw and understood the downfall of many of his Plain brethren. It rode on his shoulders like a heavy burden. Yes, he was a failure where finances and management were concerned. But he laid up treasures in heaven far above anything any of us has ever experienced."

She paused for breath.

"You can't ask Dat for a loan!" Rachel exclaimed.

"You'll never pay it back!" Emma echoed.

So there it was. The only part of Sarah's speech they had heard was about the loan, which to them meant that Sarah was taking a portion of their inheritance, resulting in less money for themselves.

"I will. I will pay back every penny, with God's help. Hannah has the will, Manny has the strength and obedience, and I will be the rock of support they will need to survive. No, not just to survive, but to flourish."

Sarah's face was pale, her hands shook as she made the coffee, but there was a new firmness, a foundation beneath her words that the sisters had never known.

Quickly, sensibly, they tried to change their erring sister's course. Sarah remained steadfast.

They went to their father, husbands in tow, and begged him to refuse Sarah's request for a loan, citing many reasons why it was only common sense to withhold the loan. Circling around their aging father like a pack of wolves, they lunged at every angle, trying to secure the amount she had asked for.

Samuel Stoltzfus was well off, and he knew it, even with the depreciation on the farm he owned. The financial markets during the Great Depression were like a smothering blanket on any gain he might have expected in the future. God had a hand in this, he knew. Monetary value had replaced the fruits of the Spirit for too many brethren, himself included.

He listened to the undertone of greed in his daughters' arguments, shored up by the desperate pleas of obedient husbands to refuse Sarah. But he remained like a rock, firm and unmovable. In his mind, he doubled the amount she had asked for, then tripled it, adding a windmill, a new well, and a decent house.

He'd ask Ben Miller's crew to install a windmill. He would. He sat at the kitchen table, his gray hair and beard surrounding his lined, aging face, weathered by hard work and a good temperament, his head and shoulders bowed by the wisdom of his years; like a head of wheat so filled with kernels, it bent him.

Once he had fully absorbed the insatiable grasping of his daughters and their collaborating spouses, there was no turning back. It was not rebellion, merely recognition of giving where giving was due. Sarah was the meek and quiet daughter, with the true love required of a married woman running in her veins. He did not doubt for a moment that she carried the same love within her heart as Ruth had for her mother-in-law and later for Boaz, as told in that beloved Old Testament story that was expounded at every Amish wedding.

"Wither thou goest, I will go. Thy God shall be my God." Hadn't Sarah proved her love, followed Mose to the ends of the earth, and believed that his God was her God?

Ah, yes, she had. Now, she was choosing to honor their love, with Mose lying beneath the plains, driven by the memory of the love that meant more to her than her own home, her own relatives, everything she had known. Sickened by the betrayal of her sisters' ravenous selfishness, she was returning to the land that had brought her to her knees, separated the worldly from the spiritual, what was true from what was a lie.

Samuel spoke with Elam and Ben and laid out his plans. At first, the sons responded with disbelief. But after hearing their father out, they slowly came to see his point. Their respect for him ran deep, so in the light of obedience, they "gave themselves up," in the often-used words of the Amish.

Hannah regained her strength, her lungs healed, and she was soon back to her forceful self. Manny told his mother that anyone as angry as Hannah probably got better by force of the strong will they lived with. But he smiled when he said it.

Sarah and the children had a long talk with her father. Hannah was wide-eyed and disbelieving. Manny grinned and all but bounced up and down.

He told them of his plans for a windmill, the crew who would install it, the cattle he would buy for them, and his plans to accompany them on the train to help give them a start. He wanted to meet the *Englische leid* around them and get a feel of the surrounding culture.

He spoke of his concern that Sarah and the children would stay true to their Amish culture and faith. He explained the need for *Ordnung*, the reason for modest dress, forgiveness, "*de lieve*," the love necessary for a successful *fottgung*. If they left Lancaster County in anger or self-righteousness, they would lose the blessing they needed to be successful.

Herr saya, God's blessing, is the ultimate goal, he said. If that is on your agenda, you will not fail.

Hannah listened, wide-eyed and silent. Her grandfather's words were priceless, but in her opinion came awfully close to her father's dreaming. Surely her grandfather didn't think along the same lines as Dat had. She knew full well it took hard work, foresight, and more hard work to get the homestead up and running. If he started in about the drought being a sign of *unsaya*, the unblessing so often spoken of—well, she didn't believe it. If it didn't rain, then it just didn't rain, and that was that. It made you tough and put every resource to use. You adapted, got a job in town to feed yourself, and you kept right on going, even if you only ate cornmeal and bread and prairie hens.

But she was grateful. She was more than grateful. Overjoyed, filled with a new and burning passion to excel. A windmill! A water tank like the Jenkinses had. Their grandfather to accompany them. It was much more than she could have ever hoped for.

Elam and Ben wanted to go. The harvest imminent, they knew they had to stay. It was hard, but they'd hear their father's account of things changing at the homestead.

Sarah was quiet, with a new resolve surrounding her like a set of fine, new clothes worn with a lift of her bowed shoulders.

CHAPTER 20

Word got around.

Samuel Stoltzfus was as bad as his son-in-law, that Mose Detweiler and his crazy venture, dead and gone now. Incredulous of his support of his widowed daughter, they tried to dissuade him, to make him see the light.

It took a month of planning, acquiring prices and agreements, and coordinating the schedules of freight trains for shipping the costly parts for the steel windmill. It was made in sections in Lancaster County by a reliable company to be shipped by train.

Most of the windmills in the West were made of wood, the lack of humidity preserving them for years of service. Windmills made of steel, used widely in the eastern United States, were better, and dozens of manufacturing companies produced them.

Ben Miller was a tall and swarthy man, red-faced and yellow-toothed from his love of a hefty wad of chewing tobacco lodged in his right cheek like a growth. Ambitious, his business of producing and installing windmills was known for many miles around. So when Samuel Stoltzfus came to see him about building one in North Dakota, his small green eyes squinted with delight. He immediately went to the door of his welding shop to spit out the long-chewed wad of tobacco before inserting a clean one.

"Ho! North Dakota! *Vass gebt?*" His voice carried well, too well in fact, leaving Samuel rubbing the ear closest to Ben.

"My daughter was married to Mose Detweiler."

Nothing further needed to be said. Ben nodded, understanding. He'd heard, knew Mose, watched the demise of a fine farm under his management. Long-suffering *schöene frau.* But nothing was said about her reason for returning. Unnecessary.

Samuel reasoned about this long before he approached Ben Miller. What the rest of Lancaster County did not know was fine with him, for he would carry a significant amount of shame from his remaining family and their overreaching concern about his charity to Sarah and her children. If Rachel and Emma wanted to air their grievances, word would spread, but so be it. Some would side with them; others would be aghast at their tightfisted selfishness.

They would need the windmill shipped as soon as possible. The prairie winters were nothing to take lightly.

Yes, yes, Ben had heard. In fact, he heard more than enough to wonder what was wrong with Samuel, thinking of supporting this venture.

"Surely you ain't leaving Sarah out there by herself?" he asked, adjusting his wide, black suspenders across the width of his barrel chest.

"She has Hannah and Manasses. Manny they call him."

Ben reached under the rusty metal desk and produced a tin can, filled halfway with the dark liquid of his spitting. Pursing his lips, he sent a stream of tobacco juice expertly into the can, landing it with a fine, splashless plunk. He scratched his stomach after replacing the can, then put a foot up on a pile of metal and turned his full attention to his customer, figuring it wasn't his business. If the man wanted a windmill, he'd do his best to give him one and install it for him, no questions asked.

After the men finished the planning and negotiating the shipping costs and the price for the job, Samuel drove his horse away from Ben Miller's shop, satisfied that he had a trustworthy person to oversee the whole transaction from start to finish, in spite of the roaring in his ears and the questionably aimed stream of tobacco juice at frequent intervals.

At home, Sarah was canning vegetables and fruit in Mason jars. Tomatoes, peaches, corn, apples turned into sauce, zucchini relish, late cucumbers, anything she thought they might need. A new respect for food that was preserved and edible in the cold winter months drove her to work tirelessly all day, laboring in the heat of the wood-fired cook stove and the boiling water in the blue agate canner. As the jars cooled, she packed them in cardboard boxes with a thick layer of newspaper, labeling each and setting it aside.

She couldn't help thinking of the journey with Mose and how he had persuaded her that the jars of food would be too heavy for the horses. They had money and would buy food along the way. Plenty of small towns. Folks were generous. They'd be all right. They had been all right, had eaten well, in fact. The only downside was the disappearance of their money, leaving them destitute, scrabbling to survive.

Oh, she tried hard not to compare her departed husband with the planning and foresight of her father, but she could not help some comparisons. The journey on the train was so much wiser, but then . . . Sarah's thoughts drifted to the joy of pleasant days on the road, the crisp mornings when a light shawl that felt good on her shoulders, the clinking of the horses' harness, the swaying of the wagon, the crunch of steel-rimmed wheels on gravel roads. She fondly remembered Mose sitting beside her, his childish joy contagious, pointing out the different flocks of birds, the thrashers and dickcissels and indigo buntings, hearing their piercing songs long before they were in sight. His heavy arm about her shoulders, drawing her close for a kiss on her cheek. My Sarah, he had called her. And his Sarah she had been, in every sense of the word.

Sometimes, she wondered if he had been slightly demented toward the end. Perhaps he was only too determined. How hard it had been to let him go. But how hard might it have been to see him slowly losing his sense, his sound mind, had he lived?

This she must leave in God's hands. It was an enormous test of her faith, to let this wondering go. She would never know. His time had come, and God took him. So now it was up to her and the children to keep the homestead. A part of her mourned the loss of Lancaster County, her childhood, her heritage. Perhaps she could never go back home, like she once thought she could.

Did she only remember the perfection? Did she view her world through the pink haze of rose-colored glasses? The most difficult task that lay ahead of her was truly forgiving her grasping sisters, especially Rachel and Emma.

Unexpectedly, a smile came to her lips, her shoulders shook with mirth, and tears rose unbidden as she thought of Hannah's version of her two sisters: "cows." Flat and unadorned, labeling them along with her least favorite animal, a milk cow. Hannah should have been sharply reprimanded, for all the amount of good it would probably not do.

But still. She knew too that Hannah would board the train with a hefty chip on her shoulder, not caring whether she forgave Rachel and Emma or if she didn't.

And so Sarah planned her own journey, allowed her father to add burlap bags of potatoes and fifty-pound paper sacks of flour, cornmeal, oatmeal, and brown sugar. They packed coffee and tea, white sugar and baking soda, stacks of canned goods and round wooden boxes of cheese. It was a carload of luxuries, a God-send of security for Sarah. She felt as if she could face the harshest winds of winter, the worst drought in years—anything. There was a song in her heart, a new purpose supported by her aging father's love, his willingness to see this homesteading undertaking through to the end.

Of course, Ben urged Hannah to go to the singing that last Sunday evening. They were leaving the next day, Monday.

Hannah had just endured the final church service, shrugging off the nosy girls' questions, glad to return home and rid herself of all these people and their sharp glances and pitying looks.

As if she had a growth on her face, or two heads, or some strange disease like leprosy. That was all right if they didn't like her, she didn't necessarily care for them either.

People just weren't Hannah's favorite thing. They were just so false, most of them. Saying nice words, their eyes full of pity that they were so dumb, returning to the West like gypsies. Wanderers. Vagabonds. Taking all her grandfather's inheritance.

She'd show every one of these superior people. She'd be known for miles around, hundreds of miles around, for her pure bloodline of the best cattle. Her most important goal was to persuade her grandfather to buy the cattle from the Klassermans, not the Jenkinses.

The tough old longhorns they mixed with any old Angus or Hereford produced scrappy calves that survived blizzards and heat and drought. But in the auction ring, they weren't worth nearly what the Klassermans' Angus were worth. Calves took more care. Hard to birth, Hod said. Well, that might be true, but what about fast weight gain? What about good bloodlines?

Oh, the list of her dreaming could go on and on, but she needed to stop and take stock of what they had now. Debt to her grandfather, the drought, the two calves, and one mad cow. All the food was nothing but charity.

She told Ben, no, she wasn't going to the singing. Then it was the usual round of coaxing followed by the usual amount of excuses from Hannah.

"What will Rebecca Lapp say?"

Hannah sat up straight. "I don't care what she says. She doesn't give a fig about me, and I don't give one about her. She doesn't even know if I'm there or not. Besides, if you don't have the nerve to ask her for a date, then I don't either. It's your problem, not mine."

Ben ground his teeth in frustration. She irked him so *hesslich*. Speaking the truth like that. Why couldn't she be nice like other girls? She honestly didn't care if she had any friends or if she didn't. She was so odd, so different, wanting to return to the West.

He left without her, disgruntled more at himself than at her, berating himself for still not having the gumption to ask Rebecca Lapp. He didn't notice Jerry Riehl watching his arrival, then turning away, or that he wasn't at the singing at all that evening.

Hannah had not yet gone to bed, too keyed up about their departure the following morning. In a way, she wished she would have gone with Ben just to make the evening go faster.

She had washed her hair, put it back with the bobby pins Doris Rocher had given her. The gold, shiny little clasps were not allowed according to the *Ordnung*. Bobby pins enabled the fast girls to adjust their hair in stylish waves, a fanciness not possible without them.

Hannah loved to experiment with bobby pins. She could pull her thick, dark hair up over her head and secure it with bobby pins, or push it forward to let it droop over her forehead like bangs. Mam would discourage this, asking her why she wasn't content to wet her hair and roll it back along the side of her head the way the other girls did, which Hannah didn't bother answering.

An object hit the window. Hail? She waited, held her breath, suddenly glad her grandfather and mother were asleep in the same house.

Ping. Ping. Two more in quick succession. Whatever could it be?

Going to the window, she pulled the retractable screen aside and pushed the wooden framed window farther up, then stuck her head out, her eyes searching the maple tree to the left and the barnyard with dark objects milling around, the driveway like a ribbon of silver in the moonlight. No dogs were barking and the cows didn't seem disturbed. The night was warm and calm, a night like any other.

"Hannah!" A whisper from the base of the maple tree.

Vass in die velt? she thought wildly.

"Hannah! It's me, Jerry."

"What do you want?" she hissed, suddenly irritated by his daring.

"Come down. I need to talk to you. Please."

"No."

"Please."

"No. I'll wake my mother."

"Then I'm coming up."

"You can't do that. You can't come to my room. That would not be *shicklich*."

"I will, if you don't come down."

Hannah snorted, replaced the screen. Well, whatever he wanted, she wasn't going to put an apron on, or a covering. Her hair was still wet.

Oh, this was so aggravating. Why couldn't he tell her what he wanted from the base of the maple tree? She hardly knew him.

She didn't bother being quiet, simply went down the steps and through the kitchen, thinking that if she woke her mother, she'd tell her the truth. Jeremiah Riehl wanted to talk to her.

Jeremiah Riehl. What a name! Like a clown or a biblical prophet. She found him by the grape arbor, in the deep shadows behind the pump house. Her first thought was, coward. *Bupp*. Why not walk up to the porch and knock like normal people?

"What?" she asked, loudly.

"Shh. Someone will hear," he hissed sharply.

"So what?"

"Your grandfather would chase me off."

"Why would he? He doesn't know you. It's not like you were after me, or anything like that."

In the dark, Jerry rolled his eyes to the night sky, exasperated. Off on the wrong foot, a rocky start for sure.

"How do you know I'm not?"

"What?"

"After you?"

The usual derisive snort. "You have an awful long way to go. I'm going home tomorrow morning."

"I know."

389

"Is that why you came to talk?"

Why did she always make him feel like a boy in the first grade? Probably he should turn and leave, simply walk away from this bluntly spoken, intimidating girl and never give her another thought.

Almost, he did just that. In fact, he turned his body as if to leave, thinking what a belligerent person she was, how different from the realm of other girls, the circle in which they moved, polite, attracted to him, giggling, some of them coquettish, flirtatious. This one couldn't care one bit whether he left or didn't.

Was that the attraction? The age-old human condition of wanting what we can't have, and if we can have it, we don't want it. All this crowded into his head, followed by indecision and not a small dose of irritation.

"I came to ask if I can have your address. I want to write to you, if I may. I thought perhaps you'd write back to me. I'd like to get to know you better."

"Really? Why is that?"

"I don't know. Maybe because I find you interesting. Different."

"Well, I'll stop any chance of you courting me by saying that I don't know if I want to be Amish. There's this guy I know, Clay Jenkins, who wants me. Hod and Abby, his parents, saved us from starving more than once. He's really nice. Polite.

I just don't know if I can do it to my mother. Leave, you know. Go English."

Jerry felt as if she'd put a fist in his stomach, leaving him scrabbling for his breath. Despair crowded out his usual sense of optimism. Boldly, without feeling, she had told him the worst. The unimaginable. He had always thought any girl who was so cold, so bereft of parental love that she could deliver the ultimate blow of *ungehorsamkeit* to undeserving parents, was not worth a passing glance.

Time stood still. The night became black, the oxygen sucked into a vacuum, leaving him without air.

"Why don't you say something?"

He had nothing to lose, so he spoke what was on his mind. "Hannah, I don't know why I have these feelings for you. I just do. I want to know you better, in spite of your leaving to go to North Dakota. I know you're not interested, but you could at least write to me every once in awhile and let me know how things are going."

"Why would you have to know? Why would you care? It's really none of your business how we're doing."

So it was that hopeless then. "I guess you're right."

"See, there are no other Amish out there. We're the only ones. And we're not worth very much. We won't own that homestead for another eight and a half years. We're getting a loan from my grandfather. We're getting all our food from him, to be shipped out with the windmill. We're just poorer than poor, taking an awful risk. And yet, it intrigues me to wonder if we're going to make it with the winter coming on and the start of our herd. Oh, you have no idea, Jerry, the things that I think."

Her voice was low, but filled with so much passion, every fiber of her being invested in the homestead in the West.

"See, if you'd see how we live, where the homestead is, how horribly poor and primitive, you would see me for what I am. You don't want to know me. Why not become interested in one of these Lancaster girls who live on a farm, in line perhaps to own the farm someday? A girl worth something. I have to look out for my mother and the rest of my family."

"You just said you might not stay Amish."

"I don't know what I'm going to do."

"Would it help if I persuaded you to stay?"

"Well, there's Clay." That statement held a bit of doubt. All was not lost.

"All right, Hannah. Then I'll have to let you go. And I will. I realize how young you are, and you need room to make your own choices. Someday, I hope to go to North Dakota to see where you live."

"No. No. Don't. Don't ever do that."

Puzzled, Jerry asked her why she said that.

"I don't know."

He stepped closer. The cloud that had obscured the silver of the full moon drifted away, bathing Hannah in the white light of moon glow, her dark hair with a sheen of diamonds, her eyes two pools of vulnerability.

He reached out to touch her hair. Instantly, she jerked away from his touch.

"I was just checking to see if it was moonlight on your hair, or diamonds."

"Smooth talker," Hannah said, but she was smiling, a small uplifting at the corners of her mouth.

Emboldened, he cupped her chin in his large, calloused hand.

"Hannah, if only you knew how beautiful you are, you would not set so much store in the state of your poverty. Don't you know that none of that means a thing to me? I don't care if you live in a cave, or a wigwam, if you have money or if you don't. That has nothing to do with . . ." Almost he said love, but caught himself just in time.

"With what?"

"With my interest in you."

She didn't answer.

Thinking he had said too much, he sighed, looked away across the darkened landscape, the black shadows behind buildings, the silver outline of the maple tree trunk.

393

"See, if I did say it was all right to exchange letters, you would lose interest. I am not a person that says entertaining things to young men the way the other girls do. I don't have anything to say."

"You talked to me that day in the rain."

"Oh, that." Suddenly she laughed, the deep laugh seldom heard.

"Do you have any idea how wet I was when I got home? I got sick, double pneumonia. The doctor wanted to put me in the hospital."

"You are surely not serious?" he asked.

"Oh, I was sick."

"See, I wanted to take you home that day."

"I know."

Then, the thought of her sickness, knowing the time of her leaving was in the morning, the permission to write to her unsecured, a great need to hold her and never let her go, keep her here with him, shook his frame.

He reached out to grasp her shoulders, surprised to find she did not immediately react and wriggle free with the usual sound of disdain.

Very softly, his hands slid down to her waist, imprisoning her arms. "Hannah, may I kiss you goodbye? Just as a token of remembrance?"

"No." She pulled away from him.

There was nothing to do but release her, let her go to stand by herself in the moonlight, her back turned to him.

"Are you afraid you'll remember me?" he asked gently.

"Of course not."

"What is it then?"

"I just want to go now. I want to forget Lancaster County and everybody in it. Why would I want to remember you? I certainly don't want to remember anyone else."

"Well, all right, Hannah. If that's what you want. May I ask you to write down your address, though? Could you please do that?"

"It takes weeks, sometimes longer, for a letter to arrive."

"That's all right."

She disappeared into the kettle house. The dim orange glow of a kerosene lamp in the window. Her bent head. A hand pushing back the curtain of dark hair.

She reappeared, handing him a slip of paper. He gave her his own on a white envelope. An exchange of promises. A slip of hope.

"Thank you, Hannah."

"Don't thank me. I didn't write to you yet."

He laughed. "Will you?"

"Maybe. If I can think of something to say."

They stood in the moonlight, each with their own thoughts, reluctant to leave, both of them now.

Hannah felt a flutter, a spark of interest, the moonlight carving his chiseled face, the dark hair that fell over his eyes, making him appear rakish, decidedly handsome. She'd go back to the homestead, sure, but what if this man actually meant what he said?

She wasn't sure how both of them stepped forward at the same time, but she found herself in his arms. One hand went up to stroke her hair, then dropped immediately when he felt her pull away.

"Hannah," he murmured. He could say that beautiful name a thousand times and never tire of it.

"May I kiss you now?" he whispered.

He smelled of sweet soap and shaving cream, toothpaste and night air, maple leaves and dew-wet grass. He was the only man that had not repelled her, even slightly. Before she could answer, she thought of Clay's slightly acrid and not too clean shirtfront, the stubble of his moustache when he had kissed her.

Without her answer, taking her slight yielding as an answer, he bent his head and found her mouth with his sweet-smelling lips. He kissed her lightly, almost like a breath.

It was Hannah who drew him closer, who would not break away. She had never imagined anything such as this. She was unprepared for the sweetness of him that rocked her and took away all of the irritation and natural rebellion that rose in her at the slightest provocation.

Her arms crept up around his shoulders, her fingers in his dark hair. It was Jerry who broke away and released her. She stayed where she was, her arms finally falling to her sides, her head lowered, ashamed now.

"Hannah," he said again. Nothing else fit into this night, this feeling.

Her hands found the edges of his black vest, clung to them. "I just . . ." She began to talk, but he stopped her with his fingers on her mouth.

"Don't talk, Hannah."

To his complete astonishment, she began to cry, softly at first, and then with childlike sobs and hiccups that threw him completely off guard. He gathered her straight back into his arms and kept her there, until the storm of weeping ceased. He produced a clean handkerchief that smelled like a different kind of soap.

"I am so sorry," she whispered.

"Sorry for what?" he asked.

"For . . . for that."

"That, if that's what you mean, was the most perfect, the most . . . There are no words to describe it. Why would you be sorry?"

"I shouldn't have allowed it. Now what am I going to do?" The old irritation welled up, her take-charge attitude firmly in place.

"You'll go to North Dakota on the train. We'll write."

She couldn't tell him that a letter from him was

the last thing she wanted. She wanted to stay here with him. No, she didn't. She had no plans of living in Lancaster County. But surely they wouldn't always live apart. She had to be with him sometime in the future.

Confused, his leaving like nothing she could begin to explain, Hannah walked slowly back to the house, went upstairs and plunked herself into bed vowing to never, ever let Jerry Riehl back into her life. She couldn't.

CHAPTER 21

How could Sarah fully describe the return trip with her father? There was no way to stave off the fear of recurring starvation, the hopeless feeling of those days with Mose. Over and over she reassured herself with her father's presence, the freight car filled with food, the later arrival of the promised windmill.

She had forgotten the desolation of the plains, the sheer expanse of it. The flagrant emptiness was like an assault, a slam to the senses. Knowing her own unpreparedness, she prayed when they got off the train and on the journey to the homestead. She knew now, it would take much more strength than she had imagined.

It helped, though, watching the children's excitement. Even Manny, who was normally subdued, seemed willing to step into their past life with renewed hope and exhilaration. Eli and Mary simply loved the freedom of the prairie, the quirky gophers and wealth of flying insects.

The view of the buildings remained unchanged, though they had turned darker and with more gray undertones, perhaps. But they remained erect, braced against the never ending wind like a proud Amish fortress.

Here was the log house with the rusty tin roof,

the door barred against the elements, windows closed and shuttered. The grass had reclaimed the yard, billowing up against the house. The barn looked half buried in it, only the tops of the barnyard fence showing.

Sarah shuddered, held her arms tight to her waist, thinking, thinking. She would never be able to clear her mind of the picture of Mose, her heart, lying battered and bleeding by the barnyard fence.

She got off the buggy as if in a dream, walked straight toward the barn and collapsed by the fence, where she stayed until her tears of sorrow were complete.

Her father helped the children unload, paid the driver, took care of the necessary steps as he let Sarah grieve. The door to the house unlatched easily. The floor was littered with the debris of the nosy rodents that had entered.

They resumed their life on the plains as before, seamlessly entering into a routine of cooking, washing, and cleaning.

Hannah remained a mystery to Sarah, during the entire journey on the train and for weeks afterward. If she didn't know better, she would have thought she had fallen in love, or was suffering from some other malady of the heart, like other girls did. But not Hannah.

Questions about her health revealed nothing. She was fine. Clipped words with her nose in the air, heavy eyelids covering any expression. Finally, Sarah decided it was the pneumonia, leaving her in a weakened condition, changing her fierce personality. Subdued, is what she was. Tamped down, the way you tamp down the good soil around a tomato plant when you put it in the earth.

Sarah stood by her garden, a withered brown patch of shriveled, dead plants. She shook her head as she scuffed a bare toe in the dust and dry grass.

Ah, but her father was here. The food would arrive in cardboard boxes. Safely. They would never go hungry, she assured herself over and over. The windmill would arrive and men to erect it and dig the well. She had to keep these thoughts, give herself over to the comfort of them, to keep the panic at bay, like a fire that keeps lurking wolves in the shadows of its heat and light. The time wasn't long, the distance between hopelessness and starvation, to this new beginning.

Her father smiled about the drought, said he'd never known there was an area in all of America where it simply didn't rain. "Our God is so much greater than we think," he said, smiling.

Sarah took solace in the fact that he did not despair in the face of the blowing grass and the emptiness. He rather liked it, he said, his hat all but leaving his head whenever it felt like it. Sarah laughed and pinned a strip of elastic from the inside of the crown to the other side, to be worn below his chin, the way they kept small boys' hats from blowing away. Rather than discard the troublesome hat, he stayed true to his teaching, the elastic cord keeping it firmly on his head.

Manny walked all the way to the Jenkinses to bring back the horses, asking Hod and the boys about the cows. Surprised to see their neighbors had already returned, they threw their hands in the air, delight creasing their weathered faces, standing there on the porch of the ranch house surrounded by their accumulation of earthly treasures, the stuff most people would label junk.

The dry brown grass, weeds, various thorny shrubs were all piled together with discarded wagon axels, wooden wheels, rusty spools of barbed wire, uneven sizes of fence posts, all things the Jenkinses viewed as useful and necessary.

Manny grinned, his shoulders already showing signs of manhood, his eyes alight with recognition.

"Yer back!" shouted Abigail.

"Howdy!" Hod yelled.

The kitchen door opened, revealing a sleepy Hank, who had been taking his noon break, followed by a jubilant Ken, who sprang out and off the porch in one leap, clapping Manny's shoulder with one hand and pumping his hand with the other.

"Glad to see you back, ol' buddy!"

"It's nice to be back," Manny said, smiling broadly.

He noticed the absence of Clay, but did not inquire, figuring he'd pop up somewhere, same as all the rest. He gladly accepted the offer of some leftover dinner, with a glass of chilled tea. He had forgotten the taste of Abby's beef steaks, rolled in flour, fried in lard in a cast-iron pan so hot the whole stove was splattered, including the wall behind it and the floor in front of it. His serving of beans would easily have fed his mother and the rest of the family, but he wasn't complaining.

Hunger was real. It was always imminent. He knew the gut-wrenching feeling of going to bed with a hollow, shriveled place inside of him, a place that was never comfortable and often kept sleep away. He knew the sacrifice of ladling small amounts of cornmeal mush in his own bowl so that Eli and Mary's stomachs could be filled, allowing them to sleep comfortably. So he dug his fork into the mound of beans, spread butter on an endless supply of leftover, cold biscuits, and was glad inside.

"So, ya gonna give it a shot without yer pa?" Hod asked, his chair pushed back, tilted on the two back legs, dangling a toothpick from his lower teeth.

Abby set to washing dishes, her mouth creased

into a smile, so glad was she to have these neighbors returned, although it wouldn't surprise her a bit if they all turned tail and ran back to wherever they had come from. They didn't stand much chance without that oldest girl.

She watched Manny from the corner of her eye as she swabbed the countertop, thought he showed some promise maybe, but these people needed a plan put firmly in place.

She stopped wiping, listening as Manny spoke. *Huh. Good thing. Hmm. Buyin' cows from the Klassermans. Well, hoity toity. Somepin' wrong with ours?* But she stayed quiet and listened. *A purebred herd of Angus. Huh. Don't ask me to help out at birthin' time. They'd have their problems, so they would. Somebody was thinkin' some big ideas.*

She turned to Manny and said, "Where's yer sister?"

"You mean Hannah?" Manny asked politely, speaking after he'd swallowed.

"Yeah. The big one."

"She's helping my mother. They're unpacking and cleaning stuff. My grandfather will be finishing our house, putting up wall board, and finishing the floors. He wants to build an addition on to the kitchen."

"Well now, ain't that nice? If you got all that help. I'm speckting yer grandpappy's got food to tide you over. Winter's comin' on."

"The windmill comin' this fall yet?" Hod broke in.

"Oh yeah. It'll be here in a couple of weeks."

Hank said he'd want to see this new contraption. The Jenkinses' ranch boasted the old wooden type, nothing wrong with it.

"Wooden, is it?"

"Oh, no. It's made of steel. Ben Miller has a welding shop in Lancaster."

Hod squinted his eyes, shifted his toothpick to a corner of his mouth, and said slowly, "Them Amish ain't all like yer pa, then?"

Manny's eyes grew wide, turned darker as he swallowed, then swallowed again. Ashamed of the quick tears that sprang up, he looked at his hands in his lap, then shook his head from side to side. "No, not all of them."

"Hey, sonny, didn't mean anything by it. Yer pa's gone now. Didn't mean to belittle him none."

Manny nodded.

Abby had her say after that, berating Hod up one side and down the other for making that boy feel bad, mentioning his pa that way, and didn't he have a brain in his head, talkin' like that?

Hank told his mother to quit talkin' to his pa that way, and was cuffed on the shoulder for it. Manny winced, trying to imagine his quiet mother hitting him or talking to his father in that manner.

Feeling uneasy, he rose to collect the horses,

405

but was met instantly by a loud clamoring of everyone wanting him to stay. Hod asked Abby to refill his coffee cup, which she did, laying a hand across his back as she did so, a warm, tender touch as if she hadn't been talking gruffly only a few minutes ago. Hank rubbed his shoulder and told Abby she carried a mean punch. Ken guffawed about that, his mouth open wide, and Abby told him if they didn't all sit up and treat her respectable, she'd throw that mean punch around a whole lot more.

Manny was bewildered, then realized their anger and hard speech had no roots; it disappeared like tumbleweed on a wind. It wasn't fastened to old grudges and jealousies. These people were different. They said what they felt, took whatever came their way, and just rolled along with it.

Hod offered to help the old man at the house. Abby said she'd bring cornbread and a pot of beans. Hank asked how many pieces the windmill was in, and Ken said probably a thousand.

They all laughed. Manny said counting nuts and bolts maybe. So it was late when he returned to the homestead, the sun low in the sky. Sarah wore a tight-lipped expression that meant she'd been watching for him too long.

Old Pete was in good shape, the horse given to them by the Jenkinses looking as skinny and lop-eared as ever, his ribs like teeth of a comb, his stomach hanging low, his knees knobby and swollen, a mean look in his half-closed eyes.

Samuel Stoltzfus stood by the barnyard fence, pushed back his hat, and scratched the bald head beneath it. His eyes crinkled, then he laughed outright. "My oh, Manny, is this what Western horses look like?"

Manny laughed, a joyous sound. "Ach, nay, Doddy. Not all of them. You have to remember that Dan died, so we had only Pete and no way to plow this grass. We had no means of buying a decent horse, so the Jenkinses gave us this one. Gave him to us for free."

Doddy Stoltzfus, as the children called him, held Mary by her small brown hand, shook his head, and said he couldn't imagine what the family had been through.

Sarah stood beside him, holding Abby, the wind tossing tendrils of her dark hair away from the bun she had coiled on the back of her head, her faded green dress skirt with the gray, patched, and mended apron flapping, her large dark eyes pools of hurt and remembrance, biting her lower lip as she swallowed her tears.

She nodded, unable to speak.

"Now, I certainly don't want to make fun of God's creatures, but this horse resembles a large, brown goat. If he was sold at the New Holland Sales Stables, I doubt we could get a bid!"

"Out here you would. Lots of horses look like that, Doddy. You know why? They live on grass or hay. No grain, most times. Sometimes corn, if it's cheap at the granary in town," Manny said, grinning.

"He looks as if he could collapse," Doddy said.

"He's a lot tougher than he looks. These horses have the best record for stamina I've ever heard. They just go and go and go, their skinny necks stretched out, their legs just keep churning."

"Ei-ya-yi," Doddy said, good humored.

Hannah walked up to the group eyeing the horses. She smiled at Manny, a look in her eyes that reminded Manny they knew things, together. They were Westerners, and they knew what this horse could do.

She strode up to Pete, stroked his neck, lifted the heavy mane and smoothed the forelocks that fell down between his ears. "Good Pete. He has a lot of miles beneath those sturdy hooves. Were you talking about the brown one, Doddy?"

"I was. He's some horse."

Hannah laughed. "Tough as leather. He'd plow all day."

"Ah, I doubt it."

"Sure he would." This from Manny, standing beside Hannah, showing Doddy they were from the West now, knew the Western ways. They were seasoned in the art of old, ugly horses and knew their worth.

Supper was a lighthearted affair that evening. The end of summer was here, the worst of the drought over, the wind cooling in the evening, making their sleep deep and restful, refreshing their bodies to face another day.

The canned beef over new potatoes and canned lima beans and applesauce was so good, eaten in the slant of yellow evening light with the front door open, the sounds of grasshoppers and locusts like a symphony to usher out the day and welcome in the night.

It was sobering to think of the scant pot of cornmeal mush, the heat and drought, the fear and foreboding taking away any sense of survival. And now, here they were, making another attempt, without their husband and father, but with a new plan, with Doddy, a loan firmly in place, the agreement written by a lawyer, signed into a legitimate pact by both Sarah and her father.

With his faith in her and the children, anything was possible. Everything. Anything. A new fierceness took hold of Sarah, a new will to do it right this time.

She sat on the front steps with her father, long after the children had gone to bed, tired out by their endless roaming, the wind and the sun and the dust. The moon rose in the east, a great white orb so close to the prairie it seemed to rise from the restless brown grass like a brilliant round flower surrounded by the dark, whispering foliage.

"Ah, Sarah, I'm afraid I have to say this. I can

see how a person like Hannah would want to return. There's a freedom out here. You can feel it in the wind, you can see it in the emptiness. It's a great land, and a restful one."

Sarah looked at her father's profile in the white-washed moonlight. Like a patriarch, an Old Testament prophet, with his white hair and full white beard surrounding his face like a curtain.

"You really think so, Dat?"

"Oh yes. Yes, I do. I can understand Mose liking it here. He had the pioneer spirit, the dislike of crowds. Too many people."

Sarah wrapped her hands around her knees, her fingers interlocked. "We just couldn't make a go of it. There was no money." She shuddered.

"I can only imagine, Sarah." Her father's voice was kind, full of caring, which brought an unexpected sob to Sarah's throat. She put a hand to her mouth, unsuccessfully suppressing the tearing sound of sorrow and remembered agony.

Quickly she coughed, trying to hide her emotion. Things like this were not easily spoken of. Far braver to hide it away.

"You will need chickens and a milk cow. A few pigs to fatten. We'll take care of that tomorrow, now that the horses are here. If you have eggs and milk, food goes a long way."

"Oh, eggs, Dat!" Sarah exclaimed, drawing in a pleased breath. "So often I was hungry for a nice soft-boiled egg with butter and salt."

Pleased at his daughter's grateful response, he spoke of perhaps not wanting to return. What if Elam and Ben wanted to come too? Here there was a simple appreciation of life's necessities, a deep thanks in everything, the way Sarah and the children bowed their heads over the most common bowl of food. They were not aware of this, he knew, but it came from the hardscrabble year they had only recently encountered.

Suddenly, thoughts of Emma, Rachel, and Lydia crowded out everything else. He could hardly contain his anger. What if he simply decided to stay? What if? He chuckled.

"What?" Sarah asked, facing her father.

"Oh, the girls. What would they say if I never returned?"

"You can't do that to them, Dat. They'd be furious. You must keep the home farm profitable."

"Until the day I die, *gel*? *Gel*, Sarah?" A brittle note of bitterness distorted the old man's normally friendly tone.

"You know they're all waiting to snatch up everything the minute I'm safely buried. They'll squabble like magpies over the kitchen cupboard that was your grandmother's. They'll fight for my collection of coins and knives. Then they'll sell all those family treasures and buy new linoleum and spanking new horses and shiny buggies, build another silo so the neighbors say, 'Must be Samuel was well off.'

"I can't stand it, Sarah. I can't believe I'm talking this way. I would never have, before. It must be the wild of the plains got into my speech. I'm sorry. You know I love all of you the same, but they have so much, and you went through so many trials. I can't see how they could possibly feel right with God. So greedy. Not wanting me to provide for my own destitute daughter."

He stopped, rubbed his hands together. Sarah could hear the rough, scraping sound of his calluses.

"What would they say of my loan to you? They'd have tried to stop the train. It breaks my heart in so many unexpected ways." He stopped, a deep sigh ending his speech.

"Ach, family. We all have our problems, some more than others. We always had a nice life together. Little squabbles, perhaps, but nothing like this. The Depression may have something to do with it. The desperation of the falling value of their land. I don't know."

Sarah nodded. She realized times were hard, in spite of the prosperous appearing farms and properties of her childhood home. She could not condemn her sisters, neither could she wallow in the mud of her own self-pity, a grudge against Rachel slowly drowning her sense of peace and goodwill. Of love and inner happiness.

If God was found in the love we have toward others, then how could Sarah continue her life with a grudge against anyone? Especially her sisters.

These thoughts chased themselves around in her head as she sat quietly with her father, the silver moon climbing steadily into the night sky. All around them, a shrill sound of insects, accompanied by the high yip of the coyotes and the bawling of the yearling calves brought a sense of being one with the earth.

The night smelled of dust, devoid of the moist dew, a dry scent of papery-thin grass, cracked, parched earth, and thirst.

"Where do the creatures find water after a summer of no rain?" her father asked quietly.

"Wherever they can, I suppose. Our well is almost dry. I don't think it would supply water through another drought."

"Ya, vell, we'll fix that." Then, "Did you want to return?"

For a long moment, Sarah searched for the right words. Finally she decided a forthright answer was best. "No."

"What made you do it?"

"Hannah. Mostly."

"And your sisters' jealousy?"

"That too."

"You do realize, Sarah, that Hannah will need company of her own kind. We cannot expect her to remain unmarried, as well as taking up with an *ausra*. With her temperament, I'd be afraid for her soul."

Better not mention Clay. "Hannah isn't like other girls her age. But without her, we would not have survived. She saw ahead the way Mose could not. She treated him with contempt many times."

Samuel shook his head, making noises of disapproval. "Children are expected to honor their parents. It doesn't say honor them if they live life according to the children's approval, or anything like that. Hannah lives her days with much confidence in her own opinion, and I imagine she often usurped his authority. Mose was a gentle person, a *mensch* of soft-hearted views, his quest for spiritual perfection sometimes overriding his good judgment. No, Sarah, he would not have made it here, had he lived. In a way, it's a mercy he could be taken home to spend eternity with his Lord and Savior."

Sarah's voice caught. "But what is to become of me? I loved him so. He treated me kindly, always caring. Some days I feel as if I can't place one foot in front of the other, going through life without him."

"You have Hannah. And Manny."

They drifted apart, sitting on the rough wooden steps, the old man lost in thought. It was well that his daughter had memories of her husband in that light of love. He knew, for him, it was more than he could honestly say.

His wife of fifty-two years. Dead now, and

gone from him, never to return. His grieving was real, but he well knew it was a different kind of sorrow than Sarah's own. His sorrow was the deep, ingrained sadness of having spent all those years with a woman he still felt as if he hadn't known in the way many husbands share a closeness with their wives.

She had simply never given him her heart. That knowledge was a deep wound in his own heart, scarred and opened, scarred again. The house, the children, the garden, the social church-going, and the quiltings, had all meant more to her than he had. He had often longed for the sharing of innermost thoughts, times spent alone, on the porch swing in the evening, or the shared intimacy of pillow talk at night.

They farmed and raised ten children, prospered with the milking of the cows, the growing of abundant crops, traveled together side by side in the gray, canvas-covered buggy, without the ties that bind. Without the love they needed.

Oh, he had loved her, as much as he was able. But a warm flame is soon extinguished if met only with the icy blast of refusal. Eyes averted, mouth downturned. Always busy, her hands moving, moving. Shelling peas, cutting corn, sewing, washing dishes. He longed for a pure light of recognition, a smile that meant *Denke*. The tiniest slice of approval, a warm and tender touch. Perhaps he had been the one who had failed. Failed to nurture the love that had withered before it could blossom.

Ah, but the children, each one more precious to his heart. Sarah, the woman of tribulation, marrying gentle Mose, and still they had so much more than himself. Thrown into poverty, perhaps, but wealthy in love.

In this way, Samuel Stoltzfus conducted himself and hid all the imperfections of the marriage away from his children, figuring they would not need all that unnecessary information, their mother dead and gone.

It was the way of it. He stretched and yawned.

"Bedtime for an old man."

"Ach, Dat, I hate to think of your leaving. Going back to Lancaster."

"Oh, but you know I have to, and soon, even before the windmill crew gets here."

"I know."

"I need to look after things at home. Elam and Ben still need teaching."

Sarah rose, tall and slender in the moonlight, her eyes large and dark. "We'll be all right."

"Yes, you will."

They stepped through the door of the house together, said their goodnights, each one to their own sleeping quarters, alone with their thoughts of the past as the moon made its way across the beauty of the clear night sky. The supplies would arrive tomorrow. The house would be covered with wall board and painted, like Abby's. The floors would be sanded smooth and varnished, making life so much cleaner, so much more normal.

Sarah knew she had nothing to fear, except the past rearing its ugly head like a horned beast, leaving her mouth dry, her heart racing. She knew the storms of the past winter. She still felt the cold in her half-frozen feet and heard the howling wind. This winter, she would not have Mose to lean on. No one to make decisions.

She gathered little Abby into her empty arms, knew there was no use wailing and pining like a weak kitten.

She must let go of her father. And somehow, bridge the gap between her and Hannah.

CHAPTER 22

One night after Doddy Stoltzfus had left but before the windmill crew arrived, Hannah woke up while it was still dark. She had no idea what time it was, but it felt like way past midnight. The flannel coverlet was drawn up well past her shoulders, half covering her ears, the nights having turned cooler as fall arrived.

Someone's voice had awoken her. It was not in the house but farther away. Instantly alert, she rolled onto her back, her arms at her sides, holding still and straining to hear.

Was it only the whisper of grass, when the wind didn't die completely away, even at night?

A banging. And most certainly voices. Low voices. Immediately, her heart set up a clamor of its own. Should she wake Mam? Manny? Wake anyone?

She lay still, listening. Yes, there it was. Someone was at the barn.

Every story she had ever heard about claim jumpers crowded into her mind. Hod Jenkins had spoken of them to her father, while she sat on the sidelines around the campfire in the yard. He had recounted tales of fist fights, even exchanges of gunfire, the law too far away and too unconcerned to help. The documents uncovered too late, many of the homesteaders, discouraged before the claim jumpers even showed up, willingly allowed them to take the land.

Knowing the subservient spirit of her mother, Hannah recognized it was up to her to save their homestead. Whether it was claim jumpers out there or cattle or horse thieves, they weren't getting away with this craziness. That was for sure.

She rolled out of bed, slipped a dark dress over her nightgown and made her way to the narrow stairs in bare feet like a ghost, her breath coming in ragged puffs.

The rifle. Beside the cupboard.

Her toe hit the leg of a kitchen chair, sending sparks of pain along her foot. Her eyes scrunched as she bit her lip to keep from crying out. She found the rifle, her hands closing around the cold metal of the barrel, down to the smooth stock. Gripping it in both hands, she let herself out the front door, holding her breath as it sent out its usual creak of hinges.

She tiptoed across the porch, wishing the silver illumination of the moon away. A dark night would be so much better, but there was nothing to do about that now.

She hunkered down in the shadows of the house, where the dark night made her disappear.

"Hey, them's horses." A volley of evil language followed.

"They come back?"

"Nah."

A shuffling followed, as they removed saddles from horses whose heads hung low, tired out, glistening with sweat in the moonlight.

One tall, thin man, accompanied by a shorter, stockier one. At that moment, Hannah realized the need of a good watchdog. A huge German shepherd, like Uncle Levi's that he kept tied to a doghouse at the side of his barn. Her father disliked that dog, saying the only thing that kept him from taking off someone's leg was the chain attached to his collar. The way that dog carried on at the slightest disturbance, he didn't know how much faith you could put in a flimsy chain, as powerful as those lunges were, coupled with the harsh barking.

She needed a dog just like that. Well, the cracking of a good rifle was all she had. Hod said that most times it spoke louder than the law. Her father had nodded, a smile playing around his gentle lips. Hannah knew well, he would never shoot a gun in any man's direction. His faith forbade it.

If a man asked him to go with him a mile, he would go twain, as the Bible required of him. If someone took his shirt, he would offer his coat as well. He lived by the righteousness of turning the other cheek. He'd get slapped around and give up the homestead, rather than lose his faith.

Nonresistant. That meant putting up no resistance when someone came to take away what was rightfully yours. There was no gray area for her father. It was all black and white. Being Amish, you lived by the articles of faith written in the small, gray booklet, and by these rules you lived your life, secure in the knowledge that they were not too much sacrifice. They were the *Ordnung*, the giving of your life to Jesus Christ, living as He had lived on this earth.

Why did these thoughts of her father come now, like a barrage of right and wrong choices, igniting an uncomfortable fire in her conscience?

Well, that was all right. That was her gentle father. She was what was left behind, and she had no plans of giving up their 320 acres of profitable grassland. The windmill was coming, and they had a checking account in her grandfather's name to buy cattle.

"Wanna try the house?"

"Yeah."

They hobbled the horses.

Hannah felt the bullet pouch, drew back the clip, and inserted one. A soft click. She held her breath. They were coming. The grass rustled in the night wind, gently. A coyote yipped, far away. It was now or never. If she spoke, they'd know it was a woman. She'd have to let the gun speak for her.

She raised the heavy rifle to her shoulder,

sighted down the black, cold barrel, aimed a few feet to the left of them, away from the barn. They should hear the bullet whistle past, but certainly not hit either one of them. Thou shalt not kill, this she knew, and had no intention of doing that.

She squeezed the trigger, her sturdy shoulder took the impact well.

Crack!

A loud yell—and another.

On they came. Hannah followed the first shot with two more. Her heart racing, a dry fear turning her mouth to cotton, she watched as they stopped, turned, and ran, silently scrambling to unhobble their horses. They threw the saddles on, jerking at the cinch, fumbling, muttering to one another about gittin' outta here.

To let them know she meant business, she fired once more, hoping her family would have the good sense not so show their faces.

She watched as they threw themselves on their mounts, turned, and galloped away into the dry, rustling moonlit night. Hannah stayed in the shadows of the house, her gun held across her raised knees, listening to the retreating hoof beats, until the quiet whispering of the grass was all that remained.

She rose from her cramped position, her knees like jelly, and stumbled up the porch steps, to find her mother and Manny, huddled by the door, Eli and Mary softly weeping.

"Hannah! Is it you? What is going on?" Manny whispered hoarsely.

"Who was shooting? Surely it wasn't you?" her mother croaked, her mouth and throat dry with the same fear.

"I was shooting. There were claim jumpers at the barn."

Sarah gasped audibly. "But, Dat, Mose, I mean . . . your father always said he didn't know what he would do if he found himself in those circumstances."

"Well, I knew. They're not getting these 320 acres." Such conviction.

Sarah shook her head, lit the kerosene lamp with shaking fingers, the glass chimney rattling between the metal prongs as she replaced it.

"Did you shoot?" Manny asked.

"Sure. I shot the rifle to scare them off. It worked."

Sarah gathered the terrified children to her side as she sat down weakly in a kitchen chair, stroking Eli's dark head as he sat on her lap. Mary stood beside her mother, arms around her shoulders, her eyes like dark pools in the light of the lamp's flame.

"But Hannah, is it right? Are we living by your father's rules?"

"Look, Mam. Dat is no longer here. We have our choices to make now, if we want to stay here in the West, all right? It isn't right to let those brazen, lawless men take what is ours. We worked hard for this, and will continue to work hard. I don't care what you say."

"But, Hannah. You know he wouldn't approve of what you just did."

Hannah took a deep breath. "Mam, listen to me. If this is how you're going to be, you may as well go back home now. We can't live by our father's dreaming if we're going to survive. I only scared them off. I didn't kill anyone. I never meant to. I know about nonresistance, but how far does that go?"

Sarah shook her head, suddenly miserable. Oh, this wild land. Amish had no business out here. How could they be expected to live by the rules of the church? Did those four gunshots mean they had crossed off one of the articles of their faith?

"Ah, but Hannah. Now we are not abiding by one rule, so now we are already started on the downward spiral, turning our backs to the teachings of our forefathers." Sarah shuddered to think of the lawlessness that had crept in so soon, like a thief in the night.

She turned to Manny, the obedient one. "What do you think?"

So much like his father, he took a few moments before he spoke. "I want to respect our father's wishes, Mam. But we can't just lay down and take the claim jumpers unlawful thievery, either. I don't know."

Hannah glowered from her stand by the door, one ear turned toward the night, alert for the sound of hoof beats.

"Here we are again. Everyone sifting through the *Ordnung*, trying to figure right from wrong, wondering, dreaming, looking back, when I am the only one who gets off my backside and does anything about anything." Her voice turned to a shout.

"You would have died without food if I hadn't gone to town. No one ever figured out if that was right or wrong, did you? Huh? No, you were too hungry." She paused for breath.

"So now, you'd better decide if you're with me or not. If this is how our future is planned, then I'll marry Clay Jenkins at the first opportunity. I want to live here. To be sensible, we might have to bend the rules sometimes."

"Oh Hannah, please. Please don't tell me you would marry an *ausra*. That is not even thinkable," Sarah said, wheedling now, begging her headstrong daughter to change her way of thinking.

As the night wore on, they remained seated around the kitchen table, hashing out the rocky path of survival and the Amish *Ordnung*, the meek and gentle spirit of Mose Detweiler the burning example, a flame to lead them in the coming years, almost extinguished by Hannah's pragmatism when compared to his righteous, biblical version of life. Sarah found herself often swayed by Hannah's power and the stark sensibility of her reasoning.

Nothing hidden, nothing sugar coated to make the swallowing of it easier. To live in the West required adaptation. Changes. Who was to care? No other Amish lived here. God saw them, of course, Hannah conceded to humor her mother.

But Sarah knew. And she could tell that Hannah knew: Hannah was wielding power over her mother and Manny by threatening to marry Clay. There was no doubt in Sarah's mind that it was possible. Hadn't she seen? Clay would marry her tomorrow. Well, Sarah had a wealth of power herself. The minute Hannah brought up the subject of Clay Jenkins becoming her husband, Sarah would mention the possibility of her grandfather's withholding his checkbook and the windmill. She knew only too well her aging father's disappointment, the deep and searing heartache he'd endure if Hannah chose to live outside the *Ordnung*, the way of righteousness by which he abided.

It was a great mystery, this heartache. Why was it so hard to see children leave the Amish? To see them openly disobey?

And Hannah on the brink of it herself. Sarah well remembered Uncle Levi's Abner, going off to war, disregarding his parents' warnings. He had lived many years untrue to the Amish

426

faith, battling side by side with the *ausra,* the English soldiers in World War I. He was shot and killed. Uncle Levi and Aunt Barbara were never the same after that. How could they be, having no hope for his soul? To burn in hell, eternal damnation. Or did he have time to repent and ask forgiveness before his final moment? They would never know. They could hope, that was all. This life was no *kinnershpiel,* no child's play. There were consequences for wrong choices. God is not mocked.

The upbringing Sarah had lived by all her life was now viewed through the microscopic lens of her self-willed oldest daughter. Things she had never questioned, that she had taken as rules written in stone, the foundation of her character, were now shaken and rattled as never before. She had given her life to her husband, and now to Hannah, faithfully and without self-pity. She had done what was required of her, and here she was, her daughter holding the threat of marriage to Clay Jenkins over her head like a fierce, flapping bird of prey that threatened to peck her eyes out.

A shot of anger sparked in Sarah. It made her feel small and helpless, like a baby bird, dependent on Hannah's offering. Well, this was not right, according to the Bible. Her husband had been a different story. This was her daughter.

She pictured herself at the base of a pedestal, an intricately chiseled Roman pillar, prostrate, worshipping at the shrine called Hannah, bidding Manny to join her. The thought was so real and so revolting that it felt as if a hot wind blew from below the bed, enveloping her in an uncomfortable steam bath. Self-recognition brought wave after wave of anxiety washing over her and then receding, only to submerge her again.

So what was she to do? What was her next step? The coming days loomed before her, formidable as the tallest mountain. It sapped her strength, leaving her floundering for oxygen, as if her trek up the mountain had already begun.

She had felt courage on the night she had the talk with her father. She had recognized the need, felt the passion directed toward the success of the homestead. Now, a far greater trial loomed: taming Hannah and reversing authority in the family.

Sarah realized the thin line of helping Hannah find the balance she would need. To be harsh and unforgiving would germinate the seed of rebellion, drawing it from the earth like a warm summer rain. To allow Hannah to control her, passive and afraid, would only bring an unchastened, unhandy spirit, one that flared up the minute her authority was questioned. Like bread dough forgotten and left to rise, Hannah had risen out of proportion and down over the pan. Such dough is ruined unless brought into submission and kneaded into shape.

Sarah shook slightly, a rare moment of laughter overcoming her as she thought of Hannah's reaction to her comparison to bread dough. Oh, mercy.

She fell asleep, a prayer on her lips, her sweet face relaxed as she breathed lightly. The moon was low in the west, luminous and orange, before the first call of the sage thrasher woke the western blue birds, until the prairie hummed and warbled and trilled.

The birdsong woke Hannah when the first of the sun's rays poked a slanted yellow beam of light on the round rafters, the rough boards placed horizontally on top of them. She would be happy to wake up in a decent room, with wall board and paint, but that was beside the point this morning.

She rolled over, stretched, then raised herself from the hay tick and padded lightly downstairs to begin her day.

She had planned on accumulating all the firewood she possibly could before the windmill crew arrived. For one thing, if the family was expected to cook for them, it would take plenty of wood to keep the stove going. Plus winter was coming, and she had no plans of being cold ever again. Between her and Manny, they'd stack the northeast side full of wood, insulating the house as well as never getting lost in an unexpected blizzard.

So Mam could make a big breakfast, after which they'd set off for the creek bed to saw wood. As soon as the new windmill was up, they'd buy the cows from the Klassermans and buy a huge dog; it didn't matter what kind, just so it was big and had a fear-inducing bark.

She wished they had some kind of food storage facility, but that could wait if it had to, she supposed.

She didn't greet her mother, just watched her set about gathering the soiled laundry from the wooden hamper in the bedroom.

Finally she asked if Sarah would make breakfast soon; she had plans for herself and Manny to chop firewood.

"I thought I might be able to get the whites on to soak before I start the wash water."

Hannah snorted. "What do you mean? That doesn't make sense."

"I have enough hot water on the cook stove to pour into the small granite tub to soak the whites in lye soap. After that, I want to start the fire to heat the rest of the water in the kettle."

"Why didn't you say so?" Hannah asked as she bent to pull on a pair of warm stockings.

Sarah's patience was as dependable as the sun's rising, so Hannah was surprised when her mother stopped sorting clothes, faced her with her hands on her hips and said firmly, "I'm busy, Hannah. The rest of the food boxes still need to be unpacked before the windmill arrives. I would appreciate your help today. You could make breakfast for all of us. It doesn't take long to make a pot of oatmeal and fry bread in a skillet."

"I can't see why that washing has to be done this minute," Hannah retorted, stretching her feet in front of her and wriggling the toes of her stockings.

"I told you," Sarah said shortly.

Hannah glared at her mother, then got up to go to the mirror above the washstand. She removed her hairpins, loosened her long dark hair, lowering her left shoulder to swing her hair behind her, raising her eyebrows to inspect a blemish on her usually flawless forehead. She claimed her head was itchy, saying she probably had lice, the way that train had been packed with people.

"Let me see. Come here." Sarah left her laundry to draw Hannah over to the doorway, where the light of the morning brought each strand of hair into keen sight. She raked the tips of her fingers through the top of Hannah's head, parting her dark hair to reveal the white scalp underneath, then lifted the heavy tresses to check thoroughly behind her ears.

The lice were harder to see than the white clusters of their eggs, and she told Hannah this, which caused her to pull away from Sarah with a sharp jerk and an exclamation of disgust.

"Well, you don't have lice, at any rate. I've seen them before, but they're most common in school-age children and smaller ones who play together. I don't believe you've been infested, Hannah."

They drew apart, each one going their own way. Hannah thought how much her mother's nearness reminded her of times when she rolled and plaited her hair to go to school, wetting it so miserably with cold water, drawing the steel-toothed comb through it without mercy, rolling it so tightly along the side of her head that it felt as if each hair was being pulled out by the root. After all that pain, she twisted the plaited hair into a bun on the back of her head, jabbing the hairpins through it without restraint. Every morning was a mild form of torture, like the one before.

But still. There was something about the smell of a mother, the soft, spicy scent that came from her clothes, the soft touch of her fingers, the way her chest rose and fell as she breathed. When her hands clamped down on her shoulders with a bit of pressure to turn her around, it was like a caress, a caring, a mother doing the duty that was like a bond between them. A part of Hannah missed this ritual, and she realized the absence of her mother's touch.

Unlike the last time she'd been held.

The thought of Jerry Riehl was so painfully embarrassing that she became rattled and forgot the bread frying in the cast-iron skillet. It burned as black as charcoal and she yelled at her mother when Sarah reminded her, her face flaming from the cookstove's heat, but mostly from her own bewildered thoughts.

She woke Manny, ate her oatmeal, and vowed to never catch sight of that man again. Why would she? Hundreds of miles away now, with no longing to return, there was no chance. So that was that.

She spread apple butter on her fried bread, drank her tea, and shivered.

"Chilly, huh?" Manny asked.

"Winter's coming," she answered soberly.

Manny lifted a spoonful of thick oatmeal and nodded. "We need firewood. And who is going to buy chickens and a cow? And pigs. Doddy told us to do that. I'll get the pens ready in the barn if you'll do the rest."

"I had planned on firewood making."

"Well, we can."

So that was what they did. Always the same. Hannah planned and Manny went along with it. Sawing and cutting all day long with only a short break at lunchtime. Manny was uneasy, watching the horizon, asking questions. He knew every minute where the rifle was, propped against a poplar tree.

"If we had a dog," he began.

Hannah put down the axe, wiped the sweat from

433

her forehead. "I'm getting one, somehow. If we had Uncle Levi's German shepherd, they never would have made it to the barn. Bold. Honestly, Manny, they were settling in. If we wouldn't have been here, they'd have some sort of false documents. Something. They'd take our claim. The only resistance they understand is the sound of a gun."

Manny shook his head. His eyes went to the horizon, afraid.

They acquired ten laying hens, brown ones, young, and laying six eggs between them. Egg production cut back in the fall as the daylight hours shortened. Two baby pigs dug in the manure in the back stall of the barn, little ones with ribs showing, runts from the Klassermans' litter of twelve.

Good-natured Owen waved away the mention of a price, said they'd likely be laid on by the mother sow anyway, as dumb as she was. Owen went on to say he'd never met an animal with less brains than a pig. Didn't understand why the good Lord made them so ugly, but he sure enjoyed the bacon and shoulder meat with the fresh sauerkraut and dumplings Sylvia made.

The milk cow was small and brown eyed, a Guernsey, he said. Good rich milk, high in fat. Said they could all use some meat on their bones, to be sure and drink it down, make plenty of butter. Nothing better on fried bread. Or biscuits. Did Sarah make biscuits?

No? Ach, he'd bring Sylvia over to show her how. Nothing like biscuits made with lard. Flaky. So soft they would melt in your mouth.

Hannah stood, shifting her weight from one foot to the other, waiting until the flowery words of praise for all things edible came to an end. She could hardly get a word in to inquire about a dog.

"A dawk? You vont a dawk? Vell, I don't haf vun. Dey kill mine sheeps. Dey luf to kill calfs and lamps. I don't haf a dawk. No, no."

"Do you know of any place we can buy one?"

"No. No. Haf no business wiss a dawk. Ornery buggers. Bite mine lamp."

It took five hours to return to the homestead, trailing the fine-boned little cow with the swinging udder behind the wagon. It was a perfect day, the heat gone, the cooling winds that carried the scent of fall, the brown grass rustling by the side of the road.

"I'm hungry, listening about all that food. It will be hours before we can eat. It almost feels like, you know, last time," Manny said.

"I know what real hunger is, that's for sure," Hannah answered.

"Think we'll make it through the winter?"

"No. We'll have to get to town for oatmeal, flour, and sugar. We have plenty of everything else. Firewood. A dog. Need to get the cattle bought and branded."

"I hate to think of branding cows. It brings

back too many memories of Dat. Poor man. I miss him every day. There's not a day goes by I don't remember his words. They're words to live by, Hannah. I will always love and remember my father."

Hannah stared intently to the right, and didn't answer at all. She didn't need to. Manny knew what she was thinking.

CHAPTER 23

When Sarah bought the cattle, Owen Klasserman was more than generous. Ten yearlings, coal black, muscular, lean, and healthy looking. One hundred dollars a head. No need to weigh them. One thousand dollars.

Sarah wrote the check with a trembling hand, struggling with her own thoughts of pessimism. Dark thoughts of disease and dying, winter blizzards, and loss. In spring, the birthing of calves. So much could go wrong, and would, she knew.

One thousand dollars in debt to her father. Another four hundred for supplies to finish the house. Then the milk cow and hens. To be in debt was a horrible thing. She would despise this loan until the day she died. She would never be free of it. But she didn't speak of this to Hannah or Manny.

The Jenkins boys rode over, with Clay this time. Hannah was waiting, trousers buttoned in place below her skirt, Pete saddled with the used saddle from Owen Klasserman. Manny was riding Goat, which was the new horse's name after Doddy Stoltzfus brought up the resemblance.

Hank and Ken were boisterous, open and friendly, their faces creased in good-natured grins. Clay hung back, his handsome, chiseled face taut, tanned to a reddish brown, the stubble on his face bleached white by the sun. He didn't greet Hannah directly. She was given a fleeting smile, a hand waved in recognition, eliciting strange stares from his brothers. Well, no time to worry about Clay's behavior now. There were cattle to be branded, and they were about a year older than they should have been.

"You need a chute," Clay observed dryly.

"We don't have one, so how are we going to do this?" Hannah asked.

"Rope 'em, hold 'em down best we kin, I spect," Hank spoke up. They were eager, up to the challenge, their horses fresh.

"Why Angus?" Clay asked. "You know these purebreds aren't as tough as our skinny cross-breeds. They're Longhorn, Angus, Hereford, and Reds. They're anything all mixed together, which makes for easy calving and getting through the winter better. They're just all around an easier breed to raise."

"And when they're sent to auction, how much less do you get per pound?" Hannah asked quickly.

"I don't know. Never asked the German what he gets."

So now it was the German. Were they actually riled, these Jenkinses? Were herds of cattle held with as much pride as the farms in Lancaster

County? For some reason, this upset Hannah, and when she was upset, she spoke what was on her mind. She faced Clay and asked him why he referred to Owen Klasserman as "the German?"

"I didn't mean anything by it. That name's a mouthful, is all." He held her gaze, his blue eyes as beautiful as she remembered, but devoid of the intense light he had always reserved for her. Bewildered, Hannah lowered her own, scuffed the toe of her worn black shoes in the dust and wondered what was going on.

As before, they cleared a large area, started a blazing fire, which Clay informed everyone was a bad idea. One spark would be all it took to get this prairie started burning. "It'll go up like tinder. Manny, you stay here and watch. Might not hurt to have a bucket of water settin' by. Get the kids to bring one."

The dust flew as the horses raced, wheeled, pulled the ropes taut, with Hannah hanging on to Pete and mostly incapable of helping at all.

Clay got mad and yelled at her to go make dinner. That stupid horse didn't know his head from his tail. He said the cows were dumb, but what could you expect from an Angus?

Hannah was seething. She had roped one, helped to hold it down. What was wrong with Clay? He acted as if there was nothing between them and never had been.

Well, she wasn't making dinner, either. She

would stand right here and watch them fail to bring down these large heifers. Good, strong, quality calves, is what they were, and she didn't care what Clay said. He didn't know everything.

But it was heart-stopping to watch those boys in action. Always a step ahead of the elusive cows, always controlling their horses with the touch of a knee, a rein draped across the horse's neck, either from the left or the right. A quick called command, followed by instant obedience.

The fire died down to a bed of hot coals, the branding iron heated, sizzled through the heavy hair and thick skin of the year-old heifers. It was a grueling job, with repeated attempts at roping gone awry. The cows charged the dancing horses, dodged the ropes, and if they were fast enough to throw one, she was quickly on her feet charging anything that moved, including the terrified barn cat.

It was well into the afternoon when the branding iron sizzled through the last hide. They released the bawling, wild-eyed heifer, extinguished the fire, and rubbed down and fed the horses.

Sarah called from the house to invite the boys to dinner, so with Manny leading the way, they all washed up on the back lean-to and went into the house.

Clay stopped short, gave a low whistle, and looked around at the painted walls, the addition to the kitchen, and the gleaming floor. "Someone was real busy, I'd say," he told Sarah, smiling at her in his best manner, which made Hannah grind her teeth in frustration.

The nerve of him, treating Mam with his flowery manners. Fuming, she slammed bowls of mashed potatoes and canned beef in gravy on the table, moving from stove to table with her head held high, her nostrils flaring in her best belligerent manner, which, seemingly, did not even faze the elegant manners Clay bestowed on Sarah.

Hank and Ken dug their forks into mounds of mashed potatoes, grinned, made conversation with Manny, and never worried about the quiet drama taking place between Clay and Hannah.

Sarah figured the roping had not gone well and left it at that, filling water glasses, talking about the water level in the old well, the windmill crew's arrival, anything, it seemed to Hannah, that would exclude her.

Sarah served a warm dried-apple pie with milk and sopped up Clay's praise like a thirsty sponge, her face shining with appreciation.

Hannah glowered and refused the slice of pie Sarah served her. "You sure?" she asked, her eyes questioning.

" 'Course I'm sure," she spat out.

Clay dipped his head to hide his amusement. Hannah ignored him when they all got up, retrieved their hats, and thanked Sarah again.

"Oh, it was nothing, really, boys. Your mother's cooking is far superior to mine. I'm just glad I have food to cook with. Glad to be able to feed you when you've done us such a big favor. Thank you."

"It was our pleasure, ma'am," Clay said, his teeth flashing white in his tanned face.

Hannah could not believe he walked out the front door and down the porch steps without looking at her. The nerve of him! What was going on? Had he forgotten the attraction, the long talks? He'd kissed her! She groaned inwardly, thinking of all the reasons he may have had to brush past her as if she were a piece of furniture.

She supposed she'd been clumsy and ill-prepared, riding poor, plodding old Pete, but could she help that? She had learned to rope and thought she'd made a good showing, helping to throw two of them, until Clay yelled at her.

Make dinner. Huh. Boy that had irked her. If she would have made him dinner just then, she would have fried him a few grasshoppers and boiled some earthworms. Oh, he made her furious!

So much for Clay Jenkins. She'd write him off as thoroughly as she'd written off the other one. She cringed in humiliation even thinking of his name. Well, this just cemented the fact that she did not need a man to keep her happy. She was much better off without anyone. Getting married was so far off on the horizon, it wasn't worth talking about.

She asked Sarah why she thought Clay was acting strange. Shocked, Sarah turned wide eyes on her daughter. "I didn't notice anything different, Hannah. He was just being Clay."

"No, he wasn't. He openly ignored me and yelled at me."

"He had a hard day, being in charge of branding those heifers."

"Puh. We could have done it without him."

"Now, Hannah, I wonder."

"If only I would have had a decent horse. Someday, Mam, I will own a fire horse with a good bloodline. I'll have a stable full of them, like Jerry Riehl."

Sarah scraped a plate and lowered it into the dish water. "Who?"

"Someone in Lancaster. Remember when I went to the feed mill that day? When I got caught in the rain?"

"Yes, I do remember well. You became sick with pneumonia."

"I got lost. Drove into a farm. Where I found him and the horses."

"Interesting."

"Yeah. Well. Someday, I'll own horses like that. I'll ride a horse that will make Clay positively green with envy. Then he won't tell me to go make dinner."

Sarah lifted the agate roaster from the cook stove. Abby fell over, bumped her head on the chair leg, and set up a howl of protest. Drying her hands on her apron, Sarah hurried over, scooped her up, and held her close, rubbing a palm across the back of her head, crooning. She dropped into the armless rocker and began to rock back and forth.

Hannah finished the dishes, then came to sit with her mother. "See, if we breed these heifers as soon as our bull arrives, in less than a year, we'll have ten calves. If we keep them till they weigh six or seven hundred pounds, and we get seventy or eighty cents a pound, that's how much?"

She stared at the ceiling, her mouth whispering the sums. "That's five hundred and sixty dollars per calf. If we sell five and keep five, that's 2,800 dollars. We can pay Doddy Stoltzfus back, plus have seven or eight hundred in the bank. If we repeat that each year, Mam, we'll be wealthy ranchers with a herd of fine black Anguses, and horses the likes of which no one on these hick plains will have ever seen. I'll enter my horses in shows, and we'll collect one blue ribbon after another. I'll take them to state fairs and festivals in all the local towns."

"Ach, Hannah, I don't want to burst your bubble with my everlasting realism, but didn't Clay mention the fact that the Angus mothers

444

have a harder time birthing their calves? I think we need to consider that. Perhaps divide the sum in half. We may have dead calves, or more unfortunate things. Maybe a hard winter."

"We have stacks and stacks of hay. If it gets too cold, they'll find their way to the barn. The Jenkinses' cows do. I'll ride every day, find the expectant mothers, bring them in, and sleep in the barn if I have to. I'll do anything, Mam. Anything to pull us out of poverty and depending on other people's charity."

There was a fierce light in Hannah's dark eyes, the set of her shoulders like granite. It frightened Sarah, this steely resolve. Unbreakable. Without bending to anyone's will. The reason she was so furious with Clay, Sarah thought, was she probably had meant to show him all she had learned, and with Pete. Well, it was sad.

How well she remembered instances during Hannah's school years. Bloodied knees, a black eye, torn clothing, notes from harried teachers needing help.

Once, she'd struck out in baseball and yelled and yelled about the unfairness of the pitch—too high or too low. Then she lost her temper completely, threw a stone, and hit the pitcher's shin, resulting in a serious injury.

Expelled from school, believing she was being treated unfairly, she never forgave the teacher fully, which always bothered Mose. He believed

Hannah would not be forgiven if she didn't learn to forgive, even at the tender age of twelve. He'd repeatedly made her copy the Lord 's Prayer, over and over, until her head drooped and fell on the tabletop. Her breathing slowed and became shallow as she fell into a deep sleep.

Sarah remembered watching her lovely daughter in repose. A beautiful tyrant. And Hannah was still was just that. She could never be described as a sweet girl, not even a good-natured one. Half the days of her life were spent either irked at someone or feeling she had been unfairly treated. Perhaps it was well that she would never marry. Perhaps it was God's will that she live her life alone, growing old and presiding over her own ranch without the added nuisance of a husband, which was all the poor man would amount to. Sarah wondered about this Jerry Riehl—or was it King? What had she called him? Had he been the reason for her black, nightmarish mood? No, it wasn't possible.

She chuckled out loud, brought back to the present by Hannah's angry, "What are you laughing about?"

"Oh, nothing, Hannah. Nothing."

"What?"

"Just a passing thought."

"You have to tell me."

"All right. I was just wondering if your poor husband will ever amount to anything other than a nuisance. A bother, like an unwanted house cat."

"I hope you know I'm not planning on having a husband. Unless, of course, I'd go English and marry Clay." She watched for Sarah's response with narrowed eyes.

Quickly, Sarah caught herself. Her instant panic, her tendency to plead. She pretended she hadn't heard and gave her full attention to Abby, getting her to say, "*Gaul*. Can you say *gaul*?" It's the Dutch word for horse.

Louder, Hannah said, "I wouldn't want anyone for a husband, except Clay. He's the best-looking man I've ever seen."

Sarah feigned unconcern. "Is he?" and turned back to teaching Abby to talk.

Hannah flounced out of the house, down to the barn, where Manny was constructing a pen for the chickens, complete with a nesting box and plenty of hay.

"Aren't they allowed out during the day, Manny? I can see penning them up at night, but they should be allowed to eat bugs and stuff."

"What? With all the eagles and hawks and falcons that hover over this prairie? They'd all be dead in less than a week!"

"You aren't serious."

"Sure I am. Haven't you seen them swoop down all the time, eating the prairie hens and gophers?" Manny bent his back and began to hammer nails into a board.

"What will we feed them?"

"Laying mash from the feed store in Pine. They deliver with that rattling old truck for fifty cents."

Hannah had forgotten. They had money now. Money to buy necessities, to feed chickens, and have eggs for breakfast. They would live like normal people. Bake cakes and pies. A surge of exhilaration crept up her spine, giving her goose bumps.

Yes, they would not only survive, but prosper, with their aging grandfather's support. She could feel it, here in the dank air of the primitive barn, a testament to their father's lack of foresight.

A hovel made of logs. And yet, Mose had brought them here, secured the documents, laid the foundation for a successful ranch on these plains. She should think along those lines, instead of undermining his abilities.

Almost, but not quite, she remembered her father with kindness.

The silo crew arrived in Pine. A flatbed truck brought the hundreds of steel parts on a cold, dry day, when the atmosphere was heavy with dust and the smell of weary grass and dead insects.

Ben Miller stuck his finger up his nose, gave a good twirl, and said every hair in his nose holes was covered with dust and dirt, soot from the train, and if he couldn't breathe through his mouth, he'd have suffocated a long time ago. Back in Indiana, to be exact.

Whoever would think of moving out here in this flat land that probably even God only remembered from time to time? He forgot the rain, sure as shootin', and most of the trees too.

He talked the whole way to the homestead, then stood in silence, speechless, when he saw the dwellings that Mose Detweiler had built in the middle of a dry desert filled with dead grass and asphyxiated bugs, stinking groundhogs, and crazy little chickens that multiplied like rabbits. They were everywhere, dashing madly across the road, chirping and squawking, pecking and fluttering.

He told Ike Lapp that you couldn't begin to shoot a fourth of them. The rest of the crew consisted of two single men, Ben Beiler and David King, bachelors both of them, aged beyond their years of *rumschpringa*, unimpressed by the thought of marriage. They worked at manufacturing and installing windmills, traveling around the states whenever they felt like it. Both lived at home enjoying the coddling of their elderly parents, figuring they had nothing to lose staying single.

Ben Beiler was known as Bennie, David as Davey. They were chaps easy to get along with. Brown haired and brown eyed, both of average height, ordinary, clean shaven young men who had no astonishing features that separated them from everyone else, one way or another, both handsome or plain. They had never met a woman they could not live without.

When the dust rolled up toward the blue, cloudless sky, Manny came dashing in from the barn, shouting about the windmill crew's arrival. Breathless with anticipation, he stayed rooted to the porch, shading his eyes, calling to his mother and Hannah when the truck reached the yard. The driver was paid and sent back to Pine, and the four men turned to greet the occupants of the house.

Homesteaders. Ben Miller strode up and shook hands with Sarah and Manny, then clutched a reluctant, limp hand belonging to Hannah. Ike Lapp, Bennie, and Davey followed, meeting the favorite Amish greeting requirement of hand shaking.

"So," Ben Miller began, hooking thumbs like sausages through his suspenders. "This is where Mose Detweiler settled then, did he?"

Sarah nodded, a half smile on her lips.

"You're planning on keeping the acreage you got off the government then? Going on without him, are you?"

"Yes, we are," Sarah nodded.

Ike Lapp stuck his thin, white nose in the air and commented nasally about the lack of rain or trees.

Hannah thought he didn't need to make fun of them, so she asked him in a voice dripping with vinegar why he thought they were erecting a windmill. That got his attention.

It got Bennie's and Davey's too. They tried to deny it to themselves, and they did deny it to each other, but this tall, confident girl with the big, dark eyes fascinated both of them. Here was a girl with some spunk. When they walked through the powder-dry grass to the site they had agreed on, Bennie watched the arrogance of her shoulders. Davey thought her steps really covered some ground.

She spoke without thinking. She told Ben Miller if he didn't like prairie hens he should try living out here with nothing else to eat. They were quite tasty.

Bennie and Davey couldn't believe the family had lived here without money, without food, and barely decent shelter. Each one watched Hannah's face intently, stealing looks when the other wasn't watching. Obviously, this Hannah Detweiler was different, a force to respect.

They planned where the windmill would go. The well-drilling rig was arriving the following morning, so everything should be finished within a week's time.

The wind blew, lifting the men's hats, tugging at their trouser legs, and parting their beards. They retrieved their straw hats and clapped them back on their heads, only to have them torn off and whirled away. Ben Miller said they'd have

451

to shut the windmill off or else their tank would overflow constantly in this kind of gale.

Sarah laughed. "It's not always this windy. I'm hoping we'll be getting some fall rains, now that the weather had cooled some." Manny squared his young shoulders and told them they'd get used to it.

Supper that evening was a lively affair. Sarah cooked generously, setting out canned sausages cooked with potatoes, lima beans, and onions, sauerkraut and fluffy white dumplings.

Ben Miller kept up a constant stream of Lancaster County news, interesting accounts of frolics, horse sales, and the high price of tomatoes. Some of his chatter bordered on gossip, blurring the line between truth and the questionable grapevine of which he was so fond.

"Elmer Beiler's Amos was scouted so bad the other night, he couldn't drive his horse and buggy home from Enos King's Emma, his girlfriend's house. They led his horse to the firehouse in Intercourse, tied it by the maple tree, there by the hitching rack. He got loose somehow and ran all the way to Bird-in-Hand without his harness.

"The buggy was taken apart so bad they still couldn't find one wheel. All the oil bled out of the hub and made a terrible mess on Enos King's barn floor. I don't know who put all that oil in the hub, but I bet the chaps who scouted them had more oil with them than what was on that wheel. Anyway, they carried his halter, whip, and neck rope all the way to the top of the windmill there at Enos King's. Henry Easch told me you could see it for miles around. They say Amos got *fer-late* with dating and told his girlfriend off. I heard the horse had a hoof condition and after galloping at that rate, he ruined a tendon in his front leg. Haven't heard if they put him down yet or not. Ach, such *dummheita*. Ain't never seen the likes. But I thought if Amos doesn't love his girlfriend better than that, she's better off without him. Amos has a quick temper. Wait till he finds out about this. The fuzz will fly."

And on and on. Ike Lapp stuck his white nose in the air from time to time, laughing uproariously, his beard sticking up like prairie grass, his Adam's apple bobbing up and down like a cork.

Hannah didn't laugh. She ate her sausage and sauerkraut and sat in her chair thinking how unattractive these windmill chaps were, greasy haired and pale as lard. She wouldn't cook for them if she was the boss. If they could sleep in the haymow, they could cook their own food. She slammed cups of coffee down and glared at all of them, including Benny and Davey, who, in her opinion, were about as helpful as two bumps on a log.

Until Manny told them about the cattle management here on the plains. They sat up, forgot making an impression on Hannah, their eyes alight, excitement in the way they sat on the edge of their chairs.

"Cowboying, you mean, son?" Bennie asked, extracting a toothpick and shoving it back between his lower teeth.

"Yeah. Oh, yeah. But there's a lot more to it than climbing on a horse and throwing a rope. It takes serious skill. I'll ask the Jenkinses to ride over and show you."

Hannah had never known Manny to be so talkative. His black eyes danced as he created pictures with his speech, his listeners rapt. Hannah broke in dryly to inform Bennie and Davey that it wasn't as exciting as Manny made it sound. There were no good horses around, so riding among those milling cattle was risking your life.

She didn't want a bunch of Lancaster County bachelors living out here on these peaceful plains. Next they'd all be raising cattle like a bunch of greenhorns, minding everyone's business but their own. Embarrassing to think about introducing Ike Lapp and Ben Miller to handsome Clay Jenkins, who, by the way, had nothing to do with her. So what should she care? She shared her thoughts to her mother after the men had gone.

"Hannah, stop it. You must not think along those lines. It's just wrong. God made these men, all individuals, loved by Him as well as all of us.

Now you stop it. They may be thinking the same thoughts about you. Did you ever think of that?"

Hannah flounced one shoulder, than the other. "They both want me. They would both like to marry me. I can tell. I wish Manny would stop painting a spectacular picture for them. He makes it sound so enticing and romantic."

Sarah watched the expression on her daughter's face and thought, she surely isn't like other girls. But she said, "Maybe it is, Hannah. Maybe it is."

CHAPTER 24

The windmill arrived. The well-drilling rig ground its way along the level road, dust rolling in huge billows, prairie chickens running ahead of it, their necks stretched with terrified squawks.

The pounding of the well drilling equipment was a ceaseless clatter as they dug deep beneath the dry soil.

Ben Miller and his crew set to work pouring the cement foundation, with Manny's help, who was completely taken by Bennie and Davey. He told Hannah he hoped with all his might they would move out here to stay. They could start a small church service on Sunday; they had the beginnings of an Amish church already.

The Jenkinses arrived midweek, the men in awe of the steel windmill's construction. Hod proclaimed it the best windmill he'd ever laid eyes on. He had a bit notion to have the guy build him one. Until Abby got wind of his plans, squelching them properly with her rapid-fire tongue lashing, saying they had a perfectly good windmill, and he wasn't going to spend no money to build another one.

Clay took up for his father, followed by Hank and Ken, who chimed in, stating their case effectively. Another familial spat ensued, with

Abby holding court like a small dog, getting everyone's attention with her wiry authority.

They stood as a group watching the windmill being set, a better construction, a better devised and assembled windmill, sturdier bolts, a gas engine in case of calm weather.

Hod laughed and told them to take that engine back to Pennsylvania. They ain't using it here, that's sure.

The well drillers hit a stream at 120 some feet, but it was a powerful one. The grizzled old man who ran the machine said it was one of the best, and he'd been digging wells for a long time.

"Lady, you ain't got nuthin' to worry about. Ye'll have good water for a thousand o' them black cows. Ain't no way this one's dryin' up. No way."

The promise of good water brought so much hope to Sarah, bolstering her spirits for days. With the dust and the wind, no rain all summer, she had repeatedly questioned their move back to the homestead when she lay alone at night with no one to talk to, no one to ask, except the fiery Hannah, who threw all Sarah's questions to the ground and stomped on them. To question, to think of quitting, was an unbearable weakness, according to Hannah. Sarah learned to keep her doubts to herself.

She wrote a check for the well driller and one for Ben Miller, cringing inwardly, wondering if this mountain of debt would ever be paid. She put her trust in God, having no one else. It came naturally, though, the submission, having practiced it all her life, although in the face of so much adversity, she needed to dig deep into the well of her soul to find the stream of trust and courage.

Sometimes, she imagined Hannah marching ahead, the flag of bravery hoisted in the air, leading her and Manny and the children. It was Hannah who had the pioneer spirit, the unflinching stoutheartedness that kept them going forward.

Had God made Hannah and given her this unusual personality for this purpose? Or was she a rebellious girl headed straight down the wrong trail? Sarah chose to believe the first as she watched Hannah sitting on the porch steps, her eyes scanning the prairie, taking in the endless possibilities of verdant, waving grass, her keen mind calculating, adding and multiplying, never dividing or subtracting.

And now, the glorious windmill and the deep, deep well, the tank of water that would never be empty. It seemed to Sarah that she could sense a new purpose in Manny, an eagerness in the glint of his dark eyes, a lifting of his young shoulders.

They were sad to see the windmill crew leave. Ben Miller's endless stories were a boon to their days. Bennie and Davey were brand new heroes for Manny. Hannah, however, could hardly wait to see them go and hoped those bachelors hadn't caught too much of the pioneer spirit. She didn't want them out here. At least Ike Lapp's nose got a bit of color. Actually, quite a lot. The sun and the wind had turned it into a deep shade of red that had started to peel like an old cherry. She just could hardly stand sitting at the supper table with that man. She told her mother to send their food down to the barn, but Sarah said no, you couldn't treat workers like ordinary barn cats.

Hannah cast her a look of disbelief. This comment, coming from her mother, surprised her. She realized that without her husband, she just might find a spark of new energy and get rid of the limp submission she had always portrayed.

The wind blew, the windmill spun effectively, the new steel water tank remained full and overflowing. The thirteen cows with the Bar S brand filed in regularly, milling around the tank, creating a quagmire of wet prairie soil, swatting their tails at the incessant flies, spreading mud and soggy grass into the clean, cold water.

Hannah didn't like that. The cows' water needed to stay clean, so every morning she strode out to the tank and skimmed the top and raked out the muck, keeping an eye out for the unpredictable black cow that had killed her father. Hod said she'd likely be all right; she'd just been riled that day from all the unusual activity with the calf branding. She had proved to be trustworthy when the new cattle from the Klassermans had arrived, so Hannah was not afraid, only vigilant.

She missed her grandfather's steady presence, his unfailing good humor. Sarah had been remarkably brave when she shook his hand, bidding him goodbye, their eyes saying the words that weren't necessary to speak.

Sarah had hoped he would stay but knew he couldn't. She knew her younger brothers would need him for the harvest. Another unspoken agreement was the telling of the loan he had given them. Her sisters would not need to know, the way they would raise a fuss. Her father knew it was probably the saving of Hannah, the keeping of her.

Ah, but it was a shaky deal, this loan, and her father knew it. It was risky, unwise perhaps. How much of it was done as a punishment to squelch Rachel's, Emma's, and Lydia's greed? Far into the night they had talked, her and her father, a golden memory so precious it was beyond description.

The bond between a father and a daughter was something she had never known existed. Always, it had been the women of the house who shared their feelings, her father always working, working, a man of few words. Now his words were priceless, each sentence laden with goodness, like mouthfuls of bread with fresh butter and honey.

The Klassermans arrived, the black Angus bull towed behind the spring wagon. Young and muscular, he was a real prize, Hannah could tell, as she stood by the barnyard fence watching their arrival.

She grinned up at their German neighbors, both rotund and sunburned at summer's end, dressed in freshly washed and ironed clothes, a broad brimmed hat setting low on Owen's head, squeezing his small blue eyes to an even smaller size. "Here comes the financial part of the Bar S," he called out. "A finer young bull ain't to be found."

Hannah nodded, still smiling. Manny came out of the barn carrying a pitchfork, his eyes alight with pleasure at the sight of their neighbors.

Sylvia heaved herself off the spring wagon, greeting them both effusively, then made her way to the house, carrying a heavy satchel.

Owen unhitched the sturdy brown horse and loosened the bull that had been tied to the spring wagon with a length of sturdy rope through the ring in his nose. "He's tired out, this vun," he chortled. "He had to run avays." True to his word, they led the black bull meekly to the tank, and released him, where he immediately stuck his chin over the side and began to drink.

Owen stood with his thumbs hooked in his fiery red suspenders and eyed the sturdy windmill, his florid face lifted to watch the spinning metal

461

panels as they whirred against the blue sky. He checked the engine, the tank, and the large steel handle to shut off the turning wheel when the tank overflowed.

"*Ach, du lieva*! Dat is qvite da setup." He clucked and shook his head, walked around the sturdy concrete base to view the windmill from different angles, and asked who the company was that designed this thing.

Manny told him, gleeful, pleased to announce the fine craftsmanship of the Amish in Lancaster County.

Hannah wished she could elbow him in the ribs to get him to shut his mouth. Next thing, that whole crew would be out here again. Likely Mam would put them up and cook for them. Half the country would want a new windmill, and Ben Miller and Ike Lapp would bring their families and take up permanent residence. Bennie and Davey would both want to marry her, and that simply was not going to happen!

Owen Klasserman was taken by that windmill, like a fish with a hook embedded in its lower lip, reeled in to lay flopping on the creek bank. He looked up, muttered to himself and put four fingers into the cold water in the tank. He kept shaking his head, his blue eyes mere slashes of calculating light.

"Vot you say diss cost?" he asked shrewdly.

Manny shrugged his shoulders, his hands in his

pockets. Hannah knew but she wasn't about to tell him. "You can't afford it," she said, cold as ice.

Owen's face whipped around to face her, his eyes opened to twice their normal size, his mouth turned into a perfect pink *O*. "Oh, ho, ho, Miss. You vatch me."

"Ben Miller is busy. He can hardly keep up with the demand."

Owen watched Hannah shrewdly. "I vait till spring. I vant to see hos dis operate in winter. How you gonna keep all dis ice avay."

"Break it," Hannah replied abruptly.

"Ah, ha. Outta da mouth of babes. You vait. Dis prairie put de Ben Miller to de test. Ah, hah."

They made an uneasy pact with Owen's announcement to delay till spring. Hannah's icy manner upped the cost of the bill by another fifty dollars, which she didn't need to know. That girl needed her wings clipped. Like a banty hen, she was.

Sarah wrote the check, thinking the amount was more than she'd bargained for, but didn't say anything. Hannah glared at Owen with large, black eyes as he pocketed the check, and he threw her a frosty look in response.

He mellowed somewhat, though, as Sarah set a wide slice of apple pie in front of him, accompanied by a cup of steaming black coffee. Sylvia asked if she had cream and sugar, Owen would appreciate it, and Hannah thought you could tell by his size that he wouldn't drink it black.

She thought of Clay, tall and lean, drinking coffee out of a thick, ironstone mug in Abby's kitchen, his blue eyes watching her without letting her know how he felt about her, now that she was back.

Sarah loved Sylvia's company. The sheer volume of her words and her heavy German accent were so *auhaemlich*, it reminded her of home and growing up among German descendants, with the flat, drawn-out vowels they uttered because the intricacies of the English language could be so hard to master. The only downside was that when speaking with Sylvia, Sarah could easily lapse into Pennsylvania Dutch, mixing it with English, sometimes in the same sentence, just like they did at home. But native-speaking Germans could not follow it.

Sylvia had brought *schnitz und knepp*, a dish Sarah had not eaten since the first move. Dried apples cooked with chunks of home-cured ham and spices, with a covering of thick, floury dumplings called *knepp*.

Sylvia also brought a pie made with thickened canned peaches that were baked into a pie crust sprinkled thickly with sugar, like sand. And *lebkucken*: butter cookies so heavy with shortening they fell apart.

The conversation flowed, Sarah's face became rich with color, laughter sparkling in her eyes, treating Sylvia like a sister.

Hannah didn't like *schnitz und knepp*. Whoever had come up with the idea of cooking ham with boiled dried apples, dark and curdled? That person surely had nothing else in the house to make for supper.

Hannah ate only a small slice of the peach pie, carefully scraping off some of the sugar and thinking it was small wonder this German couple resembled clean, pink pigs. But she didn't say it.

Sylvia had a fit about the house. She couldn't believe what a difference it made—the wall board and paint, the varnish on the newly sanded floors, curtains and colorful handmade rugs. A sink with a counter for Sarah to cook, roll out dough, and make pies and bread.

"Blessed. Blessed among vimmen. Eye-ya-yi. Viss da poor man dead and gone, so many udder blessings."

Hannah rolled her eyes and snickered. Sarah threw her a dark look. After the Klassermans took their leave, she turned to Hannah and delivered a firm lecture on good manners and resisted Hannah's pouting around after that.

When Hod and Abby came over a few days later, Hannah was in a better frame of mind—until she found out why they were visiting. They wanted a windmill!

Hod had won Abby over. She sat in the armless rocker and held Baby Abby on her lap, cooing and making the most ridiculous baby talk, which always came as a surprise to Hannah. This wiry, little woman, tough as nails, was reduced to the softness of flowery baby talk.

Abby loved this baby, who was growing up too fast. Her very own namesake was already crawling on the floor, prattling to herself, and stealing Abby Jenkins's heart so thoroughly that she never regained it.

Eli and Mary were fond of Abby Jenkins too. She always carried hard candies in her apron pocket for them. She asked about their schooling, her lined face softening like stiff dough turned out to rise. Her boys had grown up too fast, away from her, lured by the cows and horses, the vast land, and the excitement of every season. Crazy bulls and diseased animals, lost calves and thunderstorms, rodeos and bull riding.

A mother had to harden her heart after she realized she meant no more to her boys than a means of being fed and keeping clean, patched jeans and denim shirts in their dresser drawers. She'd thought she was through with the young 'uns till these people arrived needing help, and the poor, innocent children as hungry as calves without proper milk, and the poor father dead now. And now Hod's hankerin' after this windmill.

Hannah heard Hod asking for an address. She watched her mother, always ready to accommodate, produce a white envelope, pleased to help her neighbors acquire a new windmill like theirs. Hannah's eyes smoldered. She slouched in her chair and wished her mother would stop being so eager to serve everyone, so happy to help out their neighbors.

She'd been right about one thing. They'd have that whole bunch living out here right under their noses, just when Mam was loosening some of the restrictions of the *Ordnung*. Hannah had taken to wearing a dress without an apron and a small men's handkerchief on her head instead of a white covering. It was much more practical when riding a horse, cutting firewood, and forking hay, all of which turned a thin white covering positively gray.

You watch, she thought balefully, glaring at her mother's kind face. They'll arrive in droves, and I'll be back to keeping the *Ordnung* to the letter. Black apron pinned around my waist, white covering on my head. She knew her mother would live by her neighbors' consciences, her neighbors' scrutiny, crumpling beneath the gasps of *fadenkas*. "What would they think?" she would ask. According to Hannah, they could think what they wanted. If she felt better wearing a men's handkerchief on her head, then she would wear it.

Although she didn't know if she could ever turn her heart into the stone that would be necessary to turn her back and leave the faith, bringing a deep and penetrating grief to her mother. That was a leap across a yawning chasm, a division that had to be done by pushing love and obedience to the side, perhaps never to find it again.

If she chose that route, would the freedom to do what she wanted really be worth it in the end? Would it be worth casting aside the ways she had been taught?

Well, she sure couldn't tell now, with that Clay acting as if he'd never known her, let alone kissed her, and acting as if he couldn't bear the thought of her returning to Pennsylvania. Now here she was, back again, and him as hard to figure out as a thunderstorm. No matter how she tried, she couldn't understand why he even came around, sitting at the kitchen table with Hod as if nothing had ever passed between them.

He had about as many feelings for her as he did for Manny. Good neighbors, good buddies, and that was it. She watched Hod's moustache droop into his coffee cup and thought that this is what Clay would look like down the road, lifting that row of hairs, beaded with moisture, out of the scalding liquid.

She swallowed and thought, "Ew." No, marriage was not for her. She had no plans of ever becoming dependent on another person. That was all marriage was. The joining of two hearts was just a nice way of putting it. What it really amounted to was just about the opposite. You lived with someone who had a big moustache or a large sunburned nose, or trousers that were too short, and let him direct your days, weeks, and months until he took over your whole life like a thief, and you weren't even aware of it.

It was yes dear, no dear, I don't know dear, until your whole self was numb and you didn't own a thought in your head. She'd never be happy like that. So, she resolved firmly, there would be no more quiet moments, no stolen times with Clay. If he loved her the way he tried to say before, he'd come around, and then he'd be in for a surprise. Sorry, sir.

Take Hod and Abby, for instance. She didn't want that windmill. Knew they couldn't afford it. The old wooden one still served its purpose. Besides, those longhorns could go days without water, like camels. But what always happens in the end? The woman give in, her words amounting to a soap bubble that rose out of the dish water and popped. And they weren't even Amish!

She thought Hod looked at her mother too much, so she got up and went outside, saddled Pete, and rode out to check on the cattle. She loved the word *cattle*. More than one cow. That's right. They had fourteen head of cattle. One big, mad cow, one unbranded bull, ten young heifers, and two bred heifers.

She wasn't sure how they would brand that bull. It seemed dangerous, no matter how mild his temperament. She'd ask the Jenkins boys. See how aloof Clay remained.

The day was perfect except for the sadness of the brittle, brown grass rasping together, the sound of no rain. Little puffs of dust rose from Pete's hooves. The wind was full of dust particles and the smell of it. She had meant to ask Hod if there would be snow in the middle of his predicted few years of no rain.

She could see the black bodies of their cattle, like lumps of coal on a great bed of hay. She rode on among them, turning to watch their ceaseless tearing at the dry grass, their long, rough tongues wrapping around it and ripping it away from the roots—chewing, chewing.

How many cattle would 320 acres support if it didn't rain? She'd ask Hod that question too. Wisps of dark hair loosened themselves from beneath her kerchief, the sleeves of her dress rippled in the stiff breeze. She should have brought a coat, a light shawl, or something, as chilly as it felt out here.

There was the new bull, easily found by its short, thick neck and rounded muscular shoulders that displayed his power. What a good bloodline they would have, Hannah thought. For miles around, their calves would be known. A goal, a dream. She'd make it a reality.

There was the large, black cow tearing peacefully at the grass, ignoring the horse and rider, intent on the business of filling her stomach. Or stomachs. Cows had two of them.

She thought Sylvia and Owen Klasserman might have two stomachs, as much as they ate.

Satisfied that all was well, she turned Pete back to the barn, her eyes searching the horizon for anything unusual. There was nothing, only the waving grass and the level horizon, the sky like a giant blue bowl above her. As far as the eye could see, there was nothing. To the east, the north, or the south. To the west were small brown lumps, the buildings of the homestead, their shelter for the coming winter. With chickens in their coop, cows roaming the acres, a milk cow in the barnyard, two horses, a wagon, a windmill, and a well, they were on their way.

Chills raised the fine hairs on her arms and ran along her spine. Anything was possible. Anything. Or impossible, if you chose to see it that way.

On the horizon now there was a shape, then a brown horse, the rider low in the saddle, the hat.

Clay Jenkins. If she would have been on any other horse, she may have been able to outrun him, but with Pete, there was no chance. So she sat, staring straight ahead, keeping her horse at a walk. She heard the dull clopping of hoof beats, the rustling of dry, brown grass, then heard her name, but she didn't acknowledge it.

"Hey!"

Slowly, she turned her head, the smile on her face forced and frozen. "Clay."

"What are you doin' out here by yourself?"

"What does it look like?"

He was close enough that she smelled the sweat off his lathered horse, heard the creaking of leather, the squeak of wood where the stirrups rubbed the leather bands that held them.

"I guess checkin' on the cows."

"Right."

There was an awkward silence, with only the sound of the wind in her ears, the snort from one of the horses as he cleared his nostrils.

"So how they doin'?"

"Good."

"Yeah, Hannah. A nice lookin' bunch. Decoratin' the plains with yer herd. All the same black color. Not an ugly one in the bunch. You wait though. Them Angus don't winter over so good. Come spring, you'll have a heap of trouble, come birthin' time. Angus is the hardest to birth."

Hannah was too busy swallowing her fury to give him the comfort of a reply. He thought he knew everything. Just everything.

When she didn't answer, he said, "Hey, I'm talkin' to you."

"Well, go ahead. I'm not talking to you."

"What was that?"

"Go away, Clay Jenkins. Just go home and leave me alone. If you rode over to make fun of my herd of Angus, then just leave."

"That's not what I come over for. My folks is at yer house."

"I know."

"Plus, I thought I might have time to catch you alone. Sort of take up where we left off, if you know what I mean."

"What do you mean?"

"You know. We were getting to be more than just friends. Getting to know each other better. Hopin' to know you even more, here shortly."

"It would be a waste of your time, Clay."

"Why?"

"I am never getting married. I have no intentions of being anyone's wife. Especially not yours, you being different from me. From our way of life."

Why was it that she so hated to use the words English and Amish? Like Angus and Longhorn, Hereford and Holstein. A labeling of a different breed, when they were all cows. So it was with humans, a label, a brand, the telling apart one from another. A necessity?

"You sound like you mean it," Clay said, quietly.

"I do."

"So if I come around tryin' to get sweet on you, it's a waste of my time? Is that what yer sayin'?"

When she nodded, she didn't look at him, knowing that if she did, it might well be her undoing. She knew the allure those blue eyes held, the look that came from beneath the brim of his brown Stetson. If she wanted to live life on her own terms, she had to watch her boundaries and know her limits.

In love, things were much the same as they were in finances and in the running of a successful homestead: You had to calculate and plan carefully. You couldn't afford any craziness. If you got caught unprepared, the way she'd been knocked off her feet by that Jerry Riehl, you wouldn't stay true to your goal.

She put that incident out of her mind, kicked her heels against an unsuspecting Pete's sides, and rode away from Clay, the triangle of the men's handkerchief on her head fluttering a farewell to the young man who leaned forward in the saddle, his forearms crossed in front of him, a light in his blue eyes, and a chuckle rumbling from his throat.

CHAPTER 25

The cold did not come gradually. One day, it was chilly, and you wished for a shawl when you rode out. The next week there was a band of frost like spiderwebs around the perimeter of the water tank.

Hannah got down to the serious business of preparing for winter. She would think the worst and prepare for blizzards. She worried about the amount of hay stacked to the west of the barn, whether it would amount to sufficient food for the cows. She fretted about this to her mother and Manny, saying if they had very many storms the size of the one they had had the previous winter, the cattle would not survive. They could not afford to lose one cow.

Sarah watched the shifting anxiety in her daughter's dark eyes and told her quietly to place her trust in God. He was the One who would see them through the winter, and if they were meant to prosper, they would.

Hannah ground her teeth to keep the onslaught of rebellious words inside, not wanting to hurt her mother's feelings. But there it was again—so much like her father.

Well, they'd go ahead and place their trust in God, but someone would have to think and plan ahead and then do the work. She asked Manny if he thought they could erect a shelter for the cows, a lean-to, sort of. Put heavy poles in the ground and cover them with sawed lumber and some tin for a roof.

They asked Owen Klasserman about a shelter. He said the cows could usually take care of themselves if they had the lee side of a barn and some haystacks. Here in the West, it was normal to lose a few cows over the winter, especially young ones. With wolves and coyotes prowling, you couldn't expect to keep them all.

Hannah told Manny that was all right for someone like them. They could afford it. The Jenkinses' rangy herd was too tough to die. They'd probably gain weight eating snow. She would not let go of the shed idea until Manny agreed to help her set poles and cut logs.

That was where Hod and his boys found them on a cold, dry October day, whacking away on some trees by the dry creek bed. Hod stopped his horse, his eyes quiet beneath his hat, watching Hannah as she laid down the axe and walked over to meet them. "Still puttin' up firewood, are you?" he asked.

Hannah shook her head and pulled the thin, patched coat tighter around her middle. Manny tipped back his battered straw hat and grinned up at the riders, his unfailing good humor intact. "We're cutting poles for a shelter for the cows," he informed them.

Clay spoke quickly, "Don't need no shelter."

Hannah chose to ignore him and turned her attention to Hod instead. "We can't afford to lose cows this winter. I thought if they have a shelter, they'd be able to survive. All of them."

Hod chuckled, a soft and low sound tinged with pity. "Clay's right. The Longhorns don't need no shelter. But you got the makings of a high-class herd, same's them other neighbors. They baby them cows. Same way with you. Yer gonna have to."

Hank, the quiet one, spoke up. "Don't know how you aimin' to set them poles. Ground's hard as a rock."

Hod nodded. "Ain't gonna be done. Not without a diggin' machine, which gets mighty expensive."

"We have money," Hannah said forcefully, hating the indication to their former shame, their hunger and desperation.

"Wal, if'n yer bent on havin' a shelter, then you best build yerselfs a lean-to on the southeast side o' the barn. That don't require no diggin' into the ground."

Hannah drew down her eyebrows, bit her lower lip. Why hadn't she thought of that before? Of course it would work. She wasn't about to tell them though. And she didn't, either.

Manny, of course, in his humble, guileless way, laughed and said, of course, of course, a great

477

idea. That rankled Hannah, this being dependent on other people's ideas. She asked them why the southeast side. How did they know which direction the storms would approach? Take the blizzard of last year. There was no direction. The snow swirled and roared from everywhere.

Clay corrected her by saying there is always a direction. Hannah gave him a black look and said she didn't agree with him. His answer was swift and solid. "Who lived here on the plains the longest? You've only been here less than a coupla years, which, to my mind, pretty well labels all of you as greenhorns." This was said with a condescension that made Hannah so angry she wanted to rip him off his horse and . . . and, well, pound him with her fists.

Greenhorns! Who did he think he was? "We're not exactly new here. We survived, which is more than some folks do. Some don't last a year," she ground out.

Hod nodded, chuckled. "That's true, Hannah. True enough."

She cast Clay a look of triumph, but he was gazing steadily across the grass to the horizon, his mind elsewhere. As if she was a pesky fly buzzing around his head, she thought. They were all riding into Pine later that day for a beef barbeque at Rocher's Hardware. Did they want to come along?

Hannah wanted to go. Manny's eyes shone,

thinking of going to town, meeting new people and tasting the local barbeque.

"S' gonna be bull riding and calf roping."

Sarah said no. Their father would not want them to go. His words spoke to her from his grave. He wanted to keep his children pure, unsullied by the world, to avoid all appearances of evil.

Her face serene and calm, Sarah spoke quietly of the Amish tradition of staying away from groups of worldly people who entertain themselves with unseemly activities. There would be music, which was a form of sin, and girls wearing jeans, uncouth men. No, it was no place for any of her children. If they obeyed her, they would stay at home.

"Just this once, Mam. Just out of curiosity. Please let us go," Hannah begged, her voice rising in a childish whine.

Eli and Mary watched, their eyes large and wondering. Manny took his mother's words as his law, his own conscience forbidding it if his deceased father had spoken of it. He could not go against his mother's wishes.

Sarah recognized this, knew the difference in her son and daughter. Hannah said she wanted to see the Rochers. They'd wonder what became of her. She was worried about Doris, knowing how easily she slipped into her melancholy state. "She probably misses me. Perhaps she needs me still, to work in the store or to clean her house."

Sarah would not budge. "No. You can visit Harry and Doris Rocher any other time. Stay away from the goings-on in town."

All afternoon Hannah struggled with her own will. She walked around by the southeast side of the barn and got nothing accomplished. How did the Jenkinses figure they'd get poles in the ground here, if they couldn't do it on the prairie? The ground was just as dry here as anywhere else. Sometimes those Jenkinses just irked her. Know it alls.

Well, if they thought an addition to the barn was in order, then they could dig the holes themselves. She wasn't going to do it.

Later that evening, she rode out on Pete, freshly bathed, wearing the triangle of dark blue on her head, a laundered and ironed blue dress with no apron, Manny's denim trousers beneath her skirt, telling her mother she was going to check on the cows.

Her hair was done to perfection, swept up along the sides and pinned in a bun low on the back of her head.

Sarah knew she was not checking on cows. Not after all that bathing and dressing. "Hannah, if you are going to town, please wear a head covering and a black apron, as our *Ordnung* requires." Hannah shrugged her shoulders and let herself out of the door without another word.

Sarah knew there would be no sleep that night.

Hannah would be riding Pete for many hours. It would turn colder and she had only the light denim coat. Well, she would have to go out and sow her wild oats. She would have to learn the hard lessons all by herself. Her daughter's will of stone left her helpless, and her inability to guide and nurture Hannah was maddening.

Left alone with a thousand fears, a thousand thoughts of all the evil Hannah was subjecting herself to, was a new form of torture. Acceptance brought the realization that it was a necessary torture, this taming of Hannah.

Manny was furious, wanting to ride after her and bring her back. His frustration brightened his eyes with unshed, little-boy tears, but the set of his shoulders reminded Sarah of his impending manhood. Dear Manasses. So much like Mose. So easy to love, to lay down his life for them. How could one child differ so much from another? She knew the tallest order was to love Hannah as she loved Manny. How could she, when the love she tried to give was flung back, discarded, unaccepted so much of the time?

Hannah rode hard, the cooling late afternoon air biting through her thin jacket. She followed the accustomed route along the dirt roads, now ground to a gray layer of dust, the dry, gray weeds hanging their heads by the side of the road as if taking the blame for the drought.

The road that led to the Klasserman ranch, the outer reaches of rusted barbed wire fence of the Jenkins ranch—she recognized it all and figured she'd have no problem returning, with the formation of the stars to guide her.

An exhilaration bloomed in her chest, like a white prairie flower touched by the morning sun. She was free and had won that freedom by asserting herself quietly, without anger or argument. She was old enough to be her own boss now, going on eighteen the way she was.

Enough of this thing of listening to her father's voice. He wasn't here. He was gone. Well, in Heaven, of course, but not here to tell her what was what.

They were just so old-fashioned, so anciently behind the times. There was nothing wrong with an evening of clean entertainment. So, well-fortified by her own cloud of justification, Hannah rode into the town of Pine, tied Pete to a clump of trees by the livery stable, and turned to enjoy the sights and sounds of a Western night in town.

The Rochers, of course, were delighted to see their Hannah back again. Harry grabbed her in a warm embrace, holding court over the large barbeque pit, his breath smelling strange and sour, which she suspected was due to an alcoholic beverage.

Immediately, the shame of her father's whiskey-making crowded out the cheers of the onlookers as Harry Rocher introduced Hannah to his loyal friends, Doris slipping a thin arm around her waist and kissing her cheek. The wonder of being loved and accepted by these friendly people erased the shame that had washed over her, so she turned a blushing, glowing face to the crowd, her large dark eyes with their lustrous light of excitement so beautiful that it took real effort for more than one man to turn their attention to their wives and keep it there.

She ate a plateful of the most delicious beef she had ever eaten. She ate a baked potato and applesauce, beans and homemade noodles. There were pies and cakes, cupcakes and cookies, breads and cinnamon rolls. Doris plied her with food, and more food. She begged her to come back and clean her house. Over and over, she did this, without taking no for an answer, her eyes too bright, her face pale and tired.

Hannah knew she should resist and tell this woman no. She had enough to do at home if she wanted to be a successful homesteader. But a part of her longed for the activities of town. Watching the ordinary people, labeled *worldly*, wearing dresses with pretty flowers and fashionable plaids, smoking cigarettes and cutting their hair, being allowed to do all these things without the threat of damnation hanging over their heads.

They were free and easy, conversation mixed

with gossip and goodwill, enjoying the elbow room of their world. There were no restraints, no *Ordnung*. They could do as they pleased, every day. No wonder it seemed everyone was so happy.

There was an allure for Hannah. She felt the strong undertow of the world, beckoning her to come and taste this life of privilege. Being born Amish was not fair. She felt the harness of her birth, an uncomfortable slot where she was wedged tightly into a stall of expectation, the path of her life chosen by someone else, dictated and ordered by the authority that manipulated her parents' consciences as well as her own.

When the music began and the dancers swirled and stomped into an intricate pattern of color and movement, she could not hold her feet still. Sitting on the sidelines, erect, showing no emotion except for her eyes and the two bright spots of color on her cheeks, she carefully hid the movement of her feet. It was all so festive, so wonderfully lighthearted and carefree. The homestead and its cares, worries about the approaching winter, the safety of the cows, wolves and coyotes, all crumbled and fell away, as her heart swelled with the emotion of plucked guitars, drums, and harmonicas, a deep voice singing of a love gone wrong.

Had her love gone wrong? The love of her faith, her Amish heritage? Guilt stabbed her chest as she sat there on the metal folding chair, disobedient, leaving her mother and Manny at home to worry far into the night.

When she felt a presence beside her, she looked up to find Clay Jenkins, blond and handsome, clean-shaven, an invitation in his eyes.

"Dance with me, Hannah?"

Her eyes turned black with refusal, her tone clipped and severe. "No, I can't."

"You can't, or you don't know how?"

"What's the difference?"

"No, I mean yer religion. Or you never danced."

Down came her eyebrows and up came her chin. "I've danced."

"Well, come on then."

Her pride held her to the metal chair, resulting in a firm shake of her head, eyes lowered.

"You're just being stubborn."

A short girl with fiery red hair and a brilliant green flowered dress sashayed over to grab Clay's hand. "Clay, you haven't asked me to dance. What's wrong with you?"

"Hey, Jennie! Good to see you!" He grabbed her around her waist and whirled her away. Soon they were lost among the couples who whirled around the grassy town square, the smoke of the barbeque pit from Rocher's Hardware low above their heads, like a mist.

Hannah's eyes narrowed. There they were. Clay was holding her much too close. Jealousy

485

and anger were hard to tell apart, but whatever it was, Hannah knew there was no way that Jennie was going to have the upper hand with Clay while she sat there like the dowdy Amish girl no one wanted. Jennie wasn't that pretty. Too short, for one thing.

Clay circled around, his eyes looking for her, and when he found her, they were a taunt, a mockery. *See, Hannah, I can have anyone I choose.*

It was too much. Like a boat tied to a dock, the winds blew and loosened the rope of restraint.

It was inevitable that he would ask her again. When he did, she rose, placed her hand in his and was brought up close by a firm hand on her waist, swept away among the crowd of dancers, a dreamlike quality enveloping her senses and erasing every negative thought.

How could anything like this be a sin? She was carried away with the looks of admiration cast their way. She knew what a startling couple they made, Clay so tall and blond and handsome, she almost as tall and dark as he was light. She reveled in the music, the joy of movement, the crisp barbeque scented evening air, being so close to Clay.

She had no trouble keeping up with the best of the dancers, whirled away from Clay on the arms of many other men who cut in, asking her to dance. She never tired, just wanted to keep dancing all night, waiting till daylight to ride home.

When it got late, the band played their farewell piece and amid thunderous applause, began to pack away their instruments.

Clay told her he would ride home with her and she accepted gladly. The night seemed very dark, the moon only a crescent that did nothing to light anything.

Without speaking, he walked her to the livery stable, saddled Pete for her as she stood watching, then went to get his own horse. She stopped to talk to Harry and Doris and promised to ride into town every Tuesday and spend the day cleaning or working in the store for a small wage. Harry promised to drive out and bring her back in the car, if her mother would allow it.

At the mention of her mother, and the word *allow,* the fairy tale of her evening of dancing in Clay's arms evaporated, leaving her heavy with dejection and an unnamed feeling of yearning.

She bid the Rochers a goodnight, and rode away with Clay, the lights of the town and its magnetism slowly fading in the distance.

The only sound was the dull clopping of the horse's hooves, the creak of leather, and the occasional yelp of a coyote. Hannah shivered beneath her thin jacket. She noticed that Clay had donned a heavy coat with a collar that looked like sheep skin. The cold night brought back the monumental worry of the fast approaching winter.

"I meant to ask your father—in the time of drought, are there winter storms, like usual? Or is the winter dry as well?"

"It depends. You can't tell. You gotta take it as it comes."

Hannah nodded, then realized he couldn't see that gesture, so she said, "Yes."

He remained quiet, after that, leaving her alone with her thoughts. Inwardly, she picked up the pieces of the responsibilities she had left behind when she rode into town. She came down to earth with a solid jolt, placed firmly back with her family, the homestead and, yes, her heritage.

She was a daughter of Mose Detweiler, the son of Mose Detweiler before him, born into a faith that would stand the test of time. Would she, herself, be able to stay true, to stand the same test? Tonight had been powerful and all-consuming; the desire for all things forbidden was too strong. She'd pulled away from her moorings, and now, with Clay beside her, she felt the loss of direction, the heaving and swelling of these turbulent waters. Waves crested around her, doubt pushing them over her creaking boat, almost sinking her.

What had her father always said? A doubter is *unfaschtendich* in all his ways. He is tossed about like the waves of the sea.

There it was, the thing she resisted the most wedging its way into her conscience—the voice of her father. Wryly, she shook her head, the darkness a comforting cloak. They stopped their horses at the corner where the barbed wire fence met the edge of the road.

"Should I ride on home with you?" Clay asked.

"No. There's no need."

"Well, Hannah, thanks for the dance." He guided his horse over until he could reach out and pull her close. She closed her eyes as he whispered, "I love you, you know."

Immediately she turned Pete and kicked the stirrups into his sides, startling the poor animal into an uneven gait that was mostly a headlong dash into the night. Tears poured down her face, the rushing night wind drying them as they fell.

Clay sat on his horse and listened to the disappearing hoof beats, shaking his head soberly before turning his horse and riding off.

Hannah rode blindly, allowing Pete to find his way in the dark, the battle within creating her helpless tears. Yes, she could love Clay, could probably be his wife, if she chose to do that. But she wasn't prepared for this evening, and now here she was, at loose ends and thoroughly rattled. She had to be careful, calculate every angle, same as with raising cattle.

Perhaps love came down on you like a winter storm, and if you weren't prepared, you'd perish, unprotected. She had to be very careful. She had to consider the truth. Her responsibility to her mother. The homestead.

Tonight had been a time away, a reprieve, a rest from the hard beating of the odds, surviving the prairie winter.

Foolish. She'd been foolish. Slipped off the path, in more ways than one. As this truth settled about her shoulders, cloaking her like a too-snug shawl, she shrugged, and then decided that all decisions were made wisely as the need arose. The time had not yet come to be forced into a decision.

Pete loped steadily along into the night. Hannah settled into his easy rocking gait as the cold wind spoke of the long prairie winter and whispered of snow and storm and fury.

GLOSSARY

Ach, du lieva—Oh, my goodness.

Auhäemlich—Something that is familiar or memorable; reminiscent of home.

Ausbund—The book of old German hymns written by Amish ancestors imprisoned in Passau, Switzerland, for their Christian faith.

Auseriche leit—People outside the Amish church; people of the world.

Ausricha; ausra—Outsiders; "those people."

Bessa-grissa—Your conscience.

Bupp—Baby, in a pejorative sense; cry baby.

Byshtant—God's "standing by."

Dat—Name used to address one's father.

Dehmut—Humility.

De lieve—Love.

Denke—Thank you.

Der Gute Mann—The Good Man; that is, God.

Der Herr—The Lord.

Die goot schtup—The guest bedroom.

Doch-veggly—Literally, a "roof wagon," it refers to a buggy with a roof that a couple usually purchases after they are married, if they could afford one.

Dummheita—Foolishness.

Englische leid—Those whose first language is English; anyone not Plain.

Englisha mon—English man.

Fadenkas—To judge a person.

Fa-sark—Take care of; look after.

Fer-flucht—Cursed.

Fer-late—Despair; loss of hope.

Fottgung—To succeed, as with a business.

Freundshaft—A person's group of friends.

Gaul—Horse.

Gel—Right; to agree with something another says.

Goldicha fauda—The golden thread.

Gottes furcht—Fear of God.

Grosfeelich—Arrogance stemming from pride; hubris.

Heiliche Schrift—Holy Bible.

Herr saya—God's blessing.

Hesslich—Ugly.

Himmlischer Vater. Meine Herre und mein Gott—Heavenly Father. My Lord and my God.

Hochmut—Loose morals.

Ketch—Catch, as in a man who is "considered quite a *ketch*."

Kinnershpeil—Child's play.

Leblein—A piece of fabric on the back of a dress; in modern times, it is a traditional sign that the woman is Amish.

Maud—A girl who lived with other Amish families in a time of need. A helper, usually in the house, to the wife and mother in a family.

Meine dochter—My daughter.

Mensch—A person; used to stress the humanity of all people created by God.

Mishting—Pooping; used when referring to animals.

Mitt unser Herren Jesu Christus—With our Lord Jesus Christ.

Mutterschprach—Mother tongue.

Ordnung—Literally, "ordinary," or "discipline," it refers to an Amish community's agreed-upon rules for living, based on the Bible, particularly the New Testament. The *Ordnung* can vary in small ways some from community to community, reflecting the leaders' interpretations, local traditions, and historical practices.

Ponhaus—Scrapple.

Rumschpringa—Literally, "running around." A time of relative freedom for adolescents, beginning at about age sixteen. The period ends when a youth is baptized and joins the church, after which the youth can marry.

Schöene frau—Nice lady.

Schrift—Scriptures.

Schnitz boy—Dried-apple pie.

Schnitz und knepp—Dried apples cooked with chunks of home-cured ham and spices, with a covering of thick, floury dumplings called *knepp*.

Shick dich—Behave yourself.

Shicklich—To present oneself properly and with good manners.

Shtrubles—Fly-away hair.

Unfaschtendich—A person not on a good spiritual foundation; something that doesn't make sense.

Ungehorsam—Disobedient.

Ungehorsamkeit—Disobedience.

Unsaya—The unblessing.

Vass geht au—What's going on?

Vass in die velt?—What in the world?

Verboten—Forbidden.

Vonn glaynem uf—From childhood on; something about a person that has been since he or she was a child.

Vass gebt?—What gives.

Youngie ihr rumschpringas—The youths' running around.

Wasser bank—Dry sink.

ABOUT THE AUTHOR

LINDA BYLER was raised in an Amish family and is an active member of the Amish church today. Growing up, Linda loved to read and write. In fact, she still does. Linda is well-known within the Amish community as a columnist for a weekly Amish newspaper.

Linda is the author of four series of novels, all set among the Amish communities of North America: Lizzie Searches for Love, Sadie's Montana, Lancaster Burning, and Hester's Hunt for Home. *The Homestead* is the first book in the Dakota Series. Linda has also written four Christmas romances set among the Amish: *Mary's Christmas Goodbye*, *The Christmas Visitor*, *The Little Amish Matchmaker*, and *Becky Meets Her Match*. Linda has co-authored *Lizzie's Amish Cookbook: Favorite Recipes from Three Generations of Amish Cooks!*

Books are
produced in the
United States
using U.S.-based
materials

Books are printed
using a revolutionary
new process called
THINKtech™ that
lowers energy usage
by 70% and increases
overall quality

Books are
durable and
flexible
because of
Smyth-sewing

Paper is
sourced using
environmentally
responsible
foresting methods
and the
paper is acid-free

Center Point Large Print
600 Brooks Road / PO Box 1
Thorndike, ME 04986-0001 USA

(207) 568-3717

US & Canada:
1 800 929-9108
www.centerpointlargeprint.com